PRUE LEITH

The Food of Love

BOOK 1 *Laura's Story*

LIBRARIES NI
WITHDRAWN FROM STOCK

Quercus

First published in Great Britain in 2015 by

Quercus Publishing Ltd
Carmelite House
50 Victoria Embankment
London EC4Y 0DZ

An Hachette UK company

Copyright © 2015 Prue Leith

The moral right of Prue Leith to be
identified as the author of this work has been
asserted in accordance with the Copyright,
Designs and Patents Act, 1988.

All rights reserved. No part of this publication
may be reproduced or transmitted in any form
or by any means, electronic or mechanical,
including photocopy, recording, or any
information storage and retrieval system,
without permission in writing from the publisher.

A CIP catalogue record for this book is available
from the British Library

HB ISBN 978 1 78429 068 9
TPB ISBN 978 1 78429 022 1
EBOOK ISBN 978 1 78429 023 8

This book is a work of fiction. Names, characters,
businesses, organizations, places and events are
either the product of the author's imagination
or used fictitiously. Any resemblance to
actual persons, living or dead, events or
locales is entirely coincidental.

10 9 8 7 6 5 4 3 2 1

Typeset by CC Book Production

Printed and bound in Great Britain by Clays Ltd, St Ives plc

For John Playfair

PART ONE

CHAPTER ONE

1940, late summer

Laura watched her father brushing his hair with his matching brushes, one in each hand. The brushes had tortoiseshell backs with silver edges which caught the light from the Anglepoise lamp on the tallboy. His signet ring on his ring finger glinted, too, and so did his hair.

'What do you think, young lady?' he asked, turning from the looking-glass. He looked, she thought, splendid. Just splendid. So elegant and smart in his blue-grey uniform.

She remembered years ago, when she'd been at the village primary school, he had come with Mummy to the Nativity play wearing his row of miniature medals on his tunic and carrying his hat. She'd been so proud of him. Then he'd retired from the RAF and worn tweeds, except when they went out to dinner or he went hunting, when he looked good, but not so good as in his uniform.

Things had changed again last year when war had been declared. He'd been re-called to the RAF and now he had some important new war job at the Moreton-in-Marsh airfield in

Gloucestershire. Mummy had had to hang his uniform on the washing line to get rid of the smell of mothballs and she'd sponged and pressed the trousers and tunic and brushed his hat. Laura had felt proud and pleased when he'd asked her to polish the buttons on his tunic: she liked using the little brass button stick to keep the Brasso off the cloth and soon she had the buttons bright and shiny again. 'You look wonderful, Daddy.'

He came over to her and lifted her chin. She could smell his lovely fresh tobacco smell.

'And you are the prettiest young lady in the country.' He held her face in his hands. 'And don't you worry about this silly war because it will soon be over. By the time you leave school it will be a distant memory, and I will make sure that my daughter has the best coming-out ball of the season, with the loveliest ball gown and the most eligible young men trailing after her. Would you like that?'

She laughed, delighted. 'I don't know. I don't like boys, 'specially if they are the trailing-about kind. And I can't dance.'

'Ah, but I have a solution to that. You will go off to Paris and learn all the airs and graces of the upper classes, including how to dance.' He kissed her forehead and grinned. 'And in the meantime you should be making friends with the right young people. That school of yours is meant to be full of the cream of young womanhood, but you spend all your time with the vet's daughter.'

Laura, stung, coloured up. 'But you like Sophie, Daddy. What's wrong with Sophie? She's my best friend.'

He gave her a reassuring hug and instantly everything was all right again. 'Of course I like her. Sophie is a jolly little thing, plump as a pudding. Not a patch on my beautiful daughter, of course. She's coming hunting with us in the morning, isn't she?'

Laura nodded, and Donald went on. 'Let's hope we get a good run. Ever since that woman took over the hunt, one hasn't a clue what will happen.'

'What woman, Daddy?'

'The Countess Frampton. The Earl has gout and can't ride to hounds anymore, and all the men are at the front or doing war jobs, so she's now the new MFH.'

'Mummy said *you* should have been the Master.'

He smiled at her. 'Well, between you and me, but never say I said so, I'd have made a much better Master than Lady Geraldine.'

'But you have a war job, too.'

'True. Two jobs really. The War Ag Committee and the airfield. But I'd have managed somehow. At least the hunt is still going, even if it is only on Saturdays. Some of the British hunts have packed up for the duration of the war. So, my girl, you should hunt all you can while you have the chance. Some of the young girls who turn out now are from very good families – you should make some excellent friends. Make up for that hopeless school of yours.'

'But Roedean is a terrific school. You said so yourself, Daddy.'

'Well, it certainly costs enough, and it should introduce you to the right people. But now the whole school has decamped to the Lake District, I doubt if there will be much chance to meet other girls' families.'

'Miss Janis says Roedean is all about education,' Laura replied.

'Not in my book. The point of boarding school is to make the right friends. For boys it is to find friends who'll help in their career. For girls it is to find friends with suitable brothers.'

She made a disapproving face. 'Suitable brothers?'

'Yes. Suitable as potential husbands for my precious only daughter.'

Donald Oliver ran the back of his index finger along the underside of his moustache, first on one side and then the other, put on his hat, straightened it in front of the glass, tucked his Balkan Sobranie pouch in his tunic pocket and patted it flat so it wouldn't look lumpy. He picked up his briar pipe with one hand and patted her on the head with the other – like a dog, she thought, but it was nice anyway.

Laura followed him down the stairs, thinking that he was everything a man should be: handsome, decisive, in control. He always looked so *smart*. 'Master of all he surveyed' came into her head. He still had all his thick black hair, neatly parted in the middle and shining with Brylcreem; his moustache was narrow and neat, like two small black wings on his top lip. When she was little she thought everyone in the RAF had to have moustaches like wings, to match the wings on their jackets.

Laura didn't know what her Roedean classmates' fathers or brothers were like. She'd never been asked to any of their houses. Since the Army had commandeered Roedean's buildings in Sussex and the pupils and staff had moved to Keswick, most of the girls were now miles away from their homes anyway.

And her friends from her village school days were children of farmers or tradesmen from Moreton-in-Marsh and neighbouring villages. The fathers were much younger than Daddy, who was fifty-four, but they were mostly ugly and wore dull brown clothes and scuffed boots. She supposed the ones in uniform would look better, but she hadn't seen them.

Her oldest brother, Hugh, also wore RAF officer's uniform, though the stripes on his sleeves were much narrower than Daddy's. Before the war he'd been in charge of their farm, but he had been called up, too, and sent away to Canada to train as a bomber pilot. Now he and his wife Grace and their baby daughter, Jane, still lived in the farmhouse, Plumtree Cottage. Daddy had 'pulled some strings', he said, because Hugh could have been posted miles away. Hugh now flew Wellington bombers from the airfield where Daddy worked.

Hugh was twenty years older than Laura, as old as most fathers, but he was wonderful. She was almost as proud of him as she was of Daddy – not many girls' brothers flew aeroplanes. When she heard the rumbling drone of the Wellingtons, she'd watch their steady progress overhead and wonder which one contained Hugh, and she'd close her eyes and pray that he'd get back safely. He laughed at her anxieties and said so far he'd been mostly dropping leaflets, not bombs. In fact, he was jealous of his mates who had been sent to bomb Berlin, and he sometimes wished he flew a Spitfire so that he could join the scrap going on in the skies over London. He spoke as if it was a game – and Hugh loved games.

But her father was her hero. He had bought her Rufus, a proper 15-hand hunter, for her birthday and together they went hunting or just hacking round the farms. He treated her like an adult; once, before the war, her father had taken her, without her mother or either of her brothers, to London for a treat. They had had lunch at the RAF Club, where he'd introduced her to other grown-ups as 'my new young lady', which was embarrassing but made her feel proud and pleased. Afterwards they'd gone to Lillywhites, where he'd bought her a proper hunting jacket, a white silk stock, a gold tie pin with a tiny leaping horse on it, and one of the new hard riding hats. Then they had tea upstairs at Fortnum's. Glen Miller's music was being played by real musicians and models swooshed between the tables wearing the most exotic clothes. She would never forget that day.

Laura's second brother, David, had had his breakfast ages ago and was long gone to start his working day. It was harvest time and he'd been out in the fields since daybreak. He'd been managing the farm since the start of the war when Hugh had been called up and their father had returned to the RAF. David had wanted to join up, too, but his gammy leg, a legacy from suffering polio as a boy, had made that impossible. So at twenty-three he was running Chorlton. Daddy said he was too young for the job, but he seemed very old to Laura. To her, both her brothers seemed ancient, David ten years older than her and Hugh ten years older than David.

Laura watched her father and Hugh clattering out of the kitchen, Hugh still eating his toast, Daddy insisting on leaving 'this minute' and Mummy fussing over them both.

Maud shut the kitchen door after them, then sat down again at the table. Laura watched her spread dripping on her toast and tried to imagine how you could have three children over twenty years. None of her friends had such old siblings. It often felt as though she had three fathers, all telling her what to do. But mostly she adored them, and Mummy said they spoiled her. Which, she had to admit, they did sometimes.

'Laura, you are dreaming again. Eat your porridge. I need you to help me with putting up the plums. Mrs Digweed has a bad cold and I have sent her upstairs to bed. And both the girls are out harvesting.'

'Oh Mummy, please. I want to go, too. Let's both go.'

Maud shook her head. 'No, there's a war on, darling, and I have to bottle plums. You can stay up there after lunch, though. But unless you help me this morning they won't get any lunch. As well as the bottling, we need to do a picnic for everyone, and then supper for when you all get back.'

So Laura spent two hours helping her mother bottle plums in water, although she did so knowing that they wouldn't be nearly as good as they used to be, before sugar was rationed, when they were done in syrup. Stacking the finished jars on the larder shelf, Laura compared them to the few left over from last year. The plums in syrup were beautiful, a lustrous orangey pink, the colour of sunset. The ones they had just bottled looked so dull by comparison.

Then they set to making sandwiches with the stodgy National Loaf. Some of them had nothing but slices of salted pork fat in them. Those were for the men, who needed more energy because they did the heavy lifting. Laura's mother greeted her moans about the bread and the lack of cheese with her usual lecture about how lucky they were to have butter from their own cows and home-made hedgerow jam. And there was a hard-boiled egg for everyone, because the hens were laying well. 'If you lived in a town, my girl, you'd get a scraping of marge and one egg a week if you were lucky.'

They packed up the picnic in a big basket, the sandwiches wrapped in greaseproof paper. Bottles of her mother's elder-flower cordial and demi-johns of cider from the Frampton Estate next door went into a second basket with a dozen enamel mugs, most of them chipped.

*

They loaded the picnic into a wheelbarrow and pushed it up the lane. Top End, reaped clean with most of the sheaves already in stooks, lay ahead of them with Twelve Acres beyond, its wheat still standing, washed pale gold by the sun.

Her mother, puffing slightly, stopped at the top of the rise. 'It's like one of those old paintings of rural life,' she said. 'All it lacks are yokels lolling on a bank and long-aproned maidens pouring cider from flagons.'

Laura agreed, but thought to herself that if David got his way one day the scene would look very different. It would be all trac- tors and harvesters. They walked round the edge of the field, and Laura could see her brother heaving sheaves upright and standing four or five together in stooks to dry in the sun. Poor David. He'd had only a year to go to get his degree at Oxford when he'd had to abandon his studies and come home. He'd been terribly cut up about it. He wanted to be a lawyer, not a farmer, and to add insult to injury, he hated being the only one not in uniform. The RAF must be mad turning him down, thought Laura. David works harder than anyone and he can lift a calf or vault a gate without a thought. And he'd make a smashing officer: the men all do what he says and he is always planning for the future, and doing sums, and pestering Daddy to buy modern equipment.

As soon as the workers saw that lunch had arrived, everyone downed tools and made their way to the edge of the field. They flopped down on the grass, the labourers pulling out their Woodbines. David patted his pockets for his tobacco, cigarette papers and the little machine, like a baby mangle, that he used to roll his cigarettes. Laura poured cider into mugs and handed them round while her mother dispensed sandwiches.

'And mind you don't tear the paper,' warned Maud. 'I want it back to use again.'

Laura sat down on the grass next to David to eat her lunch. As soon as he'd finished, he threw himself back and stretched his arms over his head.

'So, Sis, are you staying to do a proper job with us, or going back to mess around in the kitchen with Mum?'

'I'm staying.' She looked down at her stocky brother, his shirt soaked under the arms and sticking to his barrel-like chest, sweat glistening on his neck. She could smell the sweat. It should be disgusting, she thought, but it isn't – though it doesn't smell positively good, like horses' sweat. How odd to think she preferred the smell of Rufus after a gallop to the smell of her brother.

She remembered when the fields up here were all grass, not wheat. She asked David why they'd been planted.

'Because we get paid an extra £2 for every acre of pasture that's ploughed up. The government wants us to plant wheat to make bread.'

'Why do we have this awful stuff then?' Laura pinched a bit off her sandwich and rolled it into a grey lump. 'It's horrible.'

'I suppose because we don't produce enough wheat. So what we grow gets mixed with whatever else is going – barley, oats, potatoes – acorns for all I know.'

David closed his eyes and Laura knew he didn't want to talk anymore. She lay back on the grass and looked at the sky, seamless and pale blue. Sometimes you saw skylarks up here, miles up, climbing in a spiral until they were almost out of sight. They sang all the way up, and then, silent, came plummeting down like a stone.

But now, she thought, you are more likely to see war planes, usually our bombers, droning steadily along in a bunch, maybe with Hugh flying one of them.

When Donald walked into the kitchen that evening, his wife was talking to Laura.

'Look,' Maud was saying, 'it's beautiful. How they manage such expensive card in the middle of a war is astonishing. It's got gold edges, and the print is embossed.'

'Oh, Mummy, can I go? I could get a weekend exeat. Surely I can go, too? I'm thirteen. And I look much older.'

'What's this?' asked Donald. His wife handed him the invitation.

The Earl and Countess of Frampton
Request the pleasure of the company of
Mr and Mrs Donald Oliver
To a ball to celebrate the coming of age
Of their son,
Captain Lord George Maxwell-Calder
At 7pm on the 30th October 1940
At Frampton Hall, Oxfordshire

Carriages: 2am
Dress: Evening dress or uniform

Donald ran his thumb over the embossed coronet at the top of the card and savoured the moment. At last, he thought. The only times he and Maud had visited Frampton were for the annual fête, and then they'd never got beyond the garden. The Earl and Countess had greeted them with the same aloof courtesy with which they greeted the blacksmith. Their own invitations to tea and dinner had been politely refused, and no reciprocal gestures had been forthcoming.

Laura was hanging on his sleeve. 'Can I go? Please, Daddy, please? I've never been to a ball. Can I go?'

Donald held his daughter's face in his hands, tipping her head back to look into his eyes. 'My dearest girl, I would love to take you to a ball. When you're eighteen you can go to all the balls and dances, dinners and nightclubs you like. But we cannot insert you into the Earl's party.'

Laura stamped out of the kitchen.

'Poor love.' Maud shook her head. 'She'll be even more upset when she learns that her brothers have both been asked.'

'Have they indeed?'

'They have. There is an invitation for David in the hall. And Grace came round for elevens with Jane, worrying about what to wear.'

'No doubt you women will have a lovely time fussing over ribbons, frills and furbelows for the next couple of months.'

'Mmm. Well, at least clothes and material aren't rationed yet. But I fear it will have to be "make do and mend". We're unlikely to get silk or satin.'

'I'll answer the invitation, my dear. I assume you want to go?'

'Yes, of course. Though I'm so awkward at parties. I wish you *could* take Laura. She'd be a much jollier companion than your frumpy old wife, and she'd enjoy it more, too.'

Donald secretly agreed with her but he patted her on the back, saying, 'Nonsense, my dear. Don't fish for compliments. You are neither frumpy nor old.'

*

Donald replied to the invitation at his wife's writing desk in the morning room, and then sat back with the newspaper. These days it was a thin affair, filled with condensed reports of the war, advice to housewives about saving fuel, and small advertisements for things like Sanatogen or Vim Scouring Powder. He laid it down and looked out of the window, pondering the change of heart that had led to the Earl inviting them to the ball.

He supposed the old snob was asking all the neighbouring gentry. Well, it was about time, too. But he'd bear no ill-feelings. It would be a good opportunity to start afresh.

Of course, he mused, pleasantries are exchanged after church and everyone is friendly out hunting. The Earl was only too glad to have an annual meet at Chorlton. Damn right he was – it cost the hunt nothing whereas it cost Donald a pretty penny: resurfacing the sweep in front of the house, using soft Cotswold gravel that wouldn't hurt their precious horses' hooves; whisky as well as stirrup cup for everyone; and trays of Maud's Yorkshire fruit cake served with Wensleydale from Brown's. It'd been lavish before the war, but even this season, he was sure, nobody would match Chorlton for a good hunt send-off. Yet not a single invitation to anything had ever resulted from his hospitality. Until now.

CHAPTER TWO

Donald's gaze dwelt for a second on his precious Bentley before he climbed into it. Good, old Sawkins had washed and waxed it. He backed the car carefully out of the garage, swung her round and drove across the back yard, scattering hens and geese, then honked his horn to alert Sawkins to open the gate to the back lane. The ancient chauffeur saw him, raised his fingers to his cap and hurried, stiff-legged, to oblige.

Sawkins stood by the gate. "Aft'noon, Guvnor,' he said, touching his cap again as Donald drove through. Donald acknowledged the greeting with a slight incline of his head. The old boy has aged a lot, he thought, like everything else round here.

The car rocked as he negotiated the potholes and resolved to do something about them before winter. Then he remembered he'd had the same thought last winter and done nothing about it. The estate was falling into disrepair. Except, of course, the bits that showed: the main drive still impressed with its raked gravel between neatly edged lawns on either side. And the front of the house, which had been repointed last year with the window frames painted, looked positively ship-shape and Bristol fashion.

He bumped down the back lane towards the main road with

Chorlton on the right and Frampton on the left, inspecting hedges and fences as he went. Both estates had failed to cut the hedges last winter. They were now ragged and overgrown and the fences had several broken rails. David intended, he'd said, to put Chorlton's perimeters right this winter. He doubted if Frampton's would ever be fixed.

From the time he'd bought Chorlton until the outbreak of war things had gone badly. They'd had to compete with cheap lamb from New Zealand, cheap wheat from North America, cheap everything from the Empire. The whole of British agriculture had been in the doldrums in the thirties and neither he nor Hugh had been able to make the farm pay.

But now young David seemed to be making a surprisingly good fist of it, even though Donald had had little hope of him succeeding. When he had taken over the farm the labour situation had been dire: their able-bodied men had gone to war, leaving only the ancient and the decrepit, and a few gormless school leavers champing at the bit to be old enough to get themselves killed.

Thank God for their land girl, Jill. Damned if she isn't the best thing that's happened to Chorlton, he mused. Who would have thought it? He remembered the conversation with his wife:

'Maud,' he'd said, 'don't be ridiculous. I'm sure she's perfectly nice, but why should we give bed and board, and a salary, to Dr Drummond's grand relation who will be perfectly useless on the land?'

'What makes you say that? Why should she be useless? Many of the land girls come from middle-class, even upper-class, homes and prove to be excellent workers.'

'Drummond says her interests are music and mathematics,

16

so she's not going to like drenching cows or digging ditches, is she? Anyway, why does she want to be a land girl?'

'I think her parents would prefer her in England rather than in the Forces. Any parent would. Also, she's opposed to war.'

'God, a Conchie to boot! I won't have it, Maud.'

But he did have it. Land girls were the only solution to the shortage of farm labour and at least he knew the girl was honest and healthy.

Jill was eighteen years old. Tall and skinny with a mop of black curls and large hazel eyes set in a handsome, slightly beaky face, she made Donald think of a crane or a heron, all legs and sudden jerks. But to everyone's astonishment, she turned out to be as capable out on the farm as with the admin. She was quickly indispensable. Please God she'd stay for the duration.

At least Donald no longer had the enormous wage bill he'd had before the war. The family shouldered a lot of the work on the farm, and they weren't paid. But he hated to see his wife darning, sewing, scrubbing, cleaning and trying to make palatable meals out of their rations. Strangely, though, Maud seemed to enjoy it. When her remaining maid-of-all-work, Phyllis, had joined the Wrens, she was left with only poor old Digweed and the village lass who came in on Mondays to scrub the floors and help with the washing. He shook his head slightly as he thought of his obstinate wife insisting on taking personal charge of the pigs, like a peasant.

Maud was a good and loyal wife, though, no doubt about that. She'd been happiest when she was a schoolteacher in Halifax and he worked in his father's mill. She hadn't wanted to sell up and come down south, didn't understand that he couldn't run a woollen mill all his life, that he was made for better things, even if she wasn't.

Donald cranked the windscreen open a crack to get a bit of cool air on his face and neck, although now he could smell the burning stubble in the fields to his right, quickly followed by the muck being spread on the left. Well, he thought, that's the price you pay to be a landowner.

That thought brought him back to Chorlton and the conversation that morning at breakfast.

Over his porridge, David had announced, 'Listen, everyone. The Ministry chaps were here yesterday, and we're to get top prices for the wheat, barley and oats. And we've exceeded our quotas by eleven per cent.'

'But that's just wonderful,' exclaimed Maud.

'Congratulations, my boy,' said Donald.

David reached for the teapot. 'It wasn't all my doing. Jill has more than played her part.'

They all looked at Jill, and Donald saw a blush running up her neck. 'I'm sure that's true, Jill. We'd never have done it without you,' he agreed.

'And having a guaranteed buyer does make life a lot easier,' said David.

Laura asked, 'Does the Ministry *have* to pay us for everything?'

'I'm glad to say they do,' said Donald. 'After all, we are planting what they demand, so it's only right.'

David added, 'But they can reject it, or pay less if the quality isn't there. So they come and inspect it. It's good news, and we still have the potatoes from Little End to come, though I'm not looking forward to lifting them. It's back-breaking work. Next year we need more machines.'

'We can't afford it, David,' said Donald. 'The war won't last forever.'

'I should hope it won't!' exclaimed Maud. 'Though it doesn't look as if it will really be over by Christmas.'

'Dad,' said David firmly, 'it's true the war helps with subsidies and prices, but the only way we will survive, war or no war, is by being more efficient.'

Donald shook his head. 'As soon as peace returns we will be back with unfair competition from abroad and no market for our produce.'

The argument, which they'd had before, continued, but with less irritation on Donald's side than usual. After all, the boy had done well, and maybe America's Lend-Lease scheme would yet come off and the Yanks would provide the equipment that David seemed so certain that they needed.

The rising and dipping road to Chipping Norton passed the Bliss Tweed Mill, which put Donald in mind of his old mill in Halifax. A smile of self-satisfaction crossed his face as he thought of his great coup: selling up in 1918, before the gravy train hit the buffers. The Olivers had done well out of the Great War and with any luck this one would put Chorlton back in the money. His father had made a fortune supplying worsted to the Army, but once the war was over, well, even a child could see . . .

With the money from the sale of the mill safely in the bank, he'd had fifteen glorious years in the RAF. He'd been in at the start, just a year after the Royal Flying Corps broke away from the Army. He'd got his wings at the Central Flying School and passed out as Pilot Officer Donald Oliver at Cranwell. That had been a truly great day. He'd never forget the joy and pride of joining Number 12 Squadron at RAF Andover and flying Heyford bi-planes. But then that idiot of a Wing Co had had him transferred to Logistics. He'd resented it at the time – flying was considered a cut above paper pushing – but at least he could still sport wings on his tunic. And his talents in administration were soon rewarded with a mix of home postings and foreign tours, which sent him steadily up the ranks.

Best of all had been their last tour, in India. He'd been in his element, with plenty of chums happy to share a snifter or a spot of lunch in the mess. In the heat of summer they'd gone up country and played a lot of polo and tennis; at weekends there were dinners and dances and every evening they'd have sundowners on the club verandah. He'd had a driver, a syce and servants to blanco his plimsoles and polish his boots.

But Maud hadn't been happy. She said she felt like a fish out of water, which she was, of course. But her attitude had riled him.

'Why won't you come to the club? It's not as if you have any work to do. You've got gardeners, kitchen staff, even an ayah for Laura.'

But she'd just smiled and said, 'You go, darling. I'm no good at the social talk and you're wonderful at it, and everyone adores you. You go.'

So he did, but it had irritated him that with all that opportunity to mix with the right set, Maud had preferred to stay at home with Laura. She also took every opportunity she could to go home to Blighty, taking Laura with her. To be with the boys, she said – Hugh was by then running Chorlton and David was at Eton.

*

Donald had long since learned to steer his mind off dwelling on the premature end to his original RAF career. But now, as he brooded on Maud's failings, he concluded that if she hadn't left him for such long periods he'd never have started the affair with Angela. And if that bloody little Squadron Leader husband of hers had had any honour he'd have tackled him himself, but of course he went weaselling off to the CO who'd said, the bastard, that Donald was lucky not to be cashiered. He'd had no option but to go on the retirement list.

Still, he thought with satisfaction, they'd had to get him back when it mattered. Funny how minor peccadilloes like a fling with a fellow officer's wife can end a career in peacetime, but when they need you for the war effort, well, that's a different story.

Donald's mood lightened as an RAC patrolman saw his badge on the front fender and saluted. Quite right, too, he thought, nodding in acknowledgement. He'd been an RAC member for over twenty years, ever since he bought his first motorcar in 1919. He liked being saluted, though of course he'd never admit it.

More cheerful now, his mind flipped to his second great coup: buying Chorlton from the receivers in 1930. The owner was a banker who'd lost everything in the crash, and he'd got it for less than half its worth.

No flies on me, he thought. I sold at the right time and bought at the right time.

Of course, in some ways Chorlton was a disappointment. He'd not expected to have to keep it going with his savings. Yet the real letdown was not the money, it was rather that, after ten years, Chorlton had not brought the social advancement he'd envisaged. He'd chosen the best public schools for his children so they'd mix in the right circles, and having Lord Frampton as a neighbour was bound, he'd thought, to open doors. Well, at least they'd been invited to the ball.

What a pity he couldn't take his darling Laura to it. She must feel like Cinderella. But of course she wasn't old enough, though she did look older than thirteen. With that great mass of auburn curls and big green eyes, she was going to be a real corker.

Poor girl, the war was robbing her of a proper childhood. But at least she was safe at school up in Keswick or here in the Cotswolds. They were all safer here, far from the Blitz in London and from Hitler's industrial targets. Still, he thought, his daughter should be spending her holidays at Pony Club or playing tennis, not salting down runner beans like a kitchen maid.

One day, he would make it up to her, of that he was certain.

Maud was taking Laura and Sophie into Stratford-on-Avon to trawl the junk shops before Laura went back to school. It was a treat for Laura, who had spent most of her summer holidays helping her mother in the kitchen or dairy or working on the farm for her brother. The war had put paid to visits to friends or trips to London.

The girls were laughing and chattering while watching the countryside glide past outside the train window. It was good to see them so carefree and excited, thought Maud.

'Where shall we start, Mummy? Do you know where the second-hand shops are?' asked Laura.

'I imagine there'll be a few stalls in Rother Market. What are you spending your pocket money on, Sophie?' asked Maud. 'Are you a collector like Laura?'

Sophie laughed, a little embarrassed. 'No, I can't understand it at all. But she's always collected things, haven't you, Laura? Do you remember your pressed flower craze?'

'Of course. I've still got all the books. I'd still do it, but you can't get the blotting paper.'

'Could we go and look at dress patterns somewhere?' asked Sophie. 'Mummy has got four yards of green taffeta which she says I can have if I make the dress myself.'

They went to the Rother Street Market and Laura bought a pale green Spode antique cup and saucer, and Maud bought a set of brown pie dishes. 'I don't need all three,' she admitted, 'but I need the big one to replace the one I broke tripping over David's dog.'

'Oh, go on, Mummy. You'll always use them.'

'Could I just have the big one?' Maud asked the salesman.

'Sorry, Madam, they're a set. And a bargain at the price. You'd pay more in a shop just for the little—'

'Would you take twenty per cent off if she buys all three?' Laura interrupted. To her surprise, the man agreed.

Maud watched in admiration, and some surprise, at her daughter's bargaining skills. Laura held an antique embroidery set, with scissors, thimble, hole punch and a latch hook, all of them nestling in dips in the blue velvet lining of a mahogany box. 'I can't afford five shillings,' she said. 'Would you take half a crown?'

The stallholder shook her head. 'That's solid silver, that thimble,' she said. 'And look at the workmanship of these handles.' She pointed to the elaborately decorated handles of the hook and the punch, then picked up the scissors. 'They're Victorian.' She seemed to consider, then said, 'I could let you have it for four.'

Laura took the scissors from the woman, and turned them in

her hand. 'Look, Mummy, aren't they beautiful? And they are really comfy to hold.'

Maud saw the longing in her daughter's eyes and shook her head in puzzlement. 'What do you want with an embroidery set, darling? You don't even like sewing.'

But Laura had turned back to the woman. 'Could you let me have it for three and sixpence?'

In the end they settled for three and nine. Laura was delighted, and Maud was baffled. 'Darling,' she said, 'that's half your saved pocket money gone.'

'I know, Mummy. But I love it. I won't regret it. I shall have it all my life.'

CHAPTER THREE

The local War Agricultural Committee met upstairs in the Crown and Sceptre in Chipping Norton. The room was stuffy, smelling strongly of last night's smoke. All four windows had blackout boards taped into them.

Donald was the first to arrive. He realised they hardly ever hired out these rooms in the day, but it was unconscionable to expect men to sit through a meeting with no air and no daylight. He took out his Swiss Army knife, slit the brown tape that secured one of the boards and prised it out. Then he removed the other three.

He settled himself with his papers at the head of the table and ran his eyes down the agenda. Good, he thought, we should get through the routine stuff in twenty minutes and have plenty of time for me to get my way over the Frampton land issue.

Gradually the other committee members drifted in. Jim Porly, the committee secretary and local pharmacist, arrived next, followed by two farmers and Sophie's father, Wenlock, the vet.

The last two to arrive were friends and they came in together. Jonathan Scruton was a wealthy landowner from Bloxham who also owned a quarry and brickworks near Dean, and Sir Thomas

Goodall was the representative of the Regional War Agricultural Office, to whom Donald's committee reported. Donald, who had not stood up to greet any of the others, sprang to his feet.

'Good afternoon, Jonathan. And very good of you to come, Sir Thomas. You must be a busy man.'

'War makes work-horses of us all, does it not?' Goodall sat down heavily next to Donald. 'And your committee has done well, Oliver. Getting farmers to give up animals and start ploughing isn't easy, I know.'

The first half of the meeting was taken up with a report on the year's progress. Almost all the farms had met their targets, sacrificing pasture for cultivation and ploughing available fallow. Donald hoped the committee would notice that Chorlton had out-performed the rest.

They finally got to the matter of Frampton, which had made no progress at all. Donald was determined to be tactful. There was no point in going in like a bull in a china shop and telling the truth – that his aristocratic neighbour couldn't run a whelk stall and was not in the habit of taking orders from anyone. Instead, he addressed his remarks to Sir Thomas.

'This is a rather delicate matter, sir. You'll remember, I'm sure, that Frampton's three Barrow farms were originally requisitioned by the Government because it was thought that RAF Moreton-in-Marsh would need the extra land. The Earl tried hard to retain the three farms, but the airfield went ahead and the land was requisitioned. Then, after the Munich Agreement, the airfield plans changed and the Frampton land was deemed surplus to requirements. Rather than let it lie fallow, the RAF allowed the Frampton tenants to stay on and work the land.'

Donald realised he had the attention of the whole room –

26

everyone enjoyed gossip about toffs – and he raised his voice a little, pleased with his delivery.

'The Earl complains that he was never paid any compensation for the land, but that is nothing to do with us. What *is* our business is the poor husbandry on those farms. I propose that we evict the tenants and put an efficient farmer in to bring the farms back to reasonable productivity.'

'I know the Maxwell-Calder family well,' said Sir Thomas. 'The Earl must be in his sixties now. Fascinating chap. But not much of a farmer, I suspect.'

'Yes, indeed. He's my closest neighbour. We'll be going to his son's coming-of-age ball soon. So you see it is a little awkward for me, but we must insist he make an effort to get Frampton productive. One problem is that both his land agent and his estate manager have joined up.'

'What about the son, George? Could you not approach him?'

'He's joined up, too. I wrote to the Earl last week suggesting we meet to discuss the matter, but I'm afraid I got a rather rude reply. Mr Secretary, perhaps the committee should hear the letter. Could you read it out, please?'

Jim Porly looked uncomfortable. 'Are you sure, Mr Chairman? I don't think his Lordship would want his private correspondence—'

'Porly, it is not private. It's a letter to me as Chair of this committee and I deem it right that the members know what we're dealing with here. Please give me the letter and I will read it.'

Jim Porly fumbled with the file catches and removed the letter. Donald took it, put on his spectacles and began to read.

Mr Oliver,

There is no point, and on my part no desire, to meet.

I flatly refuse to plough up my three-hundred-year-old park to plant potatoes. The idea is preposterous. I am deeply insulted by your ludicrous offer of £2 an acre for this proposed vandalism. Two hundred pounds an acre would not make me despoil my park.

Equally, your committee's command that I plough fallow land and pasture on the Barrow farms will similarly be ignored. Even had I the inclination, which I do not, I do not have the manpower. I assume you have noticed that the same authorities who are requesting ever more production have simultaneously deprived me of the means of achieving it – my son, land agent, estate manager and all my able-bodied labourers. And please don't tell me that you can provide me with land girls. Land girls are a national joke.

Finally, I refuse to hack down my magnificent and irreplaceable wrought iron railings and gates to be melted down for war material. If the Minister insists, I will take a shotgun to him and a horsewhip to anyone he sends to do it.

Frampton

Donald handed the letter back to Porly and sat back.

'Well, obviously that last paragraph, about the railings, is nothing to do with us, and I suggest we refer it to the proper authorities.'

There were nods of agreement. Sir Thomas said, 'I hope we can convey the fact that he refuses to take down his gates without passing on his threats to the Minister's life. If that gets into official channels, he could end up prosecuted.'

Serve him right, too, thought Donald. He knew that the War Ags had the power to dispossess owners of their land if they were unable or unwilling to cultivate it, and hand it to others who would farm it better. Chorlton was a natural to take over the farms. But he needed the suggestion to come from someone else.

'Perhaps Sir Thomas could help here,' he said, turning to him. 'You must have experience from other local War Ags. How do they persuade the reluctant to co-operate?'

'Well, it's difficult, of course. Many farmers have good reason for not meeting targets: no labour, for example. There's been a lot of opposition to the land girls, and to school children working on the farms. And there's a severe shortage of modern equipment, as I don't need to tell you . . .'

God, the old boy is going to waffle on for hours, thought Donald. He forced himself to say nothing. Oh, just get on with it, he prayed. Tell us about dispossession, for God's sake.

Sir Thomas continued, 'There is one thing, a last resort. We can confiscate land and hand it to a more competent farmer. Someone in the locality who has a proven record of good husbandry.'

There was a silence while the committee members digested this. Donald sat very still, thinking, For Pete's sake, someone wake up and make the obvious suggestion. It's staring you in the face.

'Chorlton marches with Frampton, doesn't it?' said Wenlock. 'And your boy is doing well, Oliver. Why don't you take it on?'

Relief flooding through him, Donald frowned and shook his head. 'It wouldn't be right, would it? I'm the Chair of this War Ag and it would look very bad if I helped myself to my neighbour's land.'

'But this is a committee, not your fiefdom,' said Scruton. 'It wouldn't be your decision. In fact, I think you would have to leave the room or something when the decision is made. Is that so, Sir Thomas?'

'Yes, I would say so.'

'Well,' said Donald, 'of course if it came to that, I would recuse myself. But I have a suggestion, if I may?' He looked round the table and received polite nods of assent.

'Sir Thomas, you are a lawyer by training, are you not?'

'I am.'

'I just thought, that as you are a friend of the Earl's, and a lawyer, and of course a renowned diplomat, you might have a quiet word with him. Just get him to understand that he has no option but to Dig for Victory like the rest of us.'

Sir Thomas finally agreed to try to bring the recalcitrant Earl to heel. If that didn't work, the land would be confiscated. Not the park, obviously, and not Home Farm, which was productive and moderately well run, but the three Barrow farms.

There was no further discussion as to who would take over the farms. Which is as it should be, thought Donald. Softly, softly, catchee monkey.

A fortnight later, Sir Thomas got agreement from the Earl to plant a section of the park with potatoes. And because the ground, which was stony, needed clearing and ploughing before the rains and frosts set in, Frampton reluctantly agreed to ask David Oliver to handle it.

He sent an imperious note to David, asking him to call round. There was a PS: *I do not wish any dealings with your father.*

They met in the Earl's study, an octagonal book-lined room

with a pale green and white Adam ceiling and carved finials to the bookcases. Not a lot has changed in here for a couple of hundred years, thought David, except the addition of ugly blackout curtains, now hooked back.

The Earl looked frail and stood up with difficulty, using both hands to push on his desk. He reached across it to shake David's hand. David noticed how cool and bony the hand was, but the grip was strong, as was the Earl's voice.

'Welcome, my boy. Good of you to come.' He indicated the chair opposite his. 'Sit down, do.'

'Thank you, sir.'

'I would offer you some tea, but the servants have gone off to a christening and Lady Frampton is down at the kennels.' He smiled. 'She's reading the kennel huntsman the riot act about some fallen stock – a deer – I think, not ending up in the hounds' bellies but at the butcher's.'

'Oh dear. I wouldn't like to be the kennel huntsman.'

'Nor I.'

David watched, fascinated, as his host filled his pipe. From his yellow tobacco pouch he extracted not loose tobacco but a short length of cigar, less than an inch long, which he dropped into his briar and lit. Noticing David's interest, he said with a smile, 'It's a lot easier, and cleaner, than messing around with loose tobacco. I like Davidoff's cigars and his Château Latour exactly fits my pipe. I cut each of them into seven blocks, which lasts me a day.'

David was both impressed and amused. 'I've never seen anyone do that before.'

The Earl offered him one of his cigar blocks, but David said, 'Thank you, sir, but I don't have a pipe. I will roll a cigarette, if I may?'

The Earl waited until David had his cigarette almost made, before getting down to business.

'Now look, young man. Let me make my position clear. I know what your father's game is, and I'm not going to let him win it. He wants to get his hands on my land and he's abusing his power on that damned committee to do so. But it won't work. You can tell him that.'

David opened his mouth to defend his father, then changed his mind.

'Sir, I haven't been involved with the War Ag Committee on the question of your land. I'm here at your request to discuss breaking new ground for potatoes.'

'Quite right. Let us stick to the matter in hand. We don't want an outright quarrel with your father just before we all celebrate George's coming of age, do we? It would be unseemly.' He drew on his pipe, the bowl invisible in his bony fist. 'You're all coming, I take it?'

'Indeed,' said David. 'We're all looking forward to it very much. George will be home on leave, I gather.'

'Yes. But not for long. You know he's been fighting in the Western Desert. I wish he was here, of course. We have two tenants and six labourers on our four farms and both my land agent and my farm manager are called up, and I am, as you see, hardly fit enough to be a farmer.'

David said, 'I'm sure I can help you, sir. We'll be finished ploughing within a week or two. And I think the War Ag will find me another tractor for your park. Next month I'll be able to spare the men if you don't have them. How much do you want to plough, and where?'

'I'm told to put twelve acres of my park down to potatoes. Can you believe it? And I have to slaughter the deer herd and sell them to the Ministry. I was going to refuse, but it seems that if I don't want to go to jail, I must comply.'

'Twelve acres. Hmm. We'll have to find open bits where we can plough without damaging your trees. What's the soil like? Is it stony?'

'Good Lord, boy. I have no idea. That land has been deer park for centuries.'

'I'd better have a look then.'

'Right. You do that then, and send me a quotation. And while you're about it, give me prices for slaughtering the herd and arranging the sale of the carcasses, too.'

David went home rather cheerful. It was the first time he had really talked to the Earl and he felt a mixture of admiration and pity for him. He had felt his anger rising when his father had been under attack, but he could understand the Earl's suspicions of his father's motives. Indeed, they were suspicions that David shared.

CHAPTER FOUR

It was the evening of the Frampton ball, and Laura was home for the weekend. She still minded that she was not invited, because she dearly wanted to be there, too.

She found Grace in the kitchen of Plumtree Cottage, preparing Jane's evening bottle.

'Hullo, Laura. Goodness, I am glad it's you. I thought it might be your mother, and I'd be in trouble . . .'

She waved an arm to encompass the clutter of her easel and paints, some stencilling kit, baby things, an open cigarette case of Passing Clouds and the remains of tea.

'I love your house. It's much cosier than ours.'

Laura crossed the kitchen to the range and stood warming her back against it. 'I hoped you'd show me what you are wearing to the ball.'

'Oh, all right. I've nothing new, of course,' said Grace. 'It's a dress I've had since Hugh and I married. It was part of my trousseau, but I've hardly worn it.'

'Can I see it?'

Grace smiled. 'Patience, young lady! First we must settle Jane.'

They carried baby and bottle upstairs and Grace tucked Jane

into the crook of her arm to feed her, her blonde hair falling down one side of her face. She looks so beautiful, like a Madonna, thought Laura.

They watched Jane snuffling gently as she sucked. After a while Laura asked, 'Can I feed her?'

'Of course.' Grace stood up and Laura took her place.

Jane, losing the teat in the transfer to Laura's lap, set up a wail. But Laura put the bottle back in her mouth, pleased that she almost immediately settled to feeding again.

'Oh Laura, I'm pleased you're here,' Grace said. 'You can do my stocking seams. I can hardly ask Hugh to do it.'

'What do you mean – do your stocking seams?'

'You know, it's a trick if you can't get silk stockings, which I can't. You draw lines down the backs of your legs, and they look like stocking seams.'

'But no one would see your legs anyway, in a ball gown.'

'Yes they would. I've cut the bottom off the dress. It was so long I had to hold it up all the time and I thought dancing would be dangerous. And so much fabric, like a train, is out of date.'

Mabel, who helped Grace out three days a week, arrived to babysit and took Jane off to the nursery. Grace and Laura went into the bedroom where Grace's dress was laid out on the bed. Laura examined it, holding it against herself in front of the looking glass while Grace smoothed make-up into her lower legs to disguise their pale nakedness.

Then Grace lay down on the bed and Laura used eyebrow pencil to draw a thick line down the middle of each leg from her ankles to her knees.

'I'll have to wear my old black court shoes, because anything else will be agony without stockings.'

Grace slipped on the dress, a pale blue-grey satin with an off-the-shoulder ruched top, tight over her waist and hips and then flaring out in kick pleats. You couldn't see much of her legs unless she swirled very fast. Grace had used the satin she'd cut off to edge a black velvet shawl and she had long white kid gloves. Laura thought she'd never seen anything so elegant, Grace so tall and blonde, her eyes a perfect match for the satin. Grace fixed a narrow silver circlet with silver and pearl drops in her hair, like a diadem.

Laura felt almost weak with envy. 'Oh Grace,' she groaned, 'why does growing up take so long?'

Grace laughed. 'But you're such a tomboy! I thought you'd never want to grow up, wear dresses, look at boys.'

'I can long to go to a ball without wanting to have anything to do with boys, can't I?'

Soon Hugh arrived home to change, and Grace busied herself with putting on her make-up, so Laura went home to check on her parents' preparations.

Her father's tailcoat was on the clothes horse and he was wearing black trousers, very shiny shoes and a white shirt. She watched, fascinated, as he added a starched shirt front with no back to it, and fixed a stiff white collar round his neck.

'I thought you would be in your uniform,' she said.

'Well, yes, that would be better. But sadly, mess dress has been suspended for the duration and obviously I can't wear my everyday tunic.'

She helped him put his studs in his shirt front and his regimental cufflinks in his sleeves, and watched him struggle with his white tie. Then they both stood in front of the tall cheval looking glass.

Donald met his daughter's eyes in the glass and said, 'I do wish we could take you, darling. I know you're too young, but you'd be the centre of attention, with all the boys like bees round a honey-pot.'

Pleased at this, Laura went through his dressing-room door to her mother's bedroom. Maud was struggling to fasten a long row of hooks that ran from her hip to her arm up the side of her lemon yellow ball gown.

Laura set about helping her, but couldn't help remarking, 'Mummy, you should have put in one of those new zip things.'

Her mother had already done her face and she did look good. She almost never wore make-up but she'd plucked her eyebrows and used the pencil to get a clean straight line, and had made up her eyes and mouth. Laura examined all the things laid out on the dressing table: Maybelline mascara in its little box with a brush, a tiny pot of eyeshadow, Helena Rubinstein's *Apple Red* lipstick and a round box of face powder with a soft-as-velvet brush. She wanted to ask if she could try making-up her own face, but decided that her mother would just say no. When they've all gone to the ball, she thought, I'll have a go and she will never know.

Maud interrupted her thoughts.

'Right, now for my hair. I wish I'd gone to a proper hairdresser.'

All day Maud had gone about her usual chores, cooking and cleaning, feeding the hens and pigs, in a scarf tied like a turban over her curling papers. Now she pulled it off and Laura helped her unravel the ringlets. Then she handed her mother the combs and bobby pins as she put up her hair. Maud swept all of it, mousey-brown and fine, back and used the combs to hold it there while she twisted and pinned up the curls on top of her head, pulling the front section down over her forehead.

She should cut it off, thought Laura. Long hair is fine for young women but Mummy is too old. But she didn't say anything.

David's voice called from the bottom of the stairs.

'Dad! Mother! It's twenty-five to. How are you doing? Sawkins has brought the car round.'

Maud, slightly panicky, delayed things a bit by forgetting her wrap and wanting to change her shoes, instructing Jill on Laura's bedtime and Laura on what was ready in the kitchen for their supper. Finally Donald, Maud and David climbed into the car to make their slow way though the unlit lanes to Frampton. Grace and Hugh followed the Bentley in their Rover. Laura watched them go, resigned to the unfairness of being so young in a family of grown-ups.

As she turned away from the window, she felt Jill's arm around her. 'Don't be sad Laura, you and I are going to amuse ourselves while they dance the night away. But first I have to wash my hair. You couldn't help me, could you? It is so awkward trying to wash it with your head over the basin.'

The Oliver family crossed the dark porch and mounted Frampton's unlit steps together.

Donald knew they made a handsome party as they emerged, blinking, into the brightly lit and crowded entrance hall of Frampton. Donald was proud of his son, already a Squadron Leader, and of his beautiful blonde daughter-in-law. And he had to hand it to her, Maud had really made an effort and looked splendid. No one would know that the shimmering silk dress had started life as a pair of curtains from their dining room in the Halifax house. I hope Maud has the sense not to tell anyone that, he thought, but she's quite capable of it.

A maid took their cloaks and then there was a slightly awkward few minutes when they did not know where to go next. But soon they were ushered into a large reception room, glittering with candles and electric chandeliers.

'Goodness,' said Maud, 'don't they know there's a war on?'

'I expect they had stocks of candles and bulbs from before the war, and this is the moment to splash out,' said Hugh.

They were in a crush, everyone heading towards the big double doors at the end of the first reception room, leading into the next. It took perhaps ten minutes before they reached the end of the receiving line and came face to face with their Frampton hosts. The Earl, leaning on his stick, and his wife, stiff and wide in a mauve ball gown, stood with their son George, the birthday boy, in his army captain's uniform. When the Olivers were asked by the Master of Ceremonies, grandly dressed in red mess jacket and a lot of gold braid, for their names, Donald answered clearly, 'Air Commodore Donald Oliver, Mrs Oliver and their sons, David Oliver and Squadron Leader Hugh Oliver, and Mrs Hugh Oliver.'

The Master of Ceremonies had not got through announcing the first of the Olivers when the Earl stopped him, reaching out to shake hands.

'How very good to see you, Oliver. And Mrs Oliver. We see so little of our neighbours, do we not?'

Before Donald could respond, he went on, 'And both young Olivers, too. And you, my dear.' He gave a little bow over Grace's hand. 'You are all most welcome.'

With that the Earl turned to greet his next guests and a second functionary of some kind, head butler probably, ushered them forward, deeper into the room. None of the Olivers had said more than a hurried 'good evening' to their hosts. And Lady Frampton had not said a word, just smiled.

The Olivers accepted coupes of champagne and surveyed their fellow guests. 'How very generous,' said Maud. 'They've invited all their tenants and neighbours. How very kind.'

Donald, though he did not say so, was dismayed. He'd thought their invitation was in recognition of their gentlefolk status, but now he felt lumped with old Cragshaw, owner of the ramshackle piggery known for miles around as 'Smelly Bottom', and the Frampton tenants, many of whom were practically yokels.

He was pleased to see that David was now talking to a young couple of obvious breeding – a naval officer, much decorated, and his lady, beautifully dressed in a mauve ball gown and amethyst jewels. Donald was approached by Sophie's father, Wenlock, which saved him, just in time, from having to talk to the farrier. The vet was hardly his social equal, but at least the man was educated.

Wenlock remarked, 'It does seem a little odd to be having such a wonderful celebration in the middle of this terrible Blitz, don't you think?'

'I don't know. I understand it was planned in the middle of the phoney war, and then when Hitler kicked off in earnest, the Earl decided that cancelling would be giving in to the little swine. Quite right, too.'

Dr Drummond and his wife joined them, and they stood about for a good thirty minutes while the Frampton party greeted the long line of guests. Now they split up and each of them, Earl,

Countess and son-and-heir, occupied a different bit of the room and went from group to group, dispensing charm. Young George was chatting to Hugh and Grace. They looked relaxed and happy, laughing with the young Viscount. Well, thought Donald, at least my boys are in the right milieu.

When dinner was announced, they followed the crowd into the ballroom where tables were laid around the dance floor, all exquisitely decorated with autumn leaves and berries and long candles in tall candelabra. Behind the dance floor was a small orchestra, all formally dressed, on a foot-high rostrum.

'Oh!' breathed Maud. 'Is it not beautiful?' There were named dance cards at every place, and the guests wandered about, looking for their names. Several waiters in tails were stationed about the room, consulting their lists to help guests find their places.

'Stay here,' Donald instructed his wife. 'I'll find out where we're seated.'

'The name is Oliver,' he said, trying to peer over the man's elbow to read the list.

The waiter turned the page, and scanned it. 'Ah,' he said. 'Oliver. Yes. Here we are, sir. I'm so sorry, I had the wrong list. Your party is seated in the Orangery, sir. If you'd care to go back through the drawing room, any of the servants will direct you.'

Donald led his family back though the hubbub of perfectly accented, confident voices. When they reached their destination, he stopped in the doorway, appalled. The dimly lit Orangery was lined with blackout material and out of it came a babble of loud laughter and country accents. Deep farmers' voices with the occasional high-pitched female shriek assailed his ears before he made out the long trestle tables with benches for seating. As his eyes grew accustomed to the dark, he saw that the tables here were also decorated, more obviously but less elegantly, with autumn foliage. Whereas silver candelabra adorned the ballroom, red oil lamps did duty here. Jugs of beer and lemonade stood on the tables and large lit lanterns hung from the iron struts of the roof.

There were no place names and most of the tables were full, or nearly full. Donald felt anger and indignation rising through his chest. 'Maud,' he expostulated, 'this is a disgrace. We're not sitting with these peasants. I will summon Sawkins at once.'

To his surprise, Maud held his sleeve, eyes burning. 'No, Donald.' She was whispering, but loudly, almost hissing. 'You'll make us look like snobs, and I'd rather be a peasant than a snob. Besides, you will spoil the evening for us all.'

She dropped his sleeve and called to her sons over his shoulder, 'David, Hugh, there are seats over there . . .' And, to Donald's astonishment, she walked into the room, weaving fast between the tables to take possession of the end of one table.

Donald, seething at both the insult of the dinner *placement* and the insurrection of his wife, hesitated. He knew his face must be bright red. He could feel the heat in his neck.

'Here, Oliver, there's a free place here.' It was Farmer Wheeler, from Enstone. Well, he was a decent man, if rough. Donald nodded. Damned if I'll sit with Maud, he thought. Looking across the room, he caught her eye, then deliberately looked away and sat down at the end of a bench next to Wheeler.

Donald was so hot with bottled anger that he was unable to speak, let alone concentrate on Wheeler's lament about the War Ag Committee. He sat silent and furious while Wheeler talked of the farmers' mistrust and suspicions of favouritism and incompetence.

Suddenly Donald could stand it no more. He stood up abruptly, turned and left the room. He marched through the reception room, now deserted except for a few attendants. One young woman, with a tray of empty glasses, tried to stop him.

'Sir, is something wrong?'

Angered by her interference, he pushed past her roughly and heard the crash of glass as he marched away. He did not look back. He had almost reached the door into the entrance hall when George, the birthday boy, stepped through it.

'Hullo, Mr Oliver. What's up? You look . . .'

George stood in the doorway, so Donald was forced to stop.

'Look here, young man, let me pass . . ..'

'Are you all right, sir? Not ill? It's hot in there, I know. That's why I came . . .'

Donald exploded. 'Of course I'm not ill. I'm leaving because I'm angry. Furious, in fact. I've never been so insulted in my life!'

He tried to push past George but George raised his arms to hold both sides of the door frame.

'Insulted? How insulted? Who has insulted you?'

'You have. Or, more accurately, your father has insulted my whole family. Damnably insulted us. My wife and boys are more forgiving than me, and are enduring dinner with the riffraff of four counties. When I think of the time and money my ladies have spent on ball gowns, only to drink beer and cider with tenants and land girls . . . Well, sir, you see why I'm leaving. Please stand aside.'

George said no more, but raised his hand to the butler standing at the front door.

'Andrews, please assist Mr Oliver. He will need his car.'

And with that he gave a formal little bow to Donald and returned to his birthday party.

Sawkins was fetched. Donald did not speak except to say, 'Home, Sawkins, and then you must return for the others as arranged.'

In the Orangery, with a couple of glasses of cider inside her, Maud was enjoying herself. At first she'd been anxious about Donald, but she made an effort to put him out of her mind and now the relaxed and convivial atmosphere engulfed her. The thought that her husband's absence might explain her mood crossed her mind, but she quickly banished it.

Dinner was splendid. The roast pork, fragrant with sage, was delicious, especially the crackling: they'd obviously slaughtered a pig, and there was apple sauce, cabbage and potatoes. Best of all there was home-made gooseberry ice cream, an almost unheard of treat.

Maud watched her daughter-in-law eating it silently. Grace was a picture of pleasure. She put small teaspoons into her mouth, closed her lips, shut her eyes to savour the moment, then slowly withdrew the spoon.

She blinked. 'Mmmm.' She looked at Maud. 'I thought ice cream was illegal?'

'Not quite, but as cream has to go for butter making and nearly all the milk is reserved for nursing mothers and children, I don't know how they made this. It would have taken gallons.'

'They must have done it in batches, skimming off a little cream at every milking,' said David.

Maud, feeling mellow and benevolent, looked at her daughter-in-law. How beautiful Grace is with that bright blonde hair, flawless skin and clear grey-blue eyes, she thought, and domestic efficiency isn't everything. If Hugh doesn't mind how hopeless a housewife Grace is, what business is it of mine?

As if reading her thoughts, Grace said,

'Maud, I've been meaning to say that I'm sorry I'm so useless on the farm and at home. It must be dreadfully annoying for you, but I do try. It's just that I wasn't cut out for this life.'

'How extraordinary. I was just thinking that being good at ironing is not the be-all and end-all of a woman's life, or shouldn't be. You have other talents, Grace, like your drawing. Those sketches of baby Jane are wonderful. And you have the most loving, tolerant nature.'

Maud became aware that Hugh was listening.

'Don't you try to change, my darling,' he said. 'You are the best of mothers and that's what matters.'

Yes, and that's the problem, thought Maud. She's so soft-hearted she'll end up spoiling the baby. The least whimper and Jane's in her arms.

David had been talking to the girls on his other side, and Maud turned to join in. She recognised them as the Frampton land girls, nicely-spoken middle-class young women from Cirencester. They worked on the Barrow farms and lived with one of the tenant farmers who, they said, had braved the Countess to get them invited to the ball.

Maud immediately thought of Jill, at home with Laura. 'David, perhaps we should have done the same for Jill?'

'I was thinking the same thing.'

After dinner they heard music strike up and most of the diners set off to the barn. Maud was persuaded by David to dance, and they followed the crowd. The path was marked by white-painted stones and the wide barn doors had two sets of blackout curtains.

Maud, eyes wide in admiration, looked round at the enormous space. Every wall was thickly decorated with greenery and the ceiling was hung with more lanterns. Round the edge were hay bales, grouped randomly as seating. The earth floor was swept clean and dampened with water to lay the dust. And the band, on a podium of crates, played an accordion, pan pipes, a saxophone and a guitar.

Maud danced a couple of reels but soon excused herself and joined Farmer Wheeler, sitting with his wife on a hay bale.

'What's up with your old man, Maud?' said Wheeler. 'He was in a fair old taking when he left.'

Maud forced herself to smile, 'Oh, you know Donald,' she said. 'He hates parties. Didn't really want to come.'

Happily, further talk of Donald was thwarted by the arrival of the owner of Bliss Tweed Mill, who engaged Maud in talk of the weaving trade.

After a while they were joined by a panting Grace and a very unruffled Hugh, so fit that his breath was perfectly steady. They all watched the dancers in near silence, unable to compete with the noise.

Maud again found herself studying her son and daughter-in-law. It was good to see Grace happy. After so many frugal suppers on her own with Hugh away on a bombing mission or dining in the officers' mess, to have a night out with her husband must be heaven.

Hugh is looking at her with the eyes of a lover, thought Maud. Well, he's not seen her dressed up and glamorous for ages. Nor without baby Jane in her arms. The couple were utterly absorbed by each other. Grace's colour was heightened by her exertions and her hair under the silver circlet was slightly awry. Hugh's eyes were on her perfect mouth as she closed her lips round her cigarette. Her eyes fluttered shut as she breathed in the smoke, then opened to return her husband's gaze. She took the Passing Cloud from her mouth and smiled slowly at him, a promise.

Maud quickly looked away, embarrassed, and just a bit jealous. Had Donald once looked at her like that?

David stood up and put his mouth to her ear. 'I'm going to get Jill,' he said.

Laura and Jill were playing Monopoly when David burst in, full of plans. Jill was in her dressing gown, a towel over her shoulders to catch the drips from her wet hair.

Jill shook her head.

'No, David, I can't. Even if I was dressed to the nines, I wouldn't leave Laura on her own.'

'Isn't Father back? And Mrs Digweed upstairs?'

'Why does everyone always think I need looking after?' Laura protested. No one answered.

'And anyway, I wasn't invited,' Jill said, 'and I wouldn't dream of going. Besides, we've only just started our game. You could join us if you like.'

So David sat down and they all played. The game went on for an hour and in the end Laura pretty well scooped the board. Jill had gone bankrupt and David was in serious debt to the bank, owned, along with most of hotel-strewn Belgravia, by Laura.

'OK, I give up,' said David. 'I declare Laura Oliver the winner.'

'No, don't give up, David,' cried Laura, pink with pleasure. 'I want to win properly, with you bankrupt, too!'

But David said it was after midnight and a good time to stop. He gave her a hug. 'Well, little sis, this calls for celebration. I'm going to get us all some scrumpy.'

David poured them each a glass. 'Well, if you won't come to Frampton, Jill, let's roll up the carpet and we can have our own barn dance,' he said. He opened up the old Dansette record player and put Count Basie on the turntable.

Jill danced a quickstep with Laura.

'How did you learn to do that?' she asked.

'At school,' replied Laura. 'We all dance with each other on Saturday nights. I can do the tango, too, and the quickstep, fox-trot, waltz. I like the polka best.'

So Laura was the one to give the dance lessons. They didn't have any Latin-American records but they had a few waltzes and fox-trots. Laura danced with each of the others to demonstrate the steps, then David and Jill danced together while Laura corrected their efforts. Laura suspected that they were humouring her, that they could both dance better than they pretended, but she didn't care. It was fun being in charge and she could feel the heat on her cheeks. She noticed that Jill, who was still in her dressing gown but now without the towel, was flushed and happy, too. She looked much prettier than usual, with her hair all wild and her eyes excited.

After they'd been galloping round the room in a six-legged polka, Jill and David collapsed together on the sofa. 'Give us another glass of scrumpy, Laura,' said David. So Laura filled their glasses and had another glass herself. She felt a little giddy and she knew she was red in the face, but hoped they'd put that down to the dancing.

David put 'Pennies from Heaven' on the turntable and he and Jill danced together. They did look funny, David in white tie and tails, Jill in her bedsocks and dressing gown. The music was really smoochy and slow, and Laura watched her brother with his face in Jill's hair and his hand spread wide on her back. And then they pulled apart a bit and David's face went all solemn as he looked into Jill's face. He wants to kiss her, thought Laura. Grown-ups are so obvious.

Jill went to bed feeling guilty and unsettled. She'd loved the dancing, and David's hand on her back, and his close attention to her, but she shouldn't have. It was all wrong. He was her boss and her friend, and it had to stay that way.

Besides, she was already spoken for. Not engaged, it was true, but she and Roger had spoken about marrying when they were older, maybe in a year or two, when the war was over and he had a job.

And he was away at the Front, probably cold and frightened. Maybe even wounded. He would be thinking of her, and she should be thinking of him, not David.

CHAPTER FIVE

Laura was home for the Christmas holidays and for once her whole family was together. Grace and Hugh (who had two nights' leave) had left Jane at home with Mabel and come to supper. Jill was sitting next to David. I bet they're holding hands under the table, thought Laura.

Laura loved Fray Bentos pies. There were two of them, bought, according to her mother, with half the family's rations for the week. It was such a treat to get beef that everyone ate in near-silence. It wasn't until they were on to the bread pudding that anyone said anything. And then the conversation returned to the well-worn subject of the Frampton farms.

David started, 'Dad, the Earl knows you want to take control of the Barrow farms. Don't you think, with your position as Chair of the War Ag, you need to be a bit careful?'

His head jerked up, his eyes challenging, and Laura felt a pang of nervous apprehension. Her father and David quarrelled a lot about the farms.

'What are you saying, boy? That I'm doing something dishonest?'

'Of course not. But the War Ags are really disliked. Everyone suspects them of favouring the landed gentry and not being fair to the small farmer.'

Laura expected an outburst from her father but instead he smiled. 'Well, the fact that we are pressing an aristocrat to do his bit for the war effort should dislodge that little prejudice.'

He sat back, looking pleased with himself.

Laura marvelled that her brother could argue without getting cross. 'But why can't you just impose a deal on him like we have for the park?' he said. 'That way, I – or some other farmer – farm the land under contract for an agreed fee, but he gets the revenue from the crops.'

David might be calm, thought Laura, but Daddy is getting angry. She silently willed them both to stop and she looked at her mother to intervene, but Maud's eyes were on her lap.

'I'm surprised at you, David. To prefer a fee to reaping the rewards of rising prices, enormous home demand and a guaranteed market is crazy. Properly farmed, the Frampton Estate could be our fortune.'

'But Dad,' said Hugh, 'surely it should be *their* fortune.'

'Well, no. As it happens the Barrow farms belong to the government already. I've no intention of paying rent to them, and, mercifully, they are not asking for any.'

'I don't understand,' said Laura. 'How can the government own the Barrows?'

'They were requisitioned before the war as it was thought they'd be needed for Moreton Airfield. But they never were.'

'So the Earl has been paid for the farms already?'

'He says not. I'm not sure I believe him.'

Laura looked troubled. 'Why don't you believe him, Daddy?

And if the airfield people don't need the land after all, why don't they give it back?'

'Don't you worry your pretty little head about it, darling. This is grown-up talk and you know nothing about it.'

Laura's face blushed hot. The unfairness of this was too much for her. She burst out, 'I *do* know about it, Daddy. I'm not stupid. The Frampton tenants don't farm properly. Your committee thing, the War Ag, wants them to grow more grain. And we are good farmers, so you think we should be given their land.'

Donald's face changed from anger to amused pride.

'Well, my girl, that's a pretty good summary of the situation, I agree. But I think you should leave it to your elders and betters to decide what's best.'

Laura thought, He's *sneering* at me. Although she was a little mollified by his partial climbdown, she told herself that if she had anything to say, she'd jolly well say it, even at the risk of her father losing his rag. She opened her mouth to speak but her mother got in first.

'What worries me is what the neighbours will think, Donald. Since the War Ag was set up we haven't been very popular with the small farmers, and since the ball, not with the gentry either. I'd hate anyone thinking we were taking advantage.'

Her father, Laura noticed, took not a blind bit of notice of her mother's contribution. Instead, he turned to Hugh.

'The Maxwell-Calders have had plenty of time to show willing, but those farms are less productive now than they were at the beginning of the war. The committee – I repeat, *the committee*, not me – may decide that the best way to get production up is to confiscate the farms.'

Her father was warming to his theme, his eyes intense.

'Are you then suggesting that we, the Olivers, should refuse to take them?' He looked from Hugh to David. 'Should we join the Earl in his lack of concern about producing food for the nation? I know where my duty lies and I will do as directed. As I hope you will, David.'

Laura's former indignation had drained away. Now she felt torn and unhappy. She did not like to see her father challenged. She had always thought he knew everything, and that his authority was respected by everyone, and that was as it should be. But over this land thing, she felt uncomfortable. It didn't sound right, and she agreed with her mother. So did Hugh and Grace, and David and Jill. If this were a democracy, she thought, he'd be out-voted.

It was good that her mother stood up to him, but of course Laura knew he would get his way. I bet it's the same at the War Ag, she thought. He probably bullies them, too. I mustn't let him bully me, she decided.

David usually worked for an hour or so in the office after supper, but tonight he was too upset by his father to concentrate. He could not stop replaying the conversation about the Frampton land, always coming to the same conclusion that thinking was pointless: he'd never in his life changed his father's mind on anything.

Jill knocked lightly on the door and slipped into the room. He made an effort to smile.

'If you've come about the milking machine prices, I haven't even compared the figures. Can't stop despairing about my impossible father.'

'No, in fact I was coming to say something about your father.

Nothing to do with milking machines. For what it's worth, I think you are absolutely right about the Frampton farms and Donald is being opportunistic and greedy.'

David sat back in his chair, his face breaking into a grin. 'Goodness, Jill. I never thought I'd hear you go against my father.'

'Well, I haven't done so publicly.' Her smile was rueful. 'I'm only the land girl, remember? But I wanted to cheer you on.'

David stood up and came round the desk. He put his arm round Jill to give her a brief hug.

'Sweet of you, and I'm grateful. But there's no chance of his listening, let alone agreeing. It's so maddening because there's an honourable solution. Two solutions, in fact: we should be paying rent for the land or we should be working it under contract for a fee.'

He looked into her face, just below the level of his, and thought how clean and honest she was. Concern for him made her eyes shine, but there was a hint of merriment behind the sympathy. She said, softly and earnestly, 'David, there must be a way.'

Suddenly her proximity, the plea in her eyes, the faint smell of soap, were all too much. He held her gaze and slowly, almost tentatively, closed the gap between their faces. His hands came up to hold her head gently as his mouth found hers.

He closed his eyes, a sort of prayer of thankfulness washing through his body: she was not pulling back, she was giving in, because she felt what he felt.

But then suddenly she stiffened and pushed him away.

'No, no, David. I can't.'

'Jill, we both feel the same thing, I know we do. What can be wrong with that?'

'It's no good. It's only happening because Roger's at the Front. If he were here . . .'

'If he were here you would leave him, Jill. You'd tell him it was over.'

He reached for her again.

She jumped back, violently shaking her head.

'No, I don't know that, do I? I haven't seen him for nearly a year. I can't just . . .' She turned to the door. 'Sorry, I'm so sorry, David.'

And she was gone.

CHAPTER SIX

1942, autumn

It was a bright, breezy day in late October and the trees had not yet lost all their leaves; the last few clung on, shining yellow and orange in the low sunshine. Grace had decided to take advantage of the fine afternoon and go for a walk with Jane. The little girl was grabbing at falling leaves and trying to jump from tussock to tussock, falling over and laughing. Grace sat on the stile at the edge of the wood and pulled her small sketchpad from her jacket pocket. As she watched her daughter and tried to catch something of her comic movements and her childish freedom, Grace felt hopeful and happier than she had for years. Everything was looking up: she was getting on better with Maud, darling Jane was growing up full of character and determination, and, best of all, news of the war was more positive. The German 6th Army was surrounded in Stalingrad and Monty had defeated Rommel at El Alamein. Soon the Allies would start to drive the Germans out of Europe, she was sure.

And Hugh was coming home tonight. She knew he would be full of the glories of the new bomber, the four-engine Lancaster.

She smiled at the thought: Hugh was like a child with a new toy, exulting over some brilliant new navigational aid that meant they could find a target even on dark nights. He was now a 'Pathfinder' Master Bomber, which meant he flew in front of the squadron, identified the target, dropped flares to mark it, and then circled round throughout the raid, making sure the bombers dropped their bombs where they should.

When he'd told her this, Grace had been horrified. 'But that means you're over the target for the longest time. All the others are in and out as soon as they have dropped their bombs.' But Hugh had just laughed and said it was an honour to get the job. He wouldn't have it any other way.

'Just think, darling,' he'd said, hugging her and smiling into her eyes, 'two years ago our chaps were flying single-engine bombers in broad daylight, or in bright moonlight, trying to pick off German ships, and Jerry was just shooting them out of the sky. And at the airfield, every few days some gung-ho young pilot would be killed on a training flight. Enough to put the wind up anyone. Flying today is a lot safer than that.'

Grace knew how deeply he felt the loss of friends, but he seldom mentioned them. He was a Wing Commander now, but he still spoke of flying bombers as if it were a game. It was one of the things she loved so much about him: Hugh's refusal to be bowed by the fear, the long hours, the lack of sleep, the appalling odds of staying alive.

It was turning chilly. Grace pocketed her sketchpad and took her daughter's hand.

'I don't want to go home,' Jane whined. 'I want to see the cows milking.'

'Being milked,' corrected Grace. 'It's not time for milking yet, darling.'

'Why?'

'Because they are milked at five o'clock and it's only three now.'

'Why isn't it time?'

'Because why's a crooked letter and you can't make it straight.'

'Why is it crooked?'

'Oh, Jane, it just means please stop asking questions.'

Jane was endlessly curious, demanding and persistent. She was also quick to tears and tantrums and as she tired the likelihood of these increased. Grace thought with relief that Mabel would be there when they got back and she would give Jane her tea and bath. And that, she thought, will give me time to change and be ready for Hugh. I may not be the best of housewives, but I do always make an effort for my husband. Then she embellished this train of thought: maybe it was time for another baby?

Grace was dressed and brushing her hair when she heard the front door bell. She quickly dabbed her neck, just below each ear, with her precious *Je Reviens* by Worth and ran down the stairs, expecting Hugh to say he'd forgotten his keys.

But it wasn't Hugh. It was a telegram boy. As soon as she opened the door and saw him standing there, perfectly still with a beige envelope in his hand, her heart closed into a tight knot. No. No . . .

'Good afternoon, madam. Are you Mrs Hugh Oliver?'

She nodded, and took the telegram.

He bowed slightly, then turned and walked down the path.

Grace stood at the door, not moving. Then she went inside, shut the door and walked through to the drawing room.

> *Deeply regret to inform you that your son 576973 Wing Commander Oliver H A is missing from our operations on the night of 20/21 October 1942 letter following please accept my most profound sympathy pending receipt of written notification from Air Ministry no information should be given to the Press.*
> *O.C H.24 Squadron*

For several minutes Grace stood stock still, her mind blank. Slowly she sank down onto the piano stool, the telegram still in her hand. Through the wall she could hear Jane's raised voice and Mabel's low-pitched responses.

Suddenly she stood up and walked through to the kitchen. Jane was scrambling down from the table and Grace scooped her up, hugging her closely as she slid into a chair. Jane immediately wriggled free and climbed down again. Grace's eyes followed her as she went to her toy box and started to pull out toys that had just been put away for the night.

Mabel, concerned, looked questioningly across the table to Grace, who passed her the telegram without speaking. Mabel glanced at it, and said at once, 'Oh, no. Is it . . .?' Grace, silent and numb, nodded.

Both women sat immobile, then Grace stood up abruptly.

'I must tell Maud,' she said. 'Can you stay with Jane?'

She retrieved the letter and put on her coat.

'Where are you going, Mummy?' Jane was clinging to her knees now. 'I want to come.'

Grace found she couldn't speak. Mabel unpeeled the child and picked her up. 'No, Jane, you and I are going to have a story now. Come along. Mummy is going to see Grandma.'

Grace felt like an automaton, putting one foot in front of the other. I should be weeping, she thought. Maybe that comes later.

It was dark by the time she got to the big house and stepped through the blackout curtain into the kitchen where Maud was laying the table for supper, a clutch of knives and forks in her hand. She looked up, smiling a welcome, then immediately dropped the silver and hurried round to Grace.

'Grace, darling, what is it?'

But before Grace spoke, Maud knew.

'Hugh's dead.'

'Oh God.' Maud's eyes, wide with shock and distress, were fixed on her daughter-in-law's. As Grace gently led Maud to sit in a chair at the table, David walked in from the drawing room.

Grace looked at him. 'Hugh's dead,' she said again. David's smile vanished as his face clamped rigid. He shut his eyes for a second, then went to kneel in front of his mother and put his arms round her. Grace stood upright, rigidly still, feeling utterly alone. Who will hug me? she thought. Not Hugh, when I really need him. In all my tiny troubles, it's been Hugh whose arms held me. No more.

This thought, of Hugh not being there to comfort her, finally broke through her carapace of shock and she put her hands to her face as a choking sob shook her shoulders. She sat down next to Maud and pressed the heels of her hands into her eyes.

David went to fetch his father, and Maud reached for Grace's hand.

After a while, Maud made tea and they all sat round the

kitchen table, silent with shock. David sent Jill to Plumtree Cottage to ask Mabel to stay the night with Jane. Grace would stay with them.

Donald asked to see the telegram. Grace pulled it from her pocket and handed it to him. He scanned it slowly, then lifted his head and flapped it between thumb and forefinger. 'This tells us almost nothing,' he said, 'just that he's missing. Maybe he came down and is a prisoner. Or he's hiding somewhere in Germany or Belgium.'

David took the telegram from his father.

'Or he could have ditched in the sea and been rescued,' he said.

Grace's head swivelled between them, hope flaring through her. 'Do you think that could be? That he's alive?'

'*Missing* generally means killed,' said Donald, 'but it takes time to confirm. There will be reports from survivors. Everyone gets thoroughly debriefed when they get home.' He stood up and made for the door.

'Where are you going, Donald?' Maud's voice was shaky.

'I'm going to the airfield, to find out what they know.'

But there was no more news when Donald returned. Hugh's squadron was on another sortie, and his commanding officer was away at a mess dinner at a neighbouring airfield.

Grace ate almost nothing for supper. She went to bed in a nightie of Maud's and slept in Hugh's old bed from his teenage days. There were still model aeroplanes hanging from the ceiling, and a photograph of all the boys in his house at Eton. Hugh must have been thirteen when it was taken, but he was instantly recognisable. Grace looked for a long time at the blond boy in the front row, smiling in that carefree way that she knew so well.

She wept steadily, until Jill, maybe forty minutes later, tapped on the door.

'I brought you some Horlicks,' she said. 'Maud says it will help you sleep.'

Grace wiped her face on her already sodden hand towel and tried, without success, to smile.

'I hope she's having some too, then. And everyone else.'

Surprisingly, Grace slept through the night, deeply and dreamlessly, but waking was terrible. The truth returned to her like a vice, and then, while they waited for more news of Hugh, the near-certainty that he was dead and the hope that he was alive took turns to twist her heart.

She was desperate to see Jane, to pick her up and hug her, kiss her protesting face, release her squirming body and watch her run about the cottage. Why had she agreed to leave her at home? By ten o'clock she was desperate and, abandoning her cup of tea, she ran back to Plumtree Cottage.

Mabel was about to give Jane her breakfast. Jane jumped down and ran to her mother, arms outstretched, demanding to be picked up. Grace hugged the child as she fought back tears. I mustn't cry, she thought. It'll upset her. She kissed her daughter's face all over, breathing in her warmth and familiar smell, until the child objected and wriggled away and they sat down together.

'Will I boil an egg for you?' asked Mabel. 'There are still two left.'

'That'd be lovely. But boil them both, and you have one, too.'

So they all had boiled eggs and soldiers. If Hugh was here, Grace thought, I'd probably have given him both the eggs. Oh

God, every little thing is going to make me think of Hugh. How will I bear it?

At midday, when Jane and Grace were making a giant's necklace out of old cotton reels, they heard the Bentley and went to the window to see Donald climbing out of it.

Grace took Jane's hand. 'Sweetheart, I have to talk to Grandpa.'

She led her daughter through to the bathroom where Mabel was scrubbing the wooden bathmat with Vim.

'You can help Mabel, and then later we will go and see Grandma.'

Donald looked terrible. The skin round his eyes was red, his usually impeccable moustache was ruffled, and his hair un-Brylcreemed. He looked old and very sad.

He took her hands and looked directly at her. He didn't say anything, just shook his head slowly.

'Please,' Grace whispered, 'tell me, Donald, I need to know. How did it happen?'

'I spoke to a pilot and an airman. They saw Hugh's plane take a direct hit, to the main body. It burst into flames at once. Nose-dived into the sea. There were no survivors, Grace.'

'Oh God,' breathed Grace, 'but couldn't they . . . didn't they . . . ?'

'They saw no one bail out.'

'But it was dark, how could they be sure? Maybe Coastal Defence will find them. Have already found them. They have those MTBs for search and rescue.'

Grace was gabbling, desperate.

Donald took her gently by the shoulders.

'Grace, it was dawn. They could see. There would not have been time to bail out, believe me.'

Grace looked at Donald for a long moment. 'He's dead then.'
'Yes, he's dead.'

Suddenly Donald's face crumpled, and Grace moved closer to put her arms round him. They held on to each other, Grace's face against the serge of her father-in-law's RAF tunic. Donald's voice was clotted with tears.

'At least it would have been quick. Over in seconds.'

CHAPTER SEVEN

The following weeks were a dark nightmare. Maud could not comfort Donald and he could not comfort her. She knew he suffered but he would not talk about it. He hadn't told her that he'd succumbed to tears when telling Grace about the certainty of Hugh's death. Grace had told her. 'He's heartbroken, like the rest of us,' she'd said. 'I've never been close to him, but that moment made me love him, I think.'

Maud understood and nodded sadly. She hadn't seen him cry in forty years of marriage. He considered displays of emotion unmanly, so she'd been pleased and touched that he'd driven up to Keswick to break the news to their youngest and bring her home for a week. Laura adored her father and he'd have been able to comfort her. She'd have liked to go too, but she could not leave the farm. And, she'd thought a little guiltily, she'd prefer to bake bread and make blackcurrant jam rather than spend hours with Donald, probably in silence, driving north.

Maud tried hard not to think of Hugh. She hardly ever sat down: sitting down led to thinking and thinking led to weeping, which was totally debilitating, leaving her weak with exhaustion and no less miserable. She supposed the old adage about a good cry being a relief might be true if there was a shoulder to cry on, but she could not burden poor Grace, and both Donald and David were of the stiff-upper-lip school.

Besides, she had no time for grief. Mrs Digweed, who used to do most of the cooking, was now too old for any job that could not be done sitting down, and now that Grace and Jane had come to live with them, feeding, washing and ironing for a full house kept her on her feet from dawn to bedtime.

She had been busy before, of course: the war made everyone busy. But now, as well as the pigs and the hens, the vegetable garden and the dairy, she filled every spare minute making bread or bottling and pickling.

Jill, sheltering in the warm kitchen during an autumn storm, challenged her on the subject.

'Maud, you don't have to do that. Mr Brown will deliver us bread. And you already have plenty of jam in the larder. Why don't you let the WI have the fruit, and give yourself a rest?'

Maud wiped her hands on her apron and put the dough to rise by the Aga.

'I like it. Better than mucking out or lifting turnips, I'm sure.'

In fact Maud found comfort in the cooking. It was a kind of balm to her soul. Kneading bread dough, even the rough stuff that made the heavy National Loaf, was somehow comforting, and there was satisfaction in seeing the neat rows of blackberry jam, hedgerow jelly and quince paste all lined up together.

So Maud dealt with her own grief by trying not to think about it, by working solidly for sixteen hours a day and falling into bed too tired to grieve. Sleep came like a blessing, the only solace.

If sometimes this strategy failed and misery overwhelmed her, she would gain strength from the thought that she was not alone: thousands of mothers had lost their sons in war; grief would come to all women, sooner or later. There was comfort in the cliché of loss being a woman's lot.

What hurt most was the fact that the world went on, indifferent: that the autumn sunsets were as lovely as ever, that the smell of burning leaves filled the air, that the basket of crab apples and hedgerow berries looked, as always, like a painting. Does God even know what is going on in this terrible war? she wondered.

Maud had not at first thought the beautiful Grace was the right woman for her eldest son. She had been intensely irritated by her domestic incompetence and inability to concentrate long enough to put a doily over a basin or her empty cigarette packet in the wastebasket. Now, though, she became her champion.

Suddenly the only thing that mattered was that Grace had loved Hugh, and had made him intensely happy. Maud realised that she had never loved her husband like Grace had loved hers. Donald had been the handsomest man for miles around, the son of the mill owner, and a great catch, but that intensity, that all-consuming devotion, was something she'd never seen before, except in the cinema.

So, partly atoning for her half-hearted welcome into the family, Maud's prime concern became giving Grace and Jane a loving home.

'Maud, it's so kind of you to have Jane and me living here,' Grace said one day. 'I know you insisted we came because you thought I'd never manage in the cottage without Hugh.' She smiled in self-deprecation. 'And you were quite right, I'd have just gone to pieces.'

Maud shook her head in denial, though there was truth in what Grace had said. She had put Grace and Jane into the two bedrooms and a bathroom that had been a guest suite before the war. For a few months after the declaration they had housed three evacuee children from the East End of London, but the youngsters were so homesick, and their parents missed them so much, that they were gone by Christmas. It was an outcome that produced in Maud both a sense of failure and one of relief: three unhappy young children were a deal of work.

Blackout curtains and a four-foot bed with painted rabbits on the white footboard and headboard remained from that time. Maud was pleased to see Jane proudly claiming this bed, but it worried her that she would build herself a nest with the blankets and eiderdown so that she could disappear completely. She kicked and screamed if anyone tampered with her 'house'. Maud issued requests to Mrs Digweed and Mabel (who had transferred her working hours to the big house) not to make Jane's bed or interfere with her elaborate foldings and burrowings. Only Jane's teddy bear was welcome.

Maud, believing her recipe of hard work would help her daughter-in-law cope with widowhood, started teaching her to cook and iron, how to turn a collar and to put worn sheets sides-to-middle, but Grace, though she tried, was not a good pupil. She had always been scatterbrained and now she was worse. One day, bringing in the washing, she carried the first armful into the kitchen and forgot the rest to await the rain.

Seeing the sheets still flapping on the line and the rain beginning to fall, Maud swallowed her irritation and fetched them in herself. Resolving to tick Grace off, she walked into the laundry room to find Grace at the ironing board, staring blankly at the wall while smoke rose from Donald's burning pyjama bottoms.

'Lord, Grace, look what you're doing.' Maud dropped her sheets and snatched the iron to put it on the trivet. Grace looked down, lifted her eyes, full of tears, to Maud's, then put her head in her hands and sobbed. 'I can't do it, Maud. I can't do it.'

Maud put her arms round Grace and led her back to the kitchen.

'Here,' she said, handing Grace the burnt pyjama bottoms. 'Cry into this. I never liked those pyjamas anyway.'

Grace tried to smile and dried her eyes on the proffered pyjama bottoms.

'Everyone says the grief will fade. But how can it? Jane will grow up without her dad, she won't even remember him.' She clenched her teeth, trying to stop crying.

'There's no cure for grief, but the thing to remember is that if you were not so unhappy, what would that say about your marriage? If you didn't miss Hugh, it would mean that you didn't love him. The greater the happiness, the sharper the loss. It's the price you pay for love.'

CHAPTER EIGHT

Laura's train home from Keswick did not leave until eleven and Miss Janis had given her permission to leave early to go to the shops for a present for her mother's birthday. In fact, this was a subterfuge: her mother's birthday was months away but Laura wanted to trawl the junk shop in the pawnbroker's basement and the dusty antique shop next door for her own collection. Almost all her pocket money had gone on what her brother considered useless junk, like her china and glass horses. Her latest enthusiasm was for antique teacups and saucers, and sometimes side plates, too, because shopkeepers wouldn't sell the cups and saucers by themselves. Her mother approved of the horses, which now filled the windowsill of her bedroom and two shelves of the bookcase. They are proper ornaments, she said, and it's good to have an artistic interest. But she didn't see the point of the cups.

'What a funny girl you are,' she'd said, 'They're far too small for a decent cup of tea, and they're so delicate you'll smash them in no time.' She shook her head. 'Cups hanging on hooks in a bedroom!'

But Laura loved them: the delicacy of the china, the colours, the variety of patterns and shapes. She liked to imagine the designers in the famous bone china companies, like Spode, Royal Doulton or Wedgwood, dreaming up the patterns; the women skilfully painting them; the excitement of the customers when they'd bought them; the polite occasions on which they'd have been used, like something out of Jane Austen; then the succession of owners and the sad breakages over the years that had reduced them to just one or two in a junk shop. Most of her collection – she had seventeen different cup-and-saucer sets plus a few plates – was Victorian, but some of them were eighteenth-century, so they'd had a long history.

Today, she was in luck. Laura found a perfect Coalport 'trio' of cup, saucer and plate. The deep blue of the band round the saucer and plate was reflected inside the cup, a little pool of pure colour against the white bottom decorated with a delicate design of forget-me-nots. The flowers were clustered in the middle of the saucer and plate, too, and the rims were gold. She had to pay 1/1d – but it was worth it. 'Only Coalport can make that blue colour,' said the shopkeeper. 'It's a trade secret.'

Today was a Friday. A few muffled-up passengers warmed their hands round their teacups in the Keswick station waiting room. Usually the room doubled as a Roedean classroom, the passengers sitting on one side while pupils took lessons on the other. The school had spread over the whole town, including occupying the entire hotel. Classes were held in the public library and in the hotel garage, as well as in the station waiting room and in several front parlours of the larger houses.

Laura knew that she would be one of the few Roedean girls whose entire school life had been spent in Cumberland. The only time she'd seen the real Roedean was before the war when

Daddy and Mummy had driven her to Sussex to visit the school before she enrolled.

Laura had a long weekend exeat, but, what with erratic war-time trains and the usual over-crowding on them, she knew she was unlikely to get home before dark. The chances were that poor David would be driving her home in the blackout. Still, as long as it wasn't cloudy there'd be moonlight to light their way. She'd have to change at Birmingham and get a bus from Banbury, then telephone him from the call box in Chipping Norton, or Banbury if she had time.

It was good to be independent. Until she had turned fifteen, she'd had to travel with a clutch of pupils shepherded by a teacher, or even, humiliatingly, under the care of Universal Aunts. This meant travelling with a label round her neck and being met at stations and helped to change trains by strange elderly women. But now that she was old enough legally to leave school, she was allowed to travel on her own.

Laura longed to be finished with education, although she had no burning ambition to do anything with her life – unlike her friend Sophie, who was nearly seventeen and next summer would be leaving Chipping Campden school to read medicine at Oxford. Laura had another term and a half at Roedean and would only be sixteen when she left. Her teachers had tried to keep her at school longer, telling her she was university material, but Laura couldn't see the point, and anyway, Daddy thought university was wasted on girls. Laura felt guilty at welcoming his attitude when she should have opposed it, but Sophie *wanted* to go to university; she had a *purpose in life,* thought Laura. She'd always wanted to be a doctor.

Jill had a purpose, too, though Laura didn't think much of it.

She was a whizz at maths and good at farming, but it seemed that she would just marry Roger after the war. Laura had only met him once, when he'd come to visit Jill at Chorlton. She'd thought him awfully dull. She'd taken him to see the pigs and the newborn lambs and he'd hardly said a word.

If Jill wanted to get married, thought Laura, she should marry David, who adored her, you could tell. Then she could continue running the farms with him like she did now.

Even Grace would have been a painter like her father if she hadn't married Hugh and become a wife and mother instead.

But Laura hadn't the faintest idea what she wanted to do, beyond being a riding teacher, or perhaps an antique dealer, and she didn't think she needed a university degree for either of those. She didn't see how she could be either with a war going on anyway. Besides, her mother and father needed her at home. Daddy had promised her that she would have a London Season when the war was over, but that seemed as far away as ever. In the meantime she'd have to work for David on the farms, or help her mother in the house.

Still, she thought, I've time yet to decide on a career. I'm much younger than all of them. Jill was twenty, and Grace was positively middle-aged, though she didn't look it. Laura worked it out on her fingers: she was the same age as David, twenty-five.

The first thing she did as the train chugged out of the station was pull her new winter dress and her black stockings from the top of her suitcase and sidle along the passage to the lavatory. She *hated* her school uniform: she was too old for a gymslip and anyway it was too small for her, and it was hideous. Of course, she'd get what for if one of the school staff spied her on the train, but she hadn't seen any, and besides, she was so near leaving school, she didn't really care.

The stockings were darned but it didn't show, and the dress, in bottle-green jersey, fitted like a glove, close but comfy. It was a pity about the clumpy school shoes, but she hadn't any others. She pulled the rubber bands from her plaits. Her hairbrush was at the bottom of her suitcase, so she shook out her hair and combed it with her fingers. She felt immediately cheerful and smiled at her reflection in the mirror above the basin. Her hair, auburn (definitely auburn, not red) and thick, had grown this term and was past her shoulders and extra curly from being plaited. Her wide-set green eyes were framed by dark lashes, not red, thank goodness. It was a pity about her freckles, but they were pale now –they got worse in summer. She turned this way and that, admiring the dress's square neckline and narrow shoulders. She couldn't see the bottom half but it felt svelte. That was the word, svelte. And grown-up.

Laura had time to telephone David before her bus left from Banbury station, and he picked her up as planned in Chipping Norton.

'We've saved the pig for this weekend,' David told her. 'They were ready a fortnight ago but Jill insisted we wait for you.'

'Oh, good. Will everyone be there? Can I ask Sophie?'

'We already did. And her dad is coming, too. He's a good sort. And the butcher, old Fitch, and most of the farm hands and their wives. We need all the help we can get. A vet and a butcher are the best pair for the job.'

'Oh, good. I hate the actual killing, the way they jerk and kick even though they are unconscious. I can't look.'

'I know, but if you want to eat meat you need to face up to killing. Between Wenlock and Fitch the beast won't suffer, I promise.'

'I know. And I do love everyone doing the work together. It's like the harvest – it's fun. Making the sausages and doing all the salting and so on.'

As they bumped over the cattle grid into the yard, David said, 'Look, there's Jill. I wonder . . . Something's wrong.' Laura followed his gaze and saw Jill stumbling, half-running, towards the barn. One hand held a flapping piece of paper, the other covered her face.

'She's crying.' Laura jumped out of the truck and ran after her into the barn. Jill was halfway up the ladder to the loft. Laura climbed after her.

'Jill, what's happened? What's wrong?'

For answer Jill held out the paper. It was a telegram.

'It's from my mother. Roger is missing in action.'

David had followed Laura into the barn and now appeared at the top of the loft ladder. Laura turned to him.

'Jill's boyfriend is missing. Her mother sent a telegram.'

David said, 'Oh God,' and went to Jill. He put his arms round her. For a second Laura thought she was trying to pull away. But then she seemed to relax and she buried her head in his shoulder. Laura looked over at her brother and thought how anguished he looked.

'Missing in Action doesn't have to mean killed, Jill,' he said, talking into her hair. 'He could be a prisoner somewhere. Or in a field hospital. Sometimes it takes a while . . .'

'Yes, yes.' Jill nodded. You could see she was trying not to cry and to speak calmly.

Laura felt a little shaft of jealousy. David and Jill stood immobile, hugging. Laura thought, he holds her like he might his sister. Only I'm his sister and he doesn't hold me like that.

And then she thought, He does love her. I knew it.

David turned to her. 'You go and say hello to Mum, Laura. I'll stay with Jill. We'll both follow you soon.'

Laura felt excluded, sent away. But she went anyway. Three's certainly a crowd round here, she thought.

The pig killing was to take place on the Sunday so the butcher and vet would be free to come. On the Saturday evening Sophie came over on her bike and she and Laura went to see the pigs and give them a bucket of bruised windfalls.

'It's a little like a last supper, poor things,' said Sophie.

To their surprise they found Grace sitting on the stile at the paddock gate, sketching the pigs. She was wearing a heavy oilskin coat, the collar turned up and the hem just clearing the muddy ground. Her cheeks were pink from the cold and her shiny blonde hair looked, thought Laura with a twinge of envy, too summery and glamorous for a pig-pen in November.

Sophie must have thought the same thing, because she said, 'Hullo, Grace. Only you could look so beautiful in a soggy field.'

'Beautiful? Hardly. I've been out here so long my nose must be blue. But I'm grateful for Hugh's old coat. Look,' she said, opening the coat to show the fur lining, 'it's moleskin. Lovely and warm.'

'Where's Jane?' asked Laura.

'She's with Maud. I thought I'd take the opportunity to immortalise the pigs while they are all here, before that chap,' she waved her pencil at the second biggest pig, 'is dispatched. They are such endearing creatures, especially the piglets.'

They looked at Grace's drawing over her shoulder.

'I wish I could draw like that,' Laura said.

Grace smiled and shrugged. 'Pigs are easy,' she replied.

There were five of them: two fully-grown pigs, two piglets and their mother, an enormous sow. The paddock was almost grassless and very muddy in places. The sow lay on her side, relaxed but with a beady eye following proceedings. One of her elder offspring lumbered towards them and the piglets followed at a trot.

'Have you always kept pigs?' asked Sophie, scratching a bristly back.

'No, only since the war began. We can slaughter one for ourselves but we must sell one to the Ministry.'

'Which ones? Not the piglets, I hope.'

'Lord, no. The piglets are for next year and the big sow lying over there is the breeding machine. They are all her babies. She's called Patricia.'

'And the piglets? What are they called?'

Laura shook her head. 'They don't have names. Mummy thinks it's easier to kill them if they're nameless.'

Laura thought she must have been very unobservant last year. She'd found the whole event fascinating, seeing a live pig turn into familiar cuts of pork, bacon and skeins and skeins of sausages in a day. And she'd loved the way everyone included her, the youngest, like a grown-up: she'd known she pulled her weight and deserved the glass of cider her father poured for her with everyone else.

But she'd been unaware of the precise organisation involved. It was like a military operation. Her father was not a farmer (well, not a real farmer – David was the farmer now) or butcher, but with the *Instructions for the Slaughtering of Pigs* issued by the Pig Meat Association in one hand, he got everyone to set up everything the night before. All except the preparations for the kitchen, which Maud firmly decreed was her department.

Laura could not but be proud of him. No wonder he's in charge of logistics at the airfield, she thought. He was in his element, organising everything with a minimum of fuss and no shouting. Nothing was left to chance – even the spills for lighting the fire and the scrubbing brush and bleach for sterilising the cutting table were placed in readiness.

The next day Maud was up first to get the kettle on, but all the women soon joined her in the kitchen and she could hear the men greeting each other in the yard. She thought, It's going to be an exhausting day, but we must try to make it enjoyable. How we do that with Hugh dead, I don't know, and now poor Jill, with her boyfriend missing.

The women took enamel mugs of tea out to the men but they kept working steadily. Mr Fitch, the butcher, arrived with a portable chopping bench, the smaller of his two mincers, and a tool roll of knives, steels and a bolt gun to dispatch the pig.

Jill and Maud stood together, looking at the preparations: the tackle for hoisting the pig, the cutting tables, washing and cleaning kit, water heating in a 50-gallon drum for scalding the pig, troughs and buckets and tubs for the butchered joints, offal and bones. No wonder it had taken them until midnight to prepare.

'Maud,' said Jill, 'wouldn't you think that, in 1942, with women taking over men's jobs everywhere, the sex divide would have crumbled? I'd *love* to learn to butcher a pig.'

Maud, shocked but amused, hugged Jill's slender shoulders. 'Nonsense, my girl. There have to be some traditions left intact. You come back in the kitchen and get on with chopping up that salt.'

When the women heard the squealing of the pig, Maud said to Grace, 'Don't worry, love. He won't feel a thing. He's just objecting to being taken away from the others.'

'I'm going to watch,' said Jill. 'I want to learn.'

The rest of the women stayed in the kitchen and at eight-thirty David bounced in, announcing that they'd killed and bled the pig, split it perfectly down the middle and extracted its innards. He plonked a basin of kidneys and liver on the table.

'Howzat?' he said proudly.

'Lovely,' said Maud, admiring the gleaming pale kidneys and purple liver. 'This will be delicious.'

She showed Laura how to halve the kidneys and remove the fine membranes. Then they sliced the kidneys and liver, fried them fast and added them to the fried onions on the warming plate of the Aga. Sophie scrambled eggs (four fresh ones and a pint of reconstituted dried) for everyone, and Laura cut thick slices of the National Loaf.

The men came into the kitchen and rapidly ate their breakfast, then were quickly out again.

Whenever the women went outside, the cold had them wrapping their arms around their bodies or pulling their collars up round their ears. But they all found it difficult to stay away. Maud had seen this routine many times, and Laura and Sophie a good few, but to Grace and Jill it was new, and Maud was anxious they should not be upset, that they enjoy it for what it was: a traditional country event.

I need not have worried, she thought. Those girls are amazing. Jill was watching as if about to be examined on the process, and Grace was sketching the men scrubbing and scraping the pig's skin until, as David said, it was white as a bride.

The men, Maud noticed, seemed not to feel the chill. In shirt-sleeves and jerkins, they worked steadily and energetically, joshing and joking, but never pausing.

'Where does it all go?' asked Jill, indicating the neat piles of meat: legs, loins, belly, slabs of back fat, skin, trotters, intestines, offal, the head. 'It looks so much, not just one pig.'

Maud laughed. 'You'll find out soon enough. Come, we need to get to work.'

Maud was proud of them all. The women worked against the clock, too, Maud leading them, explaining, teaching, encouraging. They used everything – even the ears and trotters were gently simmered to make jellied stock for the pies, and then the meat from them was chopped to add to the pie mix.

Grace, usually dilly and vague, was diligently salting down belly pork to make streaky bacon and chopping up back fat to render it down for lard and scratchings. She said, 'You know, Maud, I'm really enjoying this. I'd never have thought I would, but it is curiously satisfying, isn't it?'

Maud, smiling broadly, went across the kitchen and gave her a kiss. 'We'll make a countrywoman of you yet, you know.'

Sophie, skimming scum from the stock with a flat perforated skimmer, nodded.

'I agree. It is satisfying. I think that's because it takes the whole family to do something so basic and vital: preserving food for the winter. It's positively medieval.'

Jill straightened up, briefly arching her back. She'd been rubbing dry salt, saltpetre, sugar and crushed juniper berries into the future Easter ham. She pushed her fringe off her forehead with the back of her hand. 'Older than that,' she said. 'The Romans shipped oysters from Colchester to Rome in pitch-lined barrels, packed in salt. Imagine! They must have been truly disgusting.'

Maud, rolling pastry for the pies, looked across at Jill. What a clever girl she is. Doesn't talk much, but she knows a lot. And God, she works hard. We all do, but Jill is worse than David. She's in the office or out on the farm seven days a week. Maud thought she worked so hard 'doing her bit' because she felt somehow guilty about not being a Wren or in the WAAF. As a conscientious objector she'd wanted to join the Ambulance service, but her parents had insisted on the Land Army.

At one o'clock Mr Wenlock came in with the brain and tongue. Maud dropped the tongue into the brine tub to soak, and put the brain into the refrigerator to chill.

Sophie was counting heads. 'With the two farm hands, the butcher, my dad and the two Olivers, there are six men out there. And with Mabel and Mrs Digweed scrubbing the chitterlings in the scullery, we are six in the kitchen, too.'

Maud smiled. 'Twelve mouths to feed again.' Then she frowned. 'And Jane. That's thirteen at the table. We can't have that.'

'Oh, never mind,' said Jill. 'We'll lay for fourteen and Jane can put her teddy on the extra chair.'

Maud sliced the brain thickly and dusted the slices with flour, dipped them into beaten egg (reconstituted from dried, but never mind), and turned them gently in breadcrumbs. Then she fried the slices carefully, two at a time, in marge.

She asked Sophie to fry the field mushrooms while she opened two Kilner jars of tomato sauce she'd put up in the summer. Jill and Laura mashed turnips and boiled cabbage. The smell of browning brains filled the kitchen and drifted out into the yard, acting like a magnet for the men. They exploded into the kitchen, pleased with themselves, eager to wash the salt, blood and fat from their hands, down a mug of cider and sit down for lunch.

It was like a party, or a pre-war shooting lunch, thought Maud; everyone was happy, having a good time. The camaraderie, the jokes between the women and the men, pleased her. And then, inevitably, the thought of Hugh washed out the moment.

It was a long afternoon, punctuated by cups of tea in the kitchen and mugs of cider in the yard, and it was almost dark by the time the men were done and ready to leave. Sophie and Mabel went with them.

Donald retired to the drawing room with his briar and his precious Balkan Sobranie and David went to his office, so only the female home team were left to finish the job and prepare supper. They had two more pies in the oven, tubs of salting pork and cooling stock for jelly to carry into the cool barn, and Mrs Digweed was patiently stuffing sausage meat into casings. When she was finally done, she took herself to bed with a cup of tea, too tired for supper, leaving Maud with just the family and Jill to feed. Thank goodness we did the apple and blackberry pie yesterday, she thought.

*

82

'That was the best pig killing yet,' said David, spearing his second sausage. 'We're a great team, no doubt of that.'

'It's because your father is a born boss,' said Maud, smiling across at her husband.

To her surprise, Donald returned the compliment. 'It's more to do with your mother's hard work. Getting a pig butchered is one thing, getting it into the larder is quite another.'

After supper Maud put an arm round her daughter and said, 'No washing up for you tonight, darling. You go to bed. You've worked like a little trooper today. Thank you.'

'She's a good girl, our Laura,' said Donald, smiling at her. 'She'll make some young man a wonderful wife one day.'

'You really have worked hard, Laura,' said Grace, and Jill agreed. 'You must be dead on your feet. I am, I know,' she said.

Laura blushed with pleasure and Maud felt as pleased with all this praise for her daughter as Laura looked.

Maud went upstairs feeling more peaceful than she had on any day since Hugh's death.

There was no one else about when, the next day, David and Jill were scrubbing down the yard. The men had left it tidy but Maud said she wanted the whole area to smell of Jeyes Fluid to discourage the flies.

When the flagstones were foamy and wet David leaned his yard brush against the wall and put his arms round Jill.

'Darling, shouldn't we come clean with the family? Tell them about us? I'm certain Laura suspects the truth.'

'I expect all the women do,' said Jill, her eyes on his. 'I wish we'd told them ages ago. But at first I thought I might still love Roger. That my infatuation for you was because I was lonely.

Now I know it was more than that. But I wanted to tell Roger in person. I didn't want him to receive a letter in some miserable dugout or camp. And now he's missing, maybe dead. Oh, David, what can we do?'

'Darling, we can wait. If he comes home, we'll tell him. And until we know, we'll just go on as we are. Loving each other in secret.'

PART TWO

CHAPTER NINE

1945, spring

It was five o'clock on the afternoon of Laura's eighteenth birth-day and she lay on her bed, her pillow over her head. She'd sneaked upstairs in the hope that her mother would think she was out on the farm and David would think she was working in the kitchen. After all, she'd reasoned, surely I have a right to *some* time to myself?

She longed to fall in love. Really, truly, forever-afterwards in love, like David and Jill so obviously were. There'd been no news of Roger since he was reported missing in action, and that was three years ago, and one day her brother and Jill would marry and live in this house. And where would she be then? A spinster sister tolerated in a cottage?

She wanted real love, love that led to a wedding, babies – a house. It had to be one in a town, not a rambling great house with sprawling farms in the middle of nowhere.

She did have a boyfriend, Marcin, but he wasn't the man in her dreams. Although, she thought, he ought to be. We love each other, don't we?

She'd met him at the village hop. It had been crowded with local girls like her, land girls and school leavers of both sexes, too young to be called up. Almost all the adult men were POWs, the ones that were allowed to come and go as they pleased. There were many more girls than boys, of course, and most of the girls were dancing with each other.

She'd arrived late because the light was broken on her bicycle and she'd had to hunt for a torch small and dim enough for her not to get a ticking off from some officious warden. As she shook off her coat she saw Marcin in a group of other men – POWs, she thought. One of them, she saw, had a hip flask and they were passing it around. As he caught her eye he took the flask, and tucked it inside his jacket.

She went to the drinks table. It was a choice between lemon-barley and blackcurrant. She bought a lemon-barley and as she turned, there he was.

'Hullo,' he said. 'What is it you are drinking?' He glanced with distaste at the cloudy liquid in her glass, looked at her and grinned. 'Is it beer, maybe?'

'No, it's made from barley. And lemon and sugar.'

'Can I taste?'

She hesitated. It seemed a bit personal to ask to try a stranger's drink. But she passed it to him. 'Have it,' she said. 'I've not touched it.'

He took a sip, pulled a face and handed it back to her, his broad smile showing perfect white teeth. 'Is horrible. But I know how to make it good.' He reached inside his jacket for his flask, a flat metal bottle, and opened the lid. 'This is real vodka. Polish vodka. It make any drink a good drink.' He didn't wait for her to answer, but poured a splash into her glass.

That night her feet had barely touched the ground, he'd spun her round the dance floor so fast. He was broad and handsome with a straight mop of blond hair, and every time she looked at him his blue eyes were fixed on her.

That was the start of it. Since then they'd taken to having long walks in the cold countryside, and they'd sat side by side holding hands in the village hall watching Charlie Chaplin in *The Great Dictator*. Afterwards, as he walked her home, he'd stopped her in the lane and kissed her.

Since then he had kissed her a lot, every time more urgently. One night it was freezing cold and they'd cuddled up in the corner of Rufus's stable, while the horse munched his hay. Marcin put his arms right round her, holding her close while one hand was kneading her breasts through her brassiere.

She squirmed sideways, turning her head, and saying, 'No, Marcin, don't,' but suddenly he slipped both hands under her jumper and shirt, and undid her brassiere from the back. Still holding her to him, he pushed her gently down on the straw, saying, 'Shh, little Laura. I not going to hurt you. Lie still, and let me look at you. You are so, so beautiful. I want only to touch you, look at you. I promise.'

Laura didn't say yes. But she didn't say no either. She let him stroke her breasts, but she would not let him see them.

'It's so cold,' she said, knowing that that was not the reason. She sat up, then stood.

'I have to go. Mummy will send out a search party, and if they find me here, they'll never let me see you again.'

Marcin visited Chorlton twice, both times at teatime when he stopped work at the quarry and before he had to report back to the camp. Laura had said that if he was her boyfriend, he should surely meet her family. The first time was OK. Her mother was nice to him and David and Jill were polite. But the second time, her father was there, and it was really awkward. Why did he have to be so unfriendly? she thought. He'd asked Marcin how he got to be in a German prisoner-of-war camp, and when Marcin explained that he'd been working in Germany as a plumber at the outbreak of war, and had escaped to France to try to join the Allies, no one believed him. Her father made it plain as a pikestaff that he didn't believe him either.

One night Laura and Marcin went to another village hop, this time arriving together, like a proper couple. She loved showing everyone she had a boyfriend.

She knew the effect she was having on him and it excited her. It crossed her mind that her mother would be shocked – say she was flirting shamelessly, laughing too loud in public, hanging on to his arm, but she dismissed the thought: her mother wasn't there and it was none of her business.

After the dance, they biked back to Chorlton in the dark and stood, kissing, on the freezing doorstep. Marcin put his hand behind her and felt for the kitchen doorknob.

'It's open. We go in? They all asleep, and we get warm.' They crept in, Laura telling herself, Why not? It's my house as well.

She put Bing Crosby's 'Don't Fence Me In' very quietly on the Dansette player and they sat together on the sofa, resuming their cuddling. But then, quite suddenly, Marcin looked into her eyes. 'Laura,' he said, 'you love me, don't you?' He groaned quietly and whispered, 'You must let me.'

She shook her head and he said, 'Don't be baby. Sometimes I think I waste my time with a child.'

That hurt. She supposed she *was* a baby, and so of course she was a disappointment to him. She kissed him on the mouth, and immediately felt his tongue, athletic and slimy, forcing itself between her teeth. She twisted her head and he dipped his head to kiss her neck, which was better.

She didn't mind when he slid his hand inside her jumper to feel her breasts. She'd got used to it, it didn't hurt, and it wasn't disgusting. If she closed her eyes like a film star it should all be wonderful.

But then he had undone the placket of her slacks, and pushed them down, his hand between her legs. She tried to stand up, to pull her trousers up, but he held her still. She struggled in silence, terrified of waking her parents upstairs. They rolled onto the carpet and he was on her, his face close to hers, his eyes stony-hard. He locked her eyes to his and said, 'I must, Laura.'

Transfixed, she lay still while he knelt and yanked her slacks and knickers off. She had a fleeting second of shame over her schoolgirl bloomers. If this was 'it' she should have silky things. Then he was on top of her, at which point her will to resist stormed back. She twisted and turned, trying to push him off, biting her lip to prevent herself crying out.

But Marcin just went ahead and did what he wanted, holding her down and forcing her legs apart. She felt a sudden deep pain. He put his hand over her mouth to stop her screaming, and thrust more urgently into her. She was sobbing now, but quietly, the need not to be heard still paramount.

And then it was over. He collapsed on top of her, gasping. She lay silent, her head turned away from him, looking across the room at the grandfather clock. It was still ticking steadily as if nothing had happened.

'Oh, Laura, Laura,' he whispered, 'you are wonderful, a

beautiful woman. I love you.' She barely heard him. She was too shocked to respond. Anyway, what was she to say?

She put her clothes back on, fetched a bucket of hot water and Sunlight soap from the scullery and washed the blood out of the carpet. Marcin didn't help or comment. He just lay there, looking satisfied and sleepy. He pulled himself up before she finished, did up his flies, then bent down to kiss her. She didn't lift her head and he kissed her hair. He said again that he loved her. 'And now you are mine, Laura.'

That was two months ago and she tried not to think about it. She didn't like to say the word, even to herself. Rape. It wasn't rape, or he said it wasn't. He said it was her fault – she'd led him on. But anyway, they loved each other and it was the most natural thing in the world.

But now he wanted it all the time, and she felt she was letting him down by not wanting it too. Why didn't she feel more? He said normal women responded with passion, they didn't just lie there, indifferent. He accused her of being frigid. Maybe she was. If she didn't start liking sex she'd become a dried-up old spinster.

David and Jill talked to each other all the time, about anything, but she couldn't talk to Marcin. And if she didn't like sex, and they had nothing to discuss, why did she go on seeing him and letting him do it?

After what he'd done that night, she thought, why had she agreed to do it again? It must be because she loved him. If her parents knew what had happened, or even if her friends did, she'd die of shame. And they'd never understand. She didn't understand herself.

Her mind flipped backwards and forwards, like a ping pong ball, playing both sides. Of course she loved Marcin. He could be wonderful and he was mad about her. When he said he needed her so much, it made her feel beautiful and desired, and then when he put his great strong arms round her she felt enveloped and protected, warm all over. But when he got that steely look in his eye, and he seemed indifferent to how she felt, so determined and demanding, then she felt scared again.

Perhaps, if they were married and she wasn't feeling guilty all the time and living in terror of getting pregnant, it would all come right.

But would it? Of course her parents didn't like Marcin because he was working class and Polish and they didn't think he was 'suitable'. Her father was such a snob. Maybe her ambitions were not so different from her father's: she wanted someone manly, handsome and delightful so she would really love him, and posh and rich so her father would accept him.

London might have given her that chance. She'd have started to have a life of her own. But the war had killed all their dreams. Hugh lost over the Channel, David's hope of a law degree abandoned to run the farms, and here she was still stuck in the country, working ten-hour days. And her poor mother! She'd lost her eldest son and buried her grief in working like a navvy. Before the war she'd had servants, but now she cooked and cleaned and watched weeds take over her garden.

I should be resigned to it, Laura thought. War is all I've known since I was twelve. A third of my life. Sometimes she thought she would scream if she heard, 'Don't you know there's a war on?' one more time. Still, now everyone said the war was as good as over, at least in Europe.

So, theoretically, next year perhaps, she could still have her 'season' in London and be presented at court with a whole lot of other girls. But even if she could, would she? Somehow it felt all wrong: she was already grown up, with a lover, and the thought of her mother orchestrating her social life and picking out a future husband was altogether too Jane Austen. But she did want her life to change. She knew, she just knew, that there was more to love than their quick couplings in the disused hayloft above the barn.

Clattering sounds from the kitchen came up through the floorboards. She knew she ought to be downstairs doing something useful, like shutting up the chickens or helping with the dinner. She was half expecting her mother's impatient call. But it was her birthday after all. She would *not* feel guilty.

Laura steered her thoughts away from her woes and onto that sunlit, well-worn path, her dream of a future far away from her current life. One day she was going to meet someone who loved books and knew about music and was probably a painter or sculptor. Someone with cool, elegant hands, not roughened by farm work and with dirt under his nails. She would lie under an apple tree, her head on his stomach, while he read to her.

The cushion hit her at the same time as her brother David's voice. 'Get up, you lazy cow. What are you doing? You're meant to be milking, remember?'

She sat up, scowling, and threw the cushion, a heavy candlewick affair stuffed with horsehair, back at her brother. He caught it with ease.

'David, I've only been here an hour. And anyway, it's my birthday.'

'So? Cows need milking, your birthday or not. And Mum wants you to get some early spuds in. A whole row for the market if they're ready, she says, not just enough for supper.'

*

The cows were already in the yard, waiting patiently, their udders enormous. David must have fetched them in. She herded seven of them into the cowshed, and fixed their chains. She fetched the bucket and went down the row, sponging each cow's udders with a wet rag, then lugged the vacuum buckets and leads over to the first three cows and attached the clusters to their teats.

Laura worked efficiently and speedily, so accustomed to the routine that her mind was only half on the job, half drifting randomly. She wondered if the cows preferred the pre-war days, when they were milked by hand. She considered whether her father would give in to David's logic and build a modern milking parlour, which could milk all the cows in twenty minutes, start to finish. She liked the cows, but washing out buckets, pumping soda through the pipes and sluicing out cow muck so the Milk Marketing Board inspector could tick his boxes was not, she prayed, her future.

Laura's thoughts went back to her father's former promises, never mentioned now, of her 'coming out' year. It was true she might not have agreed to any of it but she'd have liked the option. The plan had been all mapped out from the time she went to boarding school: she was to leave at sixteen, not to labour on the farms but to spend a year at finishing school for a smattering of literature, music and art, learning to dance, curtsey, step elegantly from a taxi and make sense of *Burke's Peerage*. Then she was to spend six months in Paris with a French family while brushing up her French at the Alliance Française, travel around Europe in suitable company (probably her mother), then come home for her London season at which, with luck, she would find herself a suitable husband. That, more or less, was what Grace had done – she'd met Hugh at a debs' dance – but the war had ruined Grace's life even more thoroughly than it had hers. Hugh was dead, and Grace was only half alive, her daughter Jane her whole shrunken world.

Laura knew that the trappings of class – her lost London season; her brothers going to Eton and Oxford, her mother's bridge lessons – were all part of her father's plan for his upward climb from minor mill owner in Halifax to landed gent in the Cotswolds. It was so obvious and embarrassing – after church last week he'd cornered the Countess and angled for an invitation to see the famous water gardens at Frampton. How could he do that? The Earl, though he had agreed to David ploughing up the park for him, would barely speak to any of them since they'd taken over the Barrow farms. And yet Daddy still thought that the Countess might ask him to tea. It was humiliating, couldn't he see that?

CHAPTER TEN

When the last cow was milked, Laura opened the yard gate for David's collie, Meg, to supervise the herd's slow progress back up the lane and into the field. By the time Laura got there to shut the gate, all but two of them were through it. The laggards swayed ponderously along, snatching a mouthful of the hedgerows as Meg threatened to nip their heels.

When she was doing the final rinse of the pipes, David appeared with the donkey cart to take the churns down to the lane.

He looked at his sister rubbing cream into her hands.

'What's that?' he asked.

'Udder ointment. Works a treat on horny hands. You should try it if you want Jill to think you're a gent in disguise.'

'Don't need to.' He held out his hands. 'Feel. I get a daily dose of lanolin from the sheep.'

Laura rubbed his fingers, suddenly feeling a wash of affection for her brother.

'You really like farm work, don't you? And I really don't.'

He put a hand on her shoulder.

'Poor Laura. It won't be long – Mussolini has been captured

and shot, and Hitler must give in any day now. And the Yanks will win the Pacific war. This year it *will* all be over by Christmas. Then you can have hands like a Countess.'

The walled kitchen garden had been a favourite place when they were children. Laura and David used to infuriate the gardener by picking the peas, eating them where they stood and dropping the pods on the gravel path, or climbing the espaliered peach trees on the walls, trying to reach the fruit at the top. Sweet peas had been grown amongst the runner beans then, and it had been her job to keep picking the flowers. Constant picking kept the blooms coming, her mother said. It was a job Laura had loved, feeling proud and responsible when her mother put her face into the big bowl, eyes closed, inhaling deeply.

Now no one had time to bother with sweet peas, nor grow rows of summer flowers. The cutting garden had gone, replaced by the hen house and chicken run, and the rest of the space was planted with long rows of every kind of vegetable. The fruit cage was still full of soft fruit but between the rows of raspberry canes were more cabbages. Even the glasshouse, which used to be full of exotic plants for the house, was now used for propagating veg and for growing tomatoes. Doing our bit, said her father. But he was doing his bit at a comfy desk at Moreton aerodrome while the rest of the family dutifully Dug for Victory.

Laura had lifted potatoes, lots of them, many times, and it was backbreaking work. But she always enjoyed the first few forays into the soil. It was like bringing up treasure, the small potatoes popping up shining white against the dark Cotswold clay. She lifted enough for dinner, but they were only marble-sized so she left the rest to grow on. Early potatoes fetched more money in the market but they would still be desirable in a few weeks' time and they'd weigh a lot more.

She picked a bunch of new mint from the herb patch and added it to her bucket. They were having the first lamb of the season and her mother would need mint for the sauce and for the potatoes.

Tonight would be, if not a coming-out ball, at least a dinner party in her honour. Her mother and Mrs Digweed had made her a new dress, a mid-calf one of blue silk with white lace over the blue. It had square shoulders, a square neckline and narrow sleeves, with a long fitted waist. Both layers had been part of her mother's trousseau, raided for unobtainable fabric: the underslip had once been a silk nightie, never worn, and the lace layer was cut from a fine Spanish tablecloth. It would be such a treat to get dressed up in something colourful, and for once to look feminine and pretty. She spent her life in dingy trousers and shirts and shapeless jerseys.

Her father was sacrificing his usual Friday night in the officers' mess to come home for dinner, and Dr Drummond and his wife Molly would be there. So would David and Jill, and Laura's friend Sophie, who had got an exeat from her college in Oxford where she was in her second year, studying medicine. She wanted to be an obstetrician or gynaecologist and seemed to work every hour that God gave, but she would be on the evening train and would stay for the weekend. And, miracle of miracles, her mother had said she could invite Marcin and his friend Aleksy.

She tipped the Jerseys into the scullery sink and called over her shoulder, 'Mummy, shall I scrub the potatoes?'

Her mother came over, picked up a potato and rubbed it

between her fingers. 'Heavens, they are small. But aren't they beautiful? The skin is so fine, let's just rinse them and put them in the steamer. Oh, you good girl, you brought some mint. Put a few sprigs in and a bit of salt and they'll be perfect.'

David called from the kitchen, 'Mum, this will be the best lamb you ever tasted. Do you want just the leg, or leg and shoulder?' He lowered the lamb onto the butcher's block.

Maud and Laura came over and peered at it, Laura making an effort not to think of the creature gambolling about the field. David had skinned and gutted it in the outhouse, but the head was still there.

'What will we do with the rest?' asked Laura.

'The Drummonds are buying a side,' said David. 'They'll take it home with them tonight. And we'll keep the head, I suppose.'

Maud poked the lamb with a finger. 'This leg will not weigh even three pounds and there are ten of us. It's criminal killing a lamb so young with a war on.'

'It was the biggest there was, Mum.'

'I know, love. And it is Laura's birthday and we haven't had roast lamb since last summer. We'll roast both leg and shoulder and confine ourselves to two slices each.' Laura thought her mother had not looked this excited and happy for ages. 'Then we'll have some for cold tomorrow and Mrs Digweed can make a stew from the neck and scrag end, shepherd's pie from the leftovers, and Scotch broth from the bones. Oh, what a treat!'

'Where *is* Mrs Digweed, Mummy?' said Laura. 'I thought she'd be helping you?'

'She is. She's polishing the silver candlesticks in the still room. Since we hardly use them now they are black with tarnish. And she likes a sit-down job these days.'

David took his knife from the sheath at his waist, and carefully cut through the skin to ease back the leg. Expertly severing it at the joint, he said, 'What's for afters, Mum?'

'Your sister's favourite. Rice pud. With the last of last year's apricot jam.'

While David sectioned the lamb, Laura watched her mother slicing cabbage, her chin wobbling a little. Laura noticed the lines on her mother's neck and the slight sagging round her eyes.

'Mummy,' she said, 'you look tired. I can finish up here. Why don't you go for a lie-down?'

But her mother wouldn't. 'No, darling, I want to dress the lamb and get it in the oven, and get the soup made. Mrs D can lay the table and if you get the hens in and David sees to the horses, we'll be fine.'

'Why don't you forget the soup? Two courses is plenty. No one needs soup.'

'I agree,' David chimed in. 'Soup is boring and this lamb—'

'Because if I don't you'll eat all the lamb! That's what soup is for: to fill you up so you aren't so hungry.'

'But I *want* to be hungry,' wailed Laura. 'What can be better than to be really hungry when you have roast lamb and rice pudding?'

'That's all very well, but . . .'

Laura caught her brother's eye. Laughing, they chorused in unison, *'Don't you know there's a war on?'*

The birthday dinner started well. The food was delicious and her father made a sweet speech and toasted her. And everyone clapped.

Afterwards the Drummonds went home, Marcin and Aleksy

biked back to the POW camp and David and Jill disappeared, allegedly to check on a lame donkey, but really, Laura suspected, to make love in the hayloft.

Her father, standing by the kitchen fireplace, lit his pipe.

'Really, Laura,' he said. 'I don't know what you see in that Marcin. Even his friend has more manners.'

Laura looked up from stacking dirty dishes on the kitchen table. 'What's wrong with his manners?'

'Where to begin? He doesn't take his cap off. I had to tell him I'd hang it up for him to get it off his head. He doesn't stand up when your mother comes into the room, he doesn't put his cup down in its saucer. He holds his knife and fork like a truck driver, elbows on the table. He makes no effort at conversation. I could go on.'

'That's so unfair, Daddy!' Laura shot back. 'He's Polish. He doesn't speak good English. And perhaps table manners are different in Poland. Maybe yours wouldn't look so good in Krakow.'

Maud cut in, 'Don't be impertinent, Laura', but her father laughed and said, 'Good point, lass. But you must admit that, at bottom, he's a peasant with no imagination. Probably a nice enough chap, but both David and I tried to get him to talk and—'

'But Daddy,' interrupted Laura, 'you only talk to him about the war or music to show him up. It's cruel.'

'Now that is impertinent, Laura. I can hardly talk to him about the joys of digging in a quarry or lifting potatoes or whatever he does.'

Laura was close to tears. She picked up a pile of dishes and Sophie gathered the rest and followed her into the scullery.

They could hear Maud remonstrating with her husband and

him protesting that Laura was too touchy, and anyway he was right.

'And you know it, Maud. She probably knows it too, in her heart of hearts. That boy is no good for Laura. The sooner she can give up farm work and get away the better.'

Laura had silenced Sophie with a warning hand so she could listen, but now she heard her parents' shoes on the stone flags as they left the kitchen.

'Poor Laura. I'm so sorry,' said Sophie.

'But the awful thing is, he's right in a way. Marcin doesn't have any education. He's no good for talking. And I don't like him making love to me.' She sniffed, lifting her new dress to find her hankie in her knickers. 'I don't know why I stay with him, really.'

Sophie put an arm round her friend. 'Laura,' she said, 'he will do until something better comes along. Which it will, never fear.'

She turned to face her friend more squarely and said, 'But, Laura, in the meantime, I hope you're taking precautions. Pregnancy would scupper your options.'

Laura could feel herself blushing.

'We use Volpar. Marcin gets it.'

Sophie nodded, and changed the subject. 'Why don't you come to Oxford? Plenty of young men who can talk, and as soon as the war's over there'll be thousands.'

'You know I can't. I should have stayed at school if I was going to go to university. Now it's too late.'

'No it's not. You could catch up. There'll be a great mix of ages with lots of older men coming back from the war. You could go in two years' time.'

Maybe I could, thought Laura. Or go to France. Or anything. Anything to get away.

CHAPTER ELEVEN

1946, March

Laura had thought that the end of the war would change everything, and suddenly everything would be better. Her father said the situation was actually worse, though. He complained of the Labour Government, of the new mood of workers' rights, of increased taxes. Her mother sighed over the continued rationing, now tougher than ever.

And here she was, still labouring on the farm, still sleeping with Marcin, still longing for something different, better, magical.

The sound of a hundred bleating ewes was deafening. Separated from their lambs, they called incessantly while pacing, turning, pushing at the fence. The lambs, corralled in a paddock across the yard, bleated back.

What a time for Derek, the old shepherd to be sick, thought Laura. I'd rather muck out the pigs or lift potatoes any day. She was sitting on a low stack of hay bales, holding lamb after lamb while her brother David castrated and docked them.

He carried the next lamb from the pen and sat it on Laura's

lap, facing forwards. Laura held its back legs open and David, crouching, lifted his knife from the can of disinfectant, swiftly cut a slit in each side of the tiny scrotum, squeezed the testicles out and dropped them into a bucket. The creature jerked in Laura's grip but did not bleat. David then cut the lamb's tail off with one swift stroke, tossing it into a second bucket and his knife back into the disinfectant. Finally, he dabbed green oil on the wounds with a finger, took the lamb from Laura and dropped it into the ewes' pen where it scuttled to its mother. The whole process had taken less than a minute and a half.

Laura's back was aching, and she was only halfway through the lambs.

'Can we have a break?' she said.

David stretched, his hands above his head, his back arched. 'OK. Just ten minutes then.'

Walking to the farmhouse, Laura remarked, 'You even like this job, don't you?'

'I don't mind it. I like to be able to do every job on the farm.' David was scanning the spring-green fields, shining in the sun. 'Then I can always fill in if needed. Also, I can tell if a man's not doing something right.'

'But castrating little lambs is horrible. Did Derek teach you?'

'Yes, he did. He's a lot quicker than me, though. He draws the balls out with his teeth.'

Laura's face wrinkled in disgust. 'I don't believe you!'

'It's true. You should watch him next year.'

I won't be here next year, thought Laura. But she didn't answer.

As they walked across the concrete yard to the kitchen door, a male voice called to them from the lane.

'Can you help me? I'm looking for Chorlton Farms.'

Laura turned round. A tall young man with curly black hair approached.

Ah, thought Laura, he looks and sounds Italian. Probably an ex-POW looking for work. For months, released prisoners had been job-hunting, mostly Italians who'd worked on the farms for a pittance throughout the war and were now keen to earn a proper wage.

'Surely,' she said. 'This is Chorlton.'

'Ah, that is good,' he said. Laura felt his eyes running swiftly over her bloody apron and boots, her filthy hands. 'I am Giovanni Angelotti. I would like to speak to the owner, if that is permitted.'

'That's our father,' said David. 'But he's working at the airfield. So I'm in charge.'

'Ah, good, then I talk to you, no? I am second chef at the Mitford Arms in Moreton.'

'Come inside,' said Laura. 'We're about to have our elevenses.'

But it turned out that Giovanni wasn't after a job. He was looking for black-market meat.

'My boss the head chef, he would like that you supply us with, you know, meat? From pigs. Or sheeps? Or beefs? Even chickens? Direct?'

David and Laura looked at each other. What the Italian was suggesting was illegal. Restaurants were subject to rationing, like everyone else.

David said, stiffly but not unpleasantly, 'We don't deal on the black market. It would be unpatriotic. And we can't afford to damage our good reputation. I'm afraid the answer is no.'

Laura was washing her hands at the sink. She turned her head to watch Giovanni while her brother made this pompous little speech. She thought she detected amusement in his eyes.

'But the war is over, no?' he said. 'And we pay good price. More than you get from selling to the wholesalers, or at the livestock market.'

'No, I'm sorry, but my father would never allow it,' said David.

The Italian was not the least put out by this rejection. He shrugged and said, 'Ah well, I have tried. My chef said I must go to every farm. Maybe someone will be less, how you say, law-caring.'

'Law-abiding,' said Laura.

'Law-abiding, yes. My English is not good you see.'

David went to deal with a delivery of fencing rails and Laura poured the tea and questioned the Italian. He had spent his wartime years working on a farm in Oddington. He missed his native Abruzzo.

'But I think I make a better life in England.'

'Do you like working at the hotel?'

'No, the chef, he is animal. Very bad person. But I am cook, you see. And I think England needs cooks, no? Good cooks?'

Laura laughed, and Giovanni did, too. 'Don't you like fish and chips?' she asked.

'Yes, I like. But fat is rationed so the chef he keep it too long and everything taste bad. And Spam fritters, they are disgusting. And you don't have any olive oil. And no ice cream. Have you had Italian ice cream?' He kissed his fingertips. 'That is, how you say? Heaven.'

Laura felt a little wave of good feeling. This Giovanni was amusing, lighthearted. She wanted to hear more, but David was back, calling from the yard.

'Those lambs need dealing with, Laura. We've been at least fifteen minutes and the ewes are still bleating their heads off.'

Giovanni walked back with them to the paddock. Laura felt suddenly embarrassed at the prospect of him seeing her doing the brutal and messy task they were engaged in. Her resentment of the job returned, redoubled. Why should she be doing this? Jill, although an official farm worker, a 'land girl' for five years, was not castrating little lambs. Just because David was sweet on her, she got all the nice jobs. Right now she was happily driving the tractor in Sawpit field.

She tried to dismiss Giovanni, get him gone before they went back to work, but he had seen the buckets.

'Are you cutting the tails?' Without waiting for an answer he vaulted over the fence and looked in the buckets. 'Ah, wonderful! *Testicoli!* What do you do with them?'

'They find their way into pies or stews. Or the dog gets them,' David replied. 'Sometimes we give them to the hunt. To feed the hounds. Or maybe the foxes.'

Giovanni's head jerked up. 'You feed the foxes? I thought you killed them? Chased them on the horses so the dogs can catch them?'

'Yes, but we want them to be fit and healthy so they'll give the hounds, and us, a good run. So sometimes the hunt leaves food for the mothers and cubs in the woods. Mostly fallen stock.'

'Fallen stock?'

'Animals that die in the field, usually lambs or very young calves.'

Giovanni shook his head, half smiling. 'You English!' He turned to Laura. 'And you, you are cutting the tails and the *testicoli*. That is crazy. That is not woman's work. In Italy it is the man that—'

David, nettled, cut in. 'Yes, well, we have just been through a war, haven't we? We don't like it either, but women have to do men's work. Where have you been for the last six years?'

Laura, sensing rising antagonism, said, 'Man's job or not, it's horrible. Poor lambs, it must hurt so much.'

'I don't think so,' countered David. 'They are right as rain in no time. Come on, let's get on with it, Laura.' He strode to the pen, grabbed the nearest lamb and turned to Giovanni. 'Maybe you'd like to do Laura's job for her?'

Laura's heart sank. Her brother was trailing his coat for a quarrel. But the Italian grinned back, unruffled. 'Sure,' he said, 'I'll do whatever you want.' He picked up the testicle bucket and tipped it slightly from side to side, inspecting the marble-sized pink balls. 'But you must let me take these, and the tails. He looked up, his eyes intense and excited. 'They are beautiful, just beautiful.'

CHAPTER TWELVE

Giovanni hefted the four boxes onto the central wooden table. It was mid-afternoon and only the head chef, Hein, was in the kitchen. His bald head, wreathed in cigarette smoke, was visible through the chef's office window, his massive shoulders moving forward and back. Giovanni couldn't see the desk but he knew Hein's right hand was alternately wrenching down the handle of the calculating machine and punching in the numbers with his fat fingers.

Bet he's working out his kickback from the suppliers, thought Giovanni, or how much butter he can sell into the black market. Giovanni wondered if the owners knew about his little scams. Probably, but good cooks were hard to find now and Hein had worked here before sitting out the war in an internment camp, lucky blighter.

Giovanni had hoped to find the kitchen empty. Still, maybe he could get his sweetbread pie made for the staff supper before Hein finished his calculations and found some other job for him, and before the English cooks and waitresses saw what it was he proposed to feed them.

He rinsed the testicles in cold water and left them soaking, hidden in the cupboard under the sink. He would treat them like sweetbreads, changing the water every time it was tinged with pink, then blanch them in simmering water, pick them over to remove the stringy bits, and cook them briefly in the sauce. For that he would have to filch a couple of ladles of Hein's stock. Hein guarded and tended his two stockpots, one white, one brown, with proprietorial zeal, and he'd never part with any for staff food. Bisto would do for them.

There were still several bags of last year's dried onions – the hotel owners had responded to the Dig for Victory campaign by volunteering the kitchen staff for the making and tending of a vegetable garden. Giovanni soaked a handful in boiling water and then put them to sweat in a bit of Spry. Butter would have been nicer, but he'd better refrain. As it was the pastry would seriously diminish their butter supply.

Giovanni was enjoying himself. He began to hum 'La donna è mobile' as he tipped the stock onto the onions, thickened the sauce with cornflour, enriched it with milk powder and added a handful of the mushrooms he had picked and dried in the autumn. He gently stirred in the cooked testicles, put a lid on the pot and stowed it among the clean saucepans. Hein had a habit of peering into anything on the stove.

Susan, the kitchen trainee, arrived at five, and Giovanni put her to scrubbing potatoes and peeling carrots, while he set about the pastry for his staff pie.

Singing softly now, Giovanni fetched flour (still the wartime coarse brown stuff) from the dry store and butter from the larder. Rationing was as draconian as ever, and they usually made pastry with lard or marge, but Giovanni told himself that as Hein had the ration books of all the live-in staff, those staff should sometimes get some butter. Besides, a farmer cousin of the owner supplied it and the hotel got more than its due.

The flour flowed coolly through his fingers as he rubbed in the fat. He noticed there was more whey in the butter than usual and he was careful not to add too much water. He wanted crumbly pastry, 'short' the English called it.

Giovanni managed to line two metal flan rings with his pastry and get them baked before Hein strutted into the kitchen, barking orders for the *mise en place*. But there weren't many reservations for dinner, and he soon went off home, saying he'd be back in time for the service.

Giovanni alternated his preparations for the customers' menu with making his gastronomic creation for the staff. In the absence of the head chef, Giovanni's crooning gave way to full-throated singing and he sang his way through most of *Rigoletto*, ignoring the protests of Susan and the kitchen porter and the laughter of the waitresses as they came into the kitchen to fetch china or silver.

Most of the hotel staff lived in the attic rooms and had to be fed. Supper for them was served before the restaurant opened and the off-duty staff blundered down to join their working colleagues. All in all there were about a dozen, half the staff count of the pre-war days. The restaurant manager, barman, barmaid, housekeeper, gardener, maintenance man, two waitresses, two cleaners and the kitchen porter formed a ragged queue. Only Hein and an off-duty cook were missing.

At 6pm Giovanni pulled his pie out of the oven, slammed it on the pass and yelled, 'OK, *buon appetito, amici miei.* And believe me, it's *bellissimo.*'

Ten minutes later there was not a scrap left. Susan said,

'Giovanni, that was as good a pie as I've eaten in years. As good as Hein's chicken and mushroom pie for the customers. What was in it?'

Giovanni kissed her on the cheek. 'Italian magic,' he said.

Laura was early: the grocer's wouldn't open for another forty minutes but she was at the door because her father had dropped her off before catching his train to London. She could see Mr Brown moving about through the gap between the ill-fitting blackout blind and the door jamb. His tin leg meant he stomped and swayed unevenly, but he moved fast. He was shaking weevils out of the walnuts, and Laura waited until the weevils were in the bin and the walnuts in the big glass jar on the shelf before she knocked on the door. Everyone knew walnuts got weevils, but maybe the grocer wouldn't want her to see him winnowing them out.

Mr Brown opened the door a crack, frowning. But when he saw it was Laura his face lifted into a smile and he swung the door wide. 'Come in, come in, young lady.'

'Oh, thank you. I knew you wouldn't mind.' He closed the door quickly behind her. 'It's going to be a lovely day, but right now it's freezing.'

'It's good to see you, Miss. And how's the family?'

'Oh, they're all fine. Everyone working too hard, of course. But we'll survive. And I've got a few hours off today.'

'Really?'

'Yes, I'm to do the shopping. My father dropped me off on the way to the station.' She peered into the pickled egg jar, sniffing the vinegar. 'I thought if you were delivering in the van, I could hitch a ride home with the groceries.'

'Of course, my dear. Are you buying just a few things or the weekly order? If it's only a basketful, you can ride on the back of the bike, though the lad will make you walk up Chastleton Hill, that's for sure. He's only sixteen and weak as water.'

Laura shook her head, smiling, 'It's the big order. And anyway I'd prefer to wait for the van because I can stroll about the town and do nothing for a while. Look in the shops.'

Mr Brown pulled his mouth down. 'That might be good if there was anything much in them. But getting supplies is as tough as ever. Tougher now that bread's on the ration, too.'

'It seems so unfair that rationing should be worse after the war than during it, doesn't it? I wonder how long it will go on for?'

'Few more years yet, I wager. Got to feed the starving Germans, haven't we? And the rest of Europe, poor things.'

Laura liked Brown's. When they were children, Mr Brown used to slip them a ginger biscuit or a liquorice ribbon when their nanny wasn't looking. And even now it was a delicious-smelling, friendly place to be. The scent of bacon drifted in from the smoker in the back yard, and there was a Bradenham ham and a flitch of bacon hanging from the ceiling. A large block of 'Government Cheddar' and a bowl each of curd cheese and cottage cheese stood on the slate slab behind the counter.

Mr Brown got on with his pre-opening routine, and Laura helped him, swathed in his wife's big apron. He brought a tongue from the brine tub and a freshly boiled bacon joint from out back, and Laura scrubbed the tongue with a hard-bristled brush, skinned the bacon, then dried them both with a muslin cloth. Then she set them ready for slicing on the table behind the counter.

When she'd wiped down the sink and polished up the jars of raisins and currants, and he had strewn the floor with sawdust, he shrugged out of his grocer's coat and pulled on a clean one.

'Right, young lady. Thanks to you, we are well ahead. The least I can do is serve you early. What can I do for you, Miss?'

Laura produced the family ration books and Mr Brown riffled through them, cancelling the coupons with practised speed. They completed her shopping in time to open the shop right on eight o'clock.

The first customer through the door was the young chef from the Mitford, the Italian who had taken over her job of holding the lambs while David castrated them.

'*Buongiorno Signorina* Laura!' He pronounced it Lowra. 'Do you work here, too? I have not seen you in the shop before.'

He gave her a formal little bow and Laura found herself pleased but oddly embarrassed. She shook her head and he turned away to shake Mr Brown's hand.

'Good morning, *Signor* Brown.'

''Morning, Giovanni. You're a lucky man. I have the dried chickpeas you asked me to get, and the white beans. I forget the name. They are from South America.'

'The cannellini? *Eccellente!* They are the best.'

While Mr Brown was fetching Giovanni's dried goods, Laura and Giovanni stood in silence for a few seconds, then both started talking at once – Laura to ask him politely how he was, Giovanni to tell her, which he did on the second attempt, how good the *testicoli* pie had been.

'Of course, I did not tell them what is inside. But they eat it all. Everyone, they eat it. And they want more.'

Laura found her voice. 'What did you do with the tails?'

'Oh, very good also. I boil them to take off skin. It smell like socks in the laundry. Not good. But then I grill them with little bit mustard and honey. We serve in the bar. "Lamb Nibbles" the barman call them. Very popular. Go like hot cakes, he say.'

They both laughed, Laura thinking what extraordinary eyes he had. They were dark brown with flashes of yellow. His skin looked sun-tanned but it must be the Italian in him: you don't get brown working in a kitchen in England. His eyebrows were as thick and curly, almost as unruly, as his hair.

When Giovanni turned to Mr Brown to ask about the rice he needed for proper Italian risotto and Mr Brown was trying to persuade him that English pudding rice would do, Laura studied his back. He was wearing a loose dark jacket, worn trousers and clogs, and yet he looked attractive. She wondered if he could dance.

They walked out of Brown's together, Laura promising to be back at eleven when the van would set off on its delivery round.

'What are you going to do for the next two hours?' asked Giovanni.

'Just walk about. Window shop. And I've got a few things to get. Maybe walk up to Batsford and look at the horses.'

'Maybe I come with you?'

Laura's heart gave a thump. 'Don't you have to work?'

'Well, yes, but Hein, my boss, he is away and it's Monday. Not many customers.'

He was looking into her face, confident and smiling.

'If you come with me, we can take my groceries back to hotel and tell Susan what to do and then we take my bicycle and go for a ride. Is that good idea?'

They walked the fifty yards to the Mitford, Giovanni talking about the spring weather, 'blue sky, like Abruzzo', and Laura concealing her pleasure. What luck, she thought. A lovely day, a few hours off, and a handsome man to share it with.

They walked through the alley behind the hotel and into the yard and Laura followed Giovanni into the kitchen. He dumped his packages on the table, calling out, 'Susanna, my lovely Susanna, where are you?'

Susan emerged from the larder, carrying a bunch of carrots. She looked shy, and pleased. 'Oh, Giovanni, my name's Susan, you know it's Susan.'

Giovanni grinned. 'Of course I know, but Susanna is better.' He put an arm round her, the girl barely reaching his shoulder. Hugging her close, he said, 'You must meet my new friend. She is Laura. We are going for a ride. Can Laura take your bicycle?'

Laura protested, 'No, Giovanni, I can sit on the back of yours, if it has a seat.'

'No, no. Too uncomfortable, and I will have to work too hard up the hills.'

Susan was looking anxious. 'But Giovanni, it's Chef's day off. You are in charge.'

'Yes, yes, but I will be back at eleven and you will be fine. There will only be five for breakfast. Are they down yet?'

'Yes, they've just left. They had porridge.'

'Good, so just bake the meatloaf for lunch. Make the sauce with about this much dried onions' (he cupped one hand) 'and tinned tomatoes. And mash some potatoes. Plenty, because we need some for the staff. And if you have time, can you mix some more dough for the oat biscuits? Can you do that? Of course you can. You are very good cook.' He was now holding her by the elbows, smiling broadly, and Laura saw that Susan would walk through fire for him.

'All right,' she said, 'but what if Hein comes in?'

'He won't. But if he comes, say I'm out talking to a farmer. Which is true. Laura is farmer.' He looked at Laura, laughing.

They set off through the town towards Batsford, Laura on Susan's bicycle. Laura felt a mixture of excitement and guilt. What if they ran into Marcin? But she dismissed the thought. He didn't own her, she'd not done anything wrong.

Giovanni slowed down to keep pace with Laura. At Batsford they stopped to watch a foal gambolling and bucking, trying to get a reaction from its dam. But she cropped the grass and took no notice.

Giovanni pulled a battered packet of Senior Service out of his pocket, shook it to partially dislodge a couple of cigarettes, and offered one to Laura.

She shook her head. 'No thank you.'

'Don't you smoke? I thought all English girls smoked.'

'No, I tried once, but it made me sick.'

'Good. I don't like girls smoking. It is too, how you say? Mannish.'

Laura thought she should be indignant at such a patronising remark, but she was flattered by the compliment. She said, 'My sister-in-law, Grace, smokes those cigarettes in the pink packet, Passing Clouds. She has a cigarette holder. She looks very elegant and feminine.'

The mare trotted over to the fence and Laura rubbed her face. But since the mare was hoping for sugar or a peppermint, she turned away out of reach and dropped her head to the grass.

'It's so good to see horses again,' Laura said, her eyes following the colt's antics. 'There used to be many more. That potato field behind the paddock, and the one to the left, have only been planted since war broke out. When I was a little girl we used to have gymkhanas there.'

'Gymkhanas?'

'Riding competitions: jumping and games and all sorts. I loved them. I had a horse called Rufus. He loved them, too. I still have a drawer full of his rosettes.'

Giovanni looked bemused.

'You get big rosettes made of ribbon,' Laura explained, 'to tie on your horse's bridle if you win.'

Giovanni smiled down at Laura. 'Your eyes shine when you talk of things you like,' he said.

Laura, embarrassed, looked away. Giovanni asked, 'What happened to the horses? Maybe they were eaten? Horsemeat is very good. In Abruzzo—'

'Stop, Giovanni!'

Giovanni laughed. 'Oh, you English, so sentimental!'

Laura's face clouded over and he changed the subject. 'Who lives in that house? It is *bella, bella.*'

'Isn't it? But it's not a house. It's the stables for Batsford House.' They both gazed at the elaborate gabled building, set against the hill with its paddocks in front.

'That is for *horses*?' Giovanni's voice was a mixture of wonder and scorn.

'Yes, isn't it just perfect? Far prettier than the house.'

'But this is a palace! Do your horses live in a fancy stable like this?'

Laura laughed. 'No. I wish they did. We used to have pretty

stone stables but they are now full of cars and tractors. The old carts and horses were sold.'

'But you are rich family. Don't you have horses for riding? For hunting?'

'Yes, but only two and they live in a shed. Rufus was sold when I got too big for him. Daddy still has a hunter and there's old Sandpiper who used to be David's but he seldom rides now. Neither of us do.'

'Why not?'

'David doesn't like it much. He had polio as a child and has a bad leg. I think he only learned to ride to please Daddy. And Mother and I are both too busy.'

They resumed their ride towards Blockley and Paxford, and Laura found herself chattering away as she might to Jill or Sophie: telling Giovanni how overbearing her father could be, how her mother and sister-in-law were always on at her to be more ladylike, how she had planned on a couple of years of touring Europe and having fun, but instead she just worked on the farm.

'But the war is over and you are young. Why can't you start now?'

Laura shook her head. 'The war changed everything. Daddy says when things get back to normal Mummy and I will go travelling, but now we are both needed at home. And anyway, I no longer know what I want. I'm only good for milking cows.' Then, thinking this sounded pathetic, she said, 'I might go to university.'

Laura was strong and fit and cycled next to Giovanni on the level, but she struggled to keep up on the hills, and sometimes they got off their bikes and pushed them. Trudging side by side made talking easy and Giovanni told her about his family: his father and his two brothers had been killed in '43. He was the lucky one, he said – he'd been captured by the British.

His mother lived on their smallholding and his elder sister, Carlotta, her husband Tomaso and two small boys had gone to live with her.

'It is good she have a man in the house. But that Tomaso, he is not a good man.'

'No?' Laura was only half listening. She kept noticing how Giovanni's face changed as he talked. He'd look young and serious, and very handsome, one minute and then he'd smile or laugh and creases would wrinkle his face, his eyes would gleam, and he'd look older and friendlier and even more attractive.

'No. He and his friend they used to steal cigarettes from the docks and sell them to the American soldiers. And before the war he had a business, my father tell me, making mushrooms look like truffles. He chopped them, dried them and put them in truffle oil.'

Laura laughed. 'Well, at least he sounds enterprising. Do you like him?'

'He is, how do you say? *Lestofante*. Con man. But he is charmer. Women like him.'

'I've never had a truffle. Are they good?'

Giovanni stopped in the middle of the road to better explain the beauties of black and white truffles and Laura listened, at first amused, then fascinated. Fascinated by the idea of something so rich, fragrant and delicious being found by pigs or dogs underground, and costing so much. But she was also fascinated by Giovanni. It was wonderful to be told things, to talk to someone who knew much more than she did, who had been somewhere other than the Cotswolds – and most of all someone so animated and attractive.

A car, a Rover, came up the hill and they pushed their bicycles to the side. Giovanni watched it purr slowly past them.

'One day I will have one of those. A motorcar. And be able to buy truffles. I will serve *Tagliatelle al tartufo bianco* in my restaurant.'

'You are going to have a restaurant?'

'Oh yes, in the West End of London. For very rich people. You can come, Laura, and I will give you truffles. For free. I will, I promise.'

They were almost at the top of the hill and Giovanni put his foot on the pedal and threw his leg over the saddle. He called over his shoulder, 'Come, Laura, this is good. We go fast down the hill, no?'

Without waiting for an answer, he disappeared over the top, one arm up and waving. Laura followed, not quite so fast. All the way down she could hear him singing 'Toreador' at the top of his lungs. Even outside, in the wind, and now quite far away, she caught the sound of his rich, full tenor. She loved it.

CHAPTER THIRTEEN

'Mummy, you look exhausted. Would you like a cup of tea?'

'Love one, darling.'

Laura put the cup by her mother's elbow, in between the packet of precious white flour and the long-hoarded dried fruits.

It was true, Maud thought. She felt raddled and tired, and at least sixty. It seemed so unfair that rationing, with the war over a year ago, was worse than ever. The only good news was the reappearance of bananas. Even potatoes, which had never been rationed in the war, now were. The national crop had failed, and so had their small patch.

And her hens had been a disaster. The fox had twice got into the hen run and what hens were left alive had not laid an egg since. The new pullets weren't laying either. She'd had to use the family's entire egg ration for this cake.

I've not been able to make the fruit-packed cakes Donald loves, she thought: no Dundee cake, no Christmas cake, no Simnel cake at Easter. Even when the hens were laying, dried fruit, ground almonds, sugar and brandy were all on the ration. So for months she had been hoarding the precious ingredients. They needed five eggs for the cake, icing and real marzipan – something no one had seen for six years. And she was using a pre-war recipe: real butter, real eggs, real everything.

She would keep the cake wrapped in greaseproof paper and muslin on the top shelf of the larder, and feed it regular small doses of sloe gin over the next few months. By Christmas it would be a treat none of them would forget.

Laura fetched the flour and eggs from Brown's delivery box in the larder, and carried them back to the kitchen. As she crossed the floor the bottom of the paper bag containing the eggs suddenly gave way, and all five eggs were on the stone flags, smashed.

Maud stared in horror at the floor, then at Laura's stricken face. But her shock turned to fury in seconds. 'You stupid, stupid girl,' she said, coming round the table and slapping her daughter's cheek. 'Everyone has gone without—'

But Laura had gone. Hands over her face, she ran outside. Once in the yard, she turned wildly around. Where to go? She ran into the barn and climbed up into the old hayloft. No one would think to look up here. She sat on a hay bale, angry, hurt, her face burning, trying not to cry.

Why did her mother have to hit her? She hadn't been smacked since she was a child, and even then hardly ever. She hadn't set out to smash the family's eggs. The unfairness overwhelmed her and she put her hands to her face as she sobbed.

'Laura! Laura, where are you?' Her mother's voice came up from the yard. Then she heard David's steps and her mother asking if he'd seen her. He would guess where she was – he knew about her and Marcin sloping off to the hayloft, just as she knew about him and Jill. But, good brother that he was, he just said no, he'd not seen her.

Laura could tell by her mother's tone that she was no longer angry, and was probably sorry for the slap. She did not answer though. There was satisfaction in making her mother wait. Serve her right. She heard her return to the kitchen, shooing out the cat and closing the door.

After ten minutes she felt calmer and a little guilty. Her mother was understandably angry – she'd been talking about that cake for weeks. And it really was stupid beyond belief not have to put a hand under the egg bag. A cracked egg wasn't unusual and of course it would make the paper soggy.

She climbed down, slowly crossed the yard and stood in the door of the kitchen.

'I'm so sorry, Mummy.' Laura felt on the edge of tears again.

Maud hurried over and put her arms round her. 'I'm sorry, too. Really sorry. Oh, and you poor darling, your cheek is still bright red.' She kissed her daughter on both cheeks, hugging her. 'Go upstairs and wash your face. You'll feel better then.'

When Laura came down her mother was stirring the cake mixture, and beside it was a slab of marzipan.

'Golly! How did you . . .'

'I just scooped the eggs off the floor. I couldn't let them go to waste. Or give them to the pigs.'

Laura laughed. 'Mummy, you are just wonderful.' She pinched a piece of marzipan off the block and tasted it. 'Oh, delicious. And no visible dog hairs or grit in it.'

'I scrubbed the floor this morning. I thought it might taste of Jeyes Fluid.'

Laura hadn't seen Marcin since her bike ride with Giovanni. She had hardly thought about him. She was hanging wet sheets on the line, struggling with the weight of them, when she saw Marcin striding towards her. Good, she thought. I could do with some muscle.

She dropped the sheet back into the basket and straightened up, smiling. But Marcin's mouth was a hard line. She thought he looked strangely ugly. Usually stolidly handsome, like those young heroes of the revolution on one of Stalin's posters, now his eyes seemed to protrude and his mouth had a sardonic twist.

'I know everything, Laura. Aleksy, he saw you with that Italian. Are you going with him?'

'Don't be silly. Of course I'm not going with him. We went for a bike ride, that's all.'

He looks like a stage policeman, thought Laura, standing with his feet apart and his arms folded like that.

'Why you lying together on the grass,' he barked, 'on Dover's Hill? Tell me.'

'Aleksy exaggerates. We were resting after biking up the hill. It was hot. We needed a rest.'

Marcin dropped his arms. 'But you are *my* girlfriend. You never go up Dover's Hill with me.'

His petulant tone fired Laura to anger and she snapped. 'That's because you never want to do anything but make love. When did you ever suggest going biking anywhere? You only suggest a *walk* with the aim of finding a ditch to do it in.'

Laura's voice had risen and she had quite shocked herself with the baldness of her language, but she didn't care.

Marcin took a step closer. Uncomfortably closer, but Laura stood her ground, her eyes challenging him. He glared at her. 'So that's your problem. You want man with no balls? Well, you found the right one. That Eyetie is nancy boy for sure. Always singing opera and bowing to the ladies. You not normal, Laura. There is something wrong with you.'

Laura felt her face flush hot and red. For a second there was silence. She was speechless. Marcin had gone too far and he seemed to realise it. She backed away but he took a step towards her, arms out, his face conciliatory.

Oh, no, you don't, thought Laura. Not this time. She turned away but Marcin caught her by the elbow. 'Stop, Laura. I'm sorry. I love you—'

Laura struggled, now shouting, 'No you don't. And anyway I don't love you. I don't even *like* you.' Marcin let go his hold and she stumbled away, breaking into a run, trying not to burst into tears till she was round the corner and out of earshot.

A couple of weeks later, on Giovanni's day off, he and Laura biked to Frampton to visit the Maxwell-Calders' gamekeeper Paul and his wife Nell. Frampton supplied the Mitford with venison and game birds, and occasionally with hares, so Paul and Giovanni had become friends.

The weather was glorious. Giovanni had prepared a picnic and the four of them went down to the river. They crossed the little bridge to the island and lay on the rough grass, eating lunch and drinking cider.

Laura was on her back, half asleep. 'Whew, that is good stuff,' Giovanni said, holding his glass out for more.

'It's the brew for the estate workers. I think the toffs have milder stuff, less cloudy. The brewery gets the best apples for that.'

After lunch, Paul and Nell had to go back to work, and they left Laura and Giovanni with the scrumpy and a punnet of strawberries. Giovanni carefully hulled a strawberry and fed it to Laura.

'Mmm,' she said, 'I think this is the definition of heaven. The smell of crushed grass, ripe strawberries, cider, rippling water, glorious day.'

'And being well fed and slightly drunk.' Giovanni leaned over and stroked the inside of her bare arm very gently. 'And in love.'

Laura kept very still. Had she heard right? Yes, she knew she had. 'Say that again,' she whispered.

'And in love.'

She could feel little shimmers of sensation up and down her arm. Especially when his fingers, light as gossamer, followed the lines of the veins on her wrist. It made her mouth water. Eyes closed, she murmured, 'Don't stop.'

They were lying side by side, Giovanni on one elbow, Laura on her back, her head on a tussock of grass, like a pillow. Laura felt the sun go in and opened her eyes to find Giovanni's head over hers, his eyes on hers. Laura could feel her heart beating, and when she spoke, her voice was unreliable.

'It isn't just the cider, is it?' she said, solemn as a child.

'No, *cara mia*, it is not the cider.'

Very slowly and deliberately he hulled the strawberries, eating one, then putting the next into her mouth. They said nothing, just quietly chewed and swallowed and held each other's gaze. When he had hulled the last strawberry he leant over Laura and held it over her mouth. She tipped her head back and opened her lips but he just brushed her mouth very gently with the fruit, not allowing her to eat it. Her eyelids fluttered with the sensation and smell, and it crossed her mind that strawberries were prob-ably an aphrodisiac in someone's culture. She watched him in silence as he put the strawberry into his own mouth, then bent over her. She shut her eyes, knowing he would kiss her. He did, and as she relaxed her mouth she tasted the strawberry, dropped from his mouth to hers. It was their first kiss, and her lips felt soft and full, and his mouth tasted of cider and strawberry and him. Oh God, she thought, this is it. This is desire. The first time I've really felt it.

They made love then, and it was like an extension of the strawberry kiss. He was very deliberate and careful, caressing every inch of her as he slowly undressed her. Naked on the grass, the sun was in her eyes, and she had to turn her head to the side. Then he buried his head in her exposed neck, and once again eclipsed the sun with his head over hers. She marvelled at how his hands could raise currents of sensation all over her, and then at the shaking desire that overtook her so that she reached to touch and stroke him all over, behind his neck, his sinewy legs, his tight hard buttocks. And when at last he lay on top of her she wanted him inside her. Yes, she thought, yes, yes. And then she was saying it aloud. Yes, yes, please don't stop.

Half an hour later the sun had gone in and Giovanni and Laura were dressed again. They were sitting on the ground, Giovanni with his back against a tree trunk, smoking, Laura sitting between his legs, her head under his chin.

Laura's voice was dreamy. 'I'd no idea it could be like that. I feel just wonderful, all drifting and happy.'

He hugged her close and asked, 'Was it the first time for you?'

Laura felt her insides clench. She couldn't, just could not, tell him that she had been sleeping with Marcin. Now the very thought of what she had done for so long was mortifying, unbelievable.

She could feel her face aflame. She dared not speak, but she nodded, and he kissed her neck. 'My darling, I am so glad. You were lucky. It can hurt the first time, and bleed. But you British girls, you ride and dig fields and by the time you make love, well, how you say, you are not intact anymore. Which makes it easier for you, and just beautiful for me.'

Laura found her voice. It was a bit hesitant and husky, but she managed to say, 'It was beautiful for me, too. I love you, Giovanni.'

That evening Laura lay in bed, wrapped in happiness. Darling Giovanni, he had not for a moment doubted her.

An unwelcome thought blew into her mind and she at once waved it away: she was starting on the love affair of her life with an enormous, unforgiveable lie.

The Mitford kitchen staff were eating supper at a table in the yard when a burly, fair haired man jumped over the gate and strode over to Giovanni. Poking him in the chest, he said, 'You, you no-good Eyetie. You stay away from my girlfriend.'

Laura had mentioned a Polish boyfriend called Marcin but assured him it was over. How dare he! Giovanni jumped up to confront the Pole. His eyes were shining, his jaw thrust forward, a grin on his face. 'You want a fight?'

Giovanni liked a fight, and he was good at it. But Marcin was burlier and stronger.

'Of course I want a fight, you nancy wop.' He squared up to Giovanni, his thick legs planted apart, fists up. Giovanni, light on his feet, danced in front of him.

Chef Hein thrust himself between them, 'Nein, nein, you idiots. Giovanni, you are working. I've told you before, no fighting at work.' He pushed his head into Marcin's face and said, 'And you, whoever you are, you are trespassing. Go home.'

But Giovanni couldn't be stopped now. He was hot for a fight and dodged behind Marcin. Before the Pole had properly turned round, Giovanni had kicked him hard in the back of his knee. As Marcin staggered to retain his balance Giovanni punched him in the face.

In seconds they were locked in a fierce fistfight and Hein, for all his size, could not separate them. So he folded his arms and watched like the rest of the staff, shouting and cheering for Giovanni.

At first Giovanni knew he had the upper hand. He jumped in, jabbed quick punches to Marcin's chest and face, and danced out of the way. Marcin's punches were wilder and he swung his arms in bear-like arcs, often missing. But after five or six minutes, when both men were bloodied and heaving, he managed to deliver a punch to Giovanni's cheek that sent him crashing to the cobbles. Then he picked up the teapot from the table, tipped its contents onto Giovanni's upturned face and walked out of the yard, this time opening the gate rather than climbing over it. They watched him go, his rolling gait expressing arrogance and contempt.

Rage and adrenalin prevented Giovanni feeling any pain and in seconds he was on his feet and struggling to go after Marcin. But the others held him back and forced him to sit down.

'Your face is scarlet,' said Susan. 'Is it from the tea? Was it hot?'

Giovanni shook his head and tried to say, 'I don't think so,' and realised something was broken. Speaking was agony, and his cheek was swelling rapidly. Susan put butter on his bright red skin in case it was a burn and said, 'Chef, he needs a doctor.'

'Yes, OK, but I have something to say to him first, then you can walk him to Dr Drummond's.'

Giovanni looked up at the chef looming over him. It hurt to tip his head back. But it hurt to look down or straight ahead too.

'You're sacked, Giovanni. I told you last time, any more fights and you are out of a job. This is your third fight.'

Giovanni tried to protest that the Pole had provoked him, but it hurt too much. Hein was still talking. 'You are a good cook but you bloody Italians, you cannot control yourselves. So go to the doctor. And then stay out of my kitchen.'

CHAPTER FOURTEEN

Laura was with David and Jill inspecting the ripening corn in Sawpit field, when she fainted. She came to with her head in Jill's lap, and with her brother leaning over her. 'Are you all right, Laura?' His voice sounded oddly far away.

'It's OK, you just fainted. It's the heat,' said Jill, putting a restraining hand on Laura's forehead as she struggled to get up. 'Lie still for a few minutes.'

It was almost lunchtime, so they walked home. As soon as they entered Gypsy Wood, she felt fine. 'Don't tell Mummy I fainted, will you? She'll only fuss.'

And then one morning, when she was cleaning her teeth, she felt sick. She didn't actually throw up, and it didn't last long. But of course she thought the worst. No, I can't be pregnant, she told herself. I can't.

She sat on the side of the bath and racked her brains trying to remember when she'd last had what her mother called her 'visitor'. But she couldn't. She had an awful feeling that it was many, many weeks ago.

She stood up, telling herself not to be stupid. Her periods had always been erratic. Don't panic, she told herself. It's nothing. It's only the heat.

But a fortnight later, there was no denying it. She was pregnant. For the third time that week she was in the bathroom, vomiting. Her reflection showed her eyes wide with fear, cheeks flushed, mouth wet.

She cupped her hand under the tap, splashed water over her face, drank a few mouthfuls and buried her face in the towel.

She had not told anyone, not even Giovanni. Her thoughts ran round her head, trapped and desperate. She'd been hoping against hope that it would not be true, that her period would come and she'd be able to laugh at her dread and panic. Oh, why had they not been more careful? When she'd been with Marcin she'd used Volpar religiously. She'd kept it hidden behind the straw bales in the hayloft. But she'd not used it with Giovanni. That first time had been so unexpected and magical neither of them had been prepared. And afterwards, how could she explain why she possessed it?

Ever since she'd started sleeping with Marcin, she'd lived with the terror of pregnancy. Maybe other girls did too, but she could not imagine any of them of her age doing 'it' either. They were saving themselves for marriage. Either that or they were pretending.

But there was no pretending for her any more. It could not be worse: Giovanni's fight with Marcin had lost him his job and his room. He had had to swallow his pride and return to the farm where he'd worked as a prisoner in the war. Now he had a bunk in a Nissen hut dormitory which he shared with itinerant fruit pickers from the East End who did not like Italians. Even if Giovanni wanted to marry her, how could he support her?

Laura took a deep breath and told herself, I must tell Daddy and Mummy. And then she shrank away from the thought. Not yet. Maybe after the weekend – she'd do it then. Sophie was coming to stay soon, thank God. She would know what to do. But first she must tell Giovanni.

Giovanni astonished her. He opened his arms and cried, 'Wonderful. A bambino. Maybe a girl. She will be beautiful, like you. Wouldn't it be good to have a *ragazzina*?' He hugged her and looked into her face, his eyes shining with excitement.

She smiled uncertainly. 'Are you really pleased? You're not angry?'

He lifted her off her feet and then as suddenly put her down, and put his hand gently on her belly. 'Oh no, maybe I cannot do that now. We must be careful of our *patatina*.'

'*Patatina*?'

'It is fat small potato. But it means little girl. Like *ragazzina*.' He kissed her eyes and said, 'Do not worry, my angel. We will be a little family. Very lucky and very happy. You will see.'

The prospect of the Cotswold Fair, and the first Harvest Festival supper in Chorlton since before the war, should have excited and delighted Laura. But the impending confrontation with her parents, which she'd been putting off for weeks, hovered over her like a black cloud. Luckily she'd stayed slim and her pregnancy hardly showed yet.

The whole family went to the fair, even her father. He had

spent the summer overseeing the removal of ammunition from the Moreton dump, the decommissioning and dismantling of tented and temporary structures and the dispersal of hundreds of personnel. He was also involved in the round of dinner dances, air shows, open days and festivities that the RAF excelled at. He complained of the workload but Laura suspected he was dreading the end of his war job. He'd have to retire for a second time and he'd hate having nothing to do and no one to order about. Oh God, she thought, I am going to be a further, worse, disappointment.

It was a glorious September day and the women had dressed in their best. They all crammed into Donald's big Bentley: Jill, the thinnest, between Donald and Maud in the front, and Laura, Sophie and Grace in the back. David was already at the fair. He'd entered Meg in the sheep dog trials.

Maud turned round. 'I expect we'll see your new boyfriend, Laura. Will he be there, do you think?'

'Yes, he will. He's selling fruit for the farmers' co-op.'

Laura studied the back of her father's head. It seemed to her that disapproval radiated from him. He said nothing, but his head gave a slight shake and he glanced at his wife as if reproving her.

Laura wanted to challenge him. Challenge them both, in fact. Why couldn't her mother say 'Giovanni'? She knew his name perfectly well. 'Your new boyfriend' was insulting. He'd been to the house at least half a dozen times over the last weeks, so he was hardly 'new'. As for her father, she wanted to shout at him, 'What have you got against Giovanni? Why don't you come out with it, instead of silently emitting distaste?'

But Sophie squeezed her leg in warning. She's right, Laura

thought, and anyway he'll be voicing his objections all too loudly soon enough.

On arrival, Jill and Grace set off to find David, while Donald and Maud headed for the Farmers' Club restaurant and bar. Sophie and Laura strolled about among the farm stalls and food stands. They both knew they were looking for the Four Shires' Co-Op, but neither mentioned it.

The broadcast announcements of horse and pony events or stock parades from the ring, and the competing oompa-pah of the brass band lifted Laura's spirits. If it wasn't for her dreadful secret, all would be wonderful. She had a man she loved, who loved her; it was a glorious day; the war was over; she had money to spend.

Giovanni was struggling to serve a long queue. As always he was full of banter and good will, but underneath Laura could tell he was feeling the pressure of impatient shoppers. Most people just wanted a single punnet of blackberries or plums to eat as they walked, or a couple of apples, and were getting impatient queuing behind housewives doing their weekly shop.

As soon as he saw Laura and Sophie he shouted to them, 'Laura, quickly, come help me!' He addressed the queue of women. 'Is she not lovely? She is Laura, and she is my girlfriend so it is OK if I make her work, I think. And the other one, also very *bella, bella*, like, how you say? A cream puff, she is Sophie. Sophie is very clever. At Oxford University. She will be able to add up everything and give the right change, eh, Sophie?'

Laura saw at once that they needed two queues. While she started to serve customers, Sophie changed two chalked price signs to *One Item Only* with an arrow to the left and *Mixed Orders* with an arrow to the right.

Giovanni was a born salesman. Now more relaxed, he chatted in deliberately broken Italian to the customers, flirted with the women and sang little bursts of opera and popular songs loudly and tunefully in his clear tenor. When the queue abated enough for Laura to look round, she noticed the adjacent stallholders watching Giovanni belting out 'O Sole Mio' while filling a paper bag with greengages. They muttered to each other and Laura felt a frisson of anxiety. If their resentfulness blossomed into open hostility, Giovanni wouldn't hesitate to take them on.

So she was relieved when two young men from another of the Co-Op's farms came to take over the stall. By two o'clock Giovanni was free to join the girls.

Laura put one arm through Giovanni's and the other through Sophie's. 'Let's get some lunch,' she said. 'I'm starving.'

They bought fried fish and ate it off the newspaper, and then sat at a café stall for tea and gingerbread. Giovanni lit a cigarette.

Sophie noticed Jill and David watching the Punch and Judy show, standing behind a crowd of children sitting on the grass, enthralled. 'I think I've been a gooseberry to you two lovebirds long enough. I'll go and be a gooseberry to your brother and Jill for a bit.'

Before they could politely protest, she was gone, and they looked at each other with relief and pleasure. 'Let's go to the fairground. I need to kiss you. Kissing is traditional in fairgrounds,' said Giovanni.

'No it's not. Not in England. We are very strait-laced.'

But Laura was wrong. There were several young men, many still in uniform, cuddled up with their girlfriends on the rides.

But Laura was too embarrassed to be kissed in public, and anyway she feared her parents might see her, so the only kisses Giovanni got were in the Tunnel of Love, for the brief few seconds when the little train was in the dark.

Laura won a tiny goldfish in a jam jar at the coconut shy and Giovanni a packet of balloons in the shooting gallery. Giovanni wanted to visit the Freak Show, which promised a bearded lady, Siamese twins and the 'Smallest Dwarf in England', but Laura wouldn't go. She didn't want to go to the Boxing Booth either, but felt she couldn't refuse this too, and they paid their entrance money and watched a short exhibition fight. Then the promoter, in top hat and tails, called for challengers from the crowd.

'Now that was a fine demonstration of the art of boxing, and both these world-famous gentlemen, Charlie Hickman and the legendary Barry Lonsdale, invite any of you brave young men to a fight. You can earn a bob or two if the crowd likes your spirit, and a lot more if, by some miracle, you defeat our licensed professionals. Do we have any challengers?'

Giovanni's hand shot up. 'Yes, sir. I will fight.' He was already shaking off his jacket and the crowd was cheering.

Laura grabbed his shirt, trying to stop him removing it. 'No, Giovanni, no, please . . .'

But he laughed and yanked it off, and thrust jacket and shirt into her arms. '*Cara mia*, I will be fine.' He kissed her on the mouth, and the crowd clapped. He climbed up into the ring where the promoter took his arm and turned him to face the crowd. 'What is your name, young man?'

'Giovanni Angelotti.'

'An Italian! And which of my celebrated fighters do you want to challenge?' Giovanni indicated the shorter, broader of the two.

Laura's heart clenched as she looked at the man's muscled chest, the hairs plastered to his skin with sweat from the previous fight. Beside him Giovanni looked so thin and young.

The promoter flourished his hat for attention. 'Very good. Ladies and gentlemen, the next fight will be three rounds between the famous Barry Lonsdale, known all over the Midlands . . .' The cheering from the crowd drowned out his words and he paused until he could be heard again, then continued, 'and the young challenger, Giovanni Angelotti.' The crowd hissed and booed until the promoter shushed them. 'Give the lad a chance, boys. He may be Italian and a bit scrawny, but he's brave as a lion to take on Barry.'

Laura watched, appalled, as Giovanni was helped into boxing gloves. Then the referee said a few words to the two men and almost at once the fight started with Barry aiming a blow at Giovanni's head, which Giovanni parried and followed up with a punch to Barry's chest.

Laura knew nothing about boxing. Most of the time she could not watch, and stood with her hands over her eyes. She could hear the shouts of 'C'mon, Barry, kill the wop', and found her fear replaced by anger. How could the crowd, who knew nothing of Giovanni other than that he was Italian, hate him so? And how could anyone enjoy a sport the object of which was to bash your opponent into submission?

When the bell rang and the boxers returned to their corners, Laura was surprised to see that Giovanni was unmarked and grinning happily at her, while his opponent was slumped on his stool, obviously tired.

Laura watched more of the second round and noticed that

Giovanni danced about, staying out of Lonsdale's reach but darting in if he found an opening and raining quick successive blows on the heavier man, then jumping out again. Once Lonsdale landed an uppercut to Giovanni's jaw and knocked him down. But Giovanni was up again on the third count and back on the attack.

The bell went for the end of the round. Laura watched Giovanni return to his corner and bend to unlace his boots. Oh God, she thought, he's going to fight barefoot. She could see why: his opponent was wearing supple leather boxing boots, and Giovanni's heavy boots must be a handicap. Thank God this was the last round.

Laura could not tell who was winning but the crowd were now divided. Not all of them wanted the 'wop' defeated anymore and there were occasional shouts of 'Come on, Italy!' And then Lonsdale, obviously tired, staggered forward into a clinch – and stamped hard on Giovanni's bare left foot. The crowd shouted and booed and there were cries of 'Foul! Foul!' The referee stopped the fight, holding his hands out one towards each fighter, bidding them to stay apart. Giovanni was swearing, hopping in pain and reaching down to hold his foot.

The crowd watched in near silence and then, when Giovanni indicated his willingness to continue, they cheered loudly. The bout restarted and Giovanni was like a man possessed. With controlled aggression, he rained successive fusillades of accurate blows to Lonsdale's, chest, upper arms and shoulders. Barry, heavy and stalwart, stayed on his feet and barely rocked under Giovanni's onslaught, but the fight had gone out of him. Laura even felt fleetingly sorry for him. Poor man, she thought, he's probably been fighting matches all day.

But by the time the final bell went and the referee held Giovanni's hand up to the cheering crowd, Laura was jumping up and down with excitement and pride, all sympathy for Lonsdale forgotten.

The promoter reappeared, removed his top hat and addressed the spectators. 'That was a fine display of skill and bravery from young Giovanni here. I will now pass my hat among you and I trust you will show your appreciation with generous nobbings for the young man.' Then, spotting members of the audience turning to go, he called, 'Don't go yet, ladies and gentlemen. The next, and last, item on the programme will be a boxing match between the Boxing Beauties, two young ladies in very short skirts and not much more. I am sure you will stay for that.'

When Laura and Giovanni left, all their pockets and Laura's handbag were stuffed with pennies and silver. They found a secluded corner of the field, between the sheep pens and the river, and sank down on the trampled grass. They tipped the money into Laura's lap.

Giovanni counted it. Seventeen shillings and sixpence. 'Not bad,' he said, 'for nine minutes' fighting.'

CHAPTER FIFTEEN

Sophie was the best friend anyone could have. Sharing her secret with her was such a relief; she made Laura feel normal, not a sinful outsider. With her arms around Laura, Sophie said, 'It happens all the time, I promise you. Of course it does. Wanting sex is built into us, and making babies is what we are born to do.'

'But my father . . .?'

'I know, that's the problem.'

They discussed the possibilities, which were few and stark: Laura could keep the baby and run away with Giovanni, or have the baby somewhere secret and have it adopted. Or she could have an illegal abortion.

Sophie said she knew a proper doctor, not a charlatan, outside Oxford. He did nothing, it seemed, but make unwanted babies go away.

'He did it for me, Laura, so I know.'

Laura stared at Sophie in astonishment. 'You? No! But you never told me. You poor, poor thing, what . . .?'

'I wanted to tell you, but I suppose I was ashamed. The father was my tutor, and married.'

Laura put her arms round her friend, but Sophie said,

'Honestly, Laura, it's fine. I was miserable, of course, but it was a year ago now, and I'm all right. I only told you because I wanted you to know about the doctor.'

Laura saw that Sophie was determined not to talk about herself. She released her and sat back. 'It costs a lot,' Sophie went on, 'but your father can afford it, and I'm sure he will pay rather than be embarrassed by a daughter with a growing belly.'

Laura listened, and could see the sense in it, but she couldn't agree. 'I can't, Sophie. I wouldn't do that. I might have if Giovanni had hated the idea of a baby. But he's so delighted, and now I find I want it too. Or rather, since it's inside me, I don't want to kill it. I can't.'

'OK, if you feel so strongly your parents cannot really be too horrified. And presumably they'd agree to your marriage to Giovanni. They'll have known of other cases, especially in war. Maybe they slept together before they were married.'

'Oh no, never!'

'Even if they didn't, they'd have wanted to. That doctor told me he reckons half the babies born during the war were illegitimate. English girls getting pregnant by Yanks, or by their English boyfriends. I mean, you'd sleep with the man you loved if he was off to the Front and might get killed, wouldn't you?'

'But the war is over, and I don't have that excuse.'

'All the better. Your parents will have a daughter they love marrying a man she loves, and who loves her, and is not going to get killed. And they'll have a grandchild. What more can they want?'

'Someone who can support me? Someone who works in the City or owns great swathes of countryside, someone who is educated, well-connected and English!' Laura laughed. 'But maybe you're right, times have changed. The trouble is, they don't know it.'

It was an impressive Harvest Home. Farms and smallholdings had been generous in their contributions. Frampton had provided the scrumpy, Fir Farm the geese, Brown's the bread, and the apples and vegetables had been begged from neighbouring smallholdings. The supper table and walls were decorated with hips and haws, greenery and crab apples, and there were lighted lanterns and corn dollies hanging from the rafters.

But Laura did not enjoy the feast. She did her best to pretend to be having a good time, but the knowledge that she must tell her parents about the baby weighed on her mind. She stood behind the laden trestle table, adding roast potatoes and apple sauce to plates piled high with goose and cabbage, and responding to banter with a half-hearted smile. She was dog-tired, and her weariness contributed to a sense of unreality.

When everyone was served she sat down with relief between Giovanni and Sophie. Under the table, Giovanni squeezed her thigh with a reassuring hand and she looked at him gratefully. She picked at her food, and refused the scrumpy.

'What's up, sister?' It was David, leaning across the table. 'Don't you want your dinner?' She shook her head, and David reached across and swapped his empty plate for her full one. He grinned at her. 'Shame to waste it.'

When Samson started to play his accordion, everyone was up and dancing in no time, the older labourers and farmhands doing the traditional country dances and mocking the younger ones for not knowing the steps.

Jill pulled Giovanni up and directed him in turning and

skipping, but Laura refused David's invitation to dance. He pulled Sophie to her feet instead and Laura was left alone at their table. She watched her burly brother and plump, pretty Sophie together and thought what an attractive couple they made. But David had fallen for Jill and that was fine. She loved Jill too. Sophie would have to find a handsome doctor or something.

Laura looked about her with a sense of disbelief. This time next year, she thought, will I be here? Will I have a baby on my lap? Will Giovanni and I be married?

When Giovanni and Jill returned to the table, Laura shook off her lethargy and joined the dancers in a reel. Normally she loved the energy and communal activity of a reel, the linked and loosened arms, the change of partners, the whole room twirling, everyone laughing, hot and sweaty, all cares miles away. And tonight, for the first few turns of Strip the Willow, her previous exhaustion vanished and she threw herself into the dance, joining the others in pushing and shoving poor Giovanni in the right direction. But then, quite suddenly, when she had just cavorted down the room with Giovanni to take their places once more at the head of the formation, the room tilted and her head swam. She clutched at Giovanni's sleeve, knowing she was going to be sick.

Giovanni half dragged, half carried her out of the barn. The other dancers barely noticed their disappearance and Giovanni brushed off Laura's father's 'What's up, Laura?' with a quick 'She's fine, just the heat, she needs some air.'

They managed to reach the back of the barn before Laura threw up. Giovanni held her round the waist until she was done, then passed her his handkerchief. She tried to apologise, but he shushed her.

'When we have our *bambino*, *cara*, there will be a lot more than this to deal with.'

The following afternoon, Maud put two plates piled high with toast on the kitchen table, one pile spread with Shippam's Bloater Paste, the other with Gentleman's Relish.

'Can't we have the remains of last night's geese? Or did the village scoff the lot?' asked David.

Maud shook her head. 'Sadly, they did. I had plans for the leftovers but there weren't any.'

Jill put the big glass jar of pickled eggs on the table. Maud sat down heavily and reached for the teapot. She served her husband first, and he smiled at her. 'Well, Maud, my congratulations. That was a very good harvest supper. The geese were delicious, and Glenn Miller sounded very well on our new phonograph.'

'Record player,' corrected David. He turned to his sister. 'Laura, what happened to you? I thought you and Giovanni would've been dancing till dawn. But he went home and you sloped off? Before the clearing up, I noticed.'

'I was tired. The dancing made me giddy. And Giovanni's foot still hurts.'

'Serve him right,' said her father. 'He should know better than to fight in a common booth at a fair. What does he expect? Queensberry Rules?'

Laura opened her mouth to challenge her father, but David cut her off with his barking laugh. 'I doubt if Giovanni has ever heard of Queensberry Rules. He just likes a fight.'

Laura felt her cheeks glow hot. She was about to protest when Sophie chipped in quickly, 'Of course you were tired. You'd been cooking and cleaning and decorating for a week.'

'And Jill and I have been loafing about chewing the fat, I

suppose?' countered David. 'We've been harvesting till ten for the last fortnight, but it didn't stop us.'

The conversation turned to the coming year. Donald looked from one to the other as he spoke. 'It will be very different. Your mother can at last hire someone young and strong so that Mrs Digweed can retire, and with luck our little Laura can finally go to France.' He sat back, smiling.

Laura caught Sophie's eye, but said nothing. Maud reached over and patted Jill's arm. 'And what about you, my dear?'

Jill looked across at Donald, her cheeks colouring. 'I don't know. I love the work, but I expect you won't need me when everyone's de-mobbed and you get your farm hands back.'

'No chance of that,' said David. 'Most of the men from round here are home already and hardly any have gone back to farm labour. Poor blighters, they want a nice warm factory, not the freezing fields.'

'And who can blame them?' said Maud. 'I was at Stow station when a trainload of lads arrived back. They all looked done in, not just the wounded ones.'

'But Jill, you are the best worker we've ever had,' said Donald. 'I don't think David could do without you now. As far as I'm concerned, you're welcome to stay for ever, even if the Land Army disbands you.'

'Besides,' said Maud, 'we love you living with us.'

Laura grinned at her brother and said, 'Especially David.'

Jill, embarrassed but pleased, ignored Laura and tried to thank Donald, but he went on. 'Of all our farm hands, I think only Jack wants to return. It's all change, that's for sure. With Laura in gay Paree, Maud and Grace ladies of leisure and David with half his mind on Oxford in the autumn, next year it will be you and me, Jill, with a couple of farm hands if we're lucky.'

David leant forward, 'Actually, Dad, I'm having second thoughts about Oxford. Turns out I really like being a farmer. I've been looking at agricultural college courses in Cirencester instead. That way I could keep an eye on the business here while studying.'

Laura watched her father gradually persuaded by David. He is much better at argument than me, she thought. I get upset and burst into tears, but he argues his case so calmly and logically. The conversation moved to the future of farming and David could not hide his enthusiasm.

'Dad, you're right we won't have many men on the land, but not just because they want to go to the towns. The truth is we won't need them. With the new milking machines, tractors, harvesters, balers, there won't be jobs for an army of labourers. Only at harvest time, but even that is mostly mechanised now.'

Laura sat silent, thinking that all this talk of Chorlton after the war did not concern her. No one was talking of her future, which was just as well. Her father had briefly mentioned France, but she wouldn't be going to France. She didn't even want to now. She wanted to go to London, with Giovanni. And she would, with or without her parents' blessing.

The following day, Giovanni, Sophie and Laura went for a walk, ostensibly to pick blackberries.

Laura had been thinking about how and when she'd approach her parents. She waited until the three of them were in the lane and had started picking, then said, 'I'll tell them both together, when we get back. When Daddy comes in for tea.'

Giovanni looked at her face. 'Don't look so scared, *cara*. I'll come with you.'

Sophie touched Laura's arm with the back of her hand so as not to stain her sleeve with blackberry juice. 'Laura, if they won't agree to your marrying, what will you do?'

Laura looked at Giovanni, her eyes questioning. He answered Sophie's question while looking into Laura's troubled face. 'We'll get married anyway.'

An hour later Laura put the trug on the kitchen table. In it was a colander filled with blackberries, surrounded by apples. Some of the apples were still on leafy twigs.

'Lovely,' exclaimed Maud. 'Where did you get the apples?'

'From the tree behind the henhouse. Mostly windfalls. They are cookers, I think.'

Laura closed her eyes for a moment, then looked at Giovanni for reassurance. 'Mummy, is Daddy in yet?'

'He's listening to the wireless in the drawing room.'

Laura reached for her mother's hand and drew her towards the door. 'Please, Mummy, please come, we need to speak to you both.'

Maud looked round, anxious. But Laura insisted and she followed her daughter into the room. Irritated, Donald looked up. 'What's up?' he said. 'Whatever it is, can't it wait? I'm listening to the news.'

'No, Daddy, it can't, I'm afraid. Sit down, Mummy.' Laura almost pushed her mother into a chair.

'Please, Mrs Oliver, please sit down. We need to talk to you.' Giovanni had followed Laura and her mother into the room and now stood next to Laura. Donald walked across to the wireless and turned the knob to silence the newsreader. But he did not resume his seat.

'Oh dear,' said Maud, looking from her daughter to Giovanni. Truth was dawning. Or something close to the truth. 'What is it, darling?'

'Mr Oliver, sir, I want very much to marry your daughter. She wants it too.' Laura saw his eyes flick to her and back to her father. 'We are asking for your permission.' Giovanni's voice had deepened with stress and Laura found herself, insanely, wanting to laugh. He sounded so formal and pompous.

There was a tiny silence, then, 'Out of the question!' Donald took two determined steps towards Laura and stood over her. 'What's this nonsense, Laura?'

Laura, who seconds before thought she'd faint with trepidation, now felt her face flush in indignation. 'Daddy, how can you call it nonsense? We love each other. Where is the nonsense in that?'

Maud stood up and said, her voice conciliatory, 'I'm sure you think you do, but you are so young—'

Laura swung round. 'Mother, I'm practically the same age you were when you married Daddy!'

'But you are about to go to Paris, and have a season in London. You will meet lots of young men.'

'I don't want to go to Paris. I don't want to meet any other men. I'm in love with Giovanni, Mummy, and we are going to get married, with . . . with . . .' Suddenly her bravado dried up. She could not say the words 'with or without your blessing' and she clamped her mouth shut in an effort not to cry. Her mother put her arms around her and Laura wept into the familiar comfort of her neck.

Then she heard Giovanni say, 'Mr Oliver, we are going to have a baby. Laura is pregnant.'

Laura felt her mother stiffen in her embrace, and silence followed.

Her father, his voice steady and steely-cold, addressed Giovanni. 'Young man, listen carefully. You will not marry Laura. You earn almost nothing, and you are a violent, penniless, working-class, Italian prisoner of war. Which is not what I have in mind as a husband for my daughter. Even if she has shown herself to be a slut. Now, I must ask you to leave this house.'

Laura let go of her mother. 'How dare you, Daddy! How can you talk to Giovanni – talk to anyone – like that? Come, Giovanni, let's go.'

Donald reached out and caught Laura by the wrist, gripping hard enough to halt her flight for the door. 'Laura, understand this. If you leave with this man, you will not enter this house again. Do you understand?'

'Yes, sir!' shouted Laura. 'I understand very clearly. And that is fine by me. Pity Mummy will never get to see her grandchild, but that's the price she'll pay for your blind prejudice, isn't it?'

She ran out of the door. Giovanni turned to Maud. 'Mrs Oliver, please, Laura loves you. She doesn't want—'

'Out!' barked Donald, standing by the door. 'Out!'

Giovanni gave the slightest shrug, then bowed briefly to Maud, and followed Laura.

He knew where she would be and followed her up to the hayloft. She was sitting on the hay bale, sobbing.

He held her for a long time, until she stopped crying, and then he kissed her eyes. 'You taste salty. It's delicious. You should cry more often.'

It was cold on the back of Giovanni's bicycle, and Laura pressed tightly against his back. By the time they got to his Nissen hut she was shivering, and thinking of all she'd left: her mother, her warm room, her clothes – especially her thick wool coat, her small hoard of money. At least she should have brought the coat and the money.

The door wasn't locked and they crept in to spend their first night together in Giovanni's single bed, sandwiched between two other workers' cots. Laura, warm at last and too tired to worry further, drifted in half-sleep to the rhythmical snores of their neighbour. This feels right, she thought. It's where I belong. Wrapped in the arms of my baby's father.

PART THREE

CHAPTER SIXTEEN

1946, autumn

Happiness, Laura thought, comes in many guises. When they'd first got to London she'd imagined they'd get married as soon as possible, but, having broken the rule of chastity before marriage, she now thought, why not break another and live in sin? She knew Giovanni loved her, she'd no need of a piece of paper to bind him to her, and she was, she thought bluntly, too tired and too poor to enjoy a wedding. It could wait.

Who would have thought I'd be happy living with a mostly-out-of-work chef, in a dingy rooming house, unmarried and pregnant? Especially in London, where we know no one and which is dirty and grey, with bombed-out houses, rubble and filth everywhere. Londoners, who had to queue for food, for buses, for the cinema, for everything, seemed exhausted and miserable. Yet we are happy, really happy.

When Giovanni had no work, especially when they first arrived, they busked in the street. Laura enjoyed it, particularly when the sun shone and the sky was clear. They didn't have any instruments, but Giovanni's clear tenor carried wonderfully as he sang his old mix of Italian opera or still popular war songs like 'Lily Marlene' or 'The White Cliffs of Dover'. Laura sang along when she knew the words, smiled at the punters and passed round Giovanni's cap.

She learnt early on that the poor were as generous as the rich, sometimes a lot more so. If she and Giovanni had the stretch of road to themselves, they would not do too badly, but sometimes there was an old soldier, missing an arm and a leg, selling matches. He, understandably, had a higher claim on public sympathy.

As the weather worsened into December, busking became unprofitable. It was cold and people hurried past, protected by their hats and turned-up collars from catching her eye.

Giovanni got a job at the Kardomah tearooms doing casual shifts and was soon promoted from making sandwiches to the hot kitchen. Laura was also accepted as a casual waitress. But the pay was poor and since she continued to suffer from nausea, she could only do the occasional shift. She did what she could, as much to get out of their rented room in Paddington as from the need for money.

Towards Christmas the café became crowded and they both worked longer hours. One freezing afternoon at about six o'clock, tired from being on her feet all day, Laura came back to their rented room in Paddington. Giovanni was staying on to do a double shift but she was glad to be on her own. It was her night for a bath and she planned to wash her hair, rub her swollen belly with Vaseline and have an early night.

For once the geyser burst into action with a satisfying hiss, pop and rumble, and boiling water spluttered out of the tap in steaming bursts. Laura did not dare fill the tub above the prescribed three inches, but she enjoyed her bath. She lay on her back, her belly with its neat round bump rising out of the water. She watched it move as the baby kicked. Except for the small bulge, she was thin, and the baby had a lot more energy than she did. She smiled, thinking of it turning somersaults, happy and safe inside her. She was certain she had conceived that first time on the grass at Frampton, which would mean the baby would be born in the last week of February. That had been the happiest day of her life, and if it was a girl they'd call her Felicity. But not Felix if a boy: Giovanni said Felix was a cartoon cat.

Laura emerged from the bathroom and met her landlady coming along the corridor with an armful of newspaper squares threaded on string to serve as lavatory paper. Laura's skin was glowing from the rough towel, her hair was wet and she felt revived, clean and cheerful. She greeted the usually grumpy Mrs Enders with a broad smile.

'Good evening, Mrs Enders.'

Mrs Enders responded with a grunt and was about to pass by, when she suddenly jerked her head forward to focus her eyes on Laura's stomach. 'I thought as much, young lady.' Her eyes had narrowed to slits and her tone was hard with accusation. 'You've got a bun in the oven, haven't you?'

Laura took a small step backwards as though fearing Mrs Enders' sharp beak would pierce her little balloon of a belly. 'Why, yes. We're going to have a baby. In February.'

'Not in my house, you're not. This is a respectable rooming house, not a bleeding refuge for women as is not as good as they ought to be. If you'd told me you was up the duff, I'd not have let you in in the first place. You and that fancy Italian pimp of yours can hop it out of my house. And sharpish.'

Laura was so taken aback it took her a second or two to reply. 'But . . . but why? What have we done? We're good tenants, aren't we? You can't just throw us out!'

'Oh yes I can. I'm not having no bawling brats, thank you very much. And don't think I don't know that you two aren't married. I turned a blind eye to that out of the goodness of me heart. An unmarried couple is one thing, as long as they behave respectable. But little bastards underfoot, screaming all night, that's quite another kettle of fish.'

Mrs Enders, breathing heavily, walked a few paces down the corridor, then turned back to the speechless Laura. 'You can stay till Friday. And count yourselves lucky I'm giving you notice. I should be pitching you out on the street, that I should.'

Laura leant against the wall, her hands protectively clutching her belly, her mind racing. How dare the woman refer to her baby as a bastard? Or to Giovanni as a pimp? Did she really think that she, Laura, was a prostitute? No, no, she was just a horrible woman, and she was using the excuse to get the room back for Christmas fortnight, when she could let it for more money. Of course they should not live here – it was a horrible place. They would go today, as soon as Giovanni came home.

But when Giovanni got home, close to midnight, Laura had already cried herself to sleep. When she woke, she thought Giovanni looked so done in, so grey with exhaustion, she postponed the discussion. Maybe, she thought, things won't be so bad after breakfast.

She and Giovanni spent the next two days looking for a room they could afford and which would have them. The war had ensured that housing was scarce and expensive and few landladies would tolerate children, let alone a baby. They could not afford the rent of the few flats that accepted families.

Laura was about to tell Giovanni that she felt too ill to go on, when a man, one of the tenants walking out of the house that had just turned them down, suggested they try the Salvation Army.

'What is that, the Salvation Army?' asked Giovanni as they walked on. Laura was about to say what had immediately sprung into her head, which was that she could not possibly go to a hostel: she had not sunk as low as that. But then she said, 'It's a charity that helps homeless people. And it looks as though we are about to qualify for their help.'

Giovanni smiled, but the smile was strained. 'Let's give it a little longer. We don't have to find a bed until tomorrow night.'

But Laura could not face looking at places any more, and she needed something starchy to eat to quell the nausea, so she sat in a café with a cup of tea and a Bath bun while Giovanni continued the search alone. It was warm in the steamy little café and Laura leant against the wall and fell asleep.

She didn't wake up until Giovanni slid onto the bench next to her and stroked her wrist to wake her. '*Cara mia*, it's no good. I tried a dozen places. We must go to the house for homeless place.'

They got directions from the café owner and walked to the Salvation Army hostel on the embankment. They knocked on the door. An old man, with the bearing of a soldier but poorly dressed, let them in. Yes, he said, they could find a bed, but this was a men's hostel. No, they could not take women. And, he said, looking at Laura's stomach, no children either. The men mostly slept in dormitories, you see.

The next day Giovanni had to work: they needed the money and the Kardomah needed him, so Laura tramped the streets alone. It was raining gently but steadily and her umbrella had a broken spike. At four o'clock, with her feet sore and her back aching, she again knocked on the Salvation Army door.

The same man opened it. He smiled kindly when he recognised her. 'I did tell you we could not take women, didn't I?' he said.

'I know, but could you take my husband? And please tell me where I'll find a women's hostel? You see, we had to leave our room this morning, and even if it's just for a few nights, until we find somewhere . . .' Her eyes suddenly filled with tears, and she had to fish out a handkerchief.

He led her into a little office, and let her shake off her wet coat and sit on his office chair. Oh, the relief to her back! It was indescribable. He brought her a mug of sweet tea and a biscuit. She did not usually have sugar in tea, but he had already stirred it in and sugar was so scarce and he was so kind, she was in danger of weeping. She thanked him, probably overdoing it, she thought, but she was so intensely grateful for a word of kindness after the stream of hard-faced landladies. The sweet tea revived her, and the biscuit steadied her stomach. She smiled at him. 'I'm so sorry,' she said.

He told her how to find St Catherine's Hostel for Fallen Women, in Soho Square. 'I'm sorry about the name,' he said, 'but you see, they only take pregnant girls and they are all unmarried.'

He advised her to say nothing about a husband: if they knew she was happily married, they might not take her in.

'Of course,' he said, 'I'm not telling you to lie, but sometimes it's best to let people jump to the wrong conclusions.'

Laura did not want to undo her previous lie about Giovanni being her husband, so she said nothing, but thanked him again and set off to walk to Soho.

The hostel turned out to be run by nuns, and the one who questioned her, Sister Viola, was efficient but kind.

'I expect you're exhausted now,' she said. 'So we will leave all the questions for tomorrow. Evening prayers are at eight and then you could have some bread and tea, and we will find you a bed. Would that do?'

Panic clutched at Laura's throat. She had to see Giovanni. She couldn't just be locked up here.

'Could I possibly come later tonight? I need to fetch my things. You see, I had a room until this morning, but the landlady only just realised I was pregnant and has told me to go. But I could not carry my bag all over town while I looked for a bed.'

Telling this sorry tale brought tears back to her eyes, and Laura struggled in silence for a few seconds, taking herself to task, thinking she'd better get a grip and toughen up if she was to live with a bevy of pregnant girls from goodness knows what sort of backgrounds.

Sister Viola made her promise to be in by 9.30pm and said she would leave a supper tray for her in the hall. The night nurse would let her in if she rang the bell and show her to the dormitory.

Giovanni was horrified. 'Laura, we cannot live in separate hostels. We are not vagrants.'

'I know, but what else can we do? It's only until we find somewhere. At least we will be out of the rain.'

She knew it distressed Giovanni that he was not looking after her: he was too male and too Italian to like taking orders from her or admit defeat. She forced a smile. 'It's not important, sweetheart. It will be interesting. An adventure. One day we will look back and tell our bambino about it, and he won't believe us.' As she said this, the thought cheered her and her smile became real. Giovanni kissed her.

'You are right, as always. But I shall not let you stay there more than a week, I promise.'

But Laura knew that Giovanni might have to break his promise. He was working long shifts at the Kardomah, with little time for house hunting. For now she was just glad they both had beds to sleep in and food to eat. She put up with the nuns' insistence on chapel and the 8pm curfew as the price to be paid for bed and board.

After a few days at the hostel, one evening Laura was alarmed when she found her knickers stained with spots of blood. Roxanne, the very pregnant Scottish girl in the bed next to hers, called the matron, who sent for Dr Ingle. If she wanted to save the baby, he said, she must lie with her feet propped up higher than her hips, and not get out of bed. She must do nothing, just eat and sleep and stay in bed. Roxanne, friendly and cheerful, offered to do meal-tray and bedpan duty.

The two young women soon became friends. Roxanne's attitude to both their predicaments was entirely practical: Laura should regard the hostel as a stop-over until she was well and she and Giovanni could set up house together. Laura wanted her baby and since the nuns didn't want her to lose it either, what better place to be? And as for her, Roxanne, this would be her second baby. She was single, had no contact with the father-to-be, and used to work (and hoped to work again) as a clippie on the buses, so the only sensible thing was to have her baby adopted, as she had the first one. Most of the girls at St Catherine's had their babies adopted. The nuns helped find suitable parents for them.

Roxanne took a message to Giovanni at the Kardomah. It was the first of many, because Laura did not get better. The bleeding stopped, but the sickness returned and she felt weak and exhausted. She was also miserable not only with the shame of being in a hostel for fallen women, but because she was bitterly homesick. Christmas at Chorlton had always been the happiest of times, busy, noisy and loving. Now she missed her mother and father, David and Jill, Grace and Jane. She longed to hear from them, but of course they had no idea where she was, nor how unhappy she was. And she could not tell them, so there was no hope on that score. When she'd been with Giovanni, he'd partly filled the warm space vacated by her family. Now her situation was compounded by loneliness and helplessness.

When they were at Mrs Enders' house, she and Sophie had been exchanging letters. She'd kept hers cheerful and full of her and Giovanni's plans for the future. She didn't mention the continuing morning sickness because she knew Sophie would worry, but she'd told her about both of them working at the Kardomah and that they were doing OK.

She wished she could see Sophie now. Sophie was so good in a crisis. But even Sophie couldn't help with this one. She could not provide a flat for them, or heal the rift with her family. But as soon as we have a flat, and as soon as I have the energy, thought Laura, I must write to her again.

More than anything Laura wanted to see Giovanni, but men,

even relatives, were not allowed into the hostel and leaving it to meet him somewhere else could risk losing the baby. And then Giovanni could only get one day off before Christmas and, he told Roxanne, he needed to spend it looking for digs. He sent her loving messages, told her to stay where she was, stay warm, eat well, rest, look after their baby.

The nuns tried to spread some Christmas cheer. A few of the girls decorated a tree in the hall, and garlanded the pictures in the chapel with holly. And there was to be a Christmas lunch.

Since Laura had had no more 'spotting' and the baby seemed to be very much alive, she was told she could get up for short periods, but must not go out. So she made an effort and got out of bed for the Christmas Eve carol service, and again on Christmas Day for Matins. She had intended to show willing and attend the festive lunch, but by noon she was exhausted and climbed back into bed.

For the next twenty-four hours, Laura slept most of the time. She knew she should eat for the baby's sake, but she couldn't. On Boxing Day afternoon the matron sent for Dr Ingle.

He examined Laura. He was gentle and kind and he sat on her bed while he took her pulse.

'Do you have any family, Laura?'

'Yes, but they don't speak to me.'

Dr Ingle nodded and said, 'Have you thought about what will happen when you have the baby?'

Laura looked at him. What did he mean?

'Have the Sisters not discussed adoption with you yet?'

Laura struggled to sit up. 'Adoption? I don't want it adopted.' She shook her head. 'We will keep our baby!'

'We? Do you have a husband, Laura? Or a boyfriend?'

'Yes . . . I . . . I . . .' Laura's mind whirled about. She had not said a word to the nuns about Giovanni, and because she had been ill, she had only been to the daily chapel services on her first few days and had not been subjected to the regime of the hostel, which, she gathered from Roxanne, was a mix of housework and moral preaching.

Twice a nun had appeared in the dormitory and tried to pump her for information as to the circumstances of her pregnancy but Laura had told her little, only that when she'd got pregnant she'd run away from home. She barely listened to the woman's homilies about repentance for the sins of the flesh. She felt sorry for the girls whose babies would be adopted, but that was nothing to do with her. She wouldn't be here when her baby was born, she'd be long gone. Just as soon as Giovanni found a room.

She liked Dr Ingle and wanted to tell him the truth, but she was too tired and dispirited. She started to cry and Dr Ingle patted her arm and told her not to worry about it now. The baby wasn't due, he reckoned, for a couple of weeks yet. It was well developed and strong and even if born today would stand a good chance of survival. The important thing now was to get better, to eat well and rest. He would leave her a tonic, and something for the nausea.

When Dr Ingle left, Laura stared at the ceiling. She could not understand why she felt so fretful and anxious. Something was nagging at her, something Dr Ingle had said.

And then she remembered. He'd said the baby was due in a fortnight. That it was mature enough to survive if born now. But that could not be right. It wasn't due until the end of February at least.

When Roxanne came in with a cup of tea for her, Laura asked,

'Roxanne, how long is a pregnancy? I mean, I know it's nine months, but is that exact, and how many weeks is that?'

'Forty, I think. Why?'

'If I got pregnant at the beginning of June when is the baby due?'

Roxanne counted on her fingers. 'Beginning of March.'

Laura felt her heart drop and she could not breathe. Or speak.

Roxanne sat on the bed and took both Laura's hands in hers.

'What is it, Laura? You are white as a sheet.'

Laura swallowed but could not answer, and Roxanne shook her hands a little. 'Laura, answer me.'

Laura shook her head. 'No, it's nothing. Nothing.'

She could not tell anyone what she feared. Not even Roxanne. What if the baby was Marcin's, not Giovanni's?

If anything, Laura was getting weaker. Dr Ingle came again to see her and pronounced her anaemic and malnourished and decided she must go to the Middlesex Hospital.

'But who will pay? I can't afford hospital! It's five guineas just to have the baby.'

'I'll write you a chit for Dr Wills. He's the obstetrician under whose care you'll be when the baby comes. St Catherine's will pay. I'll arrange a bed.'

Laura lay back on her pillows and felt control of her life slipping away from her. It was a relief really. She shut her eyes, then opened them again. She must ask him.

'Dr Ingle, how pregnant am I? When will I have the baby?'

'I can't be certain, and you'll probably have a better idea yourself. When was your last period?'

'I think in the middle of May, but it may have been April. I

168

can't really remember. I have always been a bit irregular. I only knew I was pregnant when I kept throwing up.'

Dr Ingle looked at the ceiling as he counted in his head. 'Your baby's head has dropped down, into the right position for birth, and that only happens towards the end of pregnancy. I'd say you were due in about a fortnight's time. Does that seem right?'

Laura closed her eyes and swallowed. Her voice was not quite steady as she said, 'I thought I had conceived at the beginning of June, which would mean the baby coming at the beginning of March. Do you think that's possible?'

Dr Ingle looked at her, kindly and sadly. He wants to say what I want to hear, thought Laura. He said, 'It's possible, of course. But I think it unlikely. You are very thin, Laura, but your baby is well-developed and pretty near full term in my judgement.'

Laura did not answer. She lay back on the bed and shut her eyes.

'Laura,' Dr Ingle went on, 'I see many, many young women in your situation. Pregnant and with no means of supporting a baby. Often with a baby in the womb that does not have the right father.' He paused but she did not open her eyes, or try to stop him talking. 'I know nothing of your circumstances, except that you say you want to keep the child. Just let me say this: if you change your mind, or you realise that the best thing for your baby would be a married couple with the means to give him or her a loving home and a good life, then Dr Wills at the Middlesex Hospital can arrange it.'

Laura felt as though she was made of stone. She could hear but she could not move. She kept her eyes closed as she felt him get up from the bed, and heard him walk to the door. She mouthed 'Thank you', but no sound came out.

The next day she felt a bit better and came down to lunch. There were few girls in the hostel during the day, because some worked in Soho, mostly as waitresses, cinema usherettes or shop assistants. But those women due to give birth any day, or those, like Roxanne, doing temporary work in the hostel, were there. Laura and Roxanne had a refectory bench to themselves.

'Laura,' exclaimed Roxanne, 'you're up. Excellent. How are you feeling?'

Laura tried to put some pleasure into her wan smile. 'Dr Ingle gave me a tonic. A pink drink, like Wincarnis. I think it must be working.'

They ate in silence for a minute. Roxanne poured them each a tumbler of water. 'When does Dr Ingle say you'll have your baby?' she asked. 'He has a reputation here for accurate predictions.'

'Before the end of the month, he says.'

Roxanne beamed. 'But that is wonderful news. I thought you were doomed to backache and wanting to wee all the time for another two months.'

'He says I should have the baby adopted.'

Roxanne frowned. 'But Laura, I thought you said you and Giovanni want the baby?' She looked closely at her friend. 'You haven't changed your mind, have you?'

Laura shook her head. 'It's not that,' she said, her eyes suddenly pricking, 'but if it is due in two weeks, it isn't Giovanni's.'

Roxanne stared at her for a moment, and then shifted along the bench to put her arm round Laura's shoulders. Laura was beginning to cry and Roxanne produced a handkerchief and Laura, grateful, sniffled into it. The young women passing their table as they left the refectory glanced at them, but girls in tears were so common a sight that no one paid them much attention. Roxanne said, 'Do you want to tell me about it?'

So Laura told her about Marcin, and how up until she'd finally told him she didn't love him, they had slept together. Not because she'd wanted to, or enjoyed it, but because she was his girlfriend and he expected it. Then she'd immediately fallen, suddenly and forever, in love with Giovanni. The first time she'd slept with him was only a few weeks after she'd quarrelled with Marcin. And no, she couldn't remember exactly when she'd last slept with the Pole. But they 'did it' a lot. Marcin insisted. If Dr Ingle was right, then the baby was Marcin's.

Roxanne sat silent, her arm round Laura. 'Does Giovanni know about Marcin?'

'Yes. But he doesn't know I was sleeping with him.'

'If he knew, would he accept the child?'

Laura lifted her eyes to Roxanne's and saw only sympathy there. 'I don't know. I don't think so. How could he?' She was twisting the hanky in her fingers. 'He hated Marcin. They had a fight. Marcin beat him up.'

'Laura, you don't have to tell him. Pretend the baby came early. He loves you. He'll believe anything you say.'

CHAPTER SEVENTEEN

Maud was in the kitchen garden. It was cold and the garden looked at its most desolate. The chicken-wire fences, twisted and unsightly, that had supported the summer's peas and beans had not been cleared away yet. The first frosts had blackened the weeds colonising the vegetable beds. Maud used her knife to cut a Savoy cabbage from among the thistles and chickweed, and pulled a few late beets. What a grim time of year, she thought – all that bounty of summer and autumn is over. Now the garden is untidy and mostly bare, the bean plants and pumpkin vines brown and dying, the beds waiting for their annual sort out and bedding-down for winter. They are not yet glamourised by snow and they're wet, cold and ugly.

This veg patch looks like I feel, she thought: *Now is the winter of my discontent.* And then at once she told herself to brace up and get on with it.

As she carried the basket back towards the house, an unfamiliar motorcar drove into the yard. She hurried forward and then stopped in her tracks. It was Sophie. She must have news of Laura, she thought, her heart beating faster.

Sophie hadn't been to Chorlton since Laura's revelation, and that was three months ago. Maud had many times wanted to ask her if she had news of Laura but she'd been constrained by Donald's categorical command that she was to have nothing whatsoever to do with their daughter. 'She's dead to us, Maud,' he'd said, 'and the sooner you accept that, the sooner you'll get over it.'

But Donald's injunction was only part of the reason. There was also the deep shame of having a daughter run away. Everyone probably guessed the truth, or at least part of it – it wasn't uncommon for a girl to vanish for several months, and then turn up right as rain with a husband and a baby. Or without either, which was worse. But Maud was trying to pretend to the world, and sometimes even to herself, that Laura was just away from home but would be back soon. Without actually lying, she'd imply her daughter was staying with a friend in London.

Of course Sophie knew the truth, so there was no pretending. 'Sophie,' she said. 'What is it? Have you heard from Laura?'

'No, Maud, that's the thing. I haven't. I came to see if you had. Until a few weeks ago we were writing to each other, but now she must have left that address. I don't know where she is.'

Even though she was desperate to talk about Laura, Maud had to observe the niceties of good manners. She invited Sophie in and they sat at the kitchen table. Sophie accepted tea and a piece of gingerbread. She looked around, her face anxious. 'Don't worry, dear,' said Maud, 'Donald's in London, at his club.'

Maud could wait no longer. 'Please tell me, Sophie. Please tell me anything you know. I can't tell you how terrible it is to know nothing, to imagine day after day the most dreadful things. That she might be ill, that Giovanni might have abandoned her—'

'Maud, he'd never do that,' interrupted Sophie. 'He's a good man. Really. One of the best.'

Maud nodded. 'I think I knew that. But it's good to hear it.'

Sophie explained that Giovanni was working as a chef, and Laura had been working as a waitress.

Maud made an effort to control her conflicting emotions. She was enormously relieved to have news of Laura, and to know that she'd been well and with a roof over her head. But the idea of her darling daughter, pregnant and working as a waitress, cut her to the quick. And now she'd disappeared. Maybe she was no longer well, no longer with Giovanni, no longer with a roof over her head.

She shook herself into action. 'Sophie, I must go to London. Find her. I must.' As she said it she knew it was hopeless. Donald would prevent it. And how would she begin? She put her head in her hands and said, 'Oh God, Sophie, she must be five or six months pregnant now. What can we do?'

Sophie promised she'd investigate, contact the address she had in Paddington. 'I'm sure she'll write to me soon. They must have moved flats or something.'

Laura dragged on the hospital gown, pulled it closed, tied it over her belly and walked down the corridor to her appointment with Dr Wills. She waited in a kind of anteroom policed by a stern-looking nurse, but was soon shown into the room with Dr Wills' name on the door.

He looked up briefly as Laura came in and, without speaking, motioned her to the chair in front of his desk. Then he went back to his paperwork. Too busy for kindness, thought Laura. He must see hundreds of pregnant girls. All the St Catherine's girls are sent to him.

Head down and staring at her lap, Laura tried to order her thoughts so that she knew what she was going to say: she must insist on keeping the baby. She must. She wanted, passionately, to keep it, and she would not be made to give it away.

But then she thought of lying to Giovanni, of pretending a blue-eyed, blond Polish child was sired by him – a black-haired, brown-eyed Italian. How could she do that? Keeping a secret for all their lives together? It was unthinkable.

Her thoughts skittered about, trying to find a way out. If she wanted the baby, she must lie. But Giovanni was not a fool. It wasn't as if she could point to a blond streak in the Oliver family: no one was fair or blue-eyed.

But even if she could explain that away, how would she explain a full-term baby arriving two months early?

But she wanted this baby. She must tell Giovanni, be honest with him. And if she lost him, because he could not accept Marcin's child, then at least she'd have the baby. Which was worse, losing Giovanni or losing her child?

Her mind swung this way and that. One thought instantly begat another, more difficult one. If she lost Giovanni and kept the baby, how would she support it? If she went home to Chorlton, even if her father let her in, he'd insist the child be adopted.

If she could just see the baby, then it would be clear. If it was blue-eyed and blond she would give it up. If it was dark-haired with dark eyes, she would steel herself to lying.

Dr Wills was speaking. Laura looked up. He wore thick spectacles and his eyes looked tiny behind them. It was hard to gauge his expression.

'Laura Oliver, isn't it?'

Laura nodded. 'Yes.'

'You want to find a home for your baby. Is that right?'

'No, I, I want to keep the baby, but . . .'

'Have you any means of supporting it?'

'Yes, my . . . er . . . my husb . . . My . . . Well, he will be my husband. We want to get married. He has a job.'

Dr Wills was frowning. He doesn't like complications, thought Laura.

'Are you not a St Catherine's girl?' he said, looking at his notes.

'Well, yes, I am. You see, we couldn't find anywhere to live so he is in the Salvation Army hostel and I . . .' Laura wiped under her eye with the back of her hand.

Dr Wills took no notice. 'You have nowhere to live?'

'But we will have. Giovanni is looking for a flat.'

He continued shuffling loose papers in a file. 'But you are considering giving the baby up for adoption?'

'I don't want to. But . . . I haven't decided. Could I not decide after the baby comes? In a few days?'

Dr Wills peered back at his notes and then looked steadily at Laura for a few seconds. 'Ah, I see. Dr Ingle says the baby is not your current boyfriend's. Does he know that?'

'No. I can't tell him. He . . .'

'Well, in that case I would definitely advise adoption. I have several childless couples who, to put it bluntly, will give your baby a much better life than you can give it. The child will have every advantage.' He reached for a folder on his desk and took what looked like a letter from it. 'This one, for example.' He laid the letter flat on the desk and Laura could see an engraving of a big house at the top of the blue notepaper. Dr Wills went on. 'He's a brigadier. Forty-five. Still in the army. Works at the War

Office. His wife is thirty-eight. They live in the country. Manor house. They have a flat in Chelsea. Been married fifteen years. Childless.'

Oh God, thought Laura, if only Daddy would accept Giovanni, and forgive me. We could have all that. The baby and I could stay at Chorlton. Mummy would help me. It would be so wonderful. And then when Giovanni had found a flat . . . She shook her head. Useless to think like that.

Dr Wills continued. 'To answer your question: no, you can't decide about adoption after the baby is born. If the baby is to be adopted it is far better that he or she is put straight into the arms of the new mother. Better for the baby and much better for you. You will not be able to make a rational decision when you have just given birth. You have to decide now.'

Laura was sniffling again, and she did not look up. She heard his weary sigh. 'Miss Oliver. You must decide before you go into labour. Which,' again he consulted his notes, 'could be any day now. And I must tell you that St Catherine's only pay medical bills for the women who are giving up their babies.'

Laura looked at him blankly. 'But we don't have any money. Won't the new National Health Service pay?'

'The NHS does not come into effect until next year. So, no.'

'Where will I have the baby then?'

'Most mothers have their babies at home, with a midwife attending. Dr Ingle put you in here because you weren't well and St Catherine's are paying in the belief that the baby will be adopted. But you are a lot better now, and could go home.'

Laura was crying in earnest now. 'But we haven't got a home. That's why I was at St Catherine's.'

'There's no doubt in my mind, Miss Oliver, that you should

give up this baby. Which would mean you could stay here until the baby is born, and for a week after the birth, by which time you'll be strong enough to cope without a newborn baby to look after. Then you and your boyfriend can start again on a better footing.'

Laura said nothing, but she could see the logic of his words. He closed the file.

'Think about it. And let me know tomorrow. Right now, I am afraid I have patients waiting.'

Laura did think about it. She thought of nothing else. Giovanni came the following afternoon, during visiting hours. He stood over her, smiling, but his anxious eyes told how shocked he was at the sight of her. She knew how awful she looked. She'd seen her pale face, her eyes dull and deep in their sockets, the skin below them bruised with sleeplessness.

He bent to kiss her, then held her face to look at her. 'What do the doctors say?'

Laura forced a smile but her lip trembled. 'Dr Wills says I'm fine now. No nausea and I'm eating.' She sniffed and made a renewed effort at smiling. 'I like it better here than St Catherine's. At least you can come and see me and they don't expect me in chapel every night.'

'Wonderful!' He sat on the bed (against hospital rules but there were no nurses in the ward) and took her hands in his. 'But if you are better, will they send you back to the hostel?'

Oh God, she thought, I must tell him the baby is due any day. But she couldn't. 'I don't know,' she said. 'I'd rather stay here but St Catherine's are paying and it must be cheaper to have me at the hostel. But I dread it. It's worse than school.'

'Well, maybe you won't have to, *cara mia*. The good news is, I have a new job – more money – in a café near the fish market. And I have three days free before I start. So I will find us a flat. I am determined. So if you can stay here for a few more days, maybe you won't have to go back to the hostel.'

Laura had little hope of his finding affordable digs, never mind a self-contained flat, but she forced herself to be positive and cheerful. She asked Giovanni about the new job. He said it was far from gastronomy, just fish and chips, egg and bacon break-fasts and cups of tea in a workmen's café in Milk Street. But he was the sole cook, the pay wasn't bad, and he'd get a small percentage of the sales too.

The quality of the fish, he said, bought direct from the market a hundred yards away, was excellent, and if he kept the deep fat fryer clean and the batter fresh, they should make good money. They did pretty well as it was and the quality of cooking was, Giovanni thought, bad. The fish went into the fat before it was properly hot, the chips came out when still limp and pale and the batter was kept in buckets on the floor. 'I can do a much better job than that,' he said, 'and maybe, when the boss trusts me, he will let me introduce something more than egg and chips and doughnuts.'

Laura never thought she'd want Giovanni out of her sight, but now she wanted him to leave. It was agony not telling him what ailed her, trying to be cheerful and act the woman she was before. She longed to drop the pretence and tell the truth, to demand comfort from this man she loved so much. But she couldn't: far from comforting her, he'd be in agony himself.

He did not come the next day. She knew that this meant he was out looking for a place for them. She did not share his opti-mism. Nothing had changed: there was still a great shortage of

THE FOOD OF LOVE

accommodation because so many houses were rubble, London was full of de-mobbed men looking for work, and landladies did not like babies, or unmarried couples, or Italians.

It was hopeless. That evening she signed the consent form. Her baby would be adopted.

Laura woke up on her back and put her hand on her belly. No tight hard ball of baby.

She pulled the blankets over her face. She wanted to go back to sleep, not to relive the horrors of yesterday. But she was awake now, and remembering: the increasing pain of each contraction, the blissful relief when it stopped, the despair as it started again, the anger that she was going through this hell, this excruciating agony, so someone else could have her baby. That was the worst. And then the ultimate searing pain, the exhortations to push, her screaming. And then it was over.

She'd not even seen the baby. She'd heard its thin high cry, heard the midwife say, 'Take him out. Right now. The nanny is there.' She'd raised her head in time to see a nurse walking out of the delivery room with a bundle in her arms.

She'd wanted to die. Too exhausted to cry, she could not even answer when they spoke to her. She just existed, somewhere else, enveloped in deep, deep sorrow.

They'd wheeled her into this ward and given her tea, and an injection of some sort. At last she'd slept.

At four o'clock, Giovanni arrived, excitement and anxiety alternating in his face,

'Oh darling Laura, was it terrible? I came last night but they would not let me into the labour ward. And this morning no one could tell me anything, how you were, how the baby is.' His words were falling over each other. He looked around. 'And where is our *bambino*? Is it all right? It must be so small . . .'

'No *bambino*.'

He clasped her by the shoulders. 'What?'

'No baby. We don't have a baby. It's gone.'

She watched Giovanni's face first go rigid, then crumble with pain. He sank to his knees by the bed and buried his head in the coverlet. 'Oh God. Our *bambino*. No, no. It can't be.'

Laura, overwhelmed by sympathy and shame, put her hand on his head, more moved by his distress than by anything else that had happened.

Giovanni raised his face to look at her. 'My poor darling Laura, I am so, so sorry. It must be because it came so early. But the doctor said it was ready, that it would survive, didn't he? Why? Why? What happened?'

I could let him think the baby died, thought Laura. A stillbirth. But she hadn't the energy to lie successfully. He'd want details. He might ask to see the doctor.

'It didn't die. I gave it away,' she said, her voice flat.

Uncomprehending, Giovanni looked at her. 'You gave it away?'

She gave the barest of nods. 'He's gone. It was a boy.' She frowned, suddenly caught by the thought that she had given birth to a baby boy. 'I heard the midwife say "him", not "her". I'm sure it was a boy.'

'You gave our son away?' His voice had a hollow menace she'd never heard before.

She made an effort: her eyes turned slowly to his. 'Giovanni, I had to. We have nowhere to live, no money, we aren't married. We're outcasts. He would be an outcast too.'

He did not reply. He just looked at her in disbelief, his face colouring and eyes hard and angry. Then he jumped up, jerked his coat from the end of the bed and strode towards the door of the ward.

Laura, at last stung into real feeling, sat up and called to him. 'Darling, please, Giovanni. It's not the end. We didn't plan to have a baby. One day, maybe . . .'

But he had pushed open the door and was gone.

CHAPTER EIGHTEEN

The next day Giovanni went back to the Middlesex, but not to see Laura.

'I would like to see Dr Wills, please.'

'May I know what your business with Dr Wills is?' asked the receptionist, without a smile.

'It's private. But it's about one of his patients, Laura Oliver.'

'Dr Wills is on his ward round. You must make an appointment, I'm afraid. Dr Wills is a busy man.'

Giovanni walked up the stairs to the Maternity floor and stopped a passing nurse. 'Could you direct me to Dr Wills' rooms?' he said, trying to look as though he was at home in the corridors of the Middlesex.

The woman obliged and Giovanni walked into the little anteroom outside his office, sat down on a chair, and waited. He was nervous that he would not recognise the doctor when he returned. He'd only seen him once, when he'd been visiting Laura and Dr Wills had been doing his rounds. But when the doctor walked in, and made for the office door, he did recognise him and he jumped up.

'Doctor, please, I need to speak to you.'

Dr Wills turned, frowning.

'What is it?'

'Please, doctor, it will only take a minute.'

Dr Wills opened the door and ushered Giovanni inside, but he did not close it after them. He stood standing at the door, holding the handle.

'You are?'

Dr Wills' tone was impatient. Giovanni could feel his blood rising. But he forced himself to remain calm. 'My name is Giovanni Angelotti, and I am the father of Laura Oliver's baby. She gave away our baby. But Laura, she was not right in the head. She said yes, but it was a mistake. We want the baby back. We cannot give him away.'

'Laura Oliver? Ah, yes, the girl from St Catherine's. I remember. She said you had no home and no money. And you are not married. Am I right?'

'But we will get married and now we have a home.' Giovanni's voice was rising. 'I have a good job. But even if I didn't, how can you just take my baby away? Are poor people not allowed to have babies?' Giovanni took a deep breath and said, more calmly, 'We must have our baby. Where is he?'

'You cannot have the baby. That is quite impossible. Once a baby is settled with a new mother it cannot be taken away again. It would be quite wrong to remove it.'

Giovanni's gave up the attempt to control his voice. 'But I am the father. I did not agree,' he shouted. 'I will never agree.' He squared up to the bespectacled doctor, his head thrust forward. 'How can you take a baby away, just like that? Without asking the father? Without even telling him? You stole my baby.'

'Listen, young man,' Dr Wills said, 'there's no point in shouting. The truth is that your young lady asked for my advice, which I gave. It was that I considered adoptive parents could give the child a much better chance in life than she could. She had the good sense to take that advice. I told her to sleep on it, and the next day she said she'd made her decision and she signed the papers. She had many hours to think about it. If she chose not to consult you, that is her affair. And the decision to agree to adoption is also her affair. If a mother is unmarried the father has nothing whatever to do with it. Now, if you'll excuse me, I have work to do.'

Few buses were running because of the weather, and Giovanni walked all the way from the Middlesex to Billingsgate, his hands deep in his overcoat pockets, cap pulled down, scarf wound round his neck. The snow was dirty and piled high in gutters and on pavements except for a treacherous foot-track down the centre. He walked carefully, wishing he had brought an umbrella to steady his progress.

It was the worst winter anyone could remember, with long weeks of gales, snow, and sleet. He thought of the half-furnished, icy flat awaiting him. He'd paid to have the chimney swept because he wanted it to be warm for the baby, but had not yet lit a fire. He'd been waiting for mother and baby to come home for that. For now he put shillings in the gas meter whenever he could, which was not often.

His mind chewed at his unhappiness like a dog with a bone. He could not believe it: that Laura, his beloved Laura, who had been as excited about the baby as he was, could do such a thing. And why? And why so suddenly? Despite their struggles, lack of money or a home, not once had there been a mention of giving the baby up for adoption. All they'd talked about was the baby: what they'd call it, how they'd bring him or her up, how many children they'd have. Never, ever about not wanting it.

It must have been those women at St Catherine's, on and on about what a sinner she was. And the doctors, too. That hard-hearted Dr Wills probably bullied her. Probably gets a fat bribe from rich couples wanting a baby, he thought. But all the same, what she'd done was unforgivable.

This is crazy, he thought. I love Laura, but I'll never forgive her. And I don't want to see her.

Laura could not stop crying. How could her life have changed so dramatically in just a few days? There was no word from Giovanni.

She spent most of the time after the birth sleeping or weeping. The nurses chivvied her to wash, get dressed, eat, and she mutely obeyed. They also insisted she walk the corridors of the hospital. To build up her strength, they said.

She was discharged six days after her baby's birth and she walked the mile from the hospital to Soho Square, carrying her bag. The pavements had been cleared but they were still slippery and she walked slowly, keeping her mind off her freezing feet by forcing herself to plan tomorrow. She would go to find Giovanni at his Billingsgate café. She could not afford pride. And if he had left her for good she'd have to go home to Chorlton and face her father's inevitable 'I told you so'.

She arrived at St Catherine's to be greeted by Sister Christina, a young Irish nun very low in the convent pecking order. Laura was relieved it was her. She was, as yet, not inoculated against compassion. She shepherded Laura through the door.

'Oh Laura, I'm very glad you've come back,' she said. 'You must be freezing. Come in, dear.'

Laura followed her into the hall, and Sister Christina chattered on. 'Dr Ingle must have persuaded Mother Superior to bend the rules and give you a bed. I've made one up for you in Blue Dormitory.'

She took Laura's bag and kept talking as Laura followed her up the stairs.

'You are meant to be pregnant to be a St Catherine's beneficiary. But we do sometimes give shelter for a few nights to young women who have just had their new babies adopted, and who have nowhere to go.'

Laura wasn't really listening but then she heard Sister Christina saying, 'Oh, and your young man was here today, and he left this for you,' fishing in the deep pocket of her habit and passing a letter to Laura.

As soon as Laura was in the dormitory, and alone (it was noon, and everyone was out or downstairs), she sat on her bed and tore open the letter.

Darling Laura,

I have been very unhappy that you have given away our boy without asking his father. I do not understand it.

I loved him while he was still in your belly, and I will love him in my heart always. But I still love my Laura, even if I do not agree with what you have done. I know that you did it because you thought it better for our baby. This I do not agree with. Money is not better than love.

But I cannot live without you, Laura. And now at last I have found a flat. I signed the lease the day after our son was born, before I came to the hospital and you told me that we have no son, he is adopted by rich strangers. It hurts me so much that if I had found it two days before, maybe we three, you, me and the baby, would be in it now, a little Italian family.

Now is too late. But you and I can live there. If you want. It is in Billingsgate, all bomb sites around, but it is cheap and we can make it nice. It is near my job.

Giovanni.

CHAPTER NINETEEN

1947, spring

Grace could not prevent a swell of maternal pride at her daughter's riding. Jane was only seven, but she sat into her saddle with relaxed confidence, her back straight, hands low, head up, her plaits bouncing against her back, her legs barely moving as she put Snowdrop into a trot and then a canter.

At the far side of the field, Grace saw George Maxwell-Calder climbing the stile and walking towards them. Since his father's death last autumn he'd been living more at Frampton than in London, and often walked round the Barrow farms. Checking up on their husbandry, said David. But he was seldom seen on Chorlton land.

He stopped to watch Jane, then came up to Grace.

'She puts on a darn good show, does she not?' he said.

'Hullo, George. Yes, she's a grand little rider.'

'She reminds me of Laura at that age. When I was eleven or twelve and she was about four she beat me at the bending race. Oh the humiliation! Laura could ride anything. Like your daughter.'

'Maybe because they were both taught by Donald. It helps if you have a good horse under you, too, and Snowdrop is a very good pony. Her grandfather spoils her.'

Just as he did Laura, thought Grace. Donald had not once mentioned Laura since she'd left seven months ago, and though Maud sometimes talked of her, it was always with a sad shake of the head, as though she were terminally ill. It was good to hear someone say something good about her. Grace wanted to continue the conversation, but Jane came cantering up to them.

'Can I do the jumps now? We've been schooling for *hours*. And Snowdrop is as sick of it as I am. Aren't you, Snowy?' Jane dropped forward, her arms right around the pony's neck, her face pressed to his sweaty neck. 'Please, Mummy?'

'Jane, where are your manners? Say good morning to His Lordship.'

'He's not His Lordship. Uncle David said the old Earl was His Lordship.'

George laughed. 'Well, how about "Good morning, George" then?'

'Sorry. Good morning, George.'

'Good morning, Jane.'

'Why did Mummy call you His Lordship?'

Grace tried to shush her daughter, but George answered her. 'Men who are lords are often called that. But I expect your mother said it because I'm the Earl now and the head of the family. It would have been confusing to call me that when my father was alive, although you could have, because I was a Viscount, so I was already a lord.' He smiled at Jane. 'It's difficult to understand, isn't it? It's all a lot of nonsense really.'

Jane was looking blank so Grace tried to explain. 'You remember George's father died, don't you? We went to his funeral in the church. Well, when an Earl dies, his eldest son becomes the new Earl.'

'Like the Prince becoming the King?'

'Exactly.'

Jane narrowed her eyes and said, 'That is *so* unfair. It's never the Princess who becomes the King, is it?'

Both Grace and George laughed, and George said, 'Maybe not the King, but she could become the Queen. When our King dies, his eldest daughter Elizabeth will be Queen.'

'We can listen to her make a speech next week,' said Grace. 'She'll be twenty-one and that is when you are truly grown up. She's in South Africa with the King and Queen and her sister, and she's going to talk to us on the radio.'

Jane digested this, her face solemn. Then she frowned. 'Can I do the jumps now?'

Grace and George watched Jane canter to the other side of the paddock and trot the pony over some poles lying spaced a few yards apart on the ground, then turn round and canter over them from the other direction. She repeated this until Grace and George had walked across the grass and were standing by the first jump.

Then she turned Snowdrop to face the first fence and called, 'Mummy, you have to watch. Say go!'

George did it, calling out clearly: 'Ready, steady, go!'

Jane set off at a canter, pony and child as eager as each other. Snowdrop leapt efficiently over the first six jumps, none of them higher than two feet. Next came three higher jumps, evenly spaced and in a row: a low brush fence, a two-foot-three set of poles and then a slightly higher set. Pony and rider, going fast now, cleared all three with ease. The last jump was a two-foot-six high double row of hay bales which required the rider to do a wide circle to face the jump, but Jane cut the corner, approached at an angle, and Snowdrop refused. He skidded to a stop and Jane was flung forward onto his neck.

The child instantly lost her temper. She scrambled back into the saddle, jerked the pony around, and beat his rump with all her seven-year-old might.

'Oh, dear,' gasped Grace. 'Jane, Jane, stop that.'

Snowdrop, tossing his head in protest, was nevertheless spurred by Jane's flailing whip and kicking heels to shimmy back to face the jump again,

But George had left Grace's side to stride across to intercept horse and rider. Grace, embarrassed by her daughter's behaviour, watched him. With a single easy movement George took the pony's bridle in one hand and yanked the riding crop from Jane's grip with the other. He didn't speak to the child or even look at her, but stroked Snowdrop's nose, soothing him.

'Shh, shh. There, there,' he said. 'That was a bit unfair, wasn't it, old chap? Poor little Snowdrop! The silly girl didn't set you square to the jump, or give you any take-off space, did she?'

Grace caught up with them in time to see George turn his attention from pony to rider. He reached up and lifted Jane out of the saddle. Then he addressed her, firmly, but without raising his voice.

'Jane, you are an excellent little rider, but if you were my daughter there would be no more riding for a week after that display of temper. And when you were allowed back on a pony you'd ride without a crop and without spurs. And next time you blamed your pony for something that was entirely your fault,

I'd take this to *your* rump.' He waggled the crop at her. 'See how you liked it.'

Grace felt a flush of indignation. How dare he speak to her daughter like that? Especially with her standing right next to them. It was her job to reprimand Jane and he had absolutely no rights in the matter. She opened her mouth to protest, but then thought how undignified it would be, in front of Jane, to upbraid him. Grown-ups had to present a united front to children in the matter of discipline. She turned to her daughter.

'That's enough for today, Jane. Better take Snowdrop back to his stable now.'

'Shan't.' Jane's mouth set in a hard line.

George said mildly, 'I don't think you should say "Shan't" to your mother, Jane. It's very rude.'

'I don't care. I want to do the jumps again. If the stupid pony hadn't refused I'd have had a clear round.'

The child's eyes met her mother's with that familiar defiance that made Grace's heart sink. She could be so difficult.

'Jane, darling, do as I say, there's a good girl.'

But her daughter ignored her. She stared boldly at them both, her chin up, eyes wide and angry, 'No. I want to do the jumps again.'

George studied her for a second. 'Mmm . . . Well, in that case, Grace, perhaps I could help. I will deal with Snowdrop. He's a lovely little fellow, and he deserves a few carrots in his feed after such a nasty time.' He led the pony off in the direction of the stables, saying over his shoulder, 'Don't worry, I'll ask Sawkins if he can't find something.'

Grace put her arm round Jane's shoulders, bending down to reason with her, but the girl dodged out of her embrace and ran off down the lane. Grace thought she heard a sob. Poor child, she thought, she is so headstrong and so emotional. She called after her, 'Jane, Jane, come back. Don't be silly, darling.' She ran after her daughter, but when she turned the corner Jane was nowhere to be seen and Grace realised she could have gone in any direction: towards the cowsheds, the house, the woods – anywhere. She turned round and started walking back to the stable yard.

George emerged from Snowdrop's loose box, carrying the grooming kit. Some of Grace's indignation at George's interference returned. 'Well,' she said, 'now she's run away. I've no idea where she's gone.'

'I wouldn't worry. She needs time. Nothing like a bit of solitude to realise you've been a chump.'

'All the same,' said Grace stiffly, 'I don't think you should have taken over. She's my child, not yours.'

George considered what she'd said for a moment.

'You are quite right. I've spent the last six years bossing squaddies around and I suppose I'm just too used to taking control. I should have stayed out of it. I'm sorry.' His blue eyes were frank with apology. Then he dipped his head, his fair hair falling across his forehead. It was almost a bow. 'I won't be a minute.' He took the brushes and bucket into the tack room.

Grace immediately softened. The truth was she was hopeless at disciplining Jane, and the girl won hands down every time. She followed George, saying, 'No, it was awfully good of you and I should be grateful, not resentful.' He turned and she smiled at him, a little tentatively. 'But when she doesn't come home and I'm frantic with worry, where will you be? Long gone!'

'No, if she doesn't reappear in short order, which I'm sure she will, then I'll lead the search party, I promise.'

They stood together at the stable door, watching Snowdrop finish his feed, then George put a head collar on him and they led him out to the field. 'It's such a lovely day, I don't think he needs a coat, do you?'

'To be honest, I have no idea. I know nothing about horses. Donald is the horsey member of the family, but he's working long hours at the airfield these days so hasn't much time. I just come to watch her because she loves an audience.'

'And she deserves one. She's very good.'

Grace frowned, shaking her head. 'I'm so sorry she behaved so badly. I know that Donald and Maud think she's a spoilt brat. Maybe she is. She doesn't take a blind bit of notice of me, and I'm hopeless at saying no.'

'But you are good at worrying. What are you going to do for the next hour or so, until young Jane comes home tearful and contrite?'

He was teasing her, but she lifted anxious eyes to his.

'Oh, poor Jane, I must find her. You are quite right, I am a worrier, but I don't want her tearful or contrite.'

'Believe me, she doesn't want to be found just yet, not until you've had an unhappy morning or there's a big flap on while the whole Chorlton household hunts for her. You need distraction. Why don't you come and pick cowslips with me?'

'You pick cowslips? You're pulling my leg!'

'Not a bit of it! I'm making cowslip wine. And dandelion. And next month I'll have a go at elderflower. But today it's cowslip. Those big baskets by the gate are mine – you have no idea how many flowers you need to make a gallon of wine.'

Grace shook her head, bemused, and George went on, 'I was on my way to Parson's Piece when I saw Jane schooling her pony and thought I'd say hello. I didn't know you were here too.'

Grace thought that last remark pretty ungallant, but then relations between his family and hers were hardly ideal. It must be tough, she thought, to have your farms taken off you and given to a neighbour, one you probably think is a Yorkshire upstart with no breeding. And yet George was always civil. 'Surely your housekeeper makes the wines? Mrs Digweed still makes ours. It's one of the few jobs she does these days. I think it's the tipples between tasks that keep her going.'

George laughed, a barking masculine laugh. 'She did, but I've taken over. You see I'm experimenting and recording the exact recipes. Mrs Broome just threw everything in and sometimes the wines were disgusting, or exploded, and sometimes – usually – they were passable. And once in a while they were sublime.'

'And you think you could do better?' Grace smiled tolerantly, as she might smile at Jane saying she'd be world dressage champion.

George was patting the pony's neck and stroking his nose, which made Snowdrop nod his head up and down, pressing into George's side, trying to get a harder rub or a scratch between the ears. 'I know I can. I've been making cowslip wine for two years, but since I'm now out of the army and your brother-in-law is doing my job, I have time.'

Grace knew that David was uncomfortable with the farm's arrangement. He thought it patently unfair that the Framptons were still being punished for being bad farmers during the war. But Donald remained adamant he had the law on his side so George was reluctantly continuing the legal battle started by his father to establish title to the Barrow farms. The legal process would take years and the subject was no longer discussed. Grace certainly did not want to discuss it with George.

'But how many wines, and how much, can one family drink?' she asked.

George unbuckled Snowdrop's head collar and slipped it off. They both watched the pony trot a few paces, then lie down for a good roll in the dusty patch by the trough.

Grace thought perhaps George was offended by her last question, but then he said, 'Well, I'll tell you a trade secret if you promise not to go into competition with me. I have dreams, probably mad ones, of Frampton Country Wines, selling everything from sloe gin and damson brandy to nettle and ginger cordial. We already make an excellent cider, I hope you agree. Why not market it? And perry made from the Mumblehead pears. You see, I'm not unambitious.'

So Grace went cowslip picking. From the time Jane could walk Grace had picked cowslips with her, perhaps a dozen at a time for a bedside table or a little vase in the morning room. It was a pleasurable, romantic thing to do, one of those sentimental memories you store up. She remembered Jane clutching the stems too tightly in her fat toddler's hands and having a tantrum when Grace tried to loosen her grip. But picking flower-heads, hundreds and hundreds of them, pinching them off without stem or leaf and tossing them into a big basket was not the same thing. It was hard work and after an hour she'd had enough.

Besides, she must find Jane. At first the task had kept her mind off her daughter but now she walked the few yards to where George was picking and tipped the cowslips from her basket into his. 'Well, there you are, one full basket,' she handed her now empty basket to him, 'and one to go. I'm off, I'm afraid.'

But he came with her. He said he was thirsty and perhaps Grace would give him a glass of water. He left both full and empty baskets half-hidden in a shady gap of the hedgerow. Then, crooking his elbow, he said, 'Take my arm – the ground at the gate is very uneven.'

Grace slipped her arm through his and they walked across the field. Grace was almost at once conscious of the firmness of his arm beneath the sleeve of his shirt and she wondered how long it was since she had walked arm in arm with a man. Apart from a brief hand from David or Donald to help her over a step or stile, not since Hugh died. As soon as they were through the gate and on the lane, dry and smooth, she took her arm out of his. She dismissed the split-second feeling of loss.

She was relieved that both Donald and David were out working. Maud was alone in the kitchen, chopping carrots and listening to the wireless. She didn't see them at first and Grace was shocked by how old and sad she seemed. She was looking down and her face drooped, pulling the skin under her eyes and hollowing her cheeks. But then Maud heard them and looked up, her smile instantly lifting her expression to her usual friendliness.

'Why, hullo, George. What a pleasure. We don't often see you here.'

Never would be more accurate, thought Grace. 'He walked me home,' she said, thinking it best not to mention the cowslip picking. 'Is Jane back?'

'She is, darling. She came storming in in one of her famous tempers so I thought I would just leave her be. She's in her room. I was surprised not to see you panting after her.'

Grace looked at George and he gave her a grin, his blue eyes crinkling at the edges and signalling 'I told you so'. She smiled back at him, feeling sheepish. 'Maud, could I get us some of your lemonade?' She fetched the flagon from the larder.

They all had a glass and George asked for another. 'Mrs Oliver, this is a definite improvement on Mrs Broome's, but please don't tell her I said so.'

Grace went to the door with him and he dropped his voice to say, 'Sure you don't want another hour of back-breaking picking?' She shook her head. 'Pity – you make a boring task a pleasure.' And then he was gone, and Grace mounted the stairs to Jane's bedroom feeling curiously light-headed.

PART FOUR

CHAPTER TWENTY

1947, April

Laura could not believe they could be so unhappy. Her whole body was thick with misery and Giovanni barely spoke. Once, and only once, had she put her arms round him and tried to nestle into his chest, seeking comfort like a child.

But he took her shoulders and pushed her, gently but firmly, away. His eyes, suddenly full of tears, met hers. He gave a slight shake of his head, then turned away.

After that they did what they had to do, going to work, coming home, trying not to feel. They slept together in their big double bed, the first they had ever owned, but they might as well have had a bolster down the middle.

Once or twice Giovanni tried to talk about the baby, but Laura clammed up. There was no point in going over it again. She could not tell him the truth and she knew Giovanni wouldn't forgive her if she did. And she was too wretched and exhausted to comfort him, or to defend herself. Besides, how could she? She agreed with him: what she had done was unforgivable. The only difference between them was that she knew why she'd done it and Giovanni didn't.

Sometimes she thought she would tell him. But then he'd know she'd lied about being a virgin. Then he'd hate her, and probably leave her.

Laura could not stop thinking about the baby. Every time she passed a pram, she would turn her face away, biting her lip, and force herself to walk on. She must not look. That baby might be hers.

She was now working at Lyons Corner House in the Strand. She was a waitress, a 'nippy', dressed in a black dress and white apron with the company's trademark starched white-cotton headdress with a wide black ribbon threaded through it.

When custom was slow the nippies helped in the larder, washing lettuce or slicing tomatoes evenly and thinly for sandwiches, dropping the end slices into the pot to be cooked down for tomato paste. Sometimes Laura, listening to the girls chat and banter around her, felt suddenly unable to go on and she would lean against the workbench, head down, resisting the desire to crumple into a ball on the floor and howl. At other times, she'd find herself weeping in the staff lavatories.

She missed her family even more than she had in the months before she had the baby. Then, when she thought of her father, it was more in anger than in sorrow. Now she mourned for him, as though he were dead.

But mostly she longed for her mother – Maud would not have refused to hold her as Giovanni had – and for Sophie.

I need a friend so badly, she thought. If only I could still talk to Sophie, like before, when I could tell her anything. When she'd moved into their flat she'd written a short note to Sophie, with her new address and news about the flat, Giovanni's job and her hopes of working at Lyons Corner House, but the old intimacy was gone. She'd not had the courage or energy to tell her that the baby was already born, and adopted. She could not put her shame and misery on paper, and she couldn't ask her to visit because Sophie would see at once that Giovanni no longer loved her.

One day, on her afternoon break, she telephoned the Middlesex Hospital and made an appointment to see Dr Wills.

But when she got there, the receptionist looked in her book, and said, 'Ah, Miss Oliver. I am afraid that Dr Wills is unable to see you, but he has briefed his assistant, Miss Bird, and she has your notes. She will see you.'

Miss Bird turned out to be a kindly middle-aged woman who asked her to sit down and smiled at her.

'What can I do for you, Miss Oliver?'

Laura, who had rehearsed her speech in expectation of confrontation, was thrown off balance by the woman's friendly tone.

'I came to see . . . I gave my baby up for adoption in January. But I want to get him back. I don't know where he is and it's killing me. And my husband can't forgive me.' She stopped, scrabbling in her pocket for a handkerchief.

'Go on, my dear, tell me what happened,'

So Laura recounted her tale, and as she spoke, she couldn't control her tears. She hadn't found a handkerchief. Miss Bird got up from the desk and fetched her a face towel from the basin.

Laura didn't say anything about her doubts as to who the baby's father was, but she explained about the homelessness, the lack of money and St Catherine's policy of only helping women prepared to give up their babies.

'Please, I'm going mad. I must know where he is, who has him.' She could feel her face twisting, ugly and desperate, and more tears coming. 'Please. If I could just speak to them . . .'

'Laura – can I call you Laura? I'm about to have a cup of tea. I will get us both one, and in the meantime, you must try to stop crying and then we can have a proper conversation.' She left the room and as she passed her, Laura felt a gentle squeeze on her shoulder.

Miss Bird was soon back with the tea. 'Oh good,' she said, 'you've stopped weeping. Are you feeling better?'

Laura nodded and Miss Bird went on, 'Now,' she said, 'let me tell you what the situation is. It is not what you want to hear, but once you know the worst, you'll be able to cope, I'm sure.'

'I can't have him back, you mean?'

'Yes, I do mean that. It is very sad, but as Dr Wills told your boyfriend, once the baby is with the new mother . . .'

'What do you mean? Dr Wills never saw Giovanni . . .'

'He did, Laura. Giovanni came to see him while you were still upstairs in the maternity ward. He wanted to get the baby back.'

Laura's eyes widened in astonishment. She said nothing, and Miss Bird went on, 'Because you were not married, there was no requirement to consult him. Dr Wills explained this. The simple truth is, Laura, that you agreed to give up your baby, and there's nothing that can be done about it now. You must start to focus on the future.'

'But how can I?' wailed Laura. 'It's all I think about. And all

Giovanni thinks about.' She twisted the towel in her hands. 'Can I at least see him? Maybe if I knew he was well and happy . . .'

Miss Bird shook her head. 'We are not allowed to tell you the address or even the names of the family. What I can tell you is that they are respectable, well off, and they can give your boy everything he needs. That must be your comfort, Laura. You did the right thing, I'm sure of it.'

When she got home, Laura wrote a short letter to her parents.

Dear Mummy and Daddy,

I had the baby in the Middlesex Hospital, but I lost it. I am not coming home. Both Giovanni and I are working, and one day we will get married and have another child.

Laura

Three days later, Laura, in the middle of her afternoon shift, stepped up to Table 16, order pad in hand, and stopped dead. The women sitting at her table were Grace, Jill and Sophie. Instantly Sophie jumped up and threw her arms round Laura.

Laura felt weak. 'What . . .? I can't believe it! Why are you here?'

'Sit down, sit down, Laura. We came to see you.' Jill was pulling at her arm.

'I can't. I'm not allowed. I'm on duty.' Laura looked around. Mr Rupert, the manager, was sure to see her. 'I can't. I'll lose my job.' Laura felt her face burning from a mixture of agitation and excitement.

'Laura, dear Laura, calm down,' Sophie said. 'I'll talk to the manager.' She let go of Laura and walked briskly to the front door where the manager was bowing in new customers. Laura closed her eyes. This could be the end. Now I'll be dismissed on top of everything else. Fraternising with the customers was absolutely forbidden.

'I tell you what, Laura,' said Grace, 'why don't you fetch us some tea and cake, any cake, while Sophie is charming your manager.'

Laura nodded gratefully and scuttled off, her heart beating against her ribs. Somehow she managed to assemble tea for three, and a stand of meringues and éclairs. They were filled with cream made out of butter, milk and gelatine, but still, they were very popular. She was picking up the heavy tray when Mr Rupert appeared. 'Put that down a minute, Laura.' He clicked his fingers at another nippy and ordered her to take it to Table 16.

Laura stood as straight as she could, determined not to cry or plead. It was not her fault if her family came into the restaurant. She would not apologise or grovel.

'I understand that the young women on that table are your friends, is that so?'

'Yes, they are, sir. I didn't know they were coming.'

'No, of course. How could you know? Anyway, we're not very busy, and they tell me they've come up especially from the country to see you. So, rather than make them wait for hours until your shift is over, I suggest you get into your civvies and join them at the table. We cannot have waitresses sitting in the dining room in their aprons and caps now, can we?'

'Certainly not sir! And thank you very, very much, Mr Rupert.'

'That's all right. You can take the rest of the day off, too, if you like. Only make sure they have their tea first. I don't want to lose their custom as well as my best nippy.' He smiled, and said, not unkindly, 'I'm afraid I'll have to dock your wages for the time off, mind.'

When Laura got back to the table she found an extra pot of tea and plate of cakes.

'Your manager – what a nice man – sent them over. Compliments of the house,' said Grace.

But Laura couldn't eat, she felt too churned up. 'Did you really come to town to see me? How did you know where to find me? And why are you all here? There's nothing wrong with Mummy or Daddy? Or anyone? Is there?' Her questions came so thick and fast that there was no hope of coherent answers.

Finally Jill put a hand on Laura's arm. 'Shush, Laura, and we will tell you,' she said. 'Go on, Sophie, you tell her.'

'OK. I was worried about you, Laura, because after Christmas you just disappeared, no word from you, and you didn't answer my letters. In the middle of January I went to see your mother, but she knew nothing. Poor woman, until then I'd not told her that you and I had started writing to each other. Your letters were mostly happy and interesting, nearly all about Giovanni and his ambitions. I just assumed you were in touch with her too.'

'I couldn't write to her.' Laura could feel something of the anguish she'd felt back then, when her mother had not taken her side, had not stood up to her father. 'I missed her dreadfully, but I felt so betrayed by her.'

Grace put a hand on her thigh. It was comforting, but, thought Laura, kindness always makes me cry. She gave Grace a brief smile of gratitude, and turned back to Sophie, who went on.

'Anyway, after I'd seen Maud I promised to try to find you. I rang the Paddington rooming house, but your landlady wouldn't say anything other than that you'd left there. I knew you'd both worked at a Kardomah, but I didn't know which one. The Kingsway one had never heard of either of you and the Piccadilly one had no address for you. I was so worried, Laura, and I thought you must be only a few weeks off giving birth, and missing your mother, and maybe frightened of the labour.'

'Oh, Sophie, I'm really sorry,' said Laura. 'I just didn't think. I was so unhappy, you see, and we'd been thrown out of the boarding house. We were living in separate hostels. I was too ashamed to admit that.'

'Poor, poor Laura. I'm afraid I stopped looking for you, because, by the end of February, I realised you must have deliberately decided you wanted to disappear. Otherwise you'd have written. We didn't know why, but we couldn't do anything. Until Giovanni wrote to me.'

Laura felt her brain was not keeping up. 'What? Giovanni wrote to you?'

She pulled a letter out of her handbag and passed it to Laura.

'*Dear Sophie,*

You are Laura's friend and you must help her. Laura had the baby in early January. It was nearly two months too soon. We had nowhere to live then, only hostels, but not together, and we had no money. The doctor at the hospital, he made Laura give the baby away to some rich people. Now it is nearly spring and she is still very unhappy, so sad. She misses her mother, I think, and Chorlton. Please come to see her.

Giovanni

Laura stared at the letter. It meant Giovanni still cared about her, that he wasn't so deep in his own unhappiness that he was unaware of hers.

'And then,' Sophie went on, 'I showed Giovanni's letter to your mother, and she told us about your note of a few weeks ago, saying you had lost the baby. She was distraught, of course. And anguished because there was no address on it and she'd no idea where you were, and I'd never told her we were in touch. Donald won't allow any talk of you.'

'Oh, poor Mummy. It's so hard for her.' Laura sighed. 'I know she'd be kind to me if it wasn't for Daddy.'

'I'm sure,' said Grace. 'It was she who said we should all come to see you. She bought the train tickets out of her dairy money, so David knows we are here, but Donald doesn't. I think she wanted you to know that all the women love you.'

After they'd had their tea, Laura became uneasy staying at the table. She felt the other nippies would resent her being allowed customers' privileges. Sophie said, 'Where do you live, Laura? Can't we go there? We have so much still to tell you.'

'And anyway, we want to see your flat,' said Jill.

So they took a cab to Billingsgate, which Grace paid for. Lord, thought Laura, that's my day's wages. And yet we used to take cabs all the time when I was a child. She had a fleeting memory of that day with her father, when they'd been to Fortnum's for tea and then to Lillywhites. It seemed another world, another age.

The cab had to drop them at the end of the street, which still sported a bomb crater and was fenced off, pending repairs. So they walked the last bit, the country women looking in fascinated horror at the devastated houses, walls blown out to reveal small patches of pre-war wallpaper and broken fireplaces on the exposed upper floors.

'It's even worse farther east,' said Laura. 'They've only really tackled the West End so far.'

'A bit unfair when the East Enders suffered the brunt of the Blitz,' said Sophie. 'Money always talks.'

The flat was in an undamaged house – only the windows had been blown in by a bomb blast, and they'd been repaired. It was sparsely furnished but it had a sofa and two armchairs in the living room. For the first time since she and Giovanni had moved in, the sofa was used for more than a dumping ground for coats, or somewhere to listen to the news on the wireless.

Laura made them tea, and they all settled down to talk. She discovered that Jill and David were engaged to marry. Jill held out her hand, the long fingers as slender as the rest of her. 'Maud gave me her engagement ring. Unbelievably kind. And Donald, who bought it for her forty-odd years ago, agreed. He said Maud never wore it – her hands were always in the sink.'

Laura felt a shaft of pain. She had a sudden clear memory of rooting through her mother's jewellery box, trying on the bangles and beads, and her mother saying, 'Be careful with that ring, darling. It's very precious. Your father gave it to me on my betrothal. And I will give it to you on yours.'

Laura wrenched her mind back to Jill's excited chatter. 'We probably won't get married for a while. We really want our own house before we do, and we're spending every spare penny and every free minute fixing up the old brew house. It's going to be perfect.'

'Jane cannot wait to be a bridesmaid,' Grace had that indulgent mother's smile. 'She talks of nothing else. You would think it was *her* wedding.'

Grace then told her, shyly, that for the past few weeks she'd been seeing something of George Maxwell-Calder. 'I really like him,' she said, surprise and wonder in her voice. 'I'd never have dreamt I could be interested in another man. After Hugh, I mean—'

'But it's the most natural thing in the world,' interrupted Jill. 'You're young. You can't be a widow for the next fifty years, can you?'

Grace laughed. 'Don't get the wrong idea. No one is talking of marriage. It's just so good to have someone who wants to be with you. We never stop talking. And he is so kind, and sympathetic . . .'

'To say nothing of handsome, aristocratic and rich!' interrupted Sophie, hooting with laughter.

'What I want to know,' said Jill, 'is why the most eligible bachelor for miles around is still unmarried? He must be thirty, isn't he?'

'He's twenty-eight,' said Grace, 'and I agree it's surprising, but I suppose the war got in the way. Still, he says his mother has sprung into action and not a weekend goes by without some titled young woman who can only talk about horses turning up with her mother at Frampton. He says what he loves about me is I don't know a fetlock from a farthingale.'

They all laughed and Laura asked, 'If he did propose, what would that old dragon, the Countess Geraldine, say?'

'Stop, stop, you two!' exclaimed Grace. 'I wish I hadn't mentioned it.'

'She wouldn't approve, for sure,' said Jill. 'Apart from anything else, she'll have to go and live in the Dower House instead of lording it in the Manor.'

'I do wish you'd stop,' Grace protested. 'I wouldn't have raised the subject if I thought you'd have us married off in two minutes.'

The conversation finally came round to Laura and her baby. She didn't want to discuss it. She dreaded being questioned about why she'd had the child adopted. But Sophie said, 'Laura, you have to stop blaming yourself. When you had your baby, of course you couldn't keep it. It was out of the question. You and Giovanni were living in separate hostels. Where would you have lived? You'd have had to pay the midwife, buy a cot, a pram, baby things.'

'I know. I know. But we'd have managed. Somehow. I should never have agreed to give him away.' She looked down, biting her lip, then suddenly she gulped and raised her head. 'I miss him so. How can you miss a baby you never even held? But I do. I think about him all the time.' Laura looked at her three friends in turn, and saw nothing but love and sympathy in their eyes. No disapproval, no judgement.

'Laura, there is a cure for that,' said Sophie gently. 'Things are different for you now. You have somewhere to live, you both have jobs. Giovanni is earning good money.' She leant forward, fixing Laura's gaze with hers. 'Have another child, Laura. You won't believe me now, but the best cure for the unhappiness of losing a baby is to have another one.'

Laura could not stop the tears.

'Oh God,' she said, trying to smile, 'I do nothing but bawl these days.'

Laura looked at her friend. Her round face, usually so merry, was solemn. 'I promise you, Laura,' she said, 'you'll stop feeling blue about that baby once you're pregnant. Your thoughts will switch to the new baby. I'm sure of it.'

Laura took her hands off her tear-stained face. 'But you don't understand. There's no chance of a new baby. Giovanni and I, we don't . . . we haven't once since . . . Well, the truth is he doesn't understand why I gave the baby up. And he's right. I should never have done it.'

'Laura, stop blaming yourself,' said Grace. 'If Giovanni is cold, maybe he thinks you gave away the baby because you had second thoughts about *him*. He needs reassurance. Tell him that you love him and want another baby. Just tell him.'

The young women left at about eight o'clock, to catch the last train from Paddington, and Laura, for once not having to work, had the house to herself. She felt more cheerful than she had for months. The women had convinced her that her mother still loved her. And it was so good to know that she was no longer alone, she still had her three wonderful friends. And Giovanni had written to Sophie. He must still love her, or at least care for her.

She went out in the dark to the little patch of garden and, by the light of the kitchen window, picked a handful of daffodils that had popped up under the hedge.

She cut the flowers short and put them in a jam jar. Then she switched the wireless on and turned the volume up so she could hear it in the bathroom. She bathed, then washed her hair to the familiar strains of Glenn Miller and his orchestra. She put on her one good red dress, the one that Giovanni liked and had insisted on buying in the second-hand shop in the Portobello Road when they'd had a particularly good day busking in Bayswater. She added her pearl necklace, her only remotely valuable possession.

She smiled ruefully at her image in the mirror. She wouldn't have that if she'd not been wearing it the day they'd walked out of Chorlton. She lipsticked her mouth – lightly. Giovanni hated too much make-up.

She set the kitchen table, boiled some potatoes and reheated the rest of the stew Giovanni had made on Sunday. She wished she had a bottle of wine. But no matter. I am going to seduce my husband, she thought, see if I don't.

CHAPTER TWENTY-ONE

Giovanni liked Billingsgate market, and he usually walked through it to work. It took a few minutes longer but he enjoyed seeing the market traders scrubbing down the counter slabs or hefting great trays of ice.

If he came early, around 3 or 4am, the market still smelled of the Jeyes Fluid used in yesterday's wash down. It amused him how cleaning seemed to be confined to the floors, which were swept with a yard broom and hosed down, while the traders' wooden desks were covered in a thick varnish of years of fish scales and dried slime.

As the deliveries were unloaded and trundled into the market by the porters, the smell of fresh fish, and of the sea, took over. Just to see the plentiful salmon, soles, trout and herrings, shiny, wet and slithery, was a joy for a cook, a far cry from the wartime stretching of a single tin of pilchards with 80 per cent potato and a dash of anchovy essence to make fish pie for eight. Giovanni would watch the men positioning their wares – wide-mouthed cod or crates of iridescent mackerel or sardines on top of a stack of unopened boxes – or transferring live crabs and navy blue lobsters into big wire baskets to be taken to the boiling house.

Occasionally a huge fish, a giant halibut almost as big as the porter or a great wide turbot, would require two men to lift it into pride of place on someone's stand.

The porters were foul-mouthed and Giovanni soon learned not to get in their way. The salesmen paid them tuppence for every stone of fish delivered to their stands, and many of them weaved their way through the crowded market with multiple boxes piled high on their heads. It was quicker than pulling a barrow.

The salesmen at their traders' desks didn't curse, and were definitely more dignified than the porters, but both traders and porters were good-humoured. True, they called him wop and Eyetie, but it was always done in jest. They would tell him to get a bleeding shift on, get the fryer going, they'd be in for their breakfast soon. When they arrived, they'd shove each other up on the bench seats and sit with only the occasional shout of 'C'mon, Valentino, how long do I have to wait, then?'

The men almost always ate the same things: egg and chips, a breakfast fry-up or fish and chips, sometimes with mushy peas. The fry-up consisted of scrambled eggs (made from powdered egg – fresh eggs were still rationed and restaurants struggled to get the real thing), deep-fried bread, four streaky bacon rashers also cooked to all-over crispness in the fryer, two pork sausages (still containing more bread than meat) and a ladleful of baked beans. Until about 6am the customers were mainly lorry drivers from ports not served by the Great Eastern Railway, which brought the bulk of fish from Grimsby or Scotland, and the Great Western which served the Welsh, Cornish and Devon fisheries.

After that it was mostly takeaways: fish and chips for drivers who would eat in their trucks on the way home to coastal ports all over the south. Giovanni or his boss Joe would wrap the food loosely in greaseproof paper and then in newsprint. The last arrivals would be the traders coming in for breakfast after the market closed at nine-thirty.

The customers, all men from the fish market, knew good fish from bad, and Joe, though forced to buy the National Loaf and Government Cheddar, never stinted on the quality or quantity of fish. If he promised six ounces of cod, he meant six ounces after filleting, and before it went in the batter. The problem, thought Giovanni, was not so much the ingredients as the cooking. Joe was not a good cook.

One day, when Joe's wife Mel was scraping dirty plates into the pig bin, Giovanni heard Joe say, 'I don't know why they order fish and chips when they leave half of it. That's a wicked waste, that is. I saw him push his plate away. It was the chap from Brassey's.'

'Well,' said Mel, 'I don't blame him. I'd not eat that. We're lucky he never complained. There's plenty as does.'

She's right, thought Giovanni, but he thought it wiser not to get between husband and wife.

Joe turned to Mel. 'What are you saying, woman?'

'Only that I'd not have eaten that batter. It's bad enough that it's made with government flour and dried egg, but it's all greasy and soggy.'

'So what's wrong with it? Of course it goes soft if he doesn't eat it straight away, but that's good cod, that is.'

'Yes, and he ate the cod, didn't he? Dug it all out and left the batter.'

Mikey, who worked in the café and seldom spoke, suddenly jerked his head at Giovanni and said, 'The new boy says it's because the fat's not hot enough.'

Mel and Joe both turned to stare at Giovanni. Joe lifted his chin and narrowed his eyes. 'Is that so, young man?'

Giovanni ignored the challenge. 'Well, I think if we had another deep fryer, not so much go in the fish fryer at a time,' he said mildly. 'So many orders go into it when we're busy, the fat can't stay hot.'

Joe and Mel stared blankly at him. Giovanni thought, Maybe they think as I'm new here I should keep my mouth shut. Well, that's daft. He went on, 'If we used it only for chips, fried bread, doughnuts – things that don't spoil the oil like bacon and fish do – the fat lasts longer. And if we get a modern fryer with two *compartimenti*, we could have one cooler for the first cooking of the chips and one hotter for the second fry and for bread and doughnuts. Then we not give them soggy chips.'

'Maybe you're right,' said Joe. 'And do you have any other suggestions?'

Giovanni thought he might be being sarcastic, but he decided he may as well keep going now he'd started. 'Well, yes, I do. I was thinking – maybe we sell a deep-fried cheese sandwich? There'd be more profit. Cheese is cheaper than fish.'

'A deep-fried sandwich? No one is going to have a sandwich for breakfast, surely?'

'Why not? In Italy it is famous snack, *mozzarella in carrozza*. *Mozzarella* – that's a cheese, really good, from buffalo cows, white, goes like elastic when is cooked – in, how you say? In carriage. Cheese in carriage.'

Mikey snorted. 'Buffalo cows?'

'Yes, their milk is very delicious. But now you cannot get mozzarella. Only on black market and very expensive. So we make with Cheddar cheese. Cheddar is OK.'

Giovanni, sensing that Joe was at least interested if not keen, pushed his advantage. 'And Joe,' he said, 'think about the office workers at the top of Pudding Lane. Now those five-bob wartime restaurants – how do you call them? British Restaurants? – are closing, surely some would come here for lunch? We aren't far from the banks and City offices. We could stay open after the fish market closes and serve the City people. What you think?'

'And who would do the serving?' demanded Mel, her voice rising in indignation. 'I've more than enough to do with an eight-hour shift here in the morning and all the queuing and housework in the afternoon.'

Giovanni, all fire and enthusiasm now, spun round to face Mel. 'Oh Mel, I can hire Italians cheap. Really cheap, very little money. And if we buy another fryer, I can make much more money *and* give you and Joe more time off.' He turned to Joe. 'Why not give it a chance, Joe? We test the deep-fried sandwich on the market workers and if they like it, we try to get the City clerks to walk down Pudding Lane for their lunch. What you say?'

'Well, young man, I see the logic of a new fryer, and I will think about it. And if you want to try out your foreign sandwich, go ahead. Then we'll see.'

Giovanni took a deep breath. 'Thank you, Joe. Thank you very much. Can I ask one more thing?'

'And what is that?'

'If we charge 11d for the sandwich, you should make a gross profit of 6d. Will you pay me a penny for every one we sell?'

Giovanni made his first fried sandwiches out of the National Loaf. White flour and white bread were still unavailable and flour was still rationed. He sliced the coarse loaf thinly, cut off the crusts and rubbed them into breadcrumbs through a drum sieve, shaking his head at the residue of wheat husks and flecks of bran left on the wire mesh. He mixed together some English mustard with margarine and a few drops of Worcester sauce and spread this thinly over half the slices of bread. Then he spooned two tablespoons of grated Government Cheddar on each buttered slice, not quite to the edge and leaving a hollow in the middle of each square. Into each hollow he dropped the yolk, and a little of the white, of a precious real hen's egg. He used the rest of the egg white, lightly beaten, to moisten the edges of the bread, covered his constructions with plain slices of bread and pinched the edges together to seal them, taking care not to press the top and burst the egg yolk. Finally he pressed breadcrumbs along the soggy edges to prevent leaks.

Joe and Mel were waiting expectantly at the corner table as Giovanni deep-fried two sandwiches. Using a fish slice he lowered each one carefully into the fat, which received them with satisfactory bubbling and sizzling. But his heart sank as he watched the grey-brown bread darken so dully. If only he could use white Italian bread like his mother made, which fried to an irresistible golden brown. This National Loaf, grey to look at, heavy in texture and universally mocked as 'Hitler's secret weapon', was not the best *carrozza* for his filling.

But Giovanni was relieved that neither sandwich burst or leaked, and in two minutes they were crisp all over. When Mel put her knife into the crusty packet, and melted cheese and just-runny yolk flowed out, he knew he was on to a winner.

'Delicious, just delicious,' exclaimed Joe.

Giovanni's fried sandwiches were an instant success. The

market traders and truck drivers loved them. Giovanni could not get enough fresh eggs to do the sandwich with the surprise runny egg in the middle, and anyway it took too much time and care to do in quantity, so they did a cheaper cheese-only version, a bacon and scrambled egg one, and one made with tomato sauce and baked beans inside.

Persuading the market men to try them wasn't difficult. They involved no 'fancy foreign stuff', and the men liked anything deep-fried anyway. Getting the City folk to walk down towards the fish market was more difficult, but Giovanni carried trays of his hot cheese sandwiches, cut into fingers, up Fish Street Hill and gave them away to people emerging from Monument Tube station. They were barely warm by then, but still crisp and tasty. Giovanni kept up his banter and handed out roneoed leaflets with directions to the café, with an offer of a free cup of tea if they bought a sandwich.

His efforts did the trick. Within a month, opening the café for lunch was proving profitable and Giovanni got permission to set up a stall near St Paul's, on the edge of a bomb site on Cheapside. They made the sandwiches in the café, then fried them in a portable gas fryer in the street, wrapping them in several sheets of newsprint so the customers would not burn their hands.

These days Giovanni woke eager to get to work, and left work eager to return to Laura. Being able to cook good food, even simple fish and chips and fried bacon sandwiches, gave him true satisfaction. He longed to make the deep-fried sandwiches with really good bread, with real mozzarella or with other cheeses. He wanted to add flavours, like basil, anchovy, salami, garlic, red peppers. If only the ingredients were available and the clientele a bit posher, he could develop them. One day soon, somehow, he would.

It pleased him that Laura had started to take an interest in cooking, too. Until now she'd done what was needed to produce simple suppers or breakfasts at home, but without much enthusiasm. Recently, however, she'd spent her weekly afternoon off in the café, watching him cook and helping if she could. She was gratifyingly full of admiration for the organised way he worked, for the care he took with making the batter or trimming the fish. He taught her chefs' techniques for chopping onions, skinning fish, snipping the rind to stop bacon rashers curling in the heat, poaching eggs to keep the whites round the yolk.

It was a pleasure to teach her: she got such a kick out of getting it right, and that pleasure was not just because she was proving such a good cookery student. The real joy was that his darling Laura had come back to him. Everything had miraculously changed that evening he'd got home to find her dressed up, smelling delicious and as eager and loving as in their early days. He smiled at the memory: she'd admitted she'd set out to seduce him. 'I wanted two things, Giovanni,' she said. 'I wanted you back, and I wanted your child.'

He would never understand why she'd given up their first baby, but sometimes it was better to accept the good things, and not dwell on the bad. And there were plenty of good things right now. Laura was happy, she wanted to have another baby, and she was increasingly interested in food and cooking.

One afternoon, watching him scrubbing mussels one by one, painstakingly removing each stringy beard, she said, 'It's as if you think you owe it to the ingredients to treat them well.'

'Well, yes, I do. That's exactly how I feel.' He grinned, amused at how perceptive she was. 'If someone has taken a lot of trouble and many months to breed and rear a chicken, feed, kill and pluck it, and deliver it to the market, then it's a crime for a cook to go and ruin it.'

Giovanni watched Laura cutting potatoes for chips. She wore an expression of focused concentration. She was doing it exactly as he'd shown her, first trimming the peeled potatoes into rectangular blocks, then into slices, then stacking the slices for the final row of cuts to get matching chips. She looks so beautiful, he thought, like a Dutch painting.

She'd put on a few pounds and there was colour in her cheeks. Laura felt his gaze, looked up and smiled, her eyes shining.

One warm evening, Giovanni came home to find Laura wearing her red dress and lipstick, and she'd used combs to tame her flaming mop into soft curls away from her face.

'What's up?' Giovanni said, putting his arms round her. 'It's not your birthday, is it? And you don't need to seduce me again, you know. I could not love you more than I do already.'

Laura was smiling at him, a wide, confident, happy smile. Giovanni looked into her eyes, so alive with excitement. And suddenly he knew. 'You're pregnant!' he said.

They held on to each other, very tight, for a minute and then Giovanni pulled away to look at her again, 'Now we have to get married. And your parents will forgive us, you'll see.' He slipped his arm round her waist and danced her around the room. 'This story has a happy ending, darling. I promise.'

The following morning Laura asked Mr Rupert for two consecutive days off. To go home to see her parents, she said. Which was true. And she needed two days because with luck they would forgive her and she could stay the night. It would be so wonderful to sleep in her old bed and wake up to the sound of her mother clattering in the kitchen. She frowned, pushing the thought away. She knew too well that wishing for things did not make them happen.

She did not send a telegram or a letter. She knew that her father would be likely to forbid her coming. It was too risky. But she was sure they'd be at home. Her mother hated to leave her garden at the best time of the year, and it was haymaking season when all hands were needed.

She stepped off the train at Moreton-in-Marsh and made her way to Mr Brown's shop. When she entered, the doorbell ringing behind her, there was no one inside and she looked round at the meagre selection of cheeses and stacks of ham and bacon. Next to the till were Mr Brown's ration stamps. You'd think we were still at war, she thought. The National Loaf was the only bread available and there was more margarine than butter on the counter. Nothing was new or exciting.

Mr Brown appeared, and stopped dead at the sight of her.

'Hullo, Mr Brown.'

'Oh my goodness! It's Miss Laura. What a wonderful surprise. And you looking so well and all! Are you stopping a while?'

'I don't know. I just stepped off the train. I was wondering if your van was going that way? It's not that far and I can walk, it's a lovely day. But if I could find someone to give me a lift it would save a lot of time.' She realised she was chattering away to disguise her nervousness.

Mr Brown walked back through the door he'd come in by,

calling up the stairs to his wife. Could she look after the shop? He was just nipping out in the van, he said. Be back in time for the deliveries.

Mr Brown brushed the passenger seat with his brown dust jacket sleeve and held the door while Laura clambered up. He talked all the way, giving her the village gossip: the Mitford hotel had been sold, and the previous owners were now running the Frampton Arms, and doing a pretty poor job of it. The under-gardener and the groom at Frampton had been arrested for using their employer's apples and equipment to brew and sell illegal scrumpy; the potato harvest would be way down because of the floods at planting time; romance was in the air: everyone talked of Jill and David's engagement, and (here he dropped his voice as if the van was full of eavesdroppers) there was talk, plenty of it, that the new Earl was sweet on Grace Oliver, Hugh's widow. Did she know anything of that?

Before Laura had set out, she'd had high hopes that her father would have missed her enough to want to make amends. She'd even dreamed, not just of reconciliation, but of a joint wedding with David and Jill, at Chorlton. And if Grace and George did marry one day, there would be three young couples, all friends. She had a fleeting vision of a bevy of toddlers, inseparable cousins, running about the lawn. Giovanni and she would come down most weekends on the train, and one day, when they could afford it, they would convert one of the outbuildings to a house, like Jill and David were doing.

But as they got nearer to Chorlton, Laura's nervousness increased. What if this were to be the last time she'd see these familiar fields and houses? What happened in the next hour would make or break her relationship with her parents. How could she bear it if she never saw her mother again? She prayed she'd find Maud on her own.

She did. Maud was sitting at the kitchen table, stringing beans. She tried to rise, but Laura was too quick for her. She fell into her mother's arms, but had barely gasped more than a few words when Donald came into the kitchen. Laura saw him over her mother's shoulder, and slowly she let her mother go. She stood for a second, tears springing to her eyes,

'Oh, Daddy,' she cried, starting towards him. But he held up his hand to stop her.

'Has something changed? You know you are not welcome here.'

'Donald, dear . . .'

'Be quiet, Maud,' he said without looking at his wife. His eyes drilled into Laura's. 'Why you are here? I expect that wop of yours has left you in the lurch. I shouldn't be surprised.'

Laura's jaw tightened with anger. How dare he! Her chin came up and her eyes flashed. 'Of course Giovanni hasn't left me. I'm here because we're getting married.' She felt her confidence wane and she stammered a little. 'And I . . . I came down to ask you to come to the wedding.' She turned back to her mother and clasped her hands.

'Please, Mummy, will you come? We do so want you there. I'm going to have another baby, and this time we will not be bullied into giving it away.'

'Oh darling.' Maud stretched out a hand towards her daughter, and Laura clasped it while looking steadily at her father.

'If it wasn't for you, Daddy, I would be so happy.'

Donald walked over the sideboard and picked up his pipe and tobacco. For a moment he seemed to be thinking, and then he slowly swung back to his wife and daughter. Laura held her breath.

'Well, I dare say that's true. But you have made your bed and you must lie in it, I'm afraid.' He lifted his chin and walked out of the kitchen to the yard.

Laura sank down on her knees with her head in her mother's lap. Her voice came in jerks as she sobbed.

'Mummy, why can't you stand up for me? Why do you let him treat me like that? And why is he so horrible? He used to be the kindest, most wonderful father . . .'

'Oh my darling daughter, if you knew how hard it is for me to be loyal to my husband and loving to you. I love you so much, and, yes, you did wrong, but to cut you off like that!' Maud was crying too now, and reached for the tea towel on the table to wipe her face. Laura looked up.

'It's all right, Mummy, don't cry . . .'

'No, no, I want to try to explain. I promised when I made my wedding vows to obey my husband. I believe I should. But lately the cost of obedience has been too high. I can't bear it. Sometimes I hate him, Laura. Isn't that terrible?'

'No, he *is* sometimes hateful. I used to hate him. But I'm getting to be indifferent, which is worse really. At least hate implies feeling.' Laura borrowed the tea towel to mop her own face. She smiled wanly. 'I just don't understand why he goes on being so beastly.'

'It's a lot of things. His pride, mostly. And jealousy. You were so much the apple of his eye and you choosing a man for yourself felt like betrayal to him. He's not happy. I think he knows it's his own fault that he will never see his grandchild.' Maud held Laura's face in her hands and looked into her eyes. Fresh tears ran down her own cheeks. 'The other girls told me about your baby. Did you see it, Laura? Was it a boy or a girl?'

'A boy. I never held him. They wouldn't let me. They took him away. I heard him cry. I'll never forget that sound.'

They held on to each other for a while, not speaking. 'I should never have been so weak,' Laura said. 'We would have managed somehow. But this time we will keep our baby.'

Wiping her eyes on her mother's apron, she tried to smile. 'Oh God, this is like a scene from a Victorian melodrama.'

She looked up into her mother's face. 'And Mummy, the other reason I came is, well, I thought if you and Daddy would just forgive me, I could come home to have the baby, and you would be with me. Last time was so awful. So frightening.'

'Oh, Laura. Of course I'd want that. But how can I . . .? I don't know . . . Your father . . .' She didn't go on. Neither of them did.

After a while, Maud stood up and filled the kettle. She put it on the stove and fetched the biscuit tin, which had mostly broken biscuits in it. 'Oh, Laura, I am longing for rationing to stop. Mr Brown is such a nice man, letting us have broken biscuits, but it seems so unfair that supplies should be worse now than in the war. How long can it go on for?'

'God knows. Brown's shop is half empty, poor man. You're right, he's really kind. He gave me a lift from Moreton, even though it wasn't on his round.'

Laura shuffled from her kneeling position onto a chair, while Maud talked on, something about David and Jill's efforts to convert the brew house, but Laura wasn't listening.

'Mummy,' she said, 'I don't understand Daddy. The truth is I'm only one among thousands of girls who get pregnant. And if it's any business of anyone's to forgive me, then I know you have. And Grace, Sophie and Jill are really good friends, as ever. You know they came to see me in the spring, and Sophie and I write to each other almost every week. And last month I sent David a present for his birthday, a white silk scarf, a real toff's scarf for when he takes Jill dancing. He wrote me such a lovely brotherly letter. I know he's not angry. They are all just sorry for me because I lost my baby. They don't give me moral lectures. They can't all be wrong.'

'But darling, don't you see? Your father had so much invested in you. All your life he spoilt you, dreaming and planning for your future. He could see you marrying into one of the grander families in the county, bearing him grandchildren he could teach to ride and take hunting like he used to take you.'

Laura sniffed. 'So I was to be a ladder for his social climb, was I? It's disgusting, Mummy. He was always a snob, but I thought he wanted me to marry well for my sake, not for his.'

She stood up. 'Where's David, Mummy? I can't leave without seeing him, and I don't suppose Daddy is such an ogre that he'll try to stop David driving me to the station?'

David was in the office and Laura felt her stomach tightening with slight anxiety as she crossed the yard. She hesitated, then knocked on the office door.

'Come in.' At the sound of her brother's voice any worries evaporated. He jumped up from his chair and opened his arms and Laura went into them, burying her nose in his flannel shirt. She'd forgotten he smelt like that, of tobacco and farmyard.

She pushed back, laughing. 'You smell of the cows. Or sheep, or something.'

'Laura, it's so good to see you back here. Are you staying? Does Dad know?'

'Yes, he does now, and I'm not staying. I just had to see Mummy. Can you drive me to the station, and we can talk on the way?'

'We can do better than that. How about lunch in the pub?' He looked at his watch. 'And can you catch a later train? There's one at two-thirty, I think.'

They sat in the new 'Ladies Bar' which contained no ladies, only two old men playing dominoes. They ordered the five-bob lunch and it was disgusting: thin grey slices of unidentifiable meat, allegedly beef, reheated in tasteless gravy, watery mashed potatoes and lurid bluey-green cabbage.

'Good Lord, what have they done to the cabbage?' exclaimed David.

Laura laughed. 'They've put a dose of bicarb into the cooking water. It makes it that horrible green, which, I suppose, is marginally better than the grey it would be without it.'

'But Mum's cabbage isn't grey.'

'No, but she doesn't cook it for an hour and then leave it in the water for another.'

Too well-trained to ever waste food, they both cleaned their plates without further comment. Then Laura sat back.

'Don't let's talk about Daddy,' she said. 'I've done so much weeping and wailing over him in the last two years that I can't bear any more.'

'OK, let's talk about us. You first. Tell me about Giovanni's business.' So she did, and then David asked her if she and Giovanni were getting married.

'Yes we are.' She laughed. 'We have to – I'm pregnant again. And this time we're keeping the baby.' She looked across at her brother. 'I used to have dreams of a double wedding, you and

Jill and me and Giovanni in the village church. But Daddy would never agree.'

'No, I suppose not.' David reached for his pint and looked at Laura over the rim. 'I think Jill told you we are finally formally engaged?'

'Yes. Congratulations. She showed me Mummy's ring. About time too, I say!'

'I know, we have been very slow about it. We'd have done it years ago if Roger hadn't been missing in action. Jill had this fixed idea that she had to break it to him in person. But since his name is on the war memorial, there's no telling him now.'

'Even so, you've been slow. It's two years since the end of the war.'

'I know, but there's no hurry and we want to finish our house first. And it's going slowly – we are both too tired at night to do much.'

'Poor Daddy. I know I'm mostly furious with him, but I do see that the world he's in now is not his world. He was the lord and master of our family and of Chorlton, but now you argue with him about the farms and you always get your way, I won't come to heel, and even Mummy is thinking rebellion. He must have thought everything would go back to how it was before the war. But nothing has. And nothing will.'

CHAPTER TWENTY-TWO

As each ewe plunged into the dip, David used a heavy forked stick to push the head under, ensuring every inch of each sheep got the treatment. He was trying not to breathe in the heavy chemical fumes.

He was surprised that Jill didn't complain. She just got on with herding the sheep into the funnel-shaped alley. Pressure from behind forced the animals, one by one, into the bath-like trough sunk into the ground and filled with liquid pesticide. Meg ran round the flock, back and forth, preventing escape.

When the last sheep was done and they were herding them up to Longmeadow, Jill said, 'The first time I did that, do you remember? The fumes made me sick. I had a headache all night.' She shrugged. 'Now I'm fine. It's extraordinary what the body gets used to.'

'That stuff is mostly arsenic,' he said, shaking his head. 'Probably gives the sheep a headache too, but if the alternative is lice and fly-strike . . .'

'I know, but all the same I wish we didn't have to do it. It feels so unnatural to dip animals into poison. And we must both stink of the stuff. What I wouldn't give for a warm soapy bath.'

David threw an arm round her neck and pulled her close so she had to stop walking. 'You don't stink. You smell like you, the best smell in the world.'

He kissed her. Suddenly serious, he said, 'You do want to be a farmer's wife, don't you? You only have three more weeks to change your mind. After that you'll be another Mrs Oliver.'

She laughed, and nuzzled into his neck. 'You know I'm not going to change my mind. You just like hearing me say I love you. Which I do, I do.' He could feel her stiffen as she said, 'Let go, David. George is heading this way.'

David turned and waved to George, still out of hearing. 'I wonder what he wants. I hope not to go over the old ground of our farming his fields. I wish the lawyers weren't taking such an age to settle it.'

But it wasn't that. 'I came to issue an invitation,' George said, removing his hat and shaking their hands. 'Would you come to dinner on Saturday? And bring the rest of the family?'

'We'd love that, of course. But George, you know my father and his stance about the land. Won't it be embarrassing?'

'Well, I agree we have the matter of these farms,' he waved his arm towards the hillside, 'but I don't take that personally. I'm not my father. Let the courts decide on the ownership, compensation, and who should get what revenue. My father would never have admitted it, but you have done the farms nothing but good, David, and your father was probably right to take them over.'

'That's very decent of you. Thank you.'

'So, will you come to dinner? And persuade your parents to come too? The last time they were in the house was years ago, at my coming-of-age ball. But it must be time to forget all that. Let me know, will you? I hope you'll all come.'

He shook their hands again and set off briskly, using both hands to pull his deerstalker straight on his head.

'Well,' said David, watching him go, 'that's a turn-up for the books.'

'It's because he's sweet on Grace.'

'You women. You're such romantics! I know you think there is something going on, but George has never said a word to me.'

'Of course not. He's a chap. Did you tell him when you fell in love with me?'

'That's not fair!'

'Of course you didn't. I can't see you sharing confidences with anyone. You don't even tell me everything going on in your noddle.'

David knew she was right. 'Of course I do!' he said, but it didn't sound convincing.

'Anyway,' said Jill, a giggle in her voice, 'George thinks it's their secret, but Sophie and I guessed a while ago, and then Grace let on. I did tell you.'

'But is it serious, do you think?'

'They're hardly walking out together in public, are they? I don't think he's asked her to marry him. She'd say yes like a shot if he did, and she'd have told me or Sophie if he had.'

David thought it was probably just girlish speculation. Women did love to gossip.

'Sounds to me like romantic fantasy on the part of the Chorlton womenfolk,' he said.

Jill laughed and pushed him in the chest, 'No! Anyway, we are sworn to secrecy. It's my guess that George wants to persuade his fearsome mother before he gets down on one knee to Grace. It will be part of the strategy to convert her.'

At Longmeadow Jill held the gate while David and Meg herded the sheep through. As they checked the water trough David returned to the subject of Grace.

'Why was Dad so opposed to her accepting the bicycle George restored for Jane? Does he suspect Grace is siding with the enemy?'

'Oh David, I gave up trying to understand your father's prejudices years ago. But I doubt it. It's not the sort of thing Donald would notice, is it? No, he'd prefer it if we had nothing to do with any of them. He's got something personal against all the Maxwell-Calders, not just George.'

Yes, thought David, he has. They look down on him, that's what, and he resents it.

'That bike was a real labour of love,' said Jill. 'It had been rusting in the barn since George was a boy. Jane is so proud of it because it's a boy's bike with a crossbar.'

As they walked home David wondered why it had taken him so long to discover that their former land girl was not just efficient and attractive. She was intelligent, wise and even-handed. She understands Donald and George, he thought. More importantly, she understands me.

Grace had thought Jane would kick up a fuss about being left with Mabel while she was at the Frampton dinner. But no, Jane was delighted. Mabel had promised her they would make drop scones together and have them with honey for supper.

So Grace was free to look forward to the outing. She was happy but also a bit anxious. She wanted to look her best and chose a pink and turquoise cocktail dress she'd bought before the war, but seldom worn. She pulled her hair up with combs each side of her head and let the wavy mass of bright blonde fall down her back. Wearing it loose, instead of plaited and pinned to her head, made her feel young and carefree.

They were only seven for dinner. George's mother Geraldine, now in her mid-sixties, had become plainer and plumper since her husband's death. She presided over her son's table with aristocratic confidence and a cut-glass voice. She was formidable and Grace wondered if she could ever be a friend.

The pre-war niceties of walking into dinner were observed, and Grace felt awkward and unsure of herself. In her parental family, such formality had never been the rule, even before the war. Maud was taken into dinner by George and ushered to the seat on his right. Behind them in the mini-procession came Donald with the Dowager Countess on his arm. He led her, or rather she led him, to her place at the other end of the table. David followed, squiring Grace and seating her on George's left. Jill was left to trail in behind them, on her own.

Grace found it difficult to take her eyes off George, so hand-some and relaxed in the newly fashionable black tie. She sat on his left, with Maud on his right, and sneaked glances at his profile when he talked to the others. He was the perfect host, dividing his attention between his guests and encouraging them to talk.

They started with *Escargots à la Bourguignonne,* the snails siz-zling in their shells.

'What a treat, Countess. We haven't eaten snails since before the war. Have we, Donald?' said Maud.

'I've never eaten them,' said David. 'Have you, Jill?''

Jill hadn't and confessed to needing a lesson to use the tongs that held the snails and the little pick for extracting them.

'What about you, Grace?' said George, turning to her.

'My parents loved them. We used to get them in tins from France. The shells came separately but my mother couldn't be bothered with them, and we didn't have these dinky tools, so we just had them in a soup bowl, swimming in butter and garlic, and with bread to mop up the juices. Nothing like as elegant as this.'

Grace secretly thought the snails not a patch on her mother's, whose melted butter sauce was heavy with garlic, black pepper and chopped fresh parsley. These were chewy and a bit tasteless.

George caught her eye. 'Maybe snails are not a great dinner party idea,' he said, smiling ruefully.

Maud had eaten hers, but Donald had given up, putting his tongs, and pick down with finality. Jill and David were struggling. George rang the little brass bell for the butler to clear the dishes.

Over the summer Grace and George had gone for many walks, always with Jane bouncing along the lanes on her bicycle, or, if they were going through the fields, showing off on Snowdrop. It was relaxed and companionable and she'd frequently told herself he was just being kind. He was an Earl, with a country estate and a house in London. He must be the most eligible man in the county, and who was she? An older widow with no money and a daughter to bring up. Sitting next to him at the glittering table, dressed in her best finery and without the cover of her daughter, made her both excited and nervous.

He said, his voice quiet and low, 'I miss our walks. I've been trapped in London too much. Shall we go blackberrying tomorrow? Jane would like that.'

'Oh yes, I would too.' He held her gaze and Grace felt a clutch in her stomach.

'Better still, I don't suppose you could leave your darling daughter with her grandmama, could you?'

Her heart gave a thud. She nodded, then whispered, 'I'll try.'

The main course was roast partridge, and Grace's heart sank. She disliked whole birds on her plate. They were such a fiddle to eat and if they were tough, which they often were, they were likely to shoot off, splashing gravy everywhere. And then, it was much too high for her. It must have been hung for weeks. She managed a few mouthfuls of the breast, but the red-raw thighs and the canapé of toast under the bird, soaked with blood and spread with near-raw liver, turned her stomach.

George bent his head to hers. 'Is it too well-hung for you?' he asked.

'I'm afraid so. And too rare. Feeble of me. I'm sorry.' Grace looked up at him, apologetic. 'But I love all the rest.' George leant across, speared her bird with his fork and lifted it onto his side plate. He signalled Andrew, the butler, to remove it.

It was swiftly done and Grace hoped the Countess hadn't noticed. She smiled gratefully at George and tucked into the traditional extras left on her plate: crumbly roast potatoes, buttery crumbs, deep-fried game chips, a creamy clove-scented bread sauce, redcurrant jelly and deep rich gravy. Delicious.

Inevitably, the conversation could not stay off the question of the Frampton land all evening. George raised the subject after the charlotte russe had been served.

'My father could never reconcile himself to the loss of the farms but yes, Donald, it was necessary,' he said, pouring himself some cream. 'The war effort demanded it—'

'Utter tosh, George,' interrupted his mother. 'It was a disgrace and your father was quite right. It was stealing. Those farms belong to Frampton.'

George smiled without rancour. 'Mother, please,' he said mildly.

Grace feared her father-in-law's reaction, but George forestalled him.

'Donald, as I've said, I think you did the right thing, at least from the patriotic point of view. But the confiscation was seven years ago, and it was the Air Ministry not the War Ag that did it, before the war. The war is over. You and I should discuss the future.'

'Nothing to discuss, old boy.'

Grace winced. Most of the time Donald plays the Cotswold gentleman, she thought, but he can't help bursts of Yorkshire bluntness.

'I think there is,' said George equably, 'and presumably, David, you make the business decisions now?'

David looked nonplussed. 'Well, yes, most of them. But not without my father's support.'

'Well, let's discuss it when the ladies have retired. The sooner we settle it, the better, otherwise the only winners will be the lawyers.'

Grace, Jill and Maud followed the Countess as she climbed the stairs, puffing a little, her right hand on the banister and her left through the butler's arm. Andrew, released from her grip on the upstairs landing, bowed politely and opened the door to the Countess's apartments.

Lady Frampton sat down heavily in the upright chair. She pointed to a side table bearing a tray with a bottle of crème de menthe and four small glasses, and said, 'Jill, would you be so kind as to do the honours? Things are so impossible now. Not a footman to be had and George says I'm not to ask my maid to serve the ladies. Apparently she must help clear the dinner table. I don't know what the world is coming to.'

While Jill did as she was told, Grace availed herself of the Countess's bathroom. It was the size of her bedroom at Chorlton, dominated by an enormous Edwardian bath with brass taps, and a porcelain basin large enough to bath a baby in, with a scalloped shelf round it containing dips on either side for soaps. An immense shower stood in one corner which Jill suspected was never used, since there were green streaks down the tiles caused by leaks from the copper pipes. There was an upholstered armchair and a full-length cheval looking-glass in the middle of the room.

She stood in front of the glass, scrutinising herself. Her hair was very slightly dishevelled, her wide blue eyes shone with health and her heightened colour (whether from excitement or wine she didn't know) suited her. She ran her fingers round her neckline, forcing it a fraction lower to better show off her bosom, the skin still smooth and creamy. Oh Lord, she thought, I am behaving like a temptress. Then she smiled at herself, thinking, Why not?

When Grace returned to the Countess's morning room the conversation was being briskly led by Lady Frampton. First she interrogated Jill about her and David's plans for marriage. Next, she questioned Maud about the new drystone wall being built along the Chorlton boundary and declared it should have been a hedge. Finally she turned her attention to Grace, who by now was feeling distinctly anxious.

'George tells me that your daughter is an excellent horse-woman. Is that so?'

'Yes, she does ride well, Lady Frampton. But she's only just turned seven.'

'And has a temper on her, I understand. You need to smack that out of her and the sooner the better. A temper in a girl is very unattractive.'

Grace, as always stung by any criticism of her daughter, found her courage flooding back. 'I agree, but I expect she will grow out of it,' she said. 'George tells me you can be pretty fiery yourself.'

The Countess looked across at Maud. 'Is your daughter-in-law always so impertinent?'

Maud said, 'Grace, dear, I am sure you didn't mean . . .'

'Don't worry about it,' said the Countess. 'I like a girl who speaks her mind. I always speak mine, which I will do now on another subject. Grace, whatever you may think or hope, my dear, George cannot marry you. I will not have it.'

Grace felt her face flame. Embarrassment was swiftly followed by anger and she opened her mouth to reply, then shut it again. What could she say?

Maud stood up, flustered. At that moment the door opened and Donald, his face more purple than red, eyes bulging with anger, stuck his head in. 'Ladies, come, this is the second time I've found myself forced to leave this house. We will not be entering it again.'

No one said anything in the car going home, on account of Sawkins at the wheel. Maud was as silent as the rest, but she was angry. How could Donald behave so rudely? To walk out of

Frampton Hall *twice* was unforgivable. She wanted to shake him and demand how he expected to be accepted by those people if he proved himself unfit for polite society. She wanted to insist that for once he listen to other people's point of view. He was a bulldozer, crushing all debate.

But as she calmed down she admitted to herself that she'd never confront him. A childhood spent learning obedience to authority and years of Donald's forceful personality meant she would, as always, swallow her opinions, or acquiesce.

As soon as they were in the Chorlton kitchen she filled the kettle and set it to boil on the Aga with an unwonted bang. She went into the larder for the milk, and when she came back David and Donald were hard at it. She poured the boiling water into the teapot, gave it a stir, and set the teacups the right way up in the saucers.

'Father, you must at least discuss it,' David was saying. 'George is not his father but he's not going to give up his family's farms lightly. And we don't know that we still have any rights to the land. There's confusion all over the country as to wartime dispossessions.'

'There's no confusion whatsoever. The Maxwell-Calders are no longer the owners. The land was passed to the Air Ministry in 1939. But even if Frampton owned the freeholds, the tenants were evicted because they were incompetent. We now hold those tenancies. Three thousand farms were taken away from farmers during the war. Do you think they've all got them back?' Donald's voice had risen, but now, to Maud's relief, he dropped it to a more normal pitch. He sounded almost cheerful as he went on. 'All we have to do is go on farming efficiently. Even if Frampton wins the legal case we cannot be kicked off until after the crop is cut.' He smiled, pleased with himself. 'And then we just go back and plant it up again.'

His triumphant tone was too much for Maud. 'But Donald, we can't do that!' she exclaimed. 'That would be disgraceful!'

'Even if that were the case,' said Jill, 'it won't be once rationing stops, surely? It must be a wartime measure, like the dispossession orders. Just because the War Ag could throw bad farmers off the land in the war it can't mean the new tenants will have the land forever. That would be very unfair.'

'Well, David,' said Donald, 'I see you have the women on your side, all sentiment and no sense. But this is business, men's business. And I tell you, I am not handing back those farms to Frampton.'

'But Dad, why can't we discuss alternatives to fighting with our neighbours? We could farm the Barrows as we do the potato fields in the park, under contract, so George pays us a fee and keeps any profit left over. George doesn't want to farm it anyway, does he, Grace?'

'No, he doesn't. If he can prove that the Air Ministry never used the land for the aerodrome, he thinks they will have to give it back. But anyway he's not going to farm it himself. He's a businessman, with City interests. He'll put it under contract or get tenant farmers back in, like before. Only better ones, he says.'

'And what better ones will he get than us? Answer me that!' Donald's face was reddening fast.

Grace forced herself to look directly at her father-in-law. Steadily she said, 'Ones that pay him a fair rent, I should think.'

'You know nothing about it, Grace. But I don't suppose I've any right to expect family loyalty from you, have I? Not now you're setting your cap at the heir to Frampton.'

Maud watched in admiration as Grace, usually so mild, lifted her head, blue eyes challenging. 'That is so unfair. And sadly typical of you, Donald. I'm just glad – I expect we all are – that David isn't like his father.' She swallowed, her eyes wide as though astonished at herself. 'George is not a fool, Donald, and he won't let Chorlton go on taking all the profits unchallenged.'

'Well, he can challenge all he likes. He won't cut any ice with me. Or in court.' Donald picked up his pipe and tobacco and left the kitchen.

Maud cleared the table. No one had had any tea.

CHAPTER TWENTY-THREE

Maud hadn't told a soul that she was making a wedding cake for Laura and Giovanni, nor that she was knitting her grandchild-to-be a matinee jacket. It would just lead to harsh words from Donald.

She thought of that time she'd been making a fruit cake when everything was on the ration, when Laura had dropped the eggs and she'd lost her temper and slapped her daughter's face. Then afterwards they'd both been so sorry and laughed about her scooping up the smashed eggs from the floor. She squeezed her eyes shut against a pang of pure longing.

Oh God, poor Laura, why can't she be home at Chorlton right now? Helping to make her own wedding cake. Making preparations for her wedding in the village church. Why isn't Donald giving his daughter away, like any proud father? Why couldn't they welcome Giovanni into the family?

I mustn't brood, she thought, I'll only end up crying again. She got the scales down from the shelf, set the 2lb and 1lb weights on one side and shook sultanas, raisins, stoned prunes, dried figs and apricots from jars or packets into the bowl on the other side. She'd long since stopped worrying about getting the exact measurements for all the different fruits right – you used what you had or could get hold of. And today she had just about everything, if not in the right quantities. As long as they added up to roughly three pounds, the fact that apricots were replacing currants didn't matter.

She tipped the dried fruit into a big bowl, one that used to be a washbasin on her dressing table in the days before they had running water and a bathroom upstairs, and added a handful of mixed candied peel. She fished the sticky glacé cherries out of the jar with a spoon and cut each one in half on the board, then added them, with their syrup, to the fruit.

Good old Brown, she thought, he's been quietly hoarding dried fruit for me ever since I told him Laura was getting married. He's always had a soft spot for the girl, ever since she was a toddler.

Maud had just added orange juice, brandy and beer to the fruit and was setting it to soak overnight in the larder, when she heard Donald behind her. She could not control a guilty start.

'Oh Maud, there you are. I've been looking for you.'

Maud recovered quickly and turned to face him. 'Hullo, Donald darling. What did you want?'

Donald peered round her shoulder. 'Something smells delicious. What is it?'

Maud made to walk out of the larder. 'Oh, it's a cake. I put some beer into it.'

'And some brandy by the smell of it,' said Donald. 'What's the special occasion?'

I'm not going to lie, thought Maud. Why should I?

'It's for Laura's wedding.'

She looked at him and he stared back at her. 'What are you doing, Maud?' His voice was cold as ice.

'I'm making a cake for our daughter's wedding, Donald.'

There was a pause. Maud remained rigid.

'So that chap still hasn't married her?' said Donald. 'Even though the stupid girl is having his baby. If it is his baby, that is. She must be the size of a house by now.'

Maud felt anger flooding through her, extinguishing her nervousness. How could he speak so crudely, so unfeelingly, about Laura?

'What is the matter with you, Donald?' she demanded, her voice loud and accusing, 'Why are you so bitter and horrible about Laura? Yes, she got pregnant by the man she loves. What is so utterly terrible about that? Have you no charity, no sympathy, no forgiveness, no love whatever for your daughter? Don't you want to see her married? Don't you want to give them your blessing? Wish them happiness?'

He did not answer at once and she could feel her fury threatening to turn to tears.

'I have nothing to say to either of them,' he said.

'You are making it very hard indeed for me to be loyal to you, Donald,' she said, and walked past him and out of the kitchen door. She would not weep in front of him.

Maud walked up through Gypsy Wood, sobbing at first but soon recovering and starting to consider her stance. She veered from the attraction of total defiance – she would go to Laura's wedding, get a room in London and stay until the baby came – and the half-measure of making the cake and the clothes, but not going so far as openly defying her husband and going to the wedding.

When she got back to the house, it was teatime and she took a cup of tea and a slice of malt loaf into Donald's study.

'Donald, it's obvious we are not going to agree about Laura, so I suggest we avoid the subject after this conversation. If you flatly refuse to go to the wedding, I would like you to agree to my going, and staying in London until Laura has her baby.'

Donald was making no effort to say anything. He just looked at her, expressionless. Maud took a breath and went on, 'But if you're adamant that I can't go either, then I'll reluctantly obey. But I will send the cake, and some baby things I am making, with David and Jill. Luckily for them, they do not owe you any obedience, any more than Grace or Sophie do. They will all be there.'

'And what if I forbid you to send the cake or the rest of your bounty?'

'I will not obey you in that. Domestic matters are my department.'

CHAPTER TWENTY-FOUR

Laura knew that as a bride-to-be she could get extra clothes coupons for her wedding dress, but feeling rather virtuous, she joined the hundreds of other 1947 brides who donated theirs to Princess Elizabeth. Anyway, she had no intention of spending a lot of money on something she'd probably never wear again. Also, she was pregnant and getting larger by the day. They were not getting married until December when Giovanni's only close relative, his sister Carlotta, could come over from Abruzzo and when Giovanni would be less busy with his revolution of the café menu and setting up new sandwich stalls.

When the royal wedding took place and the papers carried photographs of the future queen in a flowing silk wedding gown embroidered with tiny crystals and 10,000 seed pearls and with a 13-foot tulle train, Laura felt a thrill of solidarity with the young bride and pride in her small contribution.

But the Princess's dress, which after years of wartime and post-war austerity seemed so luxurious and romantic, did make Laura a little dreamy-eyed. Maybe she *should* have enjoyed the once-in-a-lifetime chance to wear a full-length white confection.

Grace was her confidante in these matters. She was now

seeing more of George, and would often come to London to partner him to some dinner or other, or to go to the theatre, and she would take the opportunity to meet Laura. One day, sitting in the lounge of the Charing Cross Hotel, they discussed the matter of Laura's wedding dress.

'It's too late now for a proper wedding dress,' said Laura. 'I gave the princess my extra coupons and I'm not sorry about that. Anyway, I couldn't afford anything remotely like her dress, so it will have to be a suit or a dress and jacket. We've enough coupons for that.'

Grace agreed to go shopping with her and in the following weeks they spent many hours at it, trying to reconcile the competing desire for something special, later usefulness, and the need to hide her baby bulk on the day. But nothing would do. The suits Laura liked were too expensive, and fabric was still scarce.

It was George who came to the rescue. Grace had been talking to him about Laura's wistfulness and her desire for a proper wedding dress, and her reluctant determination to be sensible.

'Mama has masses of cloth,' he said. 'She calls it her ragbag but there are chests full of stuff – bolts of silk they brought back from the Far East, and old curtains, and God knows what. She'll never miss a few yards.'

'But she'd never help Laura!'

'She needn't know. I will enlist the aid of the redoubtable Mrs Broome.'

Grace agreed, her only stipulation being that he wasn't to help himself to any new fabric – no cutting into Chinese silk or embroidered Indian cotton.

The following weekend George arrived at Chorlton with an enormous brown paper parcel, tied up with string. He left it on the passenger seat of his Daimler while he had a cup of tea in the kitchen with Maud and Grace and then, when Maud went out to tend to her pigs, he brought in the parcel and they opened it up carefully on the kitchen table. There was a single ivory silk bedroom curtain with a fine damask stripe.

'There are another three where that came from, but Mrs Broome thought one would be enough. There's six yards of material in this one, she says. But, obviously, there's more if you need it.'

The lining had gone a dirty brown at the edges, which George pointed out, but Grace said, 'No, it's perfect. We wouldn't use the lining anyway. The silk is wonderful, so lustrous and beautiful.'

'And,' he said, pulling a length of cream tulle with a wide lace border from under the folded curtain, 'there's this, too. Mrs Broome thought it might make a collar or something.'

'Or a veil!' exclaimed Grace. 'It's lovely. You're a genius, Lord Frampton!' She leant to give his cheek a quick kiss, and he pulled her to him, looking into her face. She closed her eyes in anticipation of a proper kiss, but the thud of Jane descending the stairs two at a time put paid to that.

'Oh good, it's George. Can we go for a ride, Mummy?'

'Say good morning to George, Jane.'

'Good morning, George.'

'Good morning, Jane, and yes, why not? Bike or pony?'

'Pony. I want to show you my new jumps.'

'You go and tack up Snowdrop, darling, and we'll come to the stable yard.'

'OK.' She was already out of the door.

'She didn't even look at this!' said George, indicating the fabric on the table.

'Just as well. She's too young to be trusted with a secret.'

While Grace re-wrapped the curtains in their paper and re-knotted the string, George said, 'Mrs Broome told me that lace curtain had once been in the downstairs loo – to stop the servants seeing in from the back yard, but perhaps better not tell Laura that.'

When George had gone, Grace sat down to write a postcard for mailing to the Billingsgate flat.

George has a surprise for you and wants to come with me on Wednesday. Can we meet at your flat rather than at the Charing Cross? Say at six to give you time to get home? If not you can leave a message at George's office CITY 4769. With love, G

When George and Grace arrived at the flat, Grace insisted Laura give George a tour. George had never been there and Grace, who had, many times, had noticed at once that Laura had made an effort: everything was clean and tidy, there was a bunch of Michaelmas daisies on the mantelpiece, the table was set for tea and the fire was lit.

'It's hardly what you're used to, George,' said Laura, smiling, 'but I can't tell you how glad we were to find it. And we can only afford it because it's in the middle of a bomb site, so it's cheap.'

'But it's really nice. And very cosy,' said George. 'Oh, and I recognise that painter!' he said, pointing to the picture over the mantelpiece. It was a watercolour of pigs rooting around a muddy paddock. He put his arm round Grace's shoulders and gave her a little shake. 'Don't I, darling?'

'You do. That's very observant of you,' she said, looking pleased.

'Yes, isn't it good?' said Laura. 'Grace gave it to me a few weeks ago.' She smiled at Grace. 'I remember that pig day so well. I was about fifteen and we used to kill a porker every year and everyone helped. It was always hard work, but such fun. Grace sat outside in the freezing weather, drawing the pigs.'

'I thought Laura needed something to remind her of Chorlton,' said Grace. 'The good memories, I mean. And also something to put on that wall. So I looked through my sketches and found the ones of the pigs, and used them to work up a proper painting.'

Laura told George how Giovanni had painted all the walls cream to cover the murky wallpaper, and how they'd had the chimney rebuilt once the landlord got his war damage compensation, so now they could have a proper fire.

'And where did you get the jolly rug?' asked George, pointing to the multi-coloured stripey hearthrug.

'Laura made that,' said Grace, turning to Laura, 'didn't you?'

'Yes,' replied Laura, 'but it's hardly difficult. I bought the scraps of material in a big bundle from the market. My mother can do chickens and cats and patterns but I'm not up to that. Stripes are all I can manage.'

'And what about this room?' asked George, looking into the empty box room, very dark on account of the ivy outside which had grown all over the window. The room was empty except for a battered suitcase and a pile of cookbooks on the floor.

'That, we hope, will be the nursery,' said Laura. 'Another work-in-progress. Or rather, work-not-started.'

'Well, you've got a few months to go,' said Grace. 'Lots of time.'

They went into the garden to look at Giovanni's efforts at clearance.

'More work-in-progress,' said Laura, looking at the heap of rubble which might one day be a rockery, and the piles of brush-wood awaiting burning. 'Giovanni is so energetic and ambitious. He forgets that he's already doing fifteen-hour days at work.'

When Laura undid the parcel of material she was beside her-self with excitement. She stroked the silk as though it were a kitten. 'Oh George,' she said, 'you are just wonderful. But does your mother know? She probably thinks I'm the devil incarnate. She wouldn't want . . .'

'Of course not. Why worry her? Anyway,' he said, grinning, 'the contents of the ragbag are technically mine. If I can't give a friend a couple of second-hand curtains, what's the point of being an Earl?'

When Laura was seven months pregnant and her back had begun to hurt too much to work a full day at the Corner House, Mr Rupert agreed she could go on half-time, which meant she had time to sew. She bought a Simplicity pattern and Grace helped her cut out the fabric pieces for the dress. The only table they had was not big enough to lay out the silk damask and pin the tissue paper pieces to it, so they did it on the carefully-swept floor. This was awkward for pregnant Laura, who found getting down and up again a struggle, so Grace did most of the pinning and cutting. Laura, taught by her mother, was a confident seam-stress and she did the sewing, making the simple scoop-necked dress with a voluminous skirt that she could change later. She split the tulle curtain in half and joined the lengths with the lace border at the ends to make a stole-cum-veil. She didn't have a machine, but she rather enjoyed the thought that the whole dress would be made by her, by hand.

Laura was nervous about Carlotta's arrival. Giovanni adored his sister. She was coming from Abruzzo to see her little brother married and Laura feared her disapproval. What if she thinks, since I'm pregnant again, that I'm repeatedly trying to trap Giovanni into marriage?

They waited for her in the arrivals hall and as soon as she saw Carlotta, Laura warmed to her. Her round face lit up at the sight of her brother and she hurried to them, hugging and kissing Giovanni and then hugging Laura.

'You are the lovely Laura,' she said, stepping back to look her up and down. 'Giovanni was right. You are *bella, bella.*' She put her hand on Laura's stomach. 'And how is the little *bambino*? It is well, I hope, doing somersaults, playing football in there? Huh?'

They all laughed and Laura wondered why she'd worried. Giovanni had said she was lovely. She should have believed him.

Mel and Joe had offered to put Carlotta up in their house across the river in Southwark and Carlotta only had a fifteen-minute walk to get to the flat or the café. She was jolly and practical, helping Laura sew and filling the little flat with the smell of fresh garlic. She'd smuggled a clutch of bulbs through customs, wrapped in her bloomers. Laughing, she'd explained that English customs officers would not dare investigate her underwear.

Laura was struck by Carlotta's English. 'It's better than yours and you've lived in England for years,' she told Giovanni.

'It's good, isn't it? She says it's because she listens to the BBC. But she's always been the bright one, good at school. Her first job was private teacher for English family in Rome. And then she studied English at university. She would love to live in England, I think.'

'Why doesn't she?'

'She has those two boys. She would need a good job if she brought them with her. Teenage boys cost a lot.'

Laura was glad of Carlotta's company, not just because she was helpful, but because it went a good way towards alleviating the longing for her mother. Carlotta was only seven years older than her, but she seemed wise, and concerned, and very loving.

Carlotta also took Giovanni shopping for a new suit, his only one being shapeless and worn. 'It will be my wedding present for you, *mio fratellino,*' she said, 'and I will buy a nice heavy pot for Laura to make *bollito,* and a big pan for *risotto.* Your wife would be a good cook if she had better equipment, Giovanni.'

On the Saturday of the wedding, Carlotta helped Laura put her hair up, and insisted on re-ironing the wedding dress. She sent Giovanni out early to buy flowers for Laura to carry, with strict instructions.

'They must smell wonderful, and they should be ivory or yellow and white, with some greenery, too. Not red, and not orange or purple. *Hai capito?* Tell the salesman it is for your bride and he will take trouble in tying them in a pretty bunch. And maybe give you a buttonhole for free. Which should be white.'

When they were ready, Carlotta insisted they get a cab.

'You cannot walk through the streets on the way to your wedding. Afterwards, it is acceptable. But before, no.' So Giovanni went out again and hailed a cab.

They were married in the Cannon Street register office and

David was there to give her away. Jill, Grace and George came, too, and so did Sophie. But not Laura's parents.

Laura thought Giovanni looked wonderful; clean-shaven, hair cut, and in his new suit, complete with buttonhole. He held her arm and steadied her as she puffed and panted up the three flights of stone steps to the registry, followed by the others. When they got to the top, he did not let her go and Laura, grateful, squeezed his arm and held on.

I wonder how many brides are this pregnant on their wedding day, thought Laura. They were greeted at the top landing by a smiling woman. 'I'm the assistant to the registrar,' she said, 'and, don't worry, I'm a midwife too.'

They all laughed, and that set the spirit of the day. Laura and Giovanni made their vows with confidence, and when the registrar pronounced them man and wife, everyone clapped, which, thought Laura, was nice and would never have happened in a church. After the ceremony, they walked down to the Billingsgate café, excited and happy.

Laura's finery was hidden by a long warm cloak lent to her by Grace, and she hugged it round her neck.

'Are you happy, *cara mia*?' said Giovanni, his arm around her.

'Of course I am.' She smiled up at him, her face alive. 'And you, my darling, are you happy?'

'It is the best thing that has ever happened to me. Yes, I am happy.'

The road was steep and a little slippery, and Giovanni gave his free arm to Jill, walking beside him. 'And what have you there, Jill?' he said, indicating the square box she was carrying. 'I hope it is a wedding present? Maybe a crown of jewels for my princess?'

Jill laughed. 'No, and it's not a treasure chest of gold either. Or a magic lamp.'

Laura said, 'So go on, Jill, what is it?'

'It's a secret. Wait and see.'

They had the café to themselves. On Saturdays, the City was deserted and so they closed when the fish market was over. Joe, Mel and Mikey were waiting for them. Mikey had pushed three tables together to make one long one, and covered it with two of Mel's white sheets, and she'd decorated it with trailing ivy from her garden and white paper flowers. On it were glasses, three bottles of Asti Spumante, a gift from Carlotta, and tea things. Carlotta had made little almond pastries and they were set out on a fancy silver epergne, borrowed from the Maxwell-Calder Eaton Square house.

There was just one moment when Laura felt the ache of sadness: Jill opened the mystery box and lifted out a beautifully iced cake which she set down in the middle of the table. 'Mum made it,' said David. 'I think the poor woman stirred more tears into that wedding cake than brandy. She so wanted to come.'

Laura thought of her mother, alone in her kitchen, longing for her daughter as Laura still longed for her lost first baby. She bit her bottom lip to stop it trembling, and to stop her thoughts heading in that direction. She met her husband's eye and he bent to whisper in her ear, 'Don't be sad, darling. Your mum is reconciled to us, and believe me, one day your dad will be, too.'

CHAPTER TWENTY-FIVE

Grace was enjoying her life. True, the Countess Geraldine patently disapproved of her, but George loved her, and that was what mattered. They would be married in the spring, Countess or no Countess. And George was so good to Jane, treating her as his own daughter.

One day when she'd agreed to go to the opera with him and another couple, leaving Jane in Maud's care, he'd suggested she stay in the house in Eaton Square rather than make the expensive taxi ride to her parents' house in Hampstead. 'We'll be very late,' he said. 'We're having dinner afterwards at the Café Royal, and your poor mother and father would have to stay up till at least one in the morning.'

So Grace reluctantly agreed. She'd always felt unwelcome in the Maxwell-Calder houses, and that had not changed even though she and George were now officially engaged. To add to her disquiet, tonight the Countess would be in residence.

George was to meet her at the house on his return from the City, so Grace arrived alone. The butler opened the door but did not smile.

'Her Ladyship is not in,' he said. 'I'm to tell you that she will return for tea at five o'clock.' He took her coat politely enough, but then held it away from his body as he carried it out, as if it smelt bad. He returned to usher her into the library where the fire wasn't laid. He did not offer her tea and no one showed her to her bedroom.

Grace sat there for perhaps ten minutes, and then decided meek acceptance was not the way to win these people over.

She stood up and looked around for a bell. There was an old-fashioned silk bell-pull on a chain to one side of the empty fireplace and she gave it a sharp yank. She could hear the distant sound of a bell ringing.

She stood looking out of the window onto the square until the butler returned.

'You rang?' There was an infinitesimal pause until he added, 'Madam.'

Grace turned to face him. 'Yes, I would like to be shown to my room,' she said, her voice firm and steady, 'and I would be grateful if you would ask for a tray of tea to be sent up. I don't think I can wait until five o'clock.'

He sighed. 'Certainly, madam.'

Presently the housekeeper arrived to show her to her room.

It was spacious and grand in an old-fashioned way but again there was no fire laid in the grate. 'Do you have an electric fire?' Grace asked her. 'I don't want to trouble anyone for a proper fire, but it is chilly in here.'

Both tea and electric fire were forthcoming and Grace felt a little glow of satisfaction.

Later that evening, for a few moments while they waited for their car to come round, George and Grace were alone.

'I've only been here a few times, to dinner twice, I think,

and once for tea – but every time I can feel the servants' disapproval.'

'Nonsense, darling. No one could disapprove of you.'

'But they do. And probably rightly.' She forced a smile and kept her voice light-hearted. 'They know I'm not grand enough for the Earl of Frampton. You are supposed to marry a rich young virgin, not a penniless widow.'

'Well, if there is anything in it, I expect they take their cue from my mother, and winning her round will take time, I'm afraid.'

'Oh George, I do try to avoid confrontation with her.' Perhaps he thinks I exaggerate, she thought. She looked earnestly into his eyes. 'But she seems so bent on putting me down.'

'Don't worry about it, darling,' George said, pulling her to him and kissing her on the forehead. 'Mama will get your measure in the end. And servants are more snobbish than the grandest nobs. They will come round, you'll see. When you are the Countess of Frampton, they will forget all their prejudices and they'll love you. And so will my mama. Of course they will.'

'Well, I hope so. But in the meantime, if it's too late to go to my parents', in future I'll stay with Laura and Giovanni. You can sleep in your grand house and I will be very happy on the Angelottis' sofa.'

Grace's friendship with Laura was another factor in her happiness. When Hugh had been alive, Laura was just the teenage little sister, bright, enthusiastic about her pony and quaintly knowledgeable about her collection of antique china. And when Grace and Jane had come to live with the rest of the family, Laura had become like a younger sister, albeit one who was much better than her at practical things – milking, mucking out, even driving the tractor.

Now Grace felt more than a big sister's dutiful love of a younger sibling. She felt real affection and admiration for Laura. Laura didn't go on about it, but Grace knew how much she missed her mother and brother. She even misses Donald, thought Grace. He used to be such an indulgent and adoring father.

Laura did occasionally complain of missing Sophie, who worked so hard in Dr Drummond's medical practice that she seldom came to London. 'The thing is,' Laura had said, 'I think every woman needs a woman friend. And Sophie used to be mine.'

'Maybe I can be her understudy?' said Grace.

'Oh Grace, I'd love that. But who is your great friend and confidante? Jill?'

'No. If anyone, it's your mother. But you'll do very nicely, too.'

In late December, Grace had a surprise for Laura. She and Maud packed up all Jane's old baby things and hired a van to take them to London. The driver and his mate carried everything into the flat. There was a pram, a cradle, a nursing chair, a layette consisting of a chest of drawers and a baby's bathtub and big china ewer to go on top, and two suitcases: one full of baby clothes, one of towelling and muslin nappies and soft toys.

Laura protested. 'Grace, you cannot give me all this! What if you and George have a child?'

'Well, then you can give it all back again. There's a cot, too, for when the baby is too big for the cradle. But since Jane and I came to live at the big house, all this has been under dust sheets in the Chorlton attic, doing no good to anyone. It's thanks to your mother that it's not been ruined by mice and moths. She's religious about mothballs.'

'But it all looks brand new. The lining of the cradle, the mattress, everything.'

'That's Maud again. She's been secretly re-lining the cradle and knitting baby clothes. Look.' She opened the suitcase and on the top were a tiny white matinee jacket and a slightly bigger pale yellow one and two pairs of booties.

Laura held the clothes to her face, the wool as soft as swans' down. She felt tears pricking her eyes. 'But how does she hide it from Daddy?'

'He's often in London at his club, and he doesn't emerge much from his study when he's at home, so she's pretty safe. Mind you, I think he might know but he says nothing.'

Laura could not resist lowering her very pregnant self slowly into the nursing chair that Grace had brought. It was low and horseshoe-shaped, with a padded back that hugged her aching back and stuffed arms that curved round to support her elbows while holding a nursing child.

'Oh,' she said. 'This is the most comfortable chair in the world!'

'I know. I used to feed Jane in it. Even if it was the middle of the night, I loved it. There's something so tender and intimate about breastfeeding a baby with no one around, in the silence of the night, with just the baby snuffling and sucking away.'

'Oh, Grace, you must long to have another baby, don't you?'

'No, oddly, I don't. I'm so happy at the prospect of marrying George, that's enough for now. And of course, I worry about Jane. I thought she'd be jealous of George but she loves him. I don't want to distress her with too much change.'

All day Grace helped Laura to turn the little box room into a nursery. There wasn't much space so the chair had to go into the sitting room. The baby bath and ewer went onto the chest of drawers with a thick towel underneath to catch the splashes. While Grace lined the drawers with paper and filled them with the nappies and baby clothes, Laura made up the cradle. It was a big oval basket, with a deep mattress and a padded cotton lining with tiny embroidered rose sprigs all over it that fitted round the sides. There was a lacy skirt that went round the outside of the basket and a frilly cover for the wicker hood. Her mother was an angel. She must have worked hours every day on these things.

When they'd finished Grace looked around the room. 'All it needs is a baby now.' She patted Laura's stomach. 'Come on, baby, get a move on.'

CHAPTER TWENTY-SIX

1948, January

'We could afford a hospital birth, *cara*, if you would prefer it,' said Giovanni, but Laura shook her head.

'You're so good, darling, but no, I'd rather have it at home. My memories of hospital are not good, and I love this place. Sophie has promised to come up to deliver the baby. She did obstetrics at the Radcliffe Infirmary, remember? And you'll be here. So it will be friendly and everyone will be on my side. I'm almost looking forward to it.'

'But how can we be sure Sophie will get here on time? Even if she jumps onto the first train, she might not make it.'

'David has promised to drive her up, and anyway, the hospital will provide a midwife if we want one. Grace will be here, too. I shall be surrounded by friendly faces.'

In the event the contractions started at 6am and were merely uncomfortable for two hours. Then they became more frequent and painful, and Giovanni lay beside her, holding her hand tightly as the pain gripped her and releasing it as Laura relaxed.

Between contractions Laura steered her mind away from that

other labour. She worried that if she thought about it she'd panic.

She shut her eyes and tried to relax, to let her mind go blank. Or at least to think positively. She was to have a new baby now, and she was not going to give it away. It would be a new start, and maybe, just maybe, she'd begin to forget her firstborn.

At nine-fifteen Sophie walked through the door, and Laura felt a wash of pleasure and relief. Trying to pretend to Giovanni that she had no anxieties was a strain, but it would upset him if she talked of that other time. They never talked of it.

Now Sophie would be in charge. Giovanni stood up and Sophie and Laura hugged each other until Laura said, 'Oh, let go, Sophie, here comes another one.' Sophie stood back and watched Laura attentively as the pain came and went.

'Did David drive you up?' asked Giovanni. 'Is he coming in?'

'He did – it only took a little over two hours. The snow isn't settling. And no, he's not coming in. I told him this was women's work and he'd only be in the way. He's driving straight home.'

Laura started to say something about David getting back before the bad weather settled in, but then another contraction drove David out of her mind.

When Giovanni went out to get them all a cup of tea, Sophie examined Laura and declared that all was exactly as it should be.

'Do you know how long your labour was last time?' she asked.

'It seemed forever, but I have no idea. All I can remember is the misery.'

'Well, this time I think it might be nice and quick and with no misery.'

Without the unhappiness surrounding her son's birth, the pain was bearable. In the intervals between contractions Laura rested, occasionally thinking how different this was from last time. She wasn't frightened, and she was being looked after by Sophie. Grace and Giovanni were just outside, all concerned and loving. If only her mother was here looking after that first baby and her father walking Giovanni round the block, it would be perfect.

By late in the evening Laura was very tired, but with the help of gas and air she managed not to cry out. She wanted to, but she was worried about Giovanni in the next-door room. If she screamed, he'd think she was dying.

'Is Giovanni all right?' she asked Sophie, not for the first time.

'You must stop worrying about Giovanni,' said Sophie, mopping Laura's head with a cold wet flannel. 'Grace has been trying to distract him. But I am going to send him out to the pub, so you can concentrate on the job in hand. Will you be all right for a minute?'

When she got back, bringing Grace with her, Laura asked again, 'Is he all right?'

Grace kissed Laura's sweaty forehead. 'He's refused tea, cake, beer, a game of cards. He can't concentrate on the wireless or a conversation. I think he was glad to go to the pub. I said I'd go and tell him when to reappear.'

The knowledge that Giovanni was not next door relaxed Laura a little. She allowed herself to groan and moan, and when the baby finally emerged to give one long scream.

When Giovanni came into the bedroom, his baby daughter was swaddled and already at his wife's breast. He looked from mother to baby in wonder, and suddenly tears were running down his face.

'Oh God, Laura, I have never felt like this in my life.' He dried his cheeks on the bed sheet then buried his face in Laura's neck. He looked up again. 'Sorry, darling, I did not know, how beautiful, how . . . I didn't know I could feel like this.'

He sat on the bed and Laura handed him the baby. He held her in the crook of one arm and stroked her head with his free hand.

'You know, Laura, anyone who does anything, hurts – how you say? – a single hair of our daughter's head, I kill him.'

'Me too. But nothing is going to hurt her. Ever.'

CHAPTER TWENTY-SEVEN

Four months after Angelica's birth, Grace and George were married in the family chapel at Frampton. They had insisted on Giovanni and Laura being there. Indeed, Grace wanted Laura to be her maid of honour.

'I would *so* love to do that, but I can't. Angelica might yell her head off in church and I'd need to shush her.'

'Giovanni can do that. He's wonderful at it,' protested Grace.

'It's not just that. Think of your new mother-in-law. Bad enough that her son is marrying a nobody with Bohemian tendencies, but that she be attended by a disgraced woman married to an ex-prisoner of war . . . Imagine!'

'To be honest, Laura, I don't care a lot what she thinks.'

'And on top of all that relations between our families is fraught enough already. My parents will be there for your sake. But who knows how Daddy will behave to me?'

'I'm sure he'd be polite. He won't want a scene, surely?'

'He'll not *want* one, but that doesn't mean he won't make one. He's quite likely to upset me and you don't want a maid of honour in floods of tears, with a bawling baby, do you?'

So Grace asked Jill, Sophie and two of her cousins to be her bridesmaids, and Laura tried not to mind. Grace had become so close she really thought she *should* be in that best friend's role.

The chapel at Frampton was only just large enough to contain the two households and Grace's family and her parents were already in the front pew when Laura and Giovanni arrived. They were directed to the pew behind the Olivers, and Laura, her heart thudding, steeled herself against a snub from her father. He looked stolidly forward but her mother turned round and briefly held her daughter's hand, looking intently into her face. Laura pulled down Angelica's shawl so Maud could see her four-month-old granddaughter's face. But they did not speak.

Afterwards, they walked out into the churchyard. The sun was shining with the clarity of early summer and the church bells were pealing loudly and merrily. Laura suddenly wanted everything to be all right, to be normal. She took Giovanni's arm.

'Come on, let's brave the lion.'

'Are you sure, my darling?' he said, concerned. 'I don't want you to get hurt.'

'I'm hurt already. Come on.' She looked up at him, forcing a smile.

With Angelica, now awake, in her arms, she approached her parents. Giovanni followed her rather more hesitantly.

'Hullo, Daddy.' Donald did not react and Laura persevered. 'This is your granddaughter. She's called Angelica.'

Her father looked at her, refusing to drop his gaze to the baby. His face was rigid but not hostile, she thought.

'I know,' he said stiffly.

'Good afternoon, Mrs Oliver,' said Giovanni, putting out a hand. Her mother took it, smiling nervously, then clasped it tightly with both hands and shook it.

Giovanni turned to Donald. 'Good afternoon, sir.'

Donald ignored the outstretched hand. He gave a brief nod, and turned away.

Laura felt her anger rising, but then she looked at her mother, who had not followed her husband. Her eyes beginning to fill with tears, Maud took her granddaughter from Laura, and clasped her close, her mouth against Angelica's downy head.

'I'm so sorry, my darling,' she said. Laura nodded, but did not trust herself to speak.

They did not stay for the wedding tea, but caught the 5pm train back to London. There was no one in the compartment so Laura could breastfeed the baby without having to hide away in the cramped lavatory at the end of the carriage.

She leant against Giovanni's shoulder with the baby at her breast. The compartment was pleasantly fuggy. The combination of the warmth of the carriage, the clickety-clack of the train and the setting sun in her eyes was sending her to sleep. I feel so comfy and so safe, she thought. And Mummy no longer feels estranged. Maybe Giovanni is right, one day Daddy will come round.

A few weeks after the wedding, George and Grace were eating with Giovanni and Laura in the Billingsgate café. Baby Angelica was sleeping in her basket on the floor.

Giovanni noticed George looking from table to table, all of them full of fish porters and traders.

'Who are you looking for?' he asked, peering through the fog of cigarette smoke.

'No one. I'm checking how many people are eating your famous sandwich.'

'There is an easier way,' said Giovanni, standing up. He walked to the counter and asked Mikey to pass him the spike on which the order slips were impaled. He pulled them off and returned the empty spike. 'Thanks, Mikey, I'll give them back in a minute.'

They checked the orders. 'Right. Well, it's 2pm and of two hundred and twenty orders, including takeaways, a hundred and seventy three of them are for deep-fried sandwiches. And that does not include the St Paul's stall, which will do another ninety or hundred, all takeaway. And any more we do today.'

George, his cigarette in his left hand, was scribbling in a small, leather-bound notebook.

'And you get a penny for every one sold, which means about a pound for the day providing you sell two hundred and forty sandwiches?'

'Which just about doubles my salary.'

'Still doesn't sound enough, though, does it?'

'Goodness, George,' said Grace. 'Your mother would be appalled! Talking about money in front of the ladies! Whatever is the world coming to!'

'Poor Lady Geraldine,' said Laura. 'The war swept away a lot of her world. But women are allowed to be interested in business now. I certainly am.'

'And Jill knows more about the business end of the farms than David, I think,' said Grace. 'She's very talented, so organised and quick with figures. And Sophie is a doctor. I'm the only one who lets the side down. I can't add for toffee and I'd be hopeless at business.'

'But you're an artist, my darling,' said George. 'And when you get hold of our musty old house, it will be a proper job transforming it, I promise you. And you'll do it beautifully. As long as we can confine my mother to the Dower House and prevent her giving you lessons.'

Their orders, all deep-fried sandwiches, arrived. For a moment there was silence except for the clink of knives and forks. Giovanni waited, a little apprehensive, for their reaction and was gratified by the oohs and aahs of appreciation.

'You know, I'd love to do an upmarket version of this,' Giovanni said, 'but we'd need to be in Mayfair or Kensington.'

'Really?' asked Grace. 'Is a deep-fried sandwich ever going to be upmarket?'

'Well, it needn't be deep-fried. It could baked, like a calzone.'

'What's a calzone?' asked George.

'It's a bit like a pizza, only folded over.'

'Giovanni,' said George, 'I'm sorry to be so ignorant, but I don't know what a pizza is either.'

Giovanni laughed. 'Oh, you English, you have not lived! A pizza is a thin flat plate of bread dough, with tomato and cheese or anchovies or sausage or anything else you like on top, baked in a very hot oven so the bread is crisp round the edges and the middle is still soft. There's nothing like it.'

'So why don't you make pizza here, then?' asked George.

'I've thought about it. But we'd need a pizza oven, which would cost a fortune, and anyway there's no room.'

'Besides,' chipped in Laura, 'until rationing stops and we can get good mozzarella, olive oil and garlic there'd be no point. A deep-fried sandwich with Government Cheddar and the National Loaf is one thing – the frying is what saves it, but anything baked needs really good ingredients.'

Giovanni laughed. 'Anyway, most of the English think olive oil is something you get from the chemist to put in your ears.'

When the laughter had died down, Laura said, 'I just wish

we could afford to set up on our own.' She turned to the others. 'Giovanni has hired two Italian apprentices and they don't cost a lot. Joe and Mel, the owners, are absolutely delighted. The business is making a lot more money so they can afford to take it easy. Some days they don't come in at all. Giovanni pretty well runs the business, but he doesn't see the profits.'

George looked thoughtful. 'How old are they? The owners?'

Giovanni frowned. 'What a funny question! In their sixties perhaps. Maybe Joe is seventy. I don't know.'

'Would they sell, do you think?'

'Oh, I'm sure they would, but it would cost too much for me. They have a long lease on the building and they'd want a lot for the business. I could never afford it.'

'But I could,' said George.

Giovanni looked at him. 'Would you do that? Really?'

'I think I would. Seems like a good business to me.'

Giovanni looked from George to Grace to Laura, speechless.

'But George,' Laura exclaimed, 'why would you be so kind? You are such good friends, but that would be far beyond the call of friendship!'

'It's got nothing to do with friendship,' George replied. 'I'm much too hard-headed to invest in something out of sentiment, believe me. No, I think you're on to something here, Giovanni. The deep-fried sandwiches are a winner. You could sell them in market stalls and other cafés, don't you think?'

'Well, yes, if we had the outlets they'd sell all right.' Giovanni, excited now, leaned forward. 'I don't know exactly what the business now makes but Joe and Mel are thrilled with the turn-around which is mostly down to better cooking and the added customers from up the hill. The City folk start queuing at noon

PRUE LEITH

and don't stop till two. They love the sandwiches, and they're more profitable than fish and chips.'

'Well, let's say I'm definitely interested. I'd need to know a bit more, of course. First to see if Joe is willing to sell, how long his lease is, who owns the freehold, if the business has any debts. All the usual questions.'

Giovanni still had a lingering suspicion that George might be acting out of charity, helping them because Grace was so fond of Laura.

'But George,' he said, 'there must be many many businesses you could back. For an Earl to be investing in what you English call a "greasy spoon" is very unusual, no?'

George laughed. 'This café is not a greasy spoon, which you know very well since you turned it from one into a clean, pleasant café with good food.' His face suddenly becoming serious, George went on. 'And I like the idea of being involved in it. It's a good hands-on business, which I prefer to complicated financial schemes. I like to put money into new enterprises.'

'Tell them about the laundry business,' said Grace.

'Yes, that's a good example. I'm backing a new business which will do your laundry for you. It's an American idea, called a washeteria or Laundromat. Anyway, you take your laundry into a high-street shop and put it into a huge washing machine big enough to take the things that are so difficult to wash at home, and when it's done you put it in a dryer. Good, don't you think?'

'I'd use one of those, certainly,' said Laura.

Giovanni was impressed, too. It was a side of George he'd never suspected.

George went on. 'We're going to change the way ordinary people get their washing done. And I think a similar revolution in eating is on the way. With less time to sit down to a proper lunch, more people are eating on park benches and in the street.'

'Giovanni, stop worrying,' said Grace. 'George would not be interested just because we're friends. He's a natural businessman and Frampton would not survive if he didn't spend his time making money in other ways: things like stocks and shares and London property.'

She turned to George, her hand on his sleeve. 'But what you really like is investing your "gambling money". Isn't that what you call it? You like risky ventures, don't you?' She looked from Laura to Giovanni. 'He's really good at it. Did you know Frampton's dandelion and oak leaf wines are now sold in Fortnum's?'

'It's true,' said George. 'I do like a flutter. But I still take a lot of care looking into ventures I back. If there's a high risk of failure, there must also be the potential for making serious money. And if I've done well, it's mostly because I only invest in people I trust and admire, and in ventures I understand.'

The deal was speedily done. George bought the lease, the equipment and the business. He was now Giovanni's landlord, and he and Giovanni owned fifty per cent each of the newly named 'Calzone'.

Joe and Mel and Giovanni, along with Laura, Grace and George, went to the lawyers' offices to sign the papers. Afterwards Giovanni insisted they have a bottle of champagne and raise a toast to the new business.

'To Calzone,' said George, lifting his glass.

'And to Joe and Mel's happy retirement,' responded Giovanni. He felt a rush of affection for everyone. Joe's willingness to sell, Grace and George's faith in him, Laura's obvious happiness – these people have made me a very lucky man, he thought.

CHAPTER TWENTY-EIGHT

Several months had passed since the birth of her granddaughter but Maud still could not talk to Donald about Laura or the baby. She'd hoped that the sight of their grandchild would soften his attitude to their daughter, but it hadn't. He still refused even to talk about her, let alone talk to her. If he walked in to find Maud or David talking to Laura on the newly installed telephone in the kitchen, he would turn on his heel and leave.

Donald seemed to have transferred all parental affection to his soon-to-be-daughter-in-law, Jill. He thought the world of her, and Maud knew that his helping with the renovation costs of the Brew House was more for Jill than for David.

And no wonder, thought Maud. Jill had proved indispensable to them all. She and David now ran the farms in an almost equal partnership, with Jill in charge of administration and David out supervising the practical work. David was irritated by his father's opposition to modern farming practices, but Jill was more patient.

One day, when she and David were in the kitchen with Maud, Jill said, 'I think Donald is on to something with his objection to putting so much that's artificial on the land. I know the nitrates and phosphates work, and DDT kills all the insects, but I can't help feeling uneasy about it. Is it good for the land and the livestock long term, do you think?'

David snorted. 'Dad isn't concerned about the land, or the animals. He just objects to the cost.'

'It can't be just that. He isn't stupid. He knows the returns are worth the extra money.'

Maud shook her head. 'Poor Donald, he just hates anything new.'

'And he has to know better than me, on principle,' said David, 'which is why I tell him as little as possible.'

'Don't be sour, darling,' Maud said. 'Deep down he's so proud of what you've achieved. And he just adores you, Jill.'

'I like talking to him. And we *should* keep him abreast of everything on the farms – he does own them after all.'

'Not the Frampton ones he doesn't,' David said, 'but he's so obstinate he'll go to his grave convinced he does.'

Donald was off to his club in London with the familiar feeling of release from the atmosphere at Chorlton: the unacknowledged unhappiness of his wife and the slight but ever-present disapproval of his son. Dressed in black tie, he was easing himself into the Bentley when Jill opened the passenger door and slid into the seat.

'Hullo,' he said, pleased. 'Am I dropping you at the village or something?'

'No, but could I just come with you until we are out of the yard? I need to talk to you in private.'

'Goodness. How mysterious.' He looked sharply at her, suddenly anxious. 'Is there anything wrong, my dear?'

'No, or at least I don't think so, but I am afraid you will. Can we just drive out of here? And then I'll tell you.'

He stopped the car a few hundred yards down the lane, where the road widened at a field gate, and turned to look at her.

She put a hand on his arm. 'I'm pregnant, Donald.'

It was like a physical blow. His eyes widened and then he shut them, as if in pain.

'Not you too? Oh, Jill.'

'Yes.'

He put his fingers up to his temples, anguish in his eyes. 'But how could you? You are such a nice girl!'

'But Donald, you must know that nice girls also fall in love. And want to make love.' Even in his shock, Donald was aware of Jill's unconcerned calm. 'Oh, don't look so shocked!' she said. 'David and I have been together since the war began. We've been sleeping together for the last seven years.'

He was finding it difficult to take in. 'Good God,' he said. 'How appalling! But where? No, I don't want to know . . . But then why didn't you get married before?'

'We often talked about it. But at first there was Roger. Then I fell in love with David but wanted to tell Roger face to face. But he didn't come here for months, and then he went missing. And there was the war and no chance of a honeymoon.'

Jill sighed and Donald thought she'd finished. But then she went on. 'After the war we thought we should get a house first.' She shrugged her shoulders. 'To be honest, Donald, I don't know the answer. Except that as we didn't want children yet, we were happy as we were.'

'Fornicating out of wedlock, you mean?' He'd said it before he could stop himself. It was a harsh accusation and he regretted it.

'Really, Donald, that's so old-fashioned!' Her look was a little reproachful, but not angry. She's amused, he thought. She thinks I'm a buffoon. She continued, 'But yes, if we had decided not to sleep together, then we'd have married earlier just so we could.'

Donald shook his head. 'I can't believe you are talking like this. Of course I understand David wanting you. Men's urges are so strong. But you?'

'Oh, Donald, women have urges too. You didn't really think we never slept together, did you?'

He was silent, staring straight ahead. The truth was he'd never thought about it. Then he said, his voice now calm and resigned, 'This is a disaster, Jill. Does Maud know?'

She smiled then. 'No it's not. It's not a disaster. It's wonderful. And yes, Maud knows. I told her yesterday. And my parents, and David of course.' She paused. 'And Laura.'

'So I am the last to know?'

'Yes. I wanted to tell you myself.' She laid a hand on his arm and her voice was gentle, conciliatory. 'And ask for your blessing. It's really important to me.'

Donald remained staring through the windscreen, silent and unseeing. Jill put her hand briefly on his shoulder, somewhere between a squeeze and a pat, and slipped out of the car. 'I'll walk back.'

By the time he parked outside the club, he'd realised he had to accept that David and Jill would marry as soon as possible and her premature pregnancy would be glossed over somehow. Once he'd got over the shock of his beloved Jill having feet of clay, he felt, to his surprise, a little thrill of pleasure at the thought of a grandchild. And then he thought, with a shaft of guilt, that he already had a grandchild, that little bundle in Laura's arms. And (with another twinge of guilt) the first little bastard, wherever he or she is.

There was a difference, surely, between a son getting his girl pregnant and a daughter being so wanton. He shook his head. It was too difficult to think about.

The club secretary reached up to a pigeonhole and extracted an envelope, 'Good morning, sir. This came for you this morning.'

He sat in the armchair in his bedroom and opened the letter. It was from Maud, dated the previous day.

My dearest,

You know about Jill and David's baby now, and I know you will be distressed. I am sorry I did not tell you before, but Jill wanted to tell you herself, and frankly I was glad not to have to do it.

But I must tell you what we propose: Jill and David will be married quietly in three weeks' time in Kent. The banns will be read for the first time on Sunday.

Next we must finish the Brew House as quickly as possible so they can move in after the wedding. I just hope you agree to this, and are not planning to throw your son and daughter-in-law out like you did Laura.

When the time comes, Jill will go to her parents for the birth and stay a couple of months before coming home. That way only the most diligent gossips will be certain the baby was conceived out of wedlock.

Jill's parents agree. They are upset, of course, but philosophical and they are delighted their daughter is to marry David. Jill was quite sure you would be philosophical too, even kind. I hope she is right.

Finally, Donald, I do think we have been unfair to Laura. She was foolish, yes, but she loves Giovanni and if we are to accept Jill's behaviour, which we must, it is high time we forgave Laura hers.

This disagreement between you and me over Laura is hurting our marriage. I do beg you to relent.

Your ever-loving wife,
Maud

Donald looked up from the letter. 'Ever-loving wife'? The tone was hardly ever-loving. But then, he thought, why would she be loving? She is loyal because she sees that as her duty. But to love your husband you need to respect and admire him, and to agree with him, at least most of the time.

He felt increasingly isolated at home, and he knew it was mostly his own fault. The rest of the family seemed more on the side of Frampton than Chorlton over the land issue. David obviously regarded him as irrelevant to the business, his children could not control their sexual urges, his daughter had run away with a wop, and now his wife was making decisions without him.

But, he thought sourly, the business needed both Jill and David, so he had no option but to accept the family plan.

As to Laura, that drama was over. No point in opening old wounds with her and that husband of hers.

Maud did not really approve of Jill and David visiting each other in the night and she hoped Donald was unaware of it. Of course she understood: since the open acknowledgment that they'd been lovers for years, it would have been patently ridiculous for them to have to go on making love in the hayloft.

But they were tactful and discreet and no one mentioned the altered sleeping arrangements. They both worked all day on the farm, and then painted and tiled the Brew House with increased urgency, until late at night.

Maud was concerned that Jill was working too hard and she begged her to take it easy for her sake and the baby's. Jill just laughed.

'I've never felt so well, or so energetic, in my life,' she declared. 'I'm fine, I promise.'

'But you should be sewing your wedding dress or your trousseau, or hemming sheets for the new house, or something, shouldn't you? Not up a ladder, painting.'

Jill came over to her and kissed her cheek.

'I don't need a trousseau,' she said, releasing Maud's shoulders. 'And since I'm a fallen woman I can hardly wear bridal white. I will wear my best dress, the pale yellow – you know, with the matching little jacket. It's comfy and I feel good in it.'

She's a dear girl, thought Maud, but obstinate.

But ten days later, Maud was washing jam jars in the scullery, when she heard David thundering downstairs, two at a time, shouting for his mother.

'Mum, quick, quick, I think Jill is losing the baby.'

Maud took one look at the bloodied sheets and she knew that David was right. She hugged her son briefly, and went down to call Dr Drummond's practice in Moreton. While they waited for the doctor, Maud gave Jill and David tea, and sat with them. She was amazed at Jill's stoicism. She did not cry, but just lay on the bed, stroking David's hand.

He is more upset than she is, thought Maud. He doesn't show

it often, but he does feel deeply. After half an hour Sophie, who was now a junior doctor in the practice, appeared, bag in hand. She looked so young and Maud was reminded of the days when she and Laura charged about in the field on their ponies. Sophie looked much the same now, plump and pretty and clean. She maintained her professional demeanour while she examined Jill, who was pale and very calm. She put her hand on Jill's forehead and looked into her face.

'I'm so sorry, Jill, but you have miscarried.'

'I know.'

David asked Sophie if it was the hard physical work that had caused the miscarriage.

'I'd be surprised,' said Sophie. 'If she felt strong and well enough, she probably was. It is more likely that there was something not quite right about the baby. Nature has a way of rejecting things that aren't perfect. Many, many women miscarry in the early months. It's just that the foetus is so small we never know about it.'

'Should I get up?' asked Jill.

'No,' said Sophie firmly. 'I'm going to give you something to help you sleep. Try not to think. There's nothing you could have done, and there is no point now in agonising about it.'

Once Jill was asleep, Maud went to find David. She didn't say anything, just put her arms round him – she had to stretch up, he was so much taller than her – and held him close. Then she said, 'She's very calm, David, but she will take time to get over it. I know. I miscarried five times.'

Jill didn't appear to dwell on the loss of her baby either. Once, when Maud told her about her own miscarriages and two still-births, she said, 'It's such a bad design, don't you think? In a flock of a hundred ewes you might lose one or two lambs, but mostly they slip out with no trouble at all.'

'True, but it's much better now than in my day. Then miscarriages and stillbirths happened to almost everyone.'

She just gets on with things, thought Maud, calmly and with her usual lack of fuss.

Maud was sorry not to go to Jill and David's wedding, which happened in Kent, with her parents as witnesses and none of the Oliver relations present. David said Jill did not feel up to a big celebration but Maud suspected that David could not face another family wedding with the tensions between his father and his sister. And he would not want to have Donald there and not Laura.

Maud sometimes felt bereft. Hugh's death, six years on, was still a dark hollow, Laura had long gone, and now David and Jill were away in Kent and would move into the Brew House on their return. All her brood were gone. Even Grace and Jane were now at Frampton.

She wished relations between Frampton and Chorlton were friendlier. She felt she couldn't drop in unannounced and see her daughter-in-law and granddaughter. She really missed Grace. When Hugh had first married her, Maud had had to hide her irritation at his fey and scatter-brained bride. But over the years Grace had grown up and settled down without losing her sweetness. She had diligently made an effort and had become a real help around the farm. She'd learnt to milk the cows, cook and bake and to make a bed with tight hospital corners. She was still sometimes scatty, starching the dishcloths or planting onions instead of daffodils, but Maud now found these episodes endearing, not maddening.

Of course she had not filled the hole left by her darling Laura, but Grace was loving and intelligent and cheerful company which, increasingly, Donald was not.

Maud missed Jane, too. The Dowager Countess Geraldine had reluctantly moved into the Dower House so that Grace could join her husband in Frampton Hall, and George had now formally adopted Jane. The child was bright and could be amusing when she wasn't showing off or losing her temper. Grace had taught her to read at four, and now, at eight, she was deeply into Dickens. She had started with *A Christmas Carol*, had read *Great Expectations* and was now halfway through *Oliver Twist*. At first, when stumped by a word or expression she didn't understand, she'd trail round Frampton Hall looking for a grown-up to ask, but now she'd learnt to use a dictionary.

Grace did bring her daughter to Chorlton, usually at weekends. One day she and Maud were drinking tea at one end of the kitchen table, and Jane was doing a jigsaw at the other. Maud decided this was a good moment to ask a question that was on her mind.

'I expect George is keen for you to have a baby?'

'He's not said so. We want to go to Europe first. As soon as Jane is happy at school, then we'll go on a little tour. But after that, maybe.'

'I wouldn't leave it too late, my dear. You're over thirty and you may have another girl, or two or three, before you give him a boy.'

Jane looked up from her jigsaw. 'Mummy, you don't want another baby, do you?'

'Well, yes, darling, I do.' Grace sounded apologetic. 'Wouldn't you like a baby sister or brother?'

'No. It would only be a half-sister or half-brother, and I don't want one anyway.'

'But why ever not? A baby would be lovely, surely?'

'No it wouldn't. I hate babies.' Her voice was rising in pitch.

'Why do you say that, darling? You don't know any babies.'

'Well, I hate them, so there.' Her voice rose to a shout. 'I hate them. Hate, hate, hate them.'

Grace jumped up and hurried round the table, 'There, there, darling. Don't be upset.' She tried to fold Jane in her arms but the child leapt out of her reach.

Maud itched to tell the child to be quiet at once, apologise and leave the room. But she had long ago sworn not to get between Grace and her daughter. Instead she said, firmly but not unkindly, 'Jane, I'm afraid if your mummy and George want to have another child you are going to have to get used to the idea. And you will love him or her. I promise.'

Jane was now standing in the middle of the kitchen, her face aflame, as she shouted, 'I won't. I won't. I'll hate him.'

Grace bent over her daughter. 'Oh darling, you mustn't be jealous of a baby that doesn't exist yet.'

'Besides,' said Maud, 'when you go to school, the other girls will be very jealous if you have a baby sister or brother. Little girls love babies.'

'Well, I don't,' said Jane, now more truculent than angry. 'I don't WANT Mummy to have a baby. She can't do what I don't want. Can you, Mummy?'

Maud was afraid Grace would promise to remain childless just to placate her spoilt daughter, so she chipped in before Grace could answer.

'Of course she can. But Jane, do you have a reason for not wanting a baby?'

'Lots of reasons.'

Maud wanted to laugh: Jane was a picture of obstinacy, her feet planted slightly apart, chin up, mouth set. She pressed her. 'What reasons, darling?'

'Mabel told me I was the heiress to Frampton, like Estella in *Great Expectations*. But if Mummy has a baby boy then he can have Frampton and all the horses and cows and everything. And he can make me go and live in the forest. I won't have anything.'

It was funny and touching, but Maud could not help the thought that Jane's response was typically selfish.

Grace's reaction was very different: how could Mabel have told the child that? Worry her and make her feel insecure and overlooked? How could she?

Grace dreaded any confrontation but she had to have it out with Mabel. She found her letting down the hem of one of Jane's pinafores.

'Mabel, Jane tells me that you told her she'd lose her inheritance if I gave birth to a boy. Is that true?'

Mabel's eyes were filled with distress. 'Well, yes, ma'am. She was reading one of those books of hers and she wanted to know what an heiress was. So I used Frampton as an example. I said she was an heiress.'

'But why tell her anything more than that?'

'Oh, I'm so sorry, ma'am. I didn't mean any harm.' Mabel's old face creased with anxiety. 'All I said was that she was lucky she didn't have a brother because if she had, he'd be the heir.'

'She thinks that if she had a brother he'd banish her to the forest.'

Mabel shook her head. 'That's the trouble with books, ma'am. They give young people ideas.'

That night at dinner, George said, 'Darling, do stop worrying about it. She's only eight and she'll have forgotten about it in the morning.'

'But she was so upset,' wailed Grace, 'you'd think the sky had fallen in.'

'That's because you allow her to be. She can be quite a little drama queen if she gets a chance. Besides, sweetheart, children have to have a few disappointments in life. It's not all buttercups and daisies. And if we do have a boy, as I trust we will, the sooner she gets used to the idea, the better.'

Grace found Jane much easier to handle in the schoolroom than out of it. Grace had resisted the idea of boarding school and was teaching her daughter herself. Jane was an eager learner and Grace took her teaching seriously and was good at it. She knew that Maud worried about the lack of other children for Jane to play with. She'd argued strongly for boarding school. What Jane needed, Maud had said, was to discover that she wasn't the centre of the universe, and that no did sometimes mean no.

'But,' Grace argued, 'she's doing so well, why make a change? She's not nine yet but she's doing arithmetic for ten-year-olds and she reads and writes better than most adults.'

'But she needs more than the three R's . . .'

'And she's getting them! We do geography, biology and history and she loves them all. I've been looking at the new GCE syllabus, and I honestly think I could handle it. We could learn together. It's more interesting than the School Certificate.'

'But she needs other children, Grace,' Maud had persisted,

'and more experiences than Frampton and Chorlton can give her. When did she last leave the estate? I doubt if she's ever even been on a bus.'

Grace had to smile. 'All right, but her education is not all academic. You teach her to cook, and she could not have a better riding teacher than Donald. And in the spring she spent a day with the gamekeeper, looking after the pheasant chicks. And George will teach her to fish and shoot. . . . It's an ideal, indeed an idyllic, education.'

'Ah well,' said Maud, 'I suppose there's plenty of time. The main thing is she gets on so well with George. It reminds me of Laura's infatuation with her father at that age.'

Grace was struck by the wistful note in Maud's voice. Poor woman, she thought, she'll never get used to Laura's absence.

Grace reached out a hand and laid it on Maud's arm. The discussion about Jane's school continued and in the end a compromise was reached. It was Grace who suggested it.

'If I could just go on teaching her until she's old enough for big school, say eleven or twelve, she will be older and by then she might have got used to, and learned to love, a sibling or two.'

PART FIVE

CHAPTER TWENTY-NINE

1950, spring

Maud was picking spring flowers – scillas, crocuses, primroses and tiny early jonquils – when suddenly David was at her side.

'This is unlike you, Mum,' he said, giving her an affectionate touch on her shoulder. 'You're usually making marmalade in industrial quantities or bashing the life out of bread dough.'

Maud stood up and smiled. 'I know, but I cannot resist these.' She held her fistful of blue and yellow flowers to his nose for him to smell. 'Besides, they're for your wife.'

David's face clouded. 'Is she still sick? I gave her one of your rusks in bed this morning and she said she felt fine.'

'Well, she came down, and then threw up. So I packed her off to get a bit more sleep. Poor Jill, morning sickness should be over by now.'

'Sophie says it may be twins,' said David, 'did Jill tell you?'

'Yes she did, and she said she doesn't want to go to the hospital to have them.' She looked up from the patch of scillas in the lawn. 'Is that wise do you think, David?'

'Well, Sophie thinks it will be fine. Jill says she's never been in hospital in her life and she doesn't want to start now. She's very healthy – strong and energetic as ever. Except, of course, for the morning sickness.'

'And that's not serious,' said Maud. 'But still, twins! I'd have thought there are more likely to be complications with twins and you don't want an emergency dash.'

'Mum, truly, don't worry. Until a few years ago nearly all babies were born at home.'

Maud forebore to say that not all of them survived. Instead she concentrated her thoughts on Jill and David's relaxed attitude. They were wonderfully practical and down to earth.

Maud went into Laura's room to raid her dresser for antique tea-cups for her flowers. She chose two, one made by Spode with a wide yellow band round cup and saucer and little posies in the middle, and one blue floral one from Royal Doulton. She took one into Jill's bedroom (Jill was asleep, and, Maud was glad to see, now had some colour in her cheeks, which had been sheet-white earlier). Maud tiptoed out of the room and went into Donald's dressing room to put the teacup of flowers on his dressing table. They looked a picture with the looking-glass doubling their number and the sun streaming in the window. I bet he won't even notice, she thought. Once upon a time I used to bring him little bunches, to his desk or his bedside table, sometimes just a sprig of larch with brown and green cones on the same twig as the purple flowers. And he'd be delighted and touched. Ah well, she thought, I expect he'd have similar complaints of me. Better not to fuss about it.

Giovanni was fuming. He'd just had a maddening and unpro-ductive meeting at Paddington Station with the bosses of British Railways' catering division, Travellers' Fare.

He'd gone into the room with a more than fair proposition, he thought – a 50/50 business partnership. He'd take over their refreshment room and turn it into a Calzone. They would share the cost of set-up, he would guarantee them no losses, and they would get half the profits.

'My English is not as good as my cooking,' he'd said, smiling and looking round the stolid faces at the table, 'but I know you will understand the figures very well.' He'd passed round his Calzone menu, and his profit projection for the first year of trading on the station.

Giovanni had done his homework and he knew that the Travellers' tearoom lost money, and no wonder: they had far too many staff hanging around chatting, and they offered an abysmal menu. The best sellers were cheese sandwiches, made too far in advance and often curling at the edges, some passable cherry cake sweating under a glass dome, and tea and coffee. The tea, he had to admit, was good. But the coffee was appalling – made, he suspected, from a liquid mix, like Camp.

Objections to his proposal came thick and fast. 'But this food is foreign. Italian, isn't it? Our customers are British. They won't like that!'

'It's very popular on the high street,' he countered, 'and almost all our customers are English.'

'Anyway,' said the most voluble of the catering committee, 'our cafés are also waiting rooms. They need to have space for passengers' luggage and for them to sit while waiting for their trains. Too many customers would be a problem.'

Giovanni could not believe what he was hearing. He wanted to shout, 'Problem? Too many customers are a problem? Well, give us more of that problem, please.' Instead he kept his voice low and polite. 'But don't you think the customers might like something nice to eat while they are waiting?'

'They are very happy with tea and a wad. We get very few complaints.'

'A wad? What is a wad, please?' asked Giovanni.

'Yes, sorry, that's railway slang for tea and a sandwich. I'll have you know that the British Rail sandwich is the most popular sandwich in the country. It's no wonder, stands to reason. It's made with Britain's most popular bread, Mother's Pride, Britain's most popular butter, New Zealand Anchor, and Britain's most popular cheese, processed cheese slices. What do you say to that?'

Giovanni would have liked to say that since British Railways had thousands of stations all selling that sandwich and not much more, or course they sold a lot. It didn't mean they were delicious and that they would not sell a great deal more if they were. But, with an effort, he smiled and suggested that real Italian ice cream, made from cream and real eggs rather than whale fat and reconstituted egg powder, would be popular, and that smart young waiters would look better than dear old ladies in mob caps. He had brought a picture of a group of Calzone staff in their trademark white shirts, navy blue mess jackets and red and navy striped ties and cummerbands.

But he knew he was losing. When he said goodbye and the leader assured him he would be in touch, Giovanni knew it was a charade. British Railways didn't want jumped-up outsiders with modern ideas on their turf, thank you. Even if they could earn more profit by it.

I need to cool down, he thought. What does it matter if they turn me down? Why should I care? I'll take a shop in Praed Street, as close to the station as I can get, and sell my sandwiches and ice cream to the passengers before they get inside the station.

He walked towards Lord Hill's Bridge over the train tracks. I'll go as far as the Calzone in Edgware Road, he thought, and check how they're doing.

As he crossed the entrance to a mews between large stucco houses he glanced along the alley and saw a row of quaint two-storey houses, newly painted. Curious, he walked down the slope to find himself in a dead-end mews, on one side the row of white painted cottages, converted, he assumed, from old stables like the near-derelict ones on the other side.

The dilapidated side cried out for redevelopment. This whole mews could be enchanting, he thought, a secret enclave, hidden behind the tall houses. The street was cobbled and widened out towards the end to allow carts and cars to turn round in it, giving the mews an open, airy feel.

There were seven unmodernised buildings, each with what had once been a stable and coach house on the ground floor, a front door to the side and a flat above for the coachmen or groom. Most of the stables were now garages or storerooms. Some looked abandoned. There was a grubby 'For Sale' notice on the nearest one.

If you fixed them up, thought Giovanni, you could paint them different colours, and they'd be like a row of seaside cottages. A breath of fresh air in grey old London.

Feeling unreasonably excited, Giovanni took out a notebook and pencil and wrote down the agent's details. It's crazy, he thought. Why am I doing this? It's just a pipe dream. I doubt if we could afford even one of these buildings, and we'd need at least two. One would be no larger than our present flat.

But he could not get the mews out of his head and eventually broached the subject with Laura.

'You know we often say that one day we must have a home of our own and stop paying rent? Well, I think I know how we could do it, but we'd have to borrow a lot of money and go into the property business.'

The following Saturday, Laura went with him to have a look. Giovanni carried two-year-old Angelica on his shoulders. There were no cars in the mews, only a barrow outside one of the locked garages, and a pram in front of a converted cottage. Giovanni set Angelica down and she ran about, first one way, then another.

Giovanni was watching Laura intently, willing her to be as excited and enthusiastic as he was. But he could not read her. She looked bemused, blank.

'What do you think, my darling? Once these derelict buildings are fixed up like the ones on that side – and sooner or later they will be – it would be like a little village, fifteen houses in a tucked-away street. Look at Angelica, running everywhere. She'd be safe here, not like living in Billingsgate, full of buses and trucks.'

'Darling Giovanni, I agree it could be a gem of a street. But we'd never afford it, surely?'

'I've spoken to the estate agent,' said Giovanni. 'These seven have been on the market for over two years and he believes they're not selling because the owner wants to sell them as a block. But he thinks, since there have been no offers, he might be prepared to break them up, sell us two perhaps.'

Laura's eyes shot wide open. 'Two? Two cottages?'

'Yes. One would be no bigger than our flat, in fact smaller.

The old stable is just big enough for a front room and kitchen, and the top floor would make a bedroom and bathroom. We'd need at least a room for Angelica, so we'd need two. But I think we might manage it.'

Laura lifted her head, listening to a train steaming out of the station. 'But what about the noise? The trains pass every few minutes.'

'We'd get used to it, don't you think? I like the sound of trains, don't you?'

'Oh Giovanni, it could be the most exciting thing in the world. But we have to be sensible. How much are they?'

'The agent doesn't know if the owner will break them up, but if he does, he reckons they'd be over a thousand pounds each. And it might cost that again to rebuild them.'

'But darling,' protested Laura, 'how can we possibly afford it? I know we have the two thousand saved, but we'd need to fix them up. What are we talking about? Four thousand? It's impossible, surely?'

Giovanni could feel his heart sinking. If he could not enthuse Laura, the dream was dead.

'Come, darling,' he said, 'let's look inside.'

Angelica was agitating to be picked up and he hoisted her back onto his shoulders and walked into the first house, which had a garage that had lost its door. It was full of rubbish and smelt damp and musty. They picked their way over the uneven floor.

'They vary a bit in size, but not much. The two best are these at the end. The end one is slightly bigger than the others,' said Giovanni. 'They're all only one room deep, but it's quite a good size, don't you think? And the first floor is the same size. So we would need two.' He could see Laura beginning to shake her head and he went on quickly, 'No, Laura, don't shake your head. Listen to me first.'

She nodded. 'Sorry, darling. Go ahead, I'm listening.'

'Good. If we use our savings and borrow the rest of the money, which I'm sure we could since the business is doing so well, I think we could just afford to knock two together and rebuild.'

'Really, darling? But we know nothing of building. Wouldn't it be a huge risk?'

'We could manage it, I think. Of course, it all depends on whether the owner will break them up and sell just two.'

Giovanni had been talking very fast, but now stopped to take a breath.

'What do you think, my darling? Am I mad?'

Giovanni had been aware of Laura's tensing up at the risk of the proposal, but now she made a visible effort to relax.

'Probably,' she said, laughing. 'But madness often works.'

Giovanni felt relief wash through him. She was going to agree. He could feel it.

Angelica, impatient at her parents' inattention, was drumming Giovanni's head with her fists.

'Hey, stop that!' he said, at which Laura reached up to take her daughter.

'Let's get out of here,' she said, carrying Angelica out into the mews. Laura gave her a quick kiss before setting her down. Giovanni was momentarily distracted by his daughter's bouncing curls as he watched her run across the cobbles.

'We should ask George,' Laura said. 'He deals in property, doesn't he?' Giovanni turned back to her.

'Good idea, but, *cara*, I need to know. It has to be our mutual dream. Would you be happy living here?'

Laura looked up at Giovanni and smiled her widest smile. 'Would I? Of course I would. I'd love it. Just love it.'

They embraced, Giovanni feeling a familiar wave of desire for his wife. Angelica, not wanting to be left out, ran back to them and forced herself between them, holding onto Laura's legs.

As they walked out of the mews through the narrow archway, they each held one of the child's hands. They swung her, squealing with pleasure, off the ground.

It still gave Giovanni a little buzz of pride and pleasure to think that his business could now support comfortable offices. Most restaurateurs had to do their accounts at a table in the dining room. Over the last few years, Giovanni's offices had gradually expanded from a desk in one of the unlovely rooms over the Billingsgate Calzone, to occupying both floors with a good-sized office for him, another for a secretary and a book keeper, a storeroom, bathroom and a changing room for the Calzone staff downstairs.

Giovanni's secretary held open the door and ushered George in. Giovanni jumped up, pleased.

'Oh good, George. I thought you'd just telephone.'

George looked round, surprised. 'Goodness, Giovanni, this is very grand. I'd no idea you had such a smart office.'

'It looks a lot better since Laura had a go at it. You know how she trawls the second-hand markets. She bought most of the furniture down the Old Kent Road.'

'And those?' asked George. He pointed to the black-and-white prints on the wall. They were of Italian artisans: a cheesemaker, a baker and a winemaker.

'Second-hand print shop, I think. But George, tell me what

303

you think of the Paddington mews?' He offered George a chair and sat himself on the edge of his desk. 'You've been to see it?'

'I have. Giovanni, I think you have found a really good deal.' Smiling, George settled back in the chair. 'I talked to the agent and then he arranged for me to meet the owner. I've just come from seeing him.'

Giovanni could feel excitement rising, and made an effort to be businesslike and calm. 'That's very good of you, George. We didn't mean to cause you so much trouble. We just wanted your opinion on the property, really.'

'Well, here's my advice: I think the trick would be to buy the whole row of buildings together.'

Giovanni was baffled. 'Don't be crazy,' he said. 'We can barely afford two. I could never borrow that much money.'

'Which is why I went to see the owner. It wasn't kindness, Giovanni, more like self-interest. I'd like to come in with you. We could do it together.'

'Good Lord. But why? You don't want a house in Paddington!'

'Hear me out. I think it could be a good investment. The fellow wants to sell all seven as a job lot. He'll only let them go individually at a big premium. At the price he's asking for all of them, which is six thousand seven hundred pounds, it makes sense.'

George took his notebook from his pocket and consulted it. 'At that price, each house will be less than a thousand, and, fixed up, will be worth about two. One of the renovated ones opposite has just gone for two thousand three hundred.'

'But George, where am I to get my half of the money?'

'If I match whatever you can put in, and we form a partnership, I know we could borrow the rest. Then when the renovation

304

is complete we can decide whether to sell any or let the extra cottages. Either way it could be profitable.'

Giovanni felt George's enthusiasm and tried to concentrate. As he thought about it he could feel the excitement return.

'Good Lord, George, are you serious? And are you sure you want to do this for good business reasons? Not out of your usual kindness?'

'Giovanni, I never risk big tranches of money for kindness. I've done very well out of your business, and I think we could do well out of this little venture, too.'

CHAPTER THIRTY

Sophie loved her job and was a passionate supporter of the new NHS. As the most junior doctor in Dr Drummond's practice in Moreton, she was first into the surgery most mornings. She still felt a little buzz of pride at the new nameplate on the door. The last name on the list, which began with Dr Gordon Drummond, was Dr Sophie Wenlock.

One Monday as she was letting herself in the front door, she heard a squeal of tyres. She turned to see David jumping out of the car. He ran towards her.

'Sophie, quick, she's started.'

Sophie smiled at him. 'Oh good. Right on time, too.' She opened the door and stepped inside. 'Come in a minute, David. I just have to open up the waiting room, and—'

'But Jill's gone into labour, Sophie. Can't you come?'

'Whoah, David! There's no rush. When did she feel the first pains?'

David looked at his watch. 'About half an hour ago.'

'Well, you are in for many hours of waiting. I'll come as soon as I can – I have to arrange for one of the other doctors to stand in for me, and I must do one or two vital things. Then I'll be there.'

She saw David was making a visible effort to be calm.

'How long will you be?'

'Not long. Maybe an hour.' She put her hands out and clasped both his wrists. 'David, this time it will be fine. She's full term, and very healthy.'

He nodded, still anxious. Sophie said, 'You should go to work. Honestly. I'll send someone to find you on the farm when your baby comes. Or babies. You know, I'm sure she's carrying twins.'

When Sophie arrived, Jill was already on her bed, timing her contractions, with Maud and Grace beside her. She was glad to see they were all calm and cheerful and they'd set up a baby bath, soap and towels on the big dressing table, and a cot in the passage. They were half-listening to the Midlands Home Service.

Jill's face tensed a little for a contraction, then relaxed. 'Sophie,' she said, 'it's so wonderful you're here. Dr Drummond did say he'd send the midwife, but I would so much rather it was you.'

'I wouldn't miss it for the world.' She turned to David. 'But you have a rather nervous husband here. I want to send him back to work, get his mind off you for a few hours.'

'Sophie's right,' said Maud.

David took Jill's hand. 'Yes, darling,' she said, 'you should go. It will be ages yet.'

'Besides,' said Sophie, 'I have to do some very undignified things, which you don't want to see.'

David's eyes opened in alarm. 'What things?'

'Well, I have to examine her. And do some preparations.'

They were interrupted by another contraction, more forceful this time, and Maud pushed David out of the door.

'Go, David. Come back for lunch as usual. Nothing much will have happened by then.'

In the early stages, Jill was smiling and even jokey. 'If I'd known I had to put up with an enema and having everything shaved down there,' she said, 'I'd have thought twice. Poor Sophie, I don't suppose the duties of a midwife were what you were expecting when you qualified as a doc.'

'Oh, I don't mind. Country doctors have to do a bit of everything. It's what I like about the job. One moment child-birth, the next a broken ankle, then an old boy's rheumatism. It's what makes it interesting.'

Jill's contractions gradually got more frequent and stronger. After one of them, she sank back into the bed and said, 'I'm so glad you pushed David out, Maud.'

'Childbirth is women's business,' said Maud.

Sophie was glad of Maud's brisk good sense. She and Grace were attentive students as she showed them how to help Jill breathe through the contractions, how to massage her back and cool her face and arms with a damp flannel.

As the hours wore on, the women took turns to be beside Jill, doing these things and giving her occasional cups of tea. Maud had tuned the wireless to the Third Programme and turned the volume right down. Beethoven's 'Pastoral' swooped and swelled, glorious and calming. This is such a good family atmosphere, thought Sophie. It's how childbirth should be.

At lunchtime Grace went down to the kitchen to feed Donald and David and, Sophie suspected, to have a cigarette.

She reappeared after twenty minutes or so.

'Poor David,' she said. 'He's in such a state. I've managed to get him to go back to work. He'll be in the office. All we have to do is ring the yard bell and he'll hear it.'

But at six o'clock, when Sophie was helping Jill breathe, or rather pant, through another painful contraction, David pushed his way into the bedroom, his face strained with anxiety. Oh, God, thought Sophie, poor David. First-time husbands should get some training for this. David took one look at Jill, her face drained of colour and yet running with sweat, and strode across the room to her.

'Darling, what's happening?' he cried. He rounded on Sophie. 'She's not right. Can't you see—?'

Maud pushed herself between the bed and David and took him by the shoulders. Sophie watched her once again leading him out of the room, saying, 'David, nothing is wrong. This is childbirth, it's what women go through. You will only make things worse. You must go away and stay away until we ring the bell. Go and find your father. He's probably in a fine old state, too.'

Maud had him out of the room before the next contraction started, which was just as well. It was much stronger than the last.

By eight o'clock Jill was exhausted. She'd been in labour for twelve hours. Her back was hurting, even between contractions, and she seemed to have almost no recovery time before another wave of pain gripped her insides like the hands of a killer. And Sophie would not let her push.

'Not yet, Jill. I know you want to, but you're not dilated enough.'

An hour later, her hair bedraggled and her face wet with sweat, Jill was not speaking any more between contractions. She was too tired to utter anything, except the cries forced from her by excruciating pain. It cut through her like knives. With each contraction she grasped the gas-and-air mask and breathed in as if her life depended on it. The pains were followed by relief so intense that she just lay there gasping, dreading the next onslaught. She was conscious of nothing but pain and fear. It was a cycle of hell.

After scaling several more mountains of pain, and sliding down again exhausted, the urge to push was irresistible. 'Sophie, I've got to push,' she said. 'Why do I want to push if I'm not ready?' Her words were barely audible. She felt close to tears but too exhausted to cry.

'Soon you can, but you have to be ready. If the baby's head can't get out because you are not properly open it will be bad for both of you.'

Jill thought, Maybe I'm going to die. But then she thought, I don't care: I just want the pain to stop. And then at last she heard Sophie saying, 'On the next one, push. Now, Jill. Push.' And she gathered strength somehow and, with the next contraction, tried to force the baby out.

'Good girl, Jill. Now again. The head is almost out. Two or three more now.'

Maud's grip on her hand tightened as she screamed. And then suddenly she felt the baby burst out. The pain dropped away and she heard Sophie say, 'He's born, Jill. A boy.' She opened her eyes, and heard a cry, a definite baby cry. She stretched her arms out to him but Sophie quickly passed him to Maud. 'Sorry, Jill, but you have to push the next one out now. I told you it was twins.'

Almost at once another contraction overtook her, but a wave of glorious happiness engulfed her and somehow this one hurt much less. She pushed and after a few more contractions felt the baby swoosh out. This time Sophie held the baby up by the ankles, and gave it a smart slap on the bottom. Instantly the baby cried, and Sophie was grinning at her.

'Another boy. Twin boys. Both hale and hearty. Oh, Jill, I'm so, so glad.'

Jill lay back, exhausted, happy, and feeling so complete that whatever Sophie was doing down there didn't concern her. She felt a warm gush of something, and Sophie was feeling around, sort of massaging her. She didn't understand it, but she didn't care. She was so tired. And so happy.

Grace was kissing her and pushing back her hair, when Maud loomed over her, smiling broadly with tears on her cheeks. Grace stepped back and Maud put a swaddled bundle into her arms.

'Here you are, darling – your firstborn son.'

Jill looked down at the crumpled face of her firstborn and was assailed by the most extraordinary rush of raw emotion, part protectiveness, part wonder.

'Where's David?' asked Jill, her voice still a croak.

'He's on his way.'

She felt extraordinary: proud and content. She'd borne two sons, both healthy. She shut her eyes for a moment, happier than she could ever remember, and oddly enjoying her utter exhaustion.

Then suddenly David was there, telling her she was wonderful. He had the other baby in his arms. They looked at their offspring, at each other, unable to speak. He bent to kiss her and she sucked the tears off his cheek. Jill was thinking, I had no idea I could be so overcome by emotion, by love. I will always, always, remember this moment.

Sophie's voice, calm but firm, pulled her back.

'Maud and David, I need to clear the room of husbands and babies. I have to see to Jill.'

Maud took the baby from Jill's arms and she and David lowered the two bundles into the cot just outside the bedroom door. Then Maud shooed David down the stairs, 'Go on, darling. I'll call you back soon.'

Jill was beginning to drift into sleep when she heard Sophie saying to Grace, 'Could you ring Dr Drummond and get him to come here as soon as he can? And ask him, or the nurse, to get an ambulance. We need to get her to hospital. Tell them it's uterine atony.'

'Uterine what?' asked Grace,

'Just tell him her uterus won't contract. He'll understand.' Then Sophie was talking to Maud, saying something about propping her up to slow the blood flow.

Jill made an effort to make sense of their words. She'd had the babies, she was fine, the babies were fine. Why would she go to hospital? She tried to sit up, but Sophie was at her side, telling her to lie down.

'Jill, darling, you're still bleeding. That should have stopped by now. Don't worry, it will all be fine, but I'd feel happier if you were in hospital. Just lie down. We're going to get a cushion under your bottom, and I'm going to give you an injection to stimulate your uterus into contracting.'

Jill obediently rolled over so that Sophie could inject her bottom. The sharp pain as Sophie slowly depressed the plunger on the syringe jerked her out of what was left of her dreamy state.

How ironic, she thought. 'Why do you want more contractions now the babies are born? I certainly don't.'

'A contraction won't hurt now the babies are out. But it will close off the blood vessels that were ruptured when the placenta came away.'

Maud was talking to her. 'You relax, Jill dear. It will soon be fine, and then you can have the babies and David back.'

But Sophie knew that Jill would not be able to relax. The massaging was uncomfortable and although Jill bore it, Sophie saw her cheeks tighten occasionally in a wince. And then, after five minutes of this, with no let-up in the steady bleeding, she had to give her another painful injection, and then continue the massage.

Oh God, thought Sophie, as the sound of David's boots thudding up the stairs reached her. How am I going to cope? I mustn't panic. That these are my adored friends is irrelevant. Jill is a patient and efficiency will be more use to her than emotion. I have to do what I'm trained to do.

The door crashed open.

'What's going on, Sophie?' David's eyes were wide with fear, his voice high and loud. 'Why are you calling an ambulance? What's wrong?'

'Shhh, shhh, David. There's no panic. Jill will be fine.' She dropped her voice very low. 'You'll frighten her, David. Don't shout.'

David strode across the room to Jill and knelt by the bed. In the few minutes since Maud had sent him downstairs his wife, so pink and elated before, had become limp, her skin much paler, sheened with sweat.

Sophie gently massaged Jill's abdomen with both hands. She hoped she was doing it properly. She'd never seen a real-life case of uterine atony before, and she knew that massage didn't always, or even very often, work. It was not a sure-fire method of kick-start-ing the uterus into contracting as it should. She looked at the dark pool of blood on the folded sheet under Jill and the bloodied one on the floor in the corner. She wasn't haemorrhaging as she had been before, but she was still steadily losing blood.

She gave Jill another injection in the buttock. Jill barely flinched.

Maud was sitting on a chair at Jill's head, stroking her arm and wrist. David was kneeling on the other side of the bed, his hands on either side of Jill's head, turning it towards him. He was calmer now, speaking softly.

'Don't worry, darling, the babies are fine. It will be all right sweetheart, just rest. Be happy. We have two lovely sons.'

He talked on, every now and then his voice faltering. He is such a good man, thought Sophie.

The wait was terrible. Sophie managed to stay calm, keep-ing up the steady massage. Grace, obviously anxious to move, busied herself taking the bloodied sheets downstairs and putting another clean, folded one under Jill. Maud and David, each side of Jill, were quiet now. Jill was pale and calm, eyes shut. No one spoke. They're all doing what I'm doing, thought Sophie, pretending there isn't a problem.

Suddenly David's voice, rising in panic, broke the silence.

'Sophie, what's wrong? I think she's going to . . .'

Jill's eyes were fluttering, and her breath was quick and shal-low. She didn't respond.

David eyes were pleading and desperate.

'For God's sake, Sophie, you're the doctor. Do something. Help her. Can't you see she's . . . she's . . . Oh God.' He shook Jill's shoulders. 'No, no Jill, you can't. Don't, darling, don't.'

'David, you're frightening her,' said Maud, hurrying round the bed to put her hands on his shoulders. 'Be quiet, darling. Let's all be calm. Sophie knows what she's doing and Dr Drummond is on his way.'

Thank God for Maud, thought Sophie. David always listens to her. Indeed, Jill's eyes opened and she gave David a weak, split-second smile. The wait continued. Sophie tried not to look at her watch.

When Sophie heard Donald's step on the stairs her heart sank. He would be impossible.

'What's happening, Sophie?' he demanded, his voice loud and accusing. 'For God's sake, woman, what have you done?'

Sophie said, 'Jill's womb isn't contracting. She's losing too much blood. We need to get her to hospital.'

'But you said she'd be fine. What do you mean?'

Sophie's hands did not stop their steady massage. 'The womb is meant to contract to expel the babies, which it did. But now it needs to contract to constrict the blood vessels that were ruptured during birth.'

'Well, squeezing her stomach like that isn't likely to help, is it?'

'I am trying to stimulate it to restart contractions.'

'I've brought the car round. We can't wait for the ambulance. We'll take her now.'

His chin was out, his eyes both anxious and belligerent.

'No, Donald, sitting up in a car would accelerate the bleeding. We must wait for Dr Drummond and the ambulance.'

Donald's face seemed to collapse, suddenly looking defeated. 'But surely you can you tie off the blood vessels or something?' It was a plea, not a demand.

'No, not here,' Sophie said firmly. Relieved that Donald had given up his badgering, she turned to Jill. 'You're doing exactly the right thing, Jill, staying very still. The less you move the less you'll bleed.'

They heard the sound of Dr Drummond's Morris Oxford pulling up, and soon after his heavy tread as he took the stairs two at a time. He went straight to Jill and put his hand on her forehead, pulling up the skin to open her eyes.

'Mmm, you don't look too good, young lady, do you? But I hear you have two bonnie wee boys. Now, anyone would look a wee bit peely-wally after that.' The corners of Jill's mouth lifted in a ghost of a smile. She looked, thought Sophie, comforted and relieved.

So did everyone else. Dr Drummond stood by Sophie, lifted the sheet to see the bleeding, examined Jill without touching her, and then said to Sophie, kindly, 'Now, Doctor, tell me where we are. The ambulance is on its way and the more we know, the better.'

Sophie was so relieved to be handing over command, she felt almost tearful. But she braced herself to remain professional and told him what had happened and answered his questions.

The ambulance arrived at eleven o'clock, forty minutes after the second boy was born. The longest forty minutes of my life, thought Sophie. Please God can that be the worst of it.

She drove behind the ambulance in which were Dr Drummond and David as well as Jill. The rest of the family, including the babies, were behind her in the Bentley.

Jill was pronounced dead on arrival.

*

When the family had finally been persuaded to go home, Sophie drove back to the surgery and sat at her desk, poring over her obstetric textbooks. It was nearly 2am but she knew she would not sleep until she had satisfied herself that she was not responsible for Jill's death. She went over and over the events of that evening, checking and re-checking that she had done everything by the book. Then, grimly, keeping grief and exhaustion at bay, she carefully filled in her report.

At four-fifteen in the morning, she closed *Obstetric Practice and Procedures,* with the report between the pages on uterine atony, and put it on Dr Drummond's desk.

It was five o'clock when Sophie closed her curtains against the dawn sun and climbed into bed, but she couldn't sleep. David's stricken face, she thought, would be with her forever. How could she bear it? Sophie knew already that David blamed her for Jill's death – he'd said as much at the hospital. And she couldn't put her hand on her heart and say he was wrong. She had done everything by the book, she was not negligent, but that didn't meant she'd made the right decision about a home birth. Jill could have lived if she'd been in hospital.

How could she bear the knowledge that she was responsible for David losing his wife? Wonderful, darling David, whom she'd worshipped when she was a child and been in love with, secretly and steadily, since the age of sixteen. No one had ever guessed and no one must ever know. Not David, of course, but not even Laura. He'd never thought of her as anything but Laura's friend, a sort of second little sister. When he'd fallen for Jill she had successfully, though with many hidden tears, swallowed down all her hopes.

Now he would hate her.

CHAPTER THIRTY-ONE

Three weeks later, Maud walked into her husband's study, determined to get a reaction out of him. Since Jill's death he'd been morose to the point where Maud's sympathy had changed to resentment, on occasions even anger. They were all devastated by the tragedy but, she thought, Donald was wallowing in his grief.

He was sitting at his desk, unshaven and slightly dishevelled. To his right was a bottle of whisky and a half-full glass. *The Times* lay, pristine and unopened, to his left.

Donald looked up as she came in but said nothing.

'Donald, this has gone on long enough. We need to talk. If David can pull himself together and run the farm, then it's time you made an effort. You should be out helping the poor boy as much as you can, but you're sitting here or at your club, feeling sorry for yourself. It's got to stop.'

Donald raised his eyes to her, but didn't answer. He did not appear to be listening.

Maud, in spite of her resolution to be tough before she entered the study, could not help her love for him interfering. A shaft of sympathy softened her face and she went round the desk and put her arm round his shoulders. She added a little shake to her hug, then sat on the desk, allowing her hand to trail down his arm. She tried to speak kindly.

'Darling husband, we need you to be the old Donald, taking a lead. And we need you here. The club secretary rang me to see if he could do anything to help. He says you sit on your own in the bar, quietly drinking, hardly speaking to anyone. What is the use of that?'

Donald didn't answer but gave the faintest of shrugs.

'No, Donald, you can't just shrug. We have a son who is so grief-stricken he can't think straight. He blames Sophie for Jill's death, and refuses to see his sons. They are three weeks old now and he hasn't held one of them since the day they were born. Do you even know this? I have tried to talk to you often enough, but you don't listen. And no one else dares talk to you, least of all David. He needs your help, Donald. So do we all.'

He looked up, making no effort to hide his misery. 'I can't help anyone, Maud. I can't even help myself.'

Maud straightened up and took her hand from Donald's arm. The steel returned to her voice as she responded loudly and firmly, 'That's nonsense, Donald, and you know it. You've been through two world wars. You've lost two infants at birth and several by miscarriage. You've lost your eldest son. You managed to cast our daughter out without a single tear. You could pull yourself together if you wanted to. But you are too selfish to do that, and that's the truth.'

Donald looked at her with a mixture of surprise and bafflement. She expected him to fight back, shout at her that she didn't know what she was talking about, but he said nothing. Suddenly Maud found tears pricking her eyes. Quietly, with a catch in her voice, she said, 'Donald, don't you see? You loved Jill so much because you were filling the gap that Laura left. This grieving for someone else's daughter has got to stop. Everyone loved Jill, but you are mourning her like a lover. The truth is, darling, you have become a burden to this household instead of its head.'

She stood up and walked to the door.

'It breaks my heart.'

Donald sat for a long time after she'd left, her words going round in his head: *you cast our daughter out without a single tear.* Maud is right, he thought, I've been a tyrant and a fool. I punished Laura so severely because I loved her so much. It wasn't her fault that I doted on her. I just could not bear the thought of any man having her, and I never, for a moment, concerned myself with what would make her happy, with what she wanted.

He held his hands over his ears, as if that would prevent him hearing his own thoughts.

Maud is right, I replaced Laura with Jill. And when Jill got pregnant she was more grown up than Laura and brave enough to tell me straight that women like sex and that it's normal, natural, good.

He slid his hands from his ears to cover his face, his thoughts coming thick and fast. If I'm honest, I already knew that. Maud and I would have slept together before we married if we'd ever been left unchaperoned. That Squadron Leader's wife in India, Angela, she certainly enjoyed it, and God knows there have been others over the years who were willing enough, even though they knew an affair was just an affair. Laura *loves* that Italian. Who am I to blame her for sleeping with him?

Ten minutes later he went upstairs, shaved, showered, and put on his standard country attire: tweed jacket, breeches, Argyle socks and boots. He stood for a moment in front of the looking-glass, then straightened his shoulders and went in search of David.

From the kitchen window, Maud watched Donald walk across the yard, his bearing once more military and his clothes impeccable. She smiled to herself, thinking that she could not remember a single time in their long marriage when she had been so forceful. But it had worked, and it might all just come right one day. She'd give David a little longer, then have a go at him, too. His infant sons, Hal and Richard, needed a father.

Sophie had found a wet nurse whose own baby had been born a few weeks before the twins. She had plenty of milk for all three. At first the twins had stayed with her in the village so she could feed them every few hours. There wasn't room at the cottage for the hired nanny, so she slept at Chorlton and went to the wetnurse's cottage each day to help. Her Norland training ensured that all three babies soon had a routine of feed, sleep, cossetting and play. So much so that in a few weeks the twins were content with four-hourly feeds and could move into Laura's old room, now the nursery. They slept together in one big cot. The wet nurse pushed her pram up to the house four times a day to feed the babies, and at night they had bottles of the new formula baby milk.

The babies were gaining weight and looking well, but Maud was worried. Sophie came repeatedly to check on them, and agreed they were blooming, but David would have nothing to do with them. He wouldn't see Sophie either, and he resisted any suggestion that the babies move into the Brew House with him.

Sophie's world was now centred on David's babies. She was spending every hour she could with them, and between Maud, Grace and her, she felt they were getting the love and attention they needed, at least for the moment. But they needed a father's love, too.

Grace bought a big baby carriage wide enough for them to sleep side by side and long enough for them to sit up, one at each end, when they were older. When it arrived she and Sophie packed the swaddled infants into it, raised the hood against the August sunshine, and set off for a walk.

They chattered contentedly about the dust taking the shine off the baby carriage's paint.

'It's meant for parading about Kensington Gardens, not bouncing along country lanes,' said Sophie.

They discussed Laura and Giovanni's success with Calzone, and how pleased they were that clothes and fabrics had finally come off ration. After a pause to admire the view from Chorlton Hill, Sophie turned to Grace and said, 'Grace, what are we to do about David?'

'You mean about these two?' Grace rocked the baby carriage and peered at the sleeping boys.

'Yes.'

'He surely doesn't want to give them up for adoption? What does he say?'

'He won't discuss them. Maud has left him alone, since that is so obviously what he wants. But it's not right for them not to have a mother or a father.'

'Maybe you should talk to him.'

Sophie shook her head. 'Oh Grace, he won't speak to me at all. Not even a "good morning". He still blames me for Jill's death. Me and the babies.' She was fingering her amber necklace, as though telling a rosary, up and down, up and down. 'Poor man, he's in such torment.'

'What a generous woman you are, Sophie. Anyone else would be indignant, or resentful at such a gross, unfair accusation.'

'I understand it. I was the one in charge. And he needs someone to blame. But I can't pretend it doesn't hurt.'

Grace put her arm around Sophie.

'It will come right. He must know in his heart of hearts that there was nothing you could have done.'

'Dr Drummond gave him a copy of my report of the birth and Jill's death, and confirmed that I did everything by the book, but I doubt that David, in his present state of mind, would have read it. Or absorbed a word of it if he tried.'

'He'll come right. In the meantime we must just prevent him giving these babies away.'

'I doubt he'll do that. Giving them up for adoption would mean he'd have to think about them, answer questions, fill in forms, meet people, talk about them. All anathema to him.'

'If he would only see them, hold them, he'd be bound to love them, wouldn't he?'

'Which might be why he won't have anything to do with them. He's making sure he doesn't love again, in case love leads to loss again.'

They talked of other things as they walked home. And then Grace stopped in the middle of the road and said, 'We need to enlist Laura. David might listen to her.'

CHAPTER THIRTY-TWO

When Maud had rung Laura to tell her of the birth of the twins and the death of Jill, Laura had at once taken a train to Chorlton, leaving Angelica with Giovanni. For most of the journey she'd stared unseeing out of the window. She was not yet grieving for Jill – the fact that she was gone forever had not properly penetrated her mind – but the thought of her poor brother, a widower after less than two years of marriage, and the twins, orphaned at an hour old, had engulfed her.

She'd known her father would not welcome her, so she'd asked her mother not to tell him she was coming. I don't care, she'd thought. What does it matter if he doesn't talk to me? He hasn't for years – I'm used to it now.

And indeed her father didn't emerge from his study. But she and Maud clung to each other in silent understanding. The fresh-bread smell of her mother was so familiar and comforting, she wondered how she'd done without it so long.

David was nowhere to be seen, out on the farm somewhere. Laura walked for a mile before getting a tractor ride to the top of Little Barrow, where she found him in the middle of a barley field, inspecting the corn.

She walked along the edge of the field until she was near enough to hail him. He looked up, not registering surprise or pleasure, or indeed anything else. But he walked towards her through the barley.

'It's ripe for combining,' he said. 'Good and dry.'

'Oh, David,' she said, throwing her arms round his stiff shoulders and hugging him tight. She felt him slowly unbend and his arms came round her. She looked into his face and she thought, This is a picture of sorrow. This is what grief looks like. It reminded her of how Giovanni looked when she told him his firstborn son was lost to adoption.

They did not speak but when she saw his eyes fill with tears, she felt her own respond, the tears spilling down her face. She did not wipe them away, just looked steadily into his eyes, until he sniffed and pulled a handkerchief from his pocket. He mopped first her face, then his, and said, 'Thanks for coming, sis.'

They walked round the fields for a while, barely talking and then only about the state of the crops, the cows, the weather. But it was good. They walked back to the house together, although David went straight to the farm office and wouldn't come into the house itself. Neither he nor their father had reappeared by the time Laura left for the station.

Over the following three weeks, Laura often spoke to her mother, but the news was not good. Donald seemed to have gone into a melancholic slump and David was blocking the whole matter from his mind. He'd been down to Kent to Jill's funeral, but since his return he would talk only of yields, of the costs of drying corn, of government fixed prices for cereals, of anything at all except his dead wife or living sons.

Laura was so glad to be back in regular touch with her mother, even though their communication was confined to phone calls and letters, and she knew Maud felt the same. Laura sensed a new determination in her mother: she would not always be led by Donald; she would see her daughter, and telephone her, whenever she liked.

'I don't care so much about Daddy,' said Laura. 'It's probably time he knew what it's like to be unhappy.' She tried to keep the bitterness out of her voice, but realised she was not succeeding. She went on quickly, 'But poor David, he doesn't deserve this. He'd be such a loving father if he'd only let himself.'

'I know. And thank God for Sophie,' replied Maud. 'She's mothering those infants. The wet nurse is very good, but she has her own baby and family to look after, and Nanny is everything you need in a nanny – efficient, experienced, and so on. But Sophie is the one who is singing the most lullabies. She's rearranged her surgery hours to be free for as many bath-and-bed-times as possible. The twins are not being short-changed on affection, but it would help David so much if he just allowed himself to love them.'

So when Grace came to see her in London, and told her she should talk to her brother, Laura made another visit to Chorlton, determined to persuade David to give fatherhood a chance. She'd chosen a day when Donald would be at his club and after lunch mother and daughter tackled David together. As he pocketed his tobacco and cigarette papers, and put his hands on the table to push himself upright, Maud said, 'Stay a minute, darling. We need to talk to you about the twins.'

'What about the twins?' David was now standing.

'David, just sit down and listen for a few minutes. Please?' said Laura.

David sat down slowly, saying, 'You know I don't want anything to do with the twins. Make any decisions you like. Just don't involve me.'

Laura could feel her stomach clench. She said as evenly as she could, 'How can we not involve you? They are your children. You can't just abandon them.'

'There's no danger of their being abandoned. This house is full of doting women.'

'But what about when they grow up? Keeping infants unable to crawl out of your sight is one thing, but are they to grow up knowing that the man who ignores them, who hates the sight of them, refuses to look at them, won't talk to them, is their father?'

'I don't think it will come to that. I'll be long gone before they're crawling.'

The two women stared at him in horror. Laura was the first to react. 'What . . .what . . . why? Where are you going to?' She was stammering.

'I haven't a clue. Australia probably. As far away as I can.'

Maud said calmly, 'Darling, you must know that you cannot run away from unhappiness. It won't be any better somewhere else.'

Laura tried to take his hand but he withdrew it. She added, 'You'd be more unhappy. You'd just add loneliness to misery.'

David stood up once more, and for the first time there was a spark of energy in his voice which grew stronger as he spoke. 'I'm sorry, Mum. But right now everything reminds me of Jill. Everything, do you understand? This room, those plates, the yard, every inch of paintwork in the Brew House, every sheep, every lamb, every tractor. I can't stand it. That's the truth.'

As David left the kitchen, Maud put her head in her hands and Laura could see she was trying to control herself. She leant over her mother as Maud's shoulders started to shake. Maud said through her tears, 'Is there anything worse than not being able to help your child in trouble?'

'Nothing,' said Laura.

That afternoon, on the train back to London, Laura did some serious thinking. On arrival at Paddington, instead of taking the Circle line home, she took the Bakerloo to Piccadilly Circus and walked the length of Piccadilly to the RAF Club. Her hands were sweaty with anxiety as the uniformed porter looked her up and down. But she brought her chin up and said with feigned confidence, 'Would you be so good as to see if Air Commodore Oliver is in? And if he is, could you tell him his daughter is here to see him?'

She waited in the lobby. It was probably only a few minutes, but that was plenty of time for Laura to contemplate abandoning her mission. Then suddenly she heard her father's voice. She thought, This is the first time in five years I've heard him say my name.

'Hullo, Daddy.' He looked much older than she remembered. And then she thought, I must look much older, too. He probably thinks of me as eighteen. He ushered her into the morning room and ordered coffee.

He doesn't look angry, she thought, just surprised. And maybe slightly nervous. 'I know you disapprove of me, Daddy, but this is not about me,' she said. 'I just wanted to tell you that Mummy is in a desperate state. You don't see it, because she tries so hard to hide it, but she feels she's trying to keep the family together all by herself. None of the rest of us is any help at all. Hugh is dead, I'm banished, and David is half mad with grief. He has disowned his sons and wants to go to Australia. You could help him, but you're never there. And you won't listen to Mummy.'

Donald looked at her without comment.

'That's it,' she went on. 'I just wanted to tell you in case you could help. But I don't expect you will.'

She stood up, hesitated as he stood, too, then said, 'Goodbye, Daddy,' and walked swiftly out of the club.

Fighting back tears, she crossed Piccadilly and half ran, half walked through Green Park and St James's Park to the Tube. Her breathing slowed and she felt calmer as she waited for her train. When, after a minute or two, it arrived, she sank into her seat, wondering why she was shaking. She hadn't meant to run away, she'd meant to try to have a proper conversation with him, but his presence was so powerful, as if he still had authority over her, that she'd not been able to bear it. Yet, she thought, I don't think Daddy said a single word other than 'Laura', and 'Coffee for two please, steward'. And I didn't stay for the coffee. Relaxing, she shut her eyes, comforted by the warmth, rattle and sway of the train.

'Laura.'

She thought she heard her father's voice speaking to her quietly. She smiled, thinking she must have been dreaming. She mustn't fall asleep: she'd end up in Upminster.

'Laura.'

Her eyes shot open, and she turned to find her father sitting next to her. 'My God, young woman, you can certainly walk at a pace. I nearly lost you at Buckingham Palace – you ducked between those taxis like a whippet after a hare.'

'Daddy, what . . .? Did you follow me?'

'I did and it wasn't easy. You were out of the club like a shot.' They were both talking loudly, over the din of the train. He leant in close and spoke in her ear. 'I need to talk to you. Let's get out of here.' He stood up as the train pulled into Westminster station and headed for the door.

Nothing changes, thought Laura. He doesn't ask me, just commands. But she followed him into the street and into a dingy café, which smelt faintly of boiled cabbage. It was half-empty and quiet.

'Right, this time will you stick around long enough to drink your coffee?'

'Coffee is fine.' With a slight frown, she said, 'I can't believe we're sitting here, you talking to me.'

'Well, I've been thinking. Your mother is probably right. I'm not much of a thinking man. Anyway, I know now that I was too hard on you. And that you were right when you told me that I was a racist. And of course I know that you were never a trollop or a slut. But I was angry. And jealous. You were the apple of my eye and you preferred Giovanni. I just hit out at both of you. And I apologise.'

He said this quite fast and without expression. It crossed Laura's mind that he'd rehearsed it and she almost felt sorry for him. But a tight little ball of anger was forming in her gut. She thought that if this was an apology, it was not much of one. She waited, to see if there was more. Donald sat back, and said, 'There, I've said it. I was wrong, and I'm sorry.' He smiled at her. 'And of course you are welcome at Chorlton.'

The ball of anger was turning to cold steel. 'Is that all?' He looked at her blankly. 'Is that all you can say? Sorry for calling me and Giovanni names?'

'Well, yes. I've said I'm sorry. And it has cost me a lot to say . . .'

'Cost *you* a lot. Cost you? It cost me my *baby*, Daddy. My beloved baby. To say nothing of my home, my family, my father! It cost me my *life*. And what about my mother? It cost her her daughter, her peace of mind, her happiness.' Her voice, which had started strident, suddenly faltered. More quietly, she said, 'I'm glad you're sorry. And I'm sorry for the pain I caused you. But I'm over that now. I no longer need you, Daddy. I've learnt to do without you.'

'Don't say that . . .'

'Why not? It's true. But I came to see you to tell you that both David and Mummy are desperately, deeply unhappy and that you should be doing something about them. Don't worry about me. I'm fine. I have a good man to look after me, who would never, ever, behave like you.' She reached for her handbag and stood up. This time she didn't say goodbye.

David was grateful for the workload that harvest brings. He worked from dawn till ten at night, and went to bed so tired he dropped into dreamless sleep. Every morning he woke to the harrowing knowledge of Jill's death, but the need to get out and on the tractor helped. Only distraction kept his misery at bay.

He pushed thoughts of leaving Chorlton to the back of his mind. He was too busy, and lacked the energy, to think about the technicalities of emigration, new jobs, travel, or what would happen to Chorlton. I'll think of it after harvest, he thought, when there's more time.

Once the harvest was in, David went to see George at Frampton. Old Andrew greeted him at the front door.

'His Lordship offers his apologies for not being here as arranged.

He's on his way, but her Ladyship, the Dowager Countess, has had an accident, and he's had to accompany her to the hospital.'

'Oh, my goodness, is it serious?'

'I believe it is, sir. She slipped in the kennels. Dr Drummond fears a broken hip as well as a dislocated shoulder.'

'I'm so sorry. Please tell the Earl that I'll come another time.'

At that moment, they heard George's car on the gravel, and a few seconds later, he was out of the car and hurrying up the steps.

'Oh good, I am glad you're still here. So sorry to keep you . . .'

David renewed his offer to come again later, but George would not hear of it. He ushered David into the study, where David had done the deal over the park with George's father.

'I'm so sorry to hear about your mother, George. Is it worse than a broken arm?'

'Sadly, yes. Poor Mother. Much worse. She has a broken hip, arm and several ribs. But worse than any of that, they've found a tumour on her spine. Bone cancer.'

'Oh my God, George. That's dreadful.'

George offered him a pink gin, 'I know the sun isn't over the yardarm,' he said, 'but I need a drink. Can't pretend my seemingly indestructible Mama being brought down isn't a hell of a shock. And, with what you've been through, you've earned the right to drink any time of the day or night.'

'Thank you.' David took the glass. 'Did they give you any prognosis? What will happen now? Will they operate on the hip?'

'We don't know yet. She's all trussed up with the arm, and she's in a sort of straitjacket. Apparently the tumour is quite advanced. They think she'll be dead in six months.'

They stood looking out of the window, from where they could see one of the large potato fields, incongruously cut into the park and fenced with barbed wire to keep out the sheep that had replaced the old Earl's beloved deer.

'One of these years we might not have to deface your park with potatoes, George.'

'We live in hope. But with so much still on the ration I doubt if I'll get it back for a while.'

'True, and the nation would starve without spuds.'

They turned back from the window and George sat at the desk, signalling for David to take the other chair.

'Look, George,' said David, 'I'll come straight to the point. My heart is not in this feud of our fathers'. I'm not certain of the rights and wrongs of it all either. But one thing is sure, the lawyers will drag it out until the crack of doom.'

'Well, I agree with you there.'

'I have no idea what I'm going to do. Sometimes I think I'll emigrate, or just quit and do something else. But whatever I do—'

George interrupted, frowning. 'What do you mean, emigrate? How will that help?'

'I don't know, maybe it won't. But whatever happens, this Barrow farms business needs to be settled. Do you think we could reach a deal ourselves?'

'I'd be glad to, old chap, and my old man is dead so he will have no say in it. But Donald won't come to the table just because we say so.'

'I don't think he'll put up a fight. Not now. He's so completely crushed by Jill's death you'd think she was married to him, not me.'

'Poor man. Poor both of you.'

David gave a small wry smile. 'You wouldn't think you could be jealous over a dead woman, would you? Well, I am. I resent his grieving. Isn't that unkind? And ridiculous?'

'No, not at all. Perfectly natural.'

'Anyway, if I tell him I won't support his claim he'll find it hard to win the case.'

'He's never had any case, but that hasn't stopped him hanging on to the profits of the land and claiming that it no longer belongs to us. It's mad.'

'Actually, George, it's not so mad. He could even be right in law. But that doesn't mean it's fair. His case is that the land was requisitioned by the Government for the airfield, then found surplus to requirements and handed to the War Ag to deal with. And they got us to farm it. So his contention is that it's not ours to hand back, and you must take it up with the government.'

'Yes, I know all that, but it's not true. We got the requisition order right enough, but they never paid us any compensation or did anything about the farms. Nothing happened until your father kicked out the tenants and put you in charge.'

'To be fair, George, that was the committee, not my father.'

'None of whom had the balls to stand up to him. But you would go against him in this?'

'I think I'd have to.' David explained his father's complicated involvement over the years. 'I cannot persuade him that, right or wrong in law, it just looks wrong.'

They talked on, and George told David what Grace had already told Donald – that he wanted good tenants for the three farms, or a good deal with a contractor. He did not want to farm the land himself and if David made him a fair offer, then fine, he could go on farming it as now, only for a fair rent or a fair profit share. He would listen to anything David came up with.

'But you'll still have the question of ownership to pursue, George. Presumably the deeds for the Barrow farms are now in the bowels of the RAF somewhere. It could take years.'

'Maybe, but tracking them down need not be expensive and if between then and now you pay me rent, and we can prove the land has been continuously farmed – which we can, the War Ags kept meticulous records through the war, crops and yields etc. – then I'm sure the Government won't hang on to the deeds.'

'I can do better than that, George. I always put what I considered a fair rent for the Barrow farms into a separate account. It was Jill's idea. She was very strong on the subject. She thought my father was profiteering. The account is called 'Frampton Farms Rent account'. The bank statements go back ten years, with rent going in every September. There's quite a pocket of money in there. That should prove the land was farmed and that I considered it part of your acreage, like the park.'

George's mouth was open, his eyes wide. 'Good God, David! Does your father know?'

'No, and I admit I used to be nervous about him finding out, but I'd have simply argued it was prudent to set money aside for rent in case we ever had to pay it.'

'Aren't you still nervous?'

'No, because last year, on my thirtieth birthday, he passed the management wholly over to me. So now it's legitimately my decision. And it's a good business decision.'

George suddenly stood up and reached to shake David's hand. 'David, I've never known anyone do anything as honourable as this.'

David had half-risen for the handshake. Now he sank back and continued to roll his cigarette in his lap. Then he lifted his eyes to George and smiled, a rather wry smile, but a smile neverthe-less. 'Now you'll be hard put not to give the new tenancies to us.'

'Not something I can do if you're in the Antipodes. That's a daft idea, David, and it would break your mother's heart. Besides, you have the twins to think of.'

David thought, If you knew how hard I try *not* to think of them. He didn't want to discuss the twins.

'I expect you're right,' he said.

A few weeks later Laura was again visiting Chorlton with Angelica, now a chattering toddler. She resolved to come as often as she could. Babies grew so fast and she didn't want her mother to miss anything: early smiles, sucking toes, efforts to crawl, first words. Besides, it was so good seeing her mother.

Sophie had spent the whole of her annual holiday looking after the boys and was sleeping in the now-vacated nanny's room next to the nursery. The nanny had only been hired for the first two months and she'd left at the beginning of September. The babies were weaned onto formula and were thriving.

Laura was touched by Sophie's dedication. When the babies were not sleeping in the nursery, they would be out in the baby carriage with Sophie, parked in the yard where she and Maud could hear them wail, or in the kitchen in her arms.

'Sophie,' she said, 'aren't you exhausted? When Angelica was the twins' age, she nearly finished me, and you're looking after two of them *and* working as a GP. How do you do it?'

'Maud and Grace do as much as I do, honestly. And Mabel helps too. But I come because I adore them. I've delivered plenty of babies, and I've got lots of them as patients, but these two have got my heart in a vice.'

On the second day of her visit, Laura noticed that the women were careful to see that when David came in to lunch, the babies were upstairs sleeping.

'Doesn't David want to see them? Surely he's not still ignoring them?'

'He's no better,' said Maud, 'and he's so devastated we haven't tackled him since the last time with you.'

'But sooner or later,' said Sophie, 'we have to stop this business of hiding the boys from him. It's ridiculous. They can't go their whole lives staying out of the sight of their father.'

Laura was aghast. 'Has he never held them?'

'Held them – no, he definitely hasn't, not since those few moments after their birth. Seen them – well, he must see the pram about the place, but I doubt he's ever looked inside.'

Laura turned to her mother. 'Mummy, this is so wrong. If David doesn't want the children, shouldn't they be adopted?'

'Oh, Laura, neither of us could bear that.'

'I'd adopt them if I could,' said Sophie, 'but unmarried women can't adopt. Maud still believes David will come round, don't you, Maud?'

'Of course he'll come round in the end – he's got to. We can't have . . .' She stopped, her eyes filling with tears.

'I pray to God he will,' said Sophie. 'But I do doubt it. He seems absolutely closed to them.'

'I think we should force the issue,' said Laura.

So the next day when David came in to lunch, Sophie had Hal in her lap and was giving him his bottle. Laura had Richard under one arm and was carrying a jug of water to the table in the other. Laura saw David stop in the doorway, notice the infants, and hesitate. He looked for a second as if he was going to turn round and go out again, but he walked to his place at the table and sat down without comment. Richard began to gurn and to twist his head against Laura's breast, rooting for a nipple. She went back to the sink and picked up his bottle.

And then, on impulse, she deposited baby and bottle in David's lap, saying, 'Here, David, just hold him for me, will you?'

The baby was now crying, his tiny pink tongue and gums on display as he yelled. Laura had to raise her voice for David to hear her. 'Put the bottle in his mouth, David.'

David did as he was told and Richard's yells quickly subsided into rhythmic grunts of satisfaction as he sucked, his tiny hands clenching and unclenching like a cat kneading a cushion.

Laura went into the larder, ostensibly to fetch something, but in truth it was to force her brother to hold his son a little longer. When she went back, she served the soup before taking the baby and bottle back. No one commented, but she noticed David's eyes following Richard, and then moving to Hal on Sophie's lap.

After that, it was tacitly admitted that the twins did not have to be purposely kept out of David's way. But he didn't embrace them, pick them up or talk to them. He might have been a visiting uncle, not a father, thought Laura, and one that doesn't like children at all.

CHAPTER THIRTY-THREE

1951

Maud wondered where the time went. The last year had flown by and the twins were now a year old.

Life at Chorlton had improved. She could not say she was happy, but her grief for Jill and sorrow for David had become less raw. She saw a lot more of Grace and Jane, since they often came over to help with the twins, and now that the Dowager Countess had followed her husband to the grave, the atmosphere at Frampton Hall was much more welcoming. Donald was, if not back to his old commanding self, at least civil to Laura on her visits, and he was helping David where he could, mostly in the farm office. Maud longed for the old closeness and physical affection that had once existed between her and Donald, but she recognised the unlikelihood of that. If she was honest, that closeness faded many years ago, probably on their move down south. But couples grew apart, and as long as they both enjoyed what they could of their marriage, and had respect for each other, they muddled along quite well.

There had been a time, on account of the Barrow farms

business, and even more because of his attitude to Laura, when she'd felt little or no respect for Donald, and that had been truly terrible. Now, it had returned, at least in part. He'd made a real effort to pull himself out of his slough and he had tried to make it up with his daughter. Of course, she understood why Laura had spurned him, but he was a proud man for whom saying sorry was near-impossible.

The twins had made an astonishing difference to the mood at Chorlton. She found herself smiling when she heard their early morning cries for attention and later their gurgles and hiccups of merriment as Sophie, having fed them, now dressed and played with them. Maud would lie in bed, waiting for seven o'clock, when Sophie, already dressed for work, would push the door open with her foot and dump Hal or Richard on her tummy, turn and go back for the other.

Both twins were thriving, largely, she thought, thanks to Sophie. After last September's sojourn spent looking after them, she had moved into Chorlton to be their surrogate mother. She still worked at the medical practice but only in the mornings and all day on Saturday. Maud was delighted with the deal that she and Sophie had done: Sophie had free board and lodging, which meant she could let her cottage in Moreton to make up for her loss of earnings at the surgery. Maud looked after the boys while Sophie was at work, but she was home to give them their lunch at 12.30. Her love for Richard and Hal was obvious, and when they were out and about strangers would assume she was their mother. Maud noticed that Sophie didn't deny it. I expect she feels she *is* their mother, she thought. She's certainly happy. 'It's my dream job,' she'd said, 'half-time doctor and half-time nanny.' And Maud had felt a glow of affection as Sophie had added, 'And living at Chorlton with you all, and eating Maud Oliver's cooking every day. What more could I want?'

Maud knew, or thought she knew, what more Sophie could want, and that was David. Neither of them had ever mentioned such a thing, but Maud had a shrewd idea that Sophie's love of the twins was something to do with love for David. When Laura and Sophie were children, Sophie's adoration of the much older David had been funny and touching. She used to trail round after him, ball-boy for him and his friends when they played tennis, fetch him a glass of lemonade. There was no doubt in Maud's mind that she'd been devastated when he'd fallen in love with Jill. She was still at school then, and David was in his early twenties, but a sixteen-year-old heart can be broken just as badly as a grown-up one.

My little dream, thought Maud, of David warming to, and one day marrying, the carer of his children is going nowhere. At lunch he might pass her a glass or plate, but he barely speaks to her. And though he's never rude, he always leaves the room soon after she enters it.

But there was progress with the twins. After that day when Laura had dumped the infant Richard in David's lap she'd noticed him watching them. He did not make any overtures, did not pick them up or play with them, but he seemed to regard them with more interest, as though looking at puppies or growing lambs. He'd sometimes pop in of a morning, ostensibly for a cup of coffee or to ask her something, but really, she thought, to look at his sons in the playpen. She sometimes saw his face soften, his habitual solemn expression fading for a moment.

And he'd not mentioned Australia again, thank God. Maud suspected that the yearly cycle of farming had taken his attention:

the tilling of the land, planting, harvesting, and tilling again. She found the inevitability of it all somehow comforting, and she wondered if David did; people died, their children lived, sheep were slaughtered and lambs were born.

In late July David received a letter from Jill's parents in Kent. They wanted him to visit them and bring the babies. They'd never seen them, partly, Maud suspected, because David could not face such a visit as it would mean pretending a love he did not feel for his sons, and partly because Jill's mother's grief had taken the form of deep depression that had lasted all through the winter and spring. The only contact between the families had been occasional phone calls which Maud had insisted on, and brief letters between her and Jill's mother.

Now they wanted to meet their grandsons. And besides, the letter said, David had not seen the headstone they'd had made for Jill's grave.

He must go, thought Maud. He must. And he must take Sophie. Perhaps a little enforced time together will make him acknowledge her worth.

'If I have to go, Mum, you'll come with me, won't you?' he said.

'No, dear, I won't. You must take Sophie. I really cannot leave Donald and I'm too busy in the dairy. With the cows producing such good milk it would be stupid to stop butter-making now.'

'Oh, Mum, just for a few days we could surely let the Milk Marketing Board take all the milk. It's not as if the dairy was big business. You only make cheese and butter for us and our neighbours, anyway.'

'That's a bit ungenerous, darling. It might not make a lot, but it turns a profit, and anyway, I cannot leave Donald.'

'Sophie can look after Dad. If he's here – he'll probably go to his club. I really don't want to take Sophie.'

'And I dare say she won't want to go with you either. You are barely civil to her, David, and it's ridiculous. You cannot go on blaming her. She was not responsible for Jill's death. And you know it.'

'Do I?'

'Yes, I think you do. If those boys of yours are happy and secure, which they are, it's thanks to Sophie. But far from grateful, you're hostile to her.'

Maud shook her head. David's continued intransigence saddened and puzzled her. Perhaps he was more like his father than she thought.

'I am not hostile! I've barely said a word to her.'

'Precisely. If that's not hostility, then it's certainly indifference. Which is almost more cruel.'

Maud saw her son's jaw set, but he didn't answer.

'Anyway, darling, if Sophie doesn't go with you I don't see how you can go at all. Which would be rude and hurtful to your parents-in-law.'

Maud had an ulterior motive in refusing to go with David. At the moment Sophie's presence kept him from his sons. If he changed his attitude to Sophie, he'd get closer to the boys.

Sophie, though anxious about the trip, felt she had no option but to agree to it. Jill's parents had a right to see the twins, and the option of a strange nurse from Universal Aunts looking after her precious Richard and Hal was unthinkable.

They borrowed Donald's old Bentley as the boot could accommodate their suitcases and all the paraphernalia of babyhood:

nappies, bottles, clothes and toys. What wouldn't fit was the huge baby carriage Grace had given them, but Jill's mother said she would borrow one.

The twins were wedged securely on the back seat, each in a new cloth carrycot. Sophie fetched a couple of sofa cushions to prevent the cots sliding. The babies fretted at first, and Sophie had to hold Hal to prevent him trying to crawl out of his cot. But the movement of the car soon sent them both to sleep.

Sophie had thought it would be difficult to sit in near total silence next to David on a lengthy trip. But long years of one-sided secret love had disciplined her to conceal emotion, and her tiredness made silence easier than conversation. They exchanged the briefest of sentences.

'Would you mind closing your window?' said Sophie.

'Not at all,' David at once turned the handle. Neither spoke again for twenty minutes, when Sophie knew she was falling asleep. 'Do you mind if I nod off, David? I'm so tired.'

'Not at all,' said David again.

Maybe 'Not at all' is all he'll say for three hours, thought Sophie as she sank back and closed her eyes. Thank God the twins are fast asleep. Richard had been awake most of the night, teething, and Sophie had been up with him, putting oil of cloves on his gums, trying to interest him in his dummy, rocking him in her arms as she walked about the nursery. But, poor little mite, he was miserable, his chin chapped from dribbling, his cheeks shiny red.

On the outskirts of London they drew up at the Uxbridge hotel. They carried the boys to the Ladies room where Sophie changed their nappies.

In the restaurant they ordered tea and sandwiches, and Sophie produced two jam jars full of cooked vegetables with fish, and two teaspoons. The children were beginning to grizzle and Sophie could not feed them both at once. She said, 'David, do you think you could feed Hal? They are so used to Maud and me feeding them both at the same time, I think he will bawl his head off if he has to wait.'

Sophie half expected him to refuse. She had not seen him with a baby in his lap since Laura forced Richard and his bottle on him – what, nine months ago? But to her surprise he said, 'I doubt I'll be as efficient as you. Why don't I hold them both and you spoon food into them alternately?'

So that was what they did, Sophie putting a teaspoon of food into Hal's open mouth, and then, while he gulped it down, one into his brother's. The babies were hungry and soon the better part of two jars of mashed fish, potatoes and carrots were gone and they would no longer open their mouths. Sophie took Hal from David and gave him a bottle for Richard.

With Hal in her lap, sucking noisily, Sophie studied David. He held Richard in the crook of his arm, but lightly. His large brown hand steadied the bottle and Richard's chubby hands clutched it, too, as if nervous it might be wrenched away. The baby's eyes were on David, studying him as he sucked. Sophie could not see David's eyes, because his thick brown hair fell over them, but he was obviously returning the baby's gaze, his face soft and relaxed.

They made good time negotiating the outskirts of London, still scarred by weed-covered bomb sites and boarded-up buildings. It was a relief when they left the main roads and were bowling down the leafy lanes of Kent. They were perhaps ten miles from their destination when a bumping motion and difficulty in steering forced David to stop the car.

'Damn and blast, a puncture,' said David. 'I thought for once we might get somewhere without one.'

Richard was awake and threatening to cry, so, fearing he would wake Hal, Sophie lifted him out of his cot. She grabbed the travelling rug and took both baby and rug onto a sunny patch of the grass verge.

Sophie thought Richard might be in for another bout of teething, but there was nothing wrong with him other than a wet nappy. Sophie changed him, gave him a few sips of diluted orange juice, and he at once reverted to his usual sunny nature. She lay on her back on the springy grass. She lifted him above her, and he looked down, whooping with pleasure. She kept her arms straight – he was getting heavier – and jiggled him. They were both absorbed in this game when she felt a shadow block out the sun. She turned to see David standing by them, wiping his hands on a cloth. She sat up, lowering the baby onto the rug.

He was looking at them intently, but she'd no idea what he was thinking. He turned back to the car, opened the boot to stow the tools. He called over his shoulder.

'All done. We're off, Sophie.'

The next days were easier than Sophie had thought they'd be, though there were awkward moments. On the first morning, when it was time for the boys' lunch, Sophie and Jill's mother each had a baby on their laps, and were spooning rice pudding into them when David came into the kitchen.

'Oh, David, I'm doing your job. So sorry.' Jill's mother struggled up and pressed Hal into his arms.

Sophie saw David's look of embarrassment as he protested. 'No, honestly, please. Please go ahead.' He tried to give Hal back. Hal, interrupted in the middle of his pudding, opened his mouth and yelled.

Sophie was torn between sympathy for Hal and for David, and laughter. She almost pushed David into the chair and handed him the pudding bowl and spoon. 'Just spoon it in,' she said, trying hard not to smile. Poor David, she thought, watching him. He looks so tentative and awkward. No wonder when you think that yesterday was the first time he'd helped feed them, and even then he didn't *do* anything, just held them.

The fact that Jill's parents had no idea of the past tensions between David and her was an absolute boon, thought Sophie. David, unable to escape as he could at home and not wanting to raise questions, found himself falling into the role expected of him. He helped with the boys, and talked to Sophie. Not much, but enough for their hosts not to notice any strain.

They pushed the children (in separate borrowed pushchairs) up to the churchyard together to visit Jill's grave.

'We won't come with you, Sophie,' Jill's mother had said. 'I think David might want to be alone. Except for you, of course.'

Sophie had wondered if that meant that as the nanny she didn't count and was invisible, or that she was accepted as an inseparable adjunct to the family. She hoped it was the latter.

Jill's gravestone was plain dressed stone, rounded at the top. The only decoration was a design of crossed sheaves of wheat carved along the top. Sophie was relieved that it was not polished marble or black granite. That would have been too pompous for Jill. The lettering was in elegant Roman capitals, just her name and dates:

JILLIAN OLIVER
1922–1950

She stood beside David, saying nothing. Sophie was determined not to weep, though she felt her eyes fill. Then Richard started to do his happy experimental shouts, half laughing, half yelping, and woke Hal up, who at once started keening. Sophie took Hal's pushchair from David and pushed it to the other side of the churchyard, where she set him down on the ground. The novelty of the lush over-long grass and the sun shining on it distracted him from his complaints and he busied himself with wrenching fistfuls of grass out of the ground.

Sophie ran back to collect Richard, leaving David on his own. He was standing still, apparently unaware of the babies' noise or her running back and forth. She wheeled Richard to join his brother and the three of them sat on the warm grass, the boys laughing and apparently chattering to each other in a secret language. Sophie lay down on her back, blinking back tears, while Richard tried to pull her beaded necklace into his mouth, succeeding only in drooling into her neck. And Hal, trying to pull himself up, fell face forward onto her thigh.

After fifteen minutes or so, his eyes red and face blotchy from tears, David was standing over them holding a bunch of wild flowers: meadowsweet, red campion and moon daisies.

'I thought the boys might enjoy strewing the grave,' he said. His voice had a break in it, and was deep and thick from crying.

So they took the twins back to Jill's grave and threw the flowers, one by one, onto it, the boys quickly getting the idea, and enjoying it, like a game.

Walking back, Sophie said, 'That was a lovely thing to do.

Jill would have much preferred that to a formal bouquet left to wilt in a vase.'

'Yes, and the boys, though they won't remember it, can be told we did it, and it will be a sort of memory for them.'

When they got back, David said to his father-in-law, 'I love the headstone. So straightforward and self-effacing, like Jill. And are the wheat sheaves because she was a farmer?'

'Yes, and also the thought of harvest, of being gathered in her prime.'

On the long drive back, Sophie felt the atmosphere very different from that of their journey to Kent. Once they'd negotiated the farm track and country lanes, and were on the main road, David looked across at her, but she kept looking straight ahead. She sensed that he had something on his mind, that he was about to say something important.

'Sophie, I want to tell you something.'

She turned her face towards him. 'I'm all ears.'

'I've been such a fool, Sophie. I had no idea how much you love the twins.'

'I do love them, that's true.'

'Mother told me I was wrong to blame you for Jill's death, but it's taken me a year to let go of that idea. I just want to tell you that I know I was wrong. And I'm really, really sorry. I think I knew it all along, ever since I read your report on Jill's death, but I just couldn't admit it.'

'You needed someone to blame. There's no comfort in saying "These things happen" – we crave explanation. It's natural.'

David glanced across at her. 'How did you get to be so wise?'

She laughed. 'I'm not wise, but I am very practical.'

'That you are. I've been watching you for a week, and you are amazing.'

Sophie felt her cheeks redden. 'Thank you, David.'

'There's something else, and I feel really terrible about it. I told myself you were looking after the boys out of guilt, substituting for the mother you had allowed to die. How could I have thought that?'

'Oh, David, I don't know.' Sophie frowned, trying to think. 'The mind tries to find a reason, however far-fetched, to explain things it does not want to face. Maybe you could not love the boys whose birth had killed Jill. Maybe you resented the fact that the doctor who failed to save her was now happy because of them, or them happy because of her.'

'Whatever mangled reasoning I was going in for, I should have understood just what I owe to you. I hadn't a clue how much work the twins are. Or how skilled you are at dealing with them, and how good at comforting them.'

'Well, I adore them. Maybe one day you will too.'

CHAPTER THIRTY-FOUR

Laura and Giovanni, fulfilling the promise made at their wedding to visit Carlotta in Abruzzo, decided to take their first real holiday. Giovanni wrote to Carlotta, proposing to come in August.

Giovanni translated her reply to Laura. '*Of course I long for you to come. It will be wonderful. But don't come in August. It can be over 40 degrees by the coast. You know that, little brother. Your pretty English wife will expire! Everyone just wants to sleep all the time, and I want to take you to see Chieti and Atri. And Angelica will want to swim in the sea, but she'll burn up if we have a heatwave, and we nearly always do. Please come in September, Giovanni, or in June. I know it's not school holidays, but I only have to teach in the mornings, and we'll have lots of time.*'

But they had to go in August. It was the only time that the Calzone business slackened off a little. The new shop in Westbourne Grove would open in June, and Giovanni was negotiating for a mini-factory in Ealing to take over the ice-cream production. He could not go before August.

'Besides,' said Laura, 'I'll be decorating and furnishing the mews. Our lease on this flat runs out at the end of July and the builders won't finish the new house until June. We must move in June. Maybe we should postpone? Go next year?'

But Giovanni was adamant. They'd be fine.

Carlotta welcomed them with characteristic warmth and affection. As soon as they were in the house, she sat down on the sofa so that her head was level with Angelica's. 'And how old are you, Angelica?' she asked.

'Three and a half.'

'And has your daddy taught you to speak any Italian yet?'

'I can say *un cono gelato, per favore.*'

They all laughed and Carlotta hugged her. 'And you shall have an ice-cream cone from the first ice-cream shop we pass.'

Ever since Carlotta's no-good husband Tomaso had, to her mixed fury and relief, walked out on her and their boys, Carlotta had run the family smallholding. She'd gone back to teaching in the high school at Atri, and she made a bit extra by growing figs, pomegranates and table grapes for the market.

She lived in a typical farmer's house, with red-tiled roof, vines growing on the terrace, red geraniums on the steps in terracotta pots, a gnarled old olive tree sharing a weedy patch of lawn with a prolific cherry tree (whose fat black fruit now filled the shelves in the larder), and a wonderful view of vineyards and olive groves rising gently to the hilltop town of Atri in the distance.

Laura stood on the terrace, entranced. 'It's an absolute picture postcard of an Italian idyll,' she said. 'I can't believe it. It even smells right, of baked earth, fresh thyme and rosemary. Carlotta, you're so lucky.'

Carlotta smiled, but she shook her head. 'It's beautiful, yes. But the roof leaks and the electrics are positively dangerous. It needs a lot of money spent on it, which I don't have. It's OK for the moment, but none of us can afford to get sick, and when I stop earning, I'll have to give it up.'

'But Silvano will be earning one day. Maybe he can take it on?'

'There's no future for the boys in the country. Or even in small towns like Atri. They'll have to go away to Sulmona or Rome for jobs, and even then, who knows? I'll have to sell sooner or later.'

Laura was happy to see Giovanni so in his element, delighted to be back in Italy, wanting to show off all its glories to her. It was hot, but not unbearably so, and they visited churches and cafés, food markets and museums while Carlotta looked after Angelica, spoiling her with sweetmeats and ice cream.

The boys, Silvano and Mario, had cleared out a row of old pigsties behind the house and claimed them as their bedrooms. They put mattresses into two of them and slept in them in the summer. They were too low to stand up in, and they had to use torches to read by, which, said Mario, attracted flying insects. But Laura thought it must feel very independent to have your own space like that, and she admired Carlotta's relaxed attitude to her boys' schemes.

Angelica watched, fascinated, as Silvano and Mario crawled into their 'houses' for a siesta.

'I want my own house,' she declared. Silvano volunteered to clear out another pigsty for her, and to look after her if she was brave enough to sleep out there all night.

But Giovanni vetoed this. 'No, she's too young. She might wake up and be frightened. Even in the house you can hear the wild boar snuffling and grunting,' he said.

Laura thought, I must be harder-hearted than Giovanni. I'd

have let her do it. Silvano would have brought her in if she was frightened. But Giovanni is so protective.

'But darling,' she said to the wailing Angelica, 'maybe if your cousins will clear one out for you, you could use it as a Wendy House, to play in in the day.'

Sometimes they all went out together. One day the whole family was having lunch in a restaurant in Chieti. The outdoor tables had encroached on the street, half of which was given up to a fenced-in square of formally laid tables with open sides to allow a bit of breeze and a canopy to keep off the sun.

Another Italian family was eating next door to them – an old woman, presumably the grandmother, and a young couple with three children.

Laura was impressed that the children were given exactly what the grown-ups had, and all of them ate their antipasti of salami, olives, tomatoes and artichokes in concentrated silence. When the pasta came (*spaghetti al pomodoro*) the two women started quarrelling, their gestures getting ever more vigorous and their voices louder.

'What's going on? Giovanni, what are they saying?' asked Laura.

He didn't answer, but he was obviously amused by the argument. Laura longed to know what it was all about, and strained to understand. But it was hopeless. They were speaking faster and faster as the argument heated up.

'Please, Giovanni, tell me what's going on,' she pleaded.

'It's ridiculous,' said Giovanni. 'The old lady is saying that no one should put Parmesan on pasta with tomato. She says *spaghetti al pomodoro* is a Roman dish and no Roman would ever do anything so wicked as add cheese to it. Her poor daughter-in-law is having a hard time defending her northern ways.'

Laura laughed. She was about to agree with Giovanni that it seemed a silly thing to go to war about, when Carlotta cut in.

'She's quite right. To teach children to smother everything with *parmigiano*, it is wrong.'

'I *like* Parmesan on my pasta,' said Mario. 'And on *minestra,* on lots of things.'

'But you will eat anything!' snapped his mother. 'What kind of a judge of food can you be?'

Laura listened in amazement. A disagreement about the sprinkling of Parmesan had spread from one table to the next. We'll have the whole restaurant joining in in a minute, she thought.

But Laura loved the Italians' obsession with food. Once, shopping with Carlotta in Atri market, she said, 'Carlotta, I love the way you shop. You go from stall to stall, inspecting everything, feeling the tomatoes, smelling the melons, prodding the fish. And half the time you don't buy anything. English stallholders would stop you touching anything.'

'But how can you know if it's good?'

'You can't, but I don't think we care like you do. You talk about food all the time, like the French. The English never do.'

Carlotta shook her head in disbelief. 'Of course we talk about food. It's important. I would rather do a good pasta with nothing but garlic and breadcrumbs than spend a lot of money on second-class, tasteless things.'

Laura began to cook with Carlotta, making stuffed baked aubergines, bruschetta with rosemary-flavoured lardo, minestrone thick with fresh vegetables from the garden. She wrote down local ways of cooking: how the women bottled red peppers and artichoke hearts, how the restaurant chefs grilled veal chops or lamb steaks with different marinades and herbs. She watched the way they cooked whole fish or chickens buried in salt.

At dinner one evening they ate pumpkin risotto followed by pink calves' liver fried with *porchini* and *cavalo nero*.

'One day, Giovanni,' Laura said, 'we'll open a proper Italian trattoria in London, with Carlotta making pasta in the basement.'

Laura was joking, and was surprised when Carlotta said, 'Anytime. I mean it. Give me a job, little brother, and I'll be there. I would love to work in London.'

Giovanni looked up. 'Are you serious?'

'Of course I'm serious. The boys would learn English and be able to make a living. What is there for them in Abruzzo? Nothing.'

CHAPTER THIRTY-FIVE

One Sunday in December, Maud and Sophie were in the Chorlton kitchen with the twins, cooking because it was too wet and cold to go out.

Richard, cheerful and confident, was the more difficult. He'd insisted on climbing right onto the table rather than sitting in his high chair like Hal. Listening is not his strong point, thought Maud. He's got a natural bent towards rebellion.

He agitated until Maud let him try to stir the cake batter. 'Richard, no.' Maud pulled Richard's fat fist out of the mixing bowl, and wiped it with a wet dishcloth. 'Darling, here, I'll help you. Stir it like this.' She gave him a teaspoon and put her hand over his to guide the spoon in the mixture. He put his other hand into the bowl, and then put his fingers in his mouth. He looked up at her, grinning, cake-mix in his open mouth and dripping off his chin. Then he flung his arms forward and giggled with pleasure as the sticky mess splattered Sophie.

Sophie fetched another cloth and cleaned up Richard, herself and the table and then she put him into the playpen on the floor. She is endlessly patient, thought Maud, watching Sophie respond to Richard's wail by giving him an empty grape-nuts box with a teaspoon dropped into it. Richard was immediately distracted, shaking it for the sound and trying to see inside.

Maud finished making the ginger cake and put it in the oven. Then she sat on a stool and watched Sophie making scones with the more thoughtful Hal. She put the scone mix onto the tray of his high chair and tried to show him how to stamp out scones with a cutter. It was too difficult a job for an eighteen-month-old, but Hal persevered, his face concentrated and determined. Maud saw with approval that Sophie didn't immediately re-make his misshapen lumps of dough. Instead she encouraged and praised him, and then surreptitiously reshaped them as she put them on the baking tray.

'Cooking with these two certainly doubles the time it takes,' said Maud, shutting the oven door on the tray of scones. She looked at the clock. 'Well, if the ginger cake hasn't cooled by teatime, we'll just have it warm. Nothing wrong with that.'

Sunday tea had been the gastronomic highlight of the week for Maud's children for years, first in Yorkshire when there was only Hugh, then ten years later with David, and finally with baby Laura. Her children had come so far apart that Maud thought she must have produced more family Sunday lunches and teas than almost anyone.

Maud considered teatime a serious business. In Yorkshire it had been high tea and included an egg or salad, and a pudding. Here it was simpler, but they still started with bread and butter, then went on to scones or teacakes and jam, and only then were they allowed treacle tart or cake.

Because Sunday tea was a special occasion, it took place in the dining room, which was hardly ever used, not even for Sunday lunch which, Maud said, was easier to serve in the kitchen.

During the war they'd had a very pared-down version of it in the kitchen, not the dining room. They'd made do with the National Loaf, spread with marge, Shippam's paste or jam, and perhaps a rhubarb or apple cake if there was enough sugar.

But now the best china came out, and the silver teapot and hot water jug, too. There was a lace tablecloth spread over the mahogany dining table and round it sat the twins in their high chairs, the whole family and Sophie.

In the middle of the table stood an old-fashioned three-tier cake stand. On the bottom layer was the bread and butter. On the next were the scones, and on the top, the ginger cake. Strawberry jam and lemon curd were in cut-glass jam pots, and Maud had even rolled the butter into balls. She looked around the table with satisfaction.

Maud was pleased to see that David arranged the high chairs so that he and Sophie sat next to each other and between the boys, each taking responsibility for one of them. His whole attitude to her, and to them, had changed radically since their visit to Jill's parents in Kent. He played with his children now, helped feed them, occasionally pushed them in the pram. Yesterday he'd piled them both into the wheelbarrow and raced them around the lawn. At last the deepest shadows of grief seemed to be passing.

He no longer blamed Sophie for Jill's death and he treated her with the same brotherly affection he'd had for her before Jill died. Maud still harboured a vestigial dream of his falling in love with her, but she admitted it was unlikely now. Just count your blessings, she told herself, and there are many.

'This bread's good, Mum,' said David, sandwiching two slices together and wolfing them down.

Maud smiled at the compliment. 'Well, it's such a joy to have flour off the ration. Baking's getting a lot easier. Now I'd just like sugar off, too.'

'And thank God for your butter, Maud,' said Sophie. 'They'll never make a marge to touch it.'

Donald reached for a scone, smeared it with butter and jam and topped it with a large teaspoon of clotted cream. Maud watched him, but forbore to say he was breaking the house rules by having butter *and* cream. He lifted his face and looked at her. She was surprised to see him smiling broadly, in that old intimate way.

'Well, Maud, praise from David and Sophie, and these urchins are scoffing away with gusto, which speaks for itself.'

Maud felt a flush of pleasure. When did Donald last pay her a compliment? He went on, 'What other family has home-made scones with home-made jam, home-made butter and cream? To say nothing of home-made bread and ginger cake?'

On New Year's Eve, as midnight approached, the family gathered in the drawing room at Chorlton. Sophie was wearing her best dress and the pearl necklace her parents had given her for her twenty-first birthday. As the strains of 'Auld Lang Syne' died away on the radio everyone kissed everyone else and Donald opened a second bottle of champagne.

'Here's to a good year on the farm,' said David.

'And to health and happiness for us,' added Donald.

Sophie clinked her glass against David's. 'And to the twins.'

'And to absent friends,' said Maud, raising her glass. Sophie noticed how deliberately she touched her glass to her husband's and held his gaze, 'Laura, Giovanni and little Angelica.'

As Donald gave his wife a wry smile, Sophie thought, You have to hand it to Maud, she never gives up, and Donald is mellowing. One day it will all be fine.

Suddenly they heard the sound of popping explosions and they all walked to the big French windows. Maud drew open the curtains in time for them to see two fireworks, great white rockets, burst in the sky from the direction of Frampton Hall.

'Good Lord,' said Donald. 'What on earth are they up to? It's not Guy Fawkes! Why are they letting off fireworks?'

'Oh, I remember now,' said Sophie, 'their Guy Fawkes party was rained off. They had to abandon the fireworks. It was to make up for cancelling Jane's birthday party when Geraldine died. Do you remember, Maud?'

'I do. Poor Grace said she went into a massive sulk. Directed, I suppose, at the Almighty for allowing it to rain.'

Sophie took David's arm. 'Let's go out and stand on the terrace. How exciting! Free fireworks.' David opened the French windows and they all stepped out.

They gazed at the starry sky, lit up by successive flowering rockets. Sophie thought they were breathtaking, so dramatic yet so brief. She felt a tiny drop of sadness every time one died and then told herself not to be so fanciful and romantic. David probably thinks them a ridiculous waste of money.

'Isn't it good to see fireworks rather than tracers and flak and firestorms?' said Maud.

'It is,' agreed David. 'I expect the whole village is getting a free show, not just us.'

After ten minutes or so the firework display seemed to be over and Maud and Donald went back inside.

'Aren't you chilly?' David asked Sophie.

'A bit, but it's lovely out here. So many stars, better than any fireworks.'

David slipped off his velvet smoking jacket and wrapped it round Sophie's shoulders. She felt a glow of pleasure and, she acknowledged, of desire as he bent to hold the lapels of the coat to imprison her in front of him.

'Sophie,' he said, looking into her upturned face. 'Shouldn't we get married?'

It wasn't much of a proposal, but Sophie's heart stopped. She'd longed for this moment for months. Her second thought, following immediately, was that she mustn't let him know how much she loved him, even now. He wasn't in love with her, she knew, but she could bear that.

'Yes,' she said. 'Perhaps we should. It must be right for the twins, mustn't it?'

'Definitely. But what about you? Could you bear being married to me?'

'Of course. We get on well now. And we both love the boys. I've thought for a while it would be a good thing for all of us. You need some wifely looking after. I couldn't bear to be separated from the boys, which would happen if you married someone else. The boys probably think I'm their mother anyway.'

David said, smiling, 'Goodness, I should have known you would be there before me, and have it all worked out.'

'Your mother is the one who had it all worked out. She's been dropping hints for a year.'

'God, you women. Men are just putty in your hands. I'm surprised you didn't propose to me!'

'I was giving you until next summer. I thought the world

might think badly of you if you remarried less than two years after Jill's death. You know how people gossip.'

David roared with laughter. 'You really have thought of everything, haven't you? When are we getting married then?'

She laughed and kissed him lightly on the cheek. 'In the summer. When the boys will be two, and can toddle down the aisle with us.'

'And you don't mind that I'm not down on my knee, declaring passionate love and undying devotion?'

Sophie laughed. 'Well, that would have been nice!' Then she looked at him seriously. 'Of course not. We're both grown up. Some of the best marriages are arranged. At least this one is agreed by us.'

Laura came bursting into Giovanni's study, Angelica at her heels. He looked up from his papers, startled. 'What's the matter, *cara*? What's happened?'

'Guess what?' she said. 'David and Sophie are getting married!'

Angelica pushed between her parents. 'What's happened, Mummy? Why are you all excited?'

'*Dio mio*,' exclaimed Giovanni. 'How extraordinary. I thought you said he blamed her for Jill dying?'

Laura flopped into the easy chair. 'Yes, he did, but every time I've gone down to Chorlton, he's seemed more relaxed and happy. And he's definitely more interested in his boys.'

'Mummy, Mummy, tell me what's happening. I want to know!' Angelica pulled at Laura's arm.

Giovanni dropped down to squat next to her. 'Sophie is going to marry your Uncle David. That is what your mama is so excited about.'

'But why? Why is it exciting?'

Giovanni wanted to laugh. 'It's probably more exciting for grown ups than for children, and more exciting for women than for men,' he replied, 'but it's still good when two people you love want to marry each other, no?'

He turned to Laura. 'But marrying Sophie! That is good for the twins, yes, for sure,' he said. 'But does he love her do you think?'

'I don't know. I've not seen them together much. When I'm there he's usually out on the farm. But anyway, she's coming up to London. She's taken two days off work at the surgery. It'll be wonderful to see her without the twins taking all her attention. We never get to talk anymore. You don't mind, do you?'

Giovanni didn't mind. It was good to see Laura so happy, and he was too. Everything was going well. Angelica was a joy: confident, sunny, energetic, as keen on good food as her father – and she adored him. The business was growing steadily. George was an ideal partner, wise and interested but never interfering. And this place, the Paddington Mews development – what a good investment. They'd finished the rebuilding. At first he and Laura had occupied just two of the cottages, knocked together, but with more Calzones opening in Belgravia and Kensington, it didn't make sense having the office in Billingsgate. So they'd let the floors over the café and taken over a third cottage, which gave them room for an office and an extra bedroom. Everything was going like a dream.

Sophie's impending visit was the spur for Laura to spring-clean the house. With Angelica 'helping', she dusted, swept and polished.

Laura was proud of their new home and longed for Sophie to see it. She had always found antique shops and second-hand markets irresistible, and, like her old bedroom at Chorlton, the house was full of her purchases. She never spent a lot of money but she had a keen eye for the interesting, unusual or beautiful. The curtains were second-hand and came from an old hotel that was being refurbished. They had huge pelmets and rope ties, which most people would have considered too grand for a cottage. They looked magnificent. She'd painted the walls a Georgian yellow, which perfectly set off the tightly packed carved mirrors and gilt-framed paintings of unknown people on the walls. On the shelves and tables was a growing clutter of antique china, silver, glass and curiosities like framed but- terflies, giant scarabs or ostrich eggs. Now that everything had been washed and polished rather than just dusted, their colours glowed and shone. Next to a wing-backed armchair, and serving as an occasional table, was a pile of enormous leather-bound account books, filled with copperplate writing.

Laura looked round the living room with pride. Oh, I do love this house, she thought. It's so exotic and comfy. Giovanni is a genius to have seen the potential in those derelict garages.

'Come on, darling,' she said to Angelica. 'We've worked very hard and you have been such a good girl, we need a treat. Let's go to the market and buy some flowers for Sophie's room, and we'll get you a lollipop or a string of liquorice. Shall we?'

Angelica skipped along the road, her plaits bouncing on her shoulders. They found the flower seller and bought early daf- fodils for Sophie's bedroom and the drawing room. They were from the Scilly Isles and expensive, but, Laura thought, her friend's visit warranted it. A little ashamed of herself, she also bought yet another glass vase. But it cost almost nothing and it would be perfect for the daffs.

Sophie arrived on the Thursday morning and was satisfyingly impressed with the house, which she was seeing for the first time.

Laura arranged for Angelica to spend the afternoon with a friend from nursery school so she and Sophie could have the whole day together. They lit the fire and sank into the deep sofa, their legs covered by a brightly coloured Mexican quilt.

It was as if they'd never been apart. The old intimacy which had been disrupted first by Laura's shame at giving up her son, and then by Sophie's workload, was immediately there.

'Oh, Sophie, it's so good to have you to myself,' said Laura. 'It's not as if we've been out of touch, but I don't think we've had a good gossip since I left Chorlton. And that was five years ago.'

'I've missed you, too,' Sophie replied. 'We should have tried harder, but what with work and the twins . . . And there are always other people around. But never mind, we've got two days now.'

They chattered on through the morning, and then went to the Edgware Road Calzone. They ate the famous deep-fried *formaggio in carozza*.

'Giovanni is desperate to find a supply of proper Italian mozzarella but English cheesemongers have never heard of it and don't want to know. We don't have the demand yet that would make them wake up and try.'

Laura watched Sophie cut her fried bread parcel in half. The melted cheddar slowly ran out and Sophie took a mouthful. A little string of cheese caught on her lip. Using her finger to push it into her mouth, she said, 'Oh, but Laura, this is delicious.'

'I know. That's the classic version and it still sells the best. It's much improved since flour came off the ration and we can make good bread. We also do a Welsh rarebit one made with mustard and a bit of beer, and one with sliced tomato. All with cheddar, which is fine, I think. But Giovanni is obsessed with the flavours of his childhood. He pines for fresh basil, mozzarella, avocado, garlic, really good tomato, fresh anchovies, aubergine, olive oil. All those things, so everyday in Italy, are hard to get here, and they're still mocked as 'fancy foreign food'. Say the word 'garlic' and people hold their noses!'

'But there are Italian restaurants in London now, aren't there?'

'Yes, there are some, but they are nothing like we'd like to have. I swear, Sophie, one day we will open an Italian restaurant with the sort of simple beautiful food we got in Abruzzo. The Italians are still really suffering from food shortages, much worse than we are, but somehow we ate better in Atri than we ever do in England.'

The weather was surprisingly mild for late January, and after lunch they went for a walk in Kensington Gardens. The conversation became more personal.

'It hits me sometimes,' Laura found herself saying, 'the knowledge that somewhere in the world is a five-year-old boy who should be with me and never, ever will be. Oh, Sophie, I just can't forgive myself for giving the baby away.' She bit her lip. She'd never talked to anyone, ever, about her recurrent longing for her lost child and doing it now threatened tears. 'In a way it's worse because Giovanni is so wonderful, and has absolutely forgiven me.'

Sophie didn't say anything, just looked steadily at her, but

Laura saw the sympathy in her face. 'The awful thing is,' she went on, 'he doesn't know entirely why I did it.'

'Was it because you thought it might be Marcin's?' she asked.

Laura felt a moment of panic. 'How did you know? Sophie, I've never told . . .'

'I wondered at the time, when you started vomiting. It happened so quickly after you'd fallen for Giovanni, it seemed too soon. But about right if it was Marcin.'

'But . . . Why did you never say?'

'Because it hadn't even occurred to you – you believed it was Giovanni's. A true love child. I'd be ruining your chance of happiness, and Giovanni's. And for what? I could have been wrong.'

They walked in companionable silence for a few minutes. Then Laura turned again to Sophie.

'What about you, Soph?' she said. 'You are happy about marrying David, aren't you?'

'Well, yes, of course. I'd not have agreed if I wasn't.'

'But do you think you're really in love with him? Mum says you were in love with him for ages, just pretending not to be. But now she thinks you have "lost some of your sparkle", as she put it. As if something is worrying you.'

Sophie did not answer for a long time. When she returned Laura's gaze her face was solemn. 'The truth is, I was in love with David long before he married Jill. Since you and I were giggling teenagers. It broke my heart when he fell for her. I think that's why I had that affair with my tutor. But I got used to it. You can get used to almost anything.'

'And now?'

'And now I'm still in love with him, but he's not in love with me. He likes me, sure. I'm his best friend, and I love his children.'

She fished a hanky out of her bag, and dabbed at her eyes. 'A year ago, I just longed for him to realise that we'd be good together, love or no love. But now I want him to be in love with me as well. For him to desire me, want to make love to me. But he doesn't.'

Laura put her arm round the stooped back of her friend, but did not say anything. What could she say?

'Laura, I won't be able to bear it if we get married and he doesn't ever make love to me,' Sophie went on. 'And that could happen. It really could.'

Laura thought for a moment. 'You will just have to seduce him, that's what. Do you remember when you and Grace and Jill came to see me when I was so unhappy at giving away our baby?'

Sophie nodded.

'And you told me to have another? Well, I did, and I had to set about seducing Giovanni to do it. We'd become so emotionally touchy we couldn't see the obvious. That we loved each other.'

'David doesn't love me. Or is not in love with me.'

CHAPTER THIRTY-SIX

One hot June Saturday, six weeks before their wedding, Sophie and David were invited to a tennis party at Frampton. The boys had been left behind at Chorlton with their grandparents and Jane had gone to a gymkhana on Snowdrop. So, for once, there was not a child in sight, and Sophie felt curiously liberated, like a young girl again.

She didn't think she'd be much good at tennis anymore, though she'd played for the second team at school. David said that was fine by him as he'd never been any good.

They were the only local couple – the other four guests were young Londoners, staying at Frampton for the weekend. Both the men were friends of George's, one a banker and the other an army captain. Their wives, Sophie noticed, looked polished and rich. She felt diminished and shy in her white shorts, school-style tennis shirt and much-blancoed tennis shoes. Both the London women had pretty tennis dresses and long brown legs with brand new plimsoles.

By lunchtime most of the couples had played each other. David and Sophie were the lowest-scoring couple and were somewhat relieved to have been knocked out early. Lunch was set up under the trees and was delicious: cold roast ham from the Frampton pigs, mustard mayonnaise, salads and new potatoes, served hot. The atmosphere was happy and relaxed, with a lot of teasing and loud laughter.

David, sitting next to Sophie at lunch, dropped his head and said, too softly for Grace or George to hear, 'Lord, this is miles away from the Frampton of the old days. When the old Countess ruled the roost, we'd have been inside that dark dining room and all on our best behaviour. Grace has done a wonderful job of lightening things up.'

'I never came here,' replied Sophie. 'Not grand enough to qualify, I suppose. Although I'd come with my dad to the stables or piggery. No one liked the Countess. The staff would gossip to Dad, complaining. But poor woman, you wouldn't wish bone cancer on your worst enemy.'

'Yet George said she died peacefully, without pain.'

'Yes, Dr Drummond is a kind man. You need a doctor like him. One who will ease the end with a slightly increased morphine dose so the patient dies quietly in their sleep.'

'Would you do that?' asked David, looking at her, his eyes steady and serious.

Sophie wished she'd not mentioned it. If David didn't approve, he'd think her callous. She thought she would duck the question, but then she thought of Geraldine's wretched last few months, too ill for an operation to mend her hip, and in excruciating pain from the cancer in her back, dying, but not dying quickly enough. She returned David's gaze and nodded. 'Yes, I would. If there was no hope, I would.'

'Good for you,' he said. 'Your dad would do it for a dog. Why should humans not have the same relief?'

He poured her another glass of wine. No longer concerned about her tennis, Sophie drank it. And David drank a good deal of Frampton's famous cider.

After lunch the non-players, relaxed by alcohol and sun, no longer felt obliged to make polite conversation with each other and they wandered about the gardens, or down to the lake. Sophie and David admired the stable yard, potting and tool sheds and the compost bays: the only areas (with the garden) of the Frampton estate that David was not in charge of. Then they wandered back to the tennis court where some of the others were sitting on the sloping lawn, watching the players. Sophie and David flopped into a wide canvas swing seat, where David rolled a cigarette.

'Have you never smoked, Sophie?'

'No, my parents were dead against it. I remember Dad giving up because he said it made him out of breath. I'm sure that's true – it would make sense.'

'Yet in the war the Red Cross put fags in parcels for the troops, didn't they? That wouldn't have happened if they were bad for you.'

'I suppose they thought tobacco calmed the soldiers. But the *BMJ* published an article last year saying tobacco can cause cancer of the lungs.'

'Are you telling me you'll nag me to stop smoking when we're married?' His eyes were shiny and teasing.

'Mmm, I just might,' Sophie nodded, 'and make you eat your greens.'

They tried to watch the tennis but the sun was in their eyes and Sophie did not have a hat. So she gave up and lay back on the seat, her eyes closed, only half conscious of the *tock, tock* of the tennis ball and the occasional 'Good shot' or 'Jolly bad luck' from the court.

'I'm falling asleep,' she said, smiling. 'I'd like to curl up and just drift off.'

'Then do,' said David, shifting into the corner. 'Use my thigh for a pillow.'

Sophie looked round and realised that the sides of the swing seat would hide her from the others – lying on David's thigh seemed a bit fast, even if they were engaged. But if she lay on her side, she could still claim to be watching the tennis. She snuggled down and put her head in his lap. Almost immediately she thought this was a mistake: he was wearing long tennis trousers – actually his cricket flannels – but she could feel the warmth of his leg through the cloth. She had to resist the urge to turn, stretch up and snuggle her whole body up against his. Does he sense how I feel? she wondered. She lay absolutely still, but she did not drift off – her mind wouldn't let her.

It was ridiculous really: they were engaged to be married, but they had never made love, had barely kissed, and when they did it was chastely on the cheek. I should not have agreed to marry him if he doesn't love me, she told herself. And then quickly retracted the thought, admitting she'd marry him under any circumstances whatsoever. She loved him and that would have to be enough.

She closed her eyes, telling herself to stop thinking. She was just beginning to drift into sleep when she felt his fingers on her hair. She kept her eyes shut, thinking maybe it was absent-minded, as he might lazily stroke one of his boys, or his dog. But then he gently pushed his fingers into her hair, massaging her scalp, then again stroked her head, warm from the sun. She stayed immobile, still telling herself that this was not love, not sex, not even affection: it was nothing.

But when he moved his hand from her head to her forehead, and then slowly brought it down over her face, his fingers caressing her eyes, her cheeks, her mouth, then she knew. She could smell his warm fingers, a characteristic male mix of tobacco and soap, and she thought there was no smell on earth so delicious.

He bent his head so that his mouth was near her ear and murmured, too softly for any of the others to hear, 'Are we really going to wait another six weeks before we make love, Sophie Wenlock?' She didn't answer, but thought, Thank God, thank God.

'I love you, Sophie.' She opened her eyes and rolled over to look at him. 'I love you, Sophie,' he repeated. His fingers were on her lips and she kissed them, she could not help it. Then she sat up and smiled.

'Well, David Oliver, I'm very glad to hear it because I've loved you since I was sixteen.'

CHAPTER THIRTY-SEVEN

The following spring, Carlotta, Silvano – who was now thirteen – and Mario – eleven – moved to London, into a fourth cottage in Paddington mews rented from the partnership for them by Giovanni. They knocked the wall down between the two back-to-back kitchens to make one big family kitchen where everyone gathered to cook and eat. Stairs came down from Carlotta's rooms to one end of the kitchen and from Laura and Giovanni's to the other.

There was only one real bone of contention between Laura and Giovanni. Try as he might, he could not persuade Laura to see sense on the subject of oven ranges. She wanted an Esse stove, or an Aga, like Maud had in the country.

'But why?' he protested. 'It's mad. There's nothing wrong with the New World cooker we have, is there? We only bought it two years ago. It's got six rings and a huge oven. Surely that's enough, even for both families. There are only six of us, after all.'

She looked at him with those earnest eyes and his heart sank. He suspected he was defeated already. 'I know, darling, and you have logic on your side,' she said, 'but even then I wanted a big heavy cooker that would warm the whole the kitchen but we didn't have the space. Now we've got plenty.'

Giovanni shook his head. 'But Laura, those stoves are ridiculous in London. Where are you going to store the anthracite? And who is going to fill it twice a day?'

'You can get oil-fired ones. The oil company comes every few months and tops it up. We'd need a tank, but we could fit that in the back of the garage.'

Giovanni sighed and made one last effort. 'Have you seen what those things cost? It will be more than the rest of the kitchen put together.'

Laura took her husband by the shoulders. 'Darling, listen. I understand you think it's crazy. Maybe it is, but I see the kitchen as the heart of the house and the stove as the heart of the kitchen. It represents home and tradition and family. After all, we're going to live in this kitchen, aren't we? We'll eat here, the children will do their homework here, we'll have our friends to supper here. And the stove will be the centrepiece, the anchor, for all that.'

So Giovanni gave in and they bought a four-oven Esse. He had to admit it was magnificent. The front was ivory and the hob had fat square lids to keep the heat of the hotplate from escaping. When you lifted one to put the heavy kettle on the hotplate, the heat rose in a blast. Seeing Laura's pleasure in it made it worth the money. He would catch her polishing the tops quite unnecessarily.

Giovanni loved the growing commune of family filling up his and George's property development. One day, he thought, I'll make one enormous house of all seven cottages.

But for now he was content. The presence of his sister and

nephews made him realise just how much he'd missed the noise of an Italian family. He'd been in England for ten years, but since he'd left the Italian prisoner-of-war camp at the end of '43, he'd hardly ever spoken Italian. Now he encouraged the boys to belt out 'O Dolci Mani' or 'Nessun Dorma' at full volume and he indulged Angelica, who regarded his knee as her rightful seat. They would sing together, her childish warble barely audible under his clear tenor. And Carlotta had taught Laura how to make the dishes of his childhood, *pasticcio di maiale, linguine alla pescatora*. The sounds and smells of Italy defined the house.

One morning he and Laura were both in the kitchen at seven o'clock. Laura was stuffing Angelica's gym shoes into her school bag while drinking a cup of coffee, and he was eating his sister's sourdough bread spread with fig jam. It was excellent, and he reached for a second slice.

Of course his eagle-eyed Laura noticed.

'Darling,' she said, 'you'll be fat as butter if you go on wolfing bread and jam.'

'I know, but a comfortable paunch is what is expected of a successful businessman, don't you think? I just need a cigar and a pin-striped suit.'

Laura kissed his cheek. 'What are you doing today?'

'I'm meeting that designer fellow, Justin, remember, to see his plans to give all the Calzones the same look.'

'Oh yes. I'm still not sure it's a good idea, though. It'll make us look so organised. You know I like the slightly chaotic Italian family feel, but I agree, we should at least listen.'

It pleased Giovanni that Laura was getting more Italian by the day. Since Carlotta and the boys' arrival her shaky grasp of the language had become really confident and she switched between English and Italian with ease.

'And what's your day to be, *cara*?'

'Checking on the cafés. I've got until teatime because Carlotta is giving Angelica her lunch and taking her swimming. But still, I'll only be able to do Kensington and Chelsea. I've got to spend some time in the Holland Park one. Gino is very proud of his new ice-cream offer but it's too American. Italian ice cream, especially our ice cream, doesn't need decoration and syrup all over it.'

Giovanni saw his chance. 'That's why we need some uniformity, darling. Every café should look the same, have the same menu, same uniforms for the staff. Everything.'

'But we'll lose the new ideas, the innovation, don't you think?'

Giovanni stood up and kissed her. 'You and Carlotta have quite enough ideas, *cara*. We don't need every member of staff having bright ideas. What customers want is consistency.'

'Well, as long as we don't lose the cosy quirkiness. The old pictures on the wall, the pretty sugar bowls and jugs, the feeling of someone's cosy house, not a commercial restaurant.'

Giovanni laughed. Laura was so transparent. 'You just like trawling the junk shops. Go on, admit it!'

The boys came thudding down the stairs from their flat. Mario gave the door a mighty shove which had it banging against the big American fridge. He was laughing at his brother.

'You are so goody goody, Silvano. I'm not volunteering to clean up some old lady's garden. Or clean out her smelly garage. She won't even give you a tip, I bet you.'

'I don't care about a tip. It's only an afternoon, and Mr Greene has a point: we are very lucky, and it won't kill us to help someone who isn't.'

'As I said, goody goody. That's you.'

Giovanni was tempted to leave for work and not say anything. But these boys had no father.

'Boys,' he said, addressing them in Italian, 'first of all, you say good morning to Laura and to me. Next, Mario, you do not slam the door against the refrigerator, and thirdly, you should not mock your brother for doing something kind.'

'I apologise, Uncle, and good morning,' said Silvano and went at once to kiss his aunt.

Mario was looking contrite. Then he smiled. 'I'm so sorry, Uncle. I really am. And good morning, Aunty Laura. I hope I've not damaged your fridge.'

As he walked towards the station, Giovanni thought how typical that exchange had been: Silvano, typically kind and quiet. Mario demonstrating his thoughtlessness and selfishness, followed by his charm. He was too much like that spiv, his father Tomaso. He'd always been bad news, that one. In the war he'd made money on the black market, selling contraband to the British troops – especially Lucky Strike cigarettes meant for the US forces. And after the war he'd run a scam selling fake truffles, for which he'd gone briefly to prison. They were dried young turnips or mushrooms, sliced, dyed in gravy browning and steeped in diluted truffle oil.

Giovanni thought it was a good thing Tomaso had abandoned Carlotta and the boys. If he'd still been around, he might have had to employ him, too.

Giovanni's thoughts shifted to his wife. What a great businesswoman Laura had become. She'd always been interested in the cafés, but now she wanted to be a real restaurateur. If they did what she wanted and opened an upmarket *ristorante*, she'd inevitably take her eye off the cafés. She was a stickler for standards and the quality of the Calzones depended on her. All the more reason why they had to tie them down to a strict formula.

CHAPTER THIRTY-EIGHT

Laura was trying hard to stay cool. She must win the argument by rational argument. No shouting or crying.

'Look at our ice-cream sales,' she said. 'They sell best in the rich areas, Belgravia and Kensington. Wall's sells best where there are lots of children: in the parks, outside schools.'

'Well, of course. That Wall's, it is made of pig fat,' responded Giovanni. '*Bambini* don't care what their ice cream is made of.'

'But people who care about good food, do. And have you noticed that the Sloane Street stall does really well with dinner-party-sized tubs? Those rich women round Eaton Square have the new refrigerators with ice compartments. They are sick of austerity. They want the best.'

Laura appealed to George for support. He had been a steady partner in the Angelotti business, providing most of the capital for the expansion of the Calzone cafés and for equipping the ice-cream production unit in Ealing with expensive imported Italian machinery and freezers.

'I'm inclined to agree with Laura,' he said, 'the rich are starting to spend their money again.' He turned to Laura. 'And in June half the world will be in London for the Coronation. Everyone will be having parties. So I'm game. I'll back this dream of yours, but we have to all want to do it.'

Giovanni jumped in. 'How do we know they will come? Why should they? The English upper classes like French food and French wine. Or Scottish salmon and beef and steak and kidney pudding!'

'But there are already Italian restaurants here,' countered Laura, 'Bertorelli's, Toscanini – lots of them.'

'Toscanini, bah! That's not Italian!' cried Giovanni. 'Their spaghetti Bolognese, it is disgusting. It is not Bolognese. It is English mince on top of cheap pasta from a box. And they serve veal *scallopini a la Holstein*! With fried egg and anchovies on top! Where you ever get veal Holstein in Italy?' He shuddered. 'All the hotels, they have French haute cuisine and the clubs, they have the potted shrimps, and smoked salmon and roast beef and the English puddings and pies. Very good. So, the rich already have French and British. They don't want Italian.'

'Laura, Giovanni could be right,' said George. 'I don't think so, but he could be. Maybe we should test the idea less expensively before we set our sights on the truly rich. Maybe we could have a halfway house.'

'But how? You can't be half-excellent, with half-luxury, or half-gastronomy.' Laura could feel her temperature rising. 'Either it is the best of Italy, or we should stick to calzone. At least they are the best calzone.'

'I agree with that,' said Giovanni. 'Whatever we do has to be the best. No half measures.'

'No, no,' said George, putting a placating hand on Giovanni's shoulder and looking at Laura. 'Both of you. I'm not suggesting compromising on quality. I mean, let us cater for the at-home market rather than the restaurant goer. You said rich housewives are taking home ice cream for the family or a dinner party. That's because those big houses no longer have fleets of servants.' He smiled ruefully. 'I know because we own one. But that doesn't mean the well-to-do don't want to eat well at home. So let's give them the best of Italian food, but to take away and eat at home. Or we could deliver. Then we don't have the overhead of an expensive restaurant. Let's open a delicatessen shop which is also a café.'

So they rented an empty shop at the Sloane Square end of King's Road, a block from the new and fashionable Peter Jones department store. They would call it Deli-Calzone, and it would be half posh deli and half Italian snack bar. Like the other Calzones, it would sell Giovanni's trademark calzone and deep-fried sandwiches. But now that it was becoming easier to get the ingredients, they'd make more sophisticated ones, say filled with gorgonzola or mozzarella, *mozzarella in carrozza*. They'd sell *pasticcio*, cakes, soups, casseroles and pasta sauces made by Carlotta. And they'd have a licence and sell wines as well as coffee.

Giovanni and Laura went to inspect the premises. There was a smallish shop front on the street and a long room at the back.

'What's it going to look like?' Giovanni asked.

'Well, in here, we won't need much in the way of décor. That will be provided by the food we sell. You know, all the hams, salamis and strings of garlic that have been unobtainable for years will hang from the ceiling; oils, vinegars, spices, tins of anchovies, packets of pulses and pastas on the shelves, slabs of cooking chocolate, cheeses and olives on the counter.'

As she spoke Laura could feel her excitement rising. 'Darling,' she said, 'do you remember how the little grocery shops in Abruzzo smelled? It makes my mouth water to think of it.'

They walked into the back room which was to be the café. 'It's a bit dark in here, don't you think?' said Laura. 'We must make sure the lighting is good. I'd like to make it different from the other cafés. More modern and bright. Very stylish.'

'Like what, darling?'

'Well, for example, maybe those Festival of Britain Hille chairs in pure white. With white Formica tables and a black-and-white tiled floor. And modern art on the walls. Of course, we can't afford the real thing. In my fantasy world I'd have bright abstract paintings or small sculptures, Henry Moore or Barbara Hepworth on glass shelves. But perhaps we can get the same effect with modern glass or ceramic pieces. Just a few, well lit. Very dramatic.'

Laura was talking fast, so anxious to get it all out before he objected, that she now had to pause for breath.

'Won't it be too clinical?' he said. 'People expect cosy warmth from Italian restaurants.'

'But we have to be different. We have to get away from prints of Tuscany, wine barrels and plastic grape vines. Italy is beginning to be known for design. Maybe we should hire a modern Italian designer?'

Laura wasn't really surprised that Giovanni wouldn't countenance a second designer for the Deli-Calzone, so she agreed to work with Justin, who was doing a good job with an overall look for all the Calzones.

The end result was much as Laura had envisaged it, although bright posters advertising exhibitions took the place of real paintings and several students from the Royal College of Art got their first commissions for sculpture.

But it was the front of the new shop that brought the customers in. In the basement kitchen, Carlotta, with a lone assistant, made pasta and sauces, soups, salads and desserts. They displayed these upstairs in a modern glass-fronted refrigerated counter. Two-thirds of it was for chilled items, one-third for ice creams, which they scooped by hand to sell in biscuit cones, mini-tubs or family-size cardboard buckets.

The place is like a real slice of Italy, thought Laura with satisfaction, with the Italians serving upstairs and Carlotta and her cook downstairs shouting to each other, and Giovanni, who preferred working there to his office, occasionally bursting into song.

Giovanni had promised to give Mario and Silvano Saturday jobs, but Carlotta refused to have them in her kitchen. Out shopping together in Portobello Market, Laura asked her why.

'I am very grateful that Giovanni gives them jobs, Laura, believe me,' she said. 'They must learn to work. And they always want money. But I will not be their teacher.'

She stopped in the street, waving her hands. 'No, no, no. It is enough that I have to wash their socks, put up with their loud jazz music, tell them: "Don't eat with your mouth open." That Mario, he does not listen to me. And Silvano, he is a sweet boy, but he is too clever for a cook, he has a mind like an adding machine. One day he said, "Mama, do you realise how much fresh apricots cost? Why don't you use the ones in tins? They will be cooked anyway in the tart."'

Laura, anxious to stop Carlotta's flow and get her out of the way of the stream of market shoppers, took her arm and walked her to the side of a vegetable stall.

'Carlotta, stop! They are both lovely young lads. Giovanni

thinks the world of Silvano. He stuffs all the invoices in a drawer and says, "It's OK, Silvano will sort them out on Saturday."'

'Good, I am glad. But just keep him out of my kitchen. Mario too.'

Laura laughed. 'To hear you talk, anyone would think you didn't adore them.'

'Of course I love them, they are my sons,' Carlotta snorted, 'but that does not make them useful in the kitchen.'

'So what's Mario doing for his Saturday job? He's working at the ice-cream factory, isn't he?'

'Ah, that brother of mine. He is clever. Next week he is giving Mario an ice-cream bicycle and he must sell *gelati* outside the cinemas. On Saturdays, children at the morning matinee, old ladies for the afternoon show, in the evening, lots of young people. All love good ice cream.'

'Yes, but will they pay for it? They can get lollies and choc ices for half our prices.'

'Well, we will see if Mario has his father's talent. Tomaso could sell, what do you say? He could sell sand to a camel.'

Laura laughed. 'Sand to a Bedouin.'

'Yes, to a Bedouin. Mario will sell the ice creams, I am sure. But he might help himself to the money, too.'

Laura was shocked as much by Carlotta's candour as by her words. 'You cannot mean that. That your boy would steal?'

'I don't know. I hope not, but even if he is honest, he's so careless. He would forget to take the money. Or lose it. Or give away ice creams to pretty girls. He is just like his father, that one.'

Carlotta was a gem. She worked long hours at Deli-Calzone and still managed to cook two or three nights a week at home. One evening she came home from work with a wrapped present for Angelica.

'But it's not her birthday,' exclaimed Laura.

'I know, but I found it in that second-hand bookshop in Praed Street. The problem is, it's in French. But her Italian is so good, she'll work it out.'

'A French book! For a five-year-old! Carlotta, you are mad.'

Angelica unwrapped the book. It was an illustrated cookbook for children. Laura watched her turn the pages, looking at the drawings, not the writing.

'Mama,' she said, 'I want to do it now. Let's make this one.' It was for rabbit with mustard. 'Please, Mama. Or this one.' Chicken baked in a salt crust.

'Not tonight, darling. Maybe tomorrow with Daddy.'

Angelica was always pestering one of them to cook with her. Carlotta was endlessly patient and let her do almost all of it herself.

Laura got impatient and tried surreptitiously to hurry things along, but Giovanni loved it, and Laura liked to see them in the kitchen together. He's a child himself, she thought, watching Angelica swirling patterns into the bowls of potato soup with spinach purée, or Giovanni carving an apple into a swan for her.

When Carlotta wasn't cooking supper, Laura did it. At first she left Italian cooking to the Italians and stuck to good old British favourites like shepherd's pie, toad in the hole and Irish stew, which Mario and Silvano wolfed down. But gradually she got more adventurous, and when Giovanni gave her copies of Elizabeth David's *A Book of Mediterranean Food* and *French Country Cooking,* she would surprise her Italian relatives with an excellent risotto or fish soup. After a while she was cooking a lot more Italian recipes than English ones.

Deli-Calzone was an instant success. The housewives of Kensington, unable to find, or afford, the cooks of the pre-war years, turned to Carlotta to fill the gap. And when the deli's offerings were not smart enough to impress their dinner party guests, Carlotta would take special orders.

These 'specials' became a useful test run for new dishes. Carlotta would cook an extra dish or two to sell in the shop. Mostly these were cold dishes, like her seafood and pasta salad, or boned sea trout with a herringbone pattern of fresh tarragon under a thin sheen of aspic. Sometimes the experiment was a failure and the family would have the unsold dishes for supper. *Vitello tonnato* was too foreign for the British housewife, even in Belgravia.

'I could have told you that wouldn't sell,' said Giovanni. 'The British don't eat veal and they don't buy tuna. So why would they buy veal covered in tuna mayonnaise?'

The best earner, though by far the most expensive, and one which required the customer to do the final baking, was a large piece of beef fillet in pastry, with a mushroom and pâté stuffing. Meat was still rationed and cuts like fillet almost all went to the restaurant trade. But Giovanni's butcher did his best for her, and sometimes Carlotta was in luck.

At first she claimed this dish as Italian, *filetto di manzo in carrozza*, but soon found her customers knew it as beef Wellington, and it sold better under that name. So beef Wellington it was.

Laura worked in the business while Angelica was in nursery school and in the afternoons they mostly went to the park. But sometimes she would give in to Angelica's pleas and take her down to Carlotta's basement. Carlotta would feed them leftover bruschetta, or the unsaleable end-slice of a rabbit pie, or, if they were lucky, a piece of almond tart or chocolate cake.

It amazed and amused Laura that Carlotta, so impatient with her sons, and argumentative with her brother, was a model teacher with Angelica. She would explain to the child what they were doing, and why. She would let Angelica crack eggs, mopping up the mess when she missed the bowl, get her to weigh the ingredients in the big old-fashioned balance scales, encourage her to taste everything.

Watching her, Laura thought what a waste her sister-in-law's life had been until she came to London. She was a born teacher, and a brilliant cook. She'd trained as a teacher but her no-good husband had been too macho to allow her a career.

One evening, Laura suggested they join the thousands lining the streets for the Coronation. 'The children should see something so historic,' she said, 'and so quintessentially British.' She looked at the boys. 'We're good at parades, and marching and colourful processions. You'll love it.'

'We'll have to wait for hours and hours, though, and it'll probably pour with rain,' protested Giovanni.

But he was outvoted. Carlotta made a picnic to take them through breakfast, elevenses, lunch and tea, and they were in The Mall by 5am. They did have to wait for hours, but no one minded: everyone was happy and excited, and their neighbours in the crowd made a great fuss of Angelica and the boys, allowing them to push forward so they could see the procession when it eventually came. Giovanni had bought the children Union flags and they waved them with gusto.

Laura stood on tiptoe to shout above the din into Giovanni's ear. 'Who would have thought, when you were fighting the British ten years ago, that today you'd be cheering their new queen?'

Giovanni gave her upturned face a quick kiss, then bellowed into her ear. 'And I wouldn't leave England for anything. Not even for Abruzzo.'

On the way home Laura bought everyone a Coronation mug – which she then refused to let them drink out of for fear they'd get broken. 'One day they will be valuable, you'll see. And then you'll thank me.'

CHAPTER THIRTY-NINE

'Laura, darling, it's your father's birthday on Saturday,' said Maud. Her mother often phoned her in the evening.

'Yes, I know. Are you doing anything special?'

'Well, I was coming to that. He's never seen your house and I think if I suggested we come to dinner with you, he'd agree.'

'Really, Mummy? Why? After all this time? We've been in this house for over two years.'

'He's mellowing, I suppose. He never says so, but, darling, I really think he regrets his behaviour to you.'

Not as much as I do, thought Laura, but she said, 'OK, Mummy, let's do it. Water under the bridge and all that. But I must speak to Giovanni. He has even more to forgive than I do.'

But in fact Giovanni encouraged the plan. 'I know it means so much to you, *cara mia*,' he said.

On the Friday afternoon, Laura and Angelica met Carlotta in the Paddington Mews kitchen. 'It's your grandpa's birthday tomorrow, isn't it?' said Carlotta, taking Angelica's school bag and hanging it behind the door.

'Yes,' said Angelica, 'and he will be sixty-seven.'

'Can you count up to sixty-seven?'

Laura smiled at the scorn on her daughter's face. 'Of *course* I can! I can count backwards down to nothing. Sixty-seven, sixty-six, sixty . . .'

'Yes, yes, *cara*, you're a clever girl,' Laura interrupted hastily. Angelica dropped her voice to a whisper and went on counting. Laura continued, 'but shall we make a special birthday dinner for him? Beef Wellington, which is beef all wrapped up in pastry.'

Angelica at once stopped counting. 'Like Tom Kitten?'

Carlotta looked puzzled, but Laura said, 'Yes,' and smiled at Carlotta. 'It's a children's story.'

Angelica hurried to wash her hands at the basin in the corner. Then she fetched a clean tea towel from the drawer, pulled a stool from under the workbench and climbed onto it.

'I'm ready,' she announced, handing the tea towel to Carlotta, who tied it round her to make an apron.

Laura laughed. 'Goodness, you do have her well trained, Carlotta!'

'It's because she loves it. She's a natural cook, I can tell.'

Laura winced as Carlotta gave Angelica a small sharp knife and helped her to remove all the outer membrane of two long pieces of beef tenderloin.

Carlotta glanced across at Laura and said, 'Don't worry. Sharp knives are much safer than blunt ones.'

'Really?' Laura sounded doubtful.

'Yes, because you don't have to put any pressure on them. And your daughter is a very good pupil, she does exactly what I tell her. And anyway, I'm watching her.'

Laura trusted Carlotta completely, but she had to leave the kitchen all the same. She hated seeing her daughter holding that knife, and standing so close to the blazing frying pan as they browned first one fillet and then the other. 'Call me when you've done with the dangerous stuff,' she said. 'I'll be in the office.'

When they called her, she found them pricking wide strips of raw pastry all over with a fork. 'What are you doing now, darling?' she asked.

'We are making the beds for the meat to lie on. Carlotta rolled them flat,' Angelica said solemnly.

'And why are you pricking them with that fork?'

'Because we have to make holes so the hot air can get out and it won't make the pastry rise up in the oven.'

Laura was impressed. 'And do you know why they are on the back of the baking sheet, not on the front?'

'Because it will be easier to slide them off when they are cooked.'

While the pastry strips were cooling, they chopped the onion, garlic and mushrooms and cooked the mixture down to a thick paste. Then they mashed it up with a tin of duck liver pâté.

Carlotta asked Angelica to sprinkle the pastry strips with semolina. 'Can you guess why?' she said.

Angelica frowned. 'Is it like the apple tart? Because it will soak up the juice and the pastry underneath won't get all soggy.'

'You are right! Only this time it's meat juices, not apple.' Carlotta gave Angelica a hug. 'What a clever girl!' She turned to Laura. 'You see, she not only listens, she remembers. It's weeks since we made the apple tart.'

The catechism went on. Every time Carlotta explained something, Angelica would listen intently and when asked, she would repeat, almost word for word, what she'd learnt.

Laura washed up and passed Carlotta and Angelica the utensils they needed, all the time consciously enjoying the pride she felt in her daughter. Angelica was a natural in the kitchen, just like Giovanni or Maud. She was obsessed with cooking in the way other little girls were obsessed with dolls or dressing up.

When it came to rolling out the puff pastry to cover the fillets, Carlotta slipped off Angelica's shoes and let her kneel on the work surface so she could use her weight to roll out her pastry.

'Why didn't you let me make the pastry with you?' Angelica wanted to know.

Carlotta laughed. 'You need a bit more practice before you make puff pastry, darling. You aren't even six yet, and it's very difficult. Even some chefs can't do it. First we'll make flaky pastry, and when you can do that, we'll make puff.'

Angelica, still copying Carlotta's actions, put one of the cooled fillets on top of a semolina-dusted pastry strip. Then she smeared it with a thick layer of mushroom stuffing. Laura had to help her daughter position the pastry sheet exactly right and use a fish slice to lift the cooked base carefully in order to tuck the raw top sheet under.

Finally Carlotta showed Angelica how to roll out the pastry trimmings and cut them into leaves, marking the veins with the back of a knife. 'The sharp side might cut right through by mistake so I use the blunt side.' Angelica copied her every move and when all the trimmings had been turned into leaves, they brushed their undersides with water and stuck them in place all over the pastry parcels.

'And that's two beef Wellingtons,' said Carlotta. She pulled Angelica off the workbench and hugged her close.

Angelica wriggled out of her grasp.

'But I want to put them in the oven. They aren't finished.'

Laura said, 'Darling, we will cook them tomorrow for Grandpa's birthday, and you will be the one who bakes them.'

Angelica's mouth turned down. 'But I want to cook them now.'

Carlotta's voice was brisk. 'Don't whine, Angelica. We can't have anyone who whines in the kitchen.'

Angelica considered that for a moment. Then she said, her voice cheerful, 'All right. I am going to be a chef when I grow up.'

Donald felt he'd been coerced into the dinner by Maud. As they'd got older, Maud had become much more forthright, in a way she hadn't been before all the Laura business. But at least relations were better between the two of them now. He'd surfaced from that awful black depression and there were moments when they felt the old tenderness for each other. But she'd not reverted to her former unquestioning loyalty.

'If Laura is generous enough to extend an olive branch,' she'd said, 'and to give a huge supper party for the whole family in your honour, then the least you can do is to be gracious about it, darling.'

He did want to make peace with his daughter. That's why he'd chased after her when she'd swept out of his club. He'd tried to explain, even to apologise. But she'd rebuffed him with a torrent of accusations and he'd had to give up. It wasn't as if he hadn't tried.

Here was another chance, initiated by her, and he had to admit he'd been wrong about the Italian. He'd turned out to be solid as a rock and very successful. Maybe he should go, be the gracious father-in-law, smooth things over.

'But my dear Maud,' he'd said, 'we must stay at my club.

Dinner is all very well, but I cannot face Giovanni and that tribe of Italians at breakfast.'

Donald was astonished by Paddington Mews. Proudly Giovanni showed him the property. He's been told by Laura to be polite to me, he thought, just as I'm under instructions from Maud. They stood in the mews, admiring the multi-coloured cottages with tubs of geraniums at their front doors and window boxes with petunias and trailing ivy. Giovanni explained his and George's ownership of the whole row of houses, that he rented four of them from the partnership and how he had knocked them together.

When they came inside, Laura said, 'Daddy, if you can bear it I'd love to give you a quick tour of the inside. Everyone else is let off the tour. They've done it before, but you have no excuse.'

Donald was almost as impressed by the interior as by the property itself. The bedrooms were all different, full of antiques, rich fabrics, old carpets and interesting objects. A Victorian rocking horse in Angelica's window, stained-glass panels from a bombed-out pub round the bathroom shower, a huge dresser, bought from a baker's shop, with a mirrored back to the shelves which was full of assorted curiosities such as a glass fisherman's float, a brass carriage clock, a row of tin soldiers.

'Well, my goodness,' said Donald. 'You always were a collector and a hoarder, but this truly amazing.'

Laura laughed. 'You should see the Calzones. They are full of stuff I've bought in junk shops, too. Except the new one in the King's Road, which is much smarter, very clean and modern. You'd like it, I think.'

Giovanni was dispensing drinks in the living room upstairs, with the help of Silvano and Mario. The room was crowded:

if you counted Hal and Richard, who would be asleep before dinner, there were fourteen of them.

It's the first time we've all been together, thought Donald, and that's my fault. I just hope there are no accusations and explosions. The Chorlton contingent, him and Maud, David, Sophie and the twins, had come up together, squashed into the now rather elderly Bentley. Once Grace, George and Jane had arrived, Laura took Angelica's hand and said she must get on with the cooking.

'Do you mind if I come too?' Donald asked.

'No, of course not.'

Donald thought she looked surprised, but pleased. Angelica insisted on helping her mother. She solemnly brushed what looked like huge pies all over with beaten egg. But Laura refused to let her put them into the top oven.

'But, Mummy, you said I could bake them. You . . .'

'I know, darling. I'm sorry, but the oven is just too hot. It has to be at its hottest to make the pastry rise.' She shielded Angelica from the blast of heat as she slid the long tray deep inside.

'But Mummy, you promised . . .'

'Yes, but I shouldn't have.' She shut the oven door, stood up and kissed her daughter's sulky face. 'I had to be quick not to let any of the heat out.' Laura looked up and caught her father's eye. 'But when they're done you can help me carry them to the table and you can put one down in front of Grandpa. He will be at the head of the table because it's his birthday.'

It was all very friendly and looked a bit chaotic, but Donald could recognise organisation when he saw it. He watched Laura setting the oven timer, while she kept an eye on her daughter

– who was perched on a wine box frying potatoes – at the same time as calmly making white sauce.

'Leeks in white sauce,' she said. 'I hope it's still your favourite, Daddy?'

'Certainly they are. All vegetables are only edible with a good white sauce. And leeks are the best.'

She tossed a handful of something green into Angelica's pan.

'What's that, Mummy?'

'Chopped fresh rosemary. Can you smell it?'

Angelica nodded. 'It smells like the stuff in the pot outside the door,' she said.

'Clever girl. That's where it came from.'

Good Lord, thought Donald, I'd no idea Laura was such a keen cook. Must be the Italians' influence. And just look at the daughter. They're all obsessed.

'Don't turn the potatoes so often, darling,' said Laura. They'll break up too much. Only roll them over when they're brown.'

Laura noticed with satisfaction that everyone had drifted down from the living room into the kitchen, drawn, she thought, by the heady smell of rosemary and browning butter.

When the potatoes were done they tipped them into a serving dish and put them in the coolest oven. She set Angelica to decorating the birthday cake – coffee and chestnut – made by Carlotta.

Jane, who was now thirteen and increasingly bossy, came over. 'Angelica,' she said, 'you should count out the sixty-seven Smarties *before* you put them on the cake, silly.'

Angelica looked up, baffled.

'You should get a plate the same size as the top of the cake

and arrange them on the plate. Then you'll know if they'll fit.'
She sounded so officious that Laura was tempted to reprimand
her. She looked across at Grace, but Grace wore her customary
expression of pride and amusement at her daughter.

Angelica reluctantly tipped out her tube of Smarties onto a
big plate. Mario, seeing this, ran over and stuffed a handful into
his mouth.

'Stop it,' shouted Angelica as Mario laughed and darted
forward to grab another fistful. Silvano stepped forward and
pinioned his brother's arms to his sides. Mario twisted about.
'Get off, Silvano.'

But Silvano, at fourteen still fractionally taller and stronger
than his eleven-year-old brother, marched him away.

'Don't be unkind, Mario. She's only five and she's trying to
decorate her grandfather's birthday cake.'

'Now there's not enough Smarties,' wailed Angelica, her eyes
filling with tears. But Carlotta came to the rescue with another
tube from the larder cupboard.

'I've been hoarding them,' she said. 'Ever since sweets came
off the ration they've been scarcer than ever.'

'I'll do it,' said Jane, reaching for the tube.

Carlotta held it out of reach, 'Oh, no you don't, young lady.
Angelica is in charge of decorating the cake and no one is to
pinch her sweets or interfere.'

Silvano helped Angelica count out the Smarties and guarded
her from further raids while she positioned them on the icing.

Laura looked around the room, thinking that this was what
family life should be. Carlotta and Giovanni were unwrapping
cheeses; Grace and Maud were laying the big pine table, which

would just about seat all of them. George was talking to Donald and smiling, and Donald was at least listening politely. David was opening bottles of wine while Sophie was sitting on a rug in a corner, playing with the twins.

And me? thought Laura. Where do I fit in? Running her eyes around the room, she thought, with a sudden wash of pride: At the moment, I'm the heart of this family, that's what. The centre of gravity has somehow moved from Mummy's kitchen at Chorlton to mine here.

The thought that everyone depended on her pleased her: the house ran smoothly because she made it so. She did not fret or fuss, but meals happened on time, sheets got washed, the house was cleaned; Carlotta was like a helpful, loving sister and she was the best possible aunt for Angelica. Giovanni, so authoritative at work and seen by the world as the *paterfamilias* of the whole clan, was domestically useless. She smiled at the thought: such a good chef and an instinctive businessman, but incapable of picking up his trousers or finding his socks, tying his bow tie, lighting the boiler, mending a fuse. She did all that.

She looked across at Sophie, helping Hal build a tower out of wooden bricks only to have Richard knock it down again. Sophie looked so happy. Her eyes were wide and clear and her skin glowed pink. Laura smiled to herself. David had at last woken up and realised he loved her. And as for Sophie, she's always loved David and she is besotted with the twins. She says she doesn't want a baby of her own, and funnily enough, I think I believe her.

All was good. Very good. Best of all, she and Giovanni were partners in every way, even if sometimes he forgot that and she had to remind him. They were a good team, and business was booming.

And one day, she was sure, one day Giovanni and Daddy would actually enjoy each other's company instead of enduring it. And I will be able to forget . . .

Immediately, as so often in the last six years, Laura knew she'd let this self-satisfied reverie take the wrong path. She made a determined effort not to slip down that tunnel. She pressed the tea towel in her hand against her mouth and turned to the wall, hoping to hide the sudden rush of grief. She stared at the dresser shelves, keeping her eyes open wide, not spilling tears, and tried to get a hold on her emotions. But it didn't work. She felt her throat tighten and quickly ducked out of the kitchen and hurried towards the street door. She stood in the little hall, struggling to divert her mind. I must not, must not, think about him anymore. These sudden stabs of misery out of the blue, like now, or hours of deep sadness when she struggled to get out of bed, had been going on intermittently for years. It was time to stop. He would be nearly seven now. What would he look like? Surely it was just possible that he'd been born prematurely and he'd now be a skinny lad, taller than Angelica, with Giovanni's dark eyes and hair?

She shook her head. It wouldn't be like that. He'd be burly, blond and beautiful. Like Marcin. And if he ever met her, he'd hate her.

CHAPTER FORTY

Relations with her father had really started to thaw a year ago, on the evening of that birthday dinner.

He'd asked to be seated between his favourite granddaughters, Jane and Angelica, and Angelica had said, 'But we're your only granddaughters, Grandpa,' and everyone had laughed.

He'd become increasingly relaxed as the evening wore on. At one point Laura caught her mother's eye. All good, her mother seemed to be signalling.

The next day Laura had taken him to the Edgware Road Calzone and then to the newest Deli-Calzone which had opened the month before in Sloane Street.

'You order for me. I don't understand a word of it,' said Donald, frowning at the menu.

'It's in English on the other side,' said Laura, trying to turn his menu over. But he handed it to her.

'You order,' he said.

She asked for *ribollita* for two, and two glasses of Soave.

'Good God, what is that?' he asked as the waitress put his bowl in front of him.

'It's a soup, with vegetables and dried beans.'

'What's that black stuff?'

'*Cavalo nero*. Black cabbage.'

'Why is it black?' he asked, prodding it with his spoon.

'Oh, Daddy, you are worse than a child. Just taste it. It's good.'

He smiled. 'I'm sorry. But you know how conservative I am.' He lifted a piece of bread out of the soup. 'And what's this? Bread?'

'Yes, it's bread. Like croutons. Only it's not fried first, but just torn up and dropped in. You use stale bread, which breaks up less. It's a peasant soup. Very cheap and nutritious. And delicious. Eat.'

That was nearly a year ago now, but in spite of his increased closeness to her, his apparent affection for Angelica and his admiration for the business, Donald had still said little more than good morning or goodbye to Giovanni.

Mother and daughter agreed that the only hope of Donald and Giovanni forgiving each other would be if they were forced to get to know each other. So they persuaded their respective husbands that everyone should be in the Cotswolds for August.

It wasn't difficult to persuade Giovanni. 'I can put up with him ignoring me but if he insults me – or you – I'll punch him in the kisser.'

Then Maud rang to say that Donald had agreed.

'Well done, Mummy. How did you manage that?'

'I asked him if he planned to spend the next ten years, and go to his grave, on bad terms with his son-in-law.'

'That's a bit strong, isn't it?'

'Well, yes, but I've decided pussyfooting around doesn't work.'

'Poor Daddy! You should tell him he won't have to endure

Giovanni all the time. He'll have to make a few trips to town, I'm sure. Someone has to keep an eye on the business.'

'I hadn't thought of that. And Carlotta will be here, too. Will they cope?'

'Oh, I think so. August is quiet anyway, and the managers are excellent. And Carlotta has a good second chef in the deli.'

Laura had a second objective for this holiday. She wanted Angelica to spend time with her Oliver cousins: they saw much less of Hal and Richard (who were only two years younger than Angelica) than of Silvano and Mario, who were too old to do more than spoil or tease her.

It was the first time that the Italian contingent had been to the Cotswolds and they lightened the atmosphere. Jane, at fourteen, was much the same age as Carlotta's boys. She volunteered to teach them to ride, and George hired two sturdy well-trained ponies from the riding school. Laura thought it was the first time for years she'd seen Grace's daughter happy and giggling like a teenager should, enjoying being teased by Mario, slightly in awe of Silvano. No sulks, no petulance.

Angelica wanted to join the riding lessons but Donald said, 'No, Jane has enough on her hands with teaching those two louts. I will teach you. We'll get Hal to lend you Applesauce. He's a good little thing. Private lessons. How would that be?'

Angelica, dismayed, looked up at her mother for help. She would much rather be with the boys she knew so well. But Laura saw at once that her father was making an effort.

'Darling, that will be lovely,' she told Angelica. 'You are very lucky. Your grandpa taught me to ride when I was your age. Say thank you to him.'

'Thank you, Grandpa,' Angelica said, not looking at him.

Although Donald never snubbed Giovanni, and would offer him a drink in the evenings, or nod good morning to him at the breakfast table, neither man made any effort.

'It's hard for him,' said Maud to Laura. 'I think he knows he will never really get his darling daughter back if he does not accept Giovanni, but he is so proud and stubborn.'

'He's not the only one to blame. I don't think Giovanni will ever forgive him. Not unless he admits he was wrong. And we know that will never happen.'

But Laura was softening. Her father *was* gradually getting her back, little by little. Until recently Laura had found forgiveness impossible. Yet now she sometimes forgot that she'd hated him so, and she would find herself taking his arm to steady him coming down steps, or handing him his pipe and tobacco to save him the effort of hauling himself out of his armchair.

Laura noticed how wobbly he was on uneven ground, and out of breath lifting saddles or grooming his big hunter, so she would fetch his horse from the field, and help him groom and tack him up. The smell of saddles and horses brought back memories of the excitement she felt trotting alongside him to the meet, her Welsh cob having to break into the occasional jog to keep up with his gleaming black seventeen-hander. She'd forgotten how happy she'd been then, how much she'd worshipped her father.

'You're a great improvement on old Sawkins,' Donald said one day as she steadied his arm while he stepped up onto the mounting block. 'He was a wonderful chauffeur, but he resented doubling as a groom, poor chap.'

Laura had a sudden vision of Sawkins opening the gate for her father, doffing his cap respectfully, Donald sailing out in the shining Bentley without a glance. When she was little, she thought he deserved such reverence. Now she was older, she wondered how Sawkins could bear her father's arrogance.

'What became of Sawkins?' she asked.

'He retired, lives with his daughter. David refuses to hire a replacement. One of the farm hands gives my car a wash and polish once a week, and the garage looks after it. Hal and Richard have to help look after their ponies, and Sophie gives a hand sometimes.'

'Aren't the horses out in the summer?'

'Yes, they are. And in the winter Farmer Wheeler's daughter does the horses in exchange for the odd day's hunting on mine.'

Towards the end of the holiday Maud was at Frampton sitting with Grace in her morning room while Jane lay on the sofa, reading.

'I thought,' said Grace, 'it would be nice to have everyone to dinner on Friday. To mark the end of a lovely holiday.'

'Oh, good,' said Jane from the sofa. 'I'll wear my new red dress.'

'Oh no, darling, I meant all the grown-ups, not the children, I'm afraid.'

Jane sat up. 'That is *so* unfair. I'm fourteen. Juliet was *married* at fourteen.'

'Not with her parents' consent,' said Maud.

'But Mummy, if I'm old enough to give riding lessons, surely I'm old enough to come to dinner?'

Maud saw Grace weakening. Of course Jane would get her way. She always did.

Grace said, 'What do you think, Maud? Shall we let her?'

Jane jumped up, a triumphant smile on her face. 'Oh, thank you, Mummy. Thank you,' she said without waiting for an answer.

'You'll have to let the big boys come too, then,' said Maud. 'Silvano is older than Jane and you can hardly leave poor Mario out if the other two are coming.'

Dinner was to be late, at 9pm, because it was harvest time and the men, once home from the fields, needed time to change. David and the farm workers had been out until sunset for over a week, but on the day of the dinner party Giovanni and Carlotta's boys had been roped in to help with the final task of baling the straw.

Donald, George and the women were already in the Frampton drawing room when Giovanni, Silvano and Mario came in.

'Oof,' said Giovanni, accepting the armchair Grace offered him and sinking into it. 'Baling uses muscles a kitchen chef does not know he has. I will be so stiff tomorrow.'

'And look at my hands!' said Silvano. He displayed them palms up, red and sore from hoisting bales by their twine ties.

'How about you, young Mario?' asked George.

Mario groaned. 'My back aches.' He arched it.

Carlotta clucked with sympathy. 'And you've caught the sun, Mario. What happened to your hat?'

David teased, 'You don't know how lucky you are. Before the war hardly anyone round here had a tractor. We used horses to pull the plough, the seed drill, the reaper. Then we stood the corn in stooks to dry. It took everyone, girls included, to do that and then we loaded it all onto carts, brought it home and threshed it with an ancient machine. We used pitchforks to make the straw into ricks. No tractors. No harvesters. We only got those in the war. And a combine harvester and a baler five years ago.'

'And that,' said Laura, laughing, 'is a short history of pre-war farming.' David made a face at her. 'And maybe Daddy would like to tell us about broadcasting seed by hand and using a scythe?'

Donald cuffed her head. 'I'm not that old, you minx. Anyway, I wasn't a farmer then. My father was weaving cloth in Yorkshire. And not by hand either! Our looms were certainly Victorian, but they were made to last.'

Once the summer pudding and whipped cream were served, Laura tapped her glass with a spoon until everyone stopped talking.

'I have a suggestion,' she began. 'Why don't we have a family picnic? We're going back to London on Monday so let's go up on Chastleton Hill on Sunday.'

'Wonderful idea, my darling,' said Giovanni, smiling at her. Laura smiled back, thinking how well and burned by the sun he looked.

There was a general clamour of approval and then Donald said, 'Let's make it a riding picnic. Go further afield and the non-riders can bring the picnic in the cars and meet us, maybe by the old mill at Kingham or in Foscot Wood.'

George offered Laura his second hunter. They had to hire another pony from the riding school for Angelica because Hal would be on Applesauce.

Sophie decided not to join the riders. She rather wanted to, especially when David said he would ride, but she didn't have a horse and felt she should help Maud with the picnic.

On the morning after the dinner, David was mending the ballcock of the trough in the yard, and Sophie was pulling dried clothes off the line. 'Why don't you ride, Soph?' he called. 'The Frampton groom, Brenda, she'll lend you her chestnut mare, won't she?' He walked across, his spanner in his hand. 'It'll be fun. We've never ridden together, you, me and the boys, have we?'

Sophie longed to agree, but she shook her head. 'No. I've hardly ridden since I was a child, and anyway we can't leave Maud and Carlotta to make the picnic. And neither of them can drive the car.'

'My darling Sophie,' he said, his voice teasing but affectionate, 'you think of everyone before yourself. But you forget Giovanni. He's a professional in the kitchen and he won't ride with us, which makes two good cooks to help Maud. Or Frampton can make the picnic. Grace doesn't ride and she has plenty of help.'

Sophie laughed. 'It's true,' she said. 'From being down to a cook and the doddery old Andrew in the war, George has got so rich again he's back to a fleet of flunkies.'

'Right. Well then, what's your next excuse?'

'Oh, all right then, I'll come.' She was barely thinking about the picnic, or the ride. She was thinking how good David looked, brown from a hot summer, his faded check shirt open at the neck, his sleeves rolled up to his elbows, revealing reddish arm hairs glinting in the sunlight. She imagined stroking his arm the wrong way, feeling the slight resistance of the hairs, the warmth of his skin. Really, she told herself, this is no way for a married woman to think.

'There's my girl,' said David, and kissed her lightly on the cheek. The touch of his lips shot through her like a charge. Their eyes met for a second and he smiled and turned away, returning to his plumbing job.

CHAPTER FORTY-ONE

Giovanni ate his eggs and bacon and observed the bustle around him – everyone was going to church and the latecomers were swallowing their food fast. Maud was cooking eggs to order, and supervising Angelica who was frying slices of bread in Spry. His darling Laura was dishing out coins to everyone for the church collection while Donald fussed about a spilt lump of porridge on his tweed jacket and Carlotta used a dishcloth to clean it off. Silvano was wolfing down sausages and eggs and David was shouting to Mario, who'd not yet appeared, from the bottom of the stairs. Sophie was sitting between the twins, spreading Marmite on toast for them.

Only one more day of this, thought Giovanni, and then we'll be home again. He'd twice escaped to London for a day or two on the pretext of checking up on the business, and it had been a relief.

This English family led a life divided between the outdoors (farming, riding, walking, playing tennis) and the kitchen, cooking and eating. He was a fish out of water. He wasn't required to cook and anyway the kitchen seemed to be women's territory. He didn't ride or play tennis, though he did, out of politeness, go on the occasional walk.

He longed to get back to Paddington. But he had to admit that the holiday, about which he'd had serious misgivings, had been a success: wonderful for Angelica who was now obsessed with horses, and good for Laura. Last night, when at last they were alone in her old bedroom, she'd said, 'I'm so glad we came here. I know things will be better between Daddy and me from now on. I'll never really understand why he chased us out – it obviously made him miserable, too – but I have forgiven him, I think.'

'But has he forgiven you?'

'I think he forgave me years ago. He just can't admit it, that's all.'

'Well, I'll never forgive him. I'll be polite, of course – what's the point of quarrelling? And I'm glad you are friends again, darling. I know how much the separation hurt.' He'd put his arms round her and kissed her cheek. 'I just hope this will mean the end of your horrible bouts of grief.'

They went to church (there wasn't a Catholic one for miles, so Carlotta and her boys cheerfully went to Frampton), changed from Sunday best to riding kit, caught the horses and tacked up. Giovanni stood with his sister to watch the preparations. It was good to see Carlotta so proud of Mario and Silvano as they saddled up competently.

'The holiday has done your boys good, don't you think?' said Giovanni. 'It's forced Silvano to abandon his books for once and get out in the fresh air and given them both plenty to do. They've loved it.'

'Absolutely, and it's also taught them things I could never teach them. It's made them conform to English manners: listen politely to the grown-ups, lay their knives and forks together on the plate when they've finished eating, argue without shouting each other down.'

'Carlotta, don't you start squeezing the Italian out of them! You don't want a couple of stiff-upper-lip *English* for sons, now do you?

Laura felt her heart lift. The stable yard was like a riding school or the unsaddling enclosure at the races: teeming with horses and busy with excited riders carrying saddles and brushing tails, horses shifting about, bystanders (in the form of Giovanni, Maud and Carlotta) getting in the way.

At noon, Jane, George and Brenda clattered into the yard.

'Goodness, George, your horses look so smart you'd think they were going to the county show,' said Laura.

'That's what a good groom is for,' said George, smiling at Brenda.

Brenda was lending her horse to Sophie, so she climbed off and gave Sophie a leg-up. As Sophie shortened her stirrups, unconcerned at the horse's sideways fidgeting, Laura thought how good she looked on a horse.

'I'd forgotten what a good horsewoman you are, Sophie,' she said.

Laura had buckled a martingale strap loosely round Angelica's pony's neck and attached a leading rein to her bridle. Angelica was indignant. 'I don't go on the leading rein any more, Mummy. Ask Grandpa.'

'I know, darling, but we don't know this pony. The riding school says she's very good, but I want to be sure. Not all ponies are as calm as Applesauce.'

And indeed the pony fidgeted continually. She was all right when they were trotting sedately along the lane, but she did not like walking. She tossed her head and skittered along sideways.

Angelica loved it and scorned her mother's suggestion of hanging on to the neck strap 'just in case'.

Donald rode up beside her. 'How is my little rider doing?' he asked. 'That's a sprightly little thing you're on, Angelica.'

'Oh, she's lovely, Grandpa. Look, she's dancing. Much more fun than Applesauce, who just plods along, but Mummy won't let me off the lead. Please tell her, Grandpa, I can ride by myself.'

'She might be better off the lead,' said Donald, watching her. 'Or maybe that pony prefers to be in the front. Did the riding school not tell you anything about her?'

'Only that she was good as gold, which she isn't,' Laura said.

'Let me take her. Maybe she doesn't like your horse.' He stretched for the leading rein but Laura hesitated.

'Would you like that, darling, to go with Grandpa?'

'Ye-es.' Angelica turned the word into a double syllable for extra emphasis.

Laura handed the rein to her father, who said, 'We'll go up front, shall we, Angelica? Some horses just fret if they're at the back.' They trotted forward, overtaking the half-dozen riders ahead of them. Laura watched anxiously, but Angelica's pony seemed to settle down as her father had predicted, giving up her sideways skittering and walking quietly. Laura smiled with relief and pride. Angelica's back was beautifully straight, her bottom deep into the saddle, her hands moving rhythmically backwards and forwards in time to her pony's spirited step. Her father really was a great teacher.

The ride over Chastleton Hill to Adlestrop and then across to Daylesford was wonderful. Laura had forgotten what fun it could be to be cantering steadily across a field in a posse of riders. It was both exhilarating and companionable and today was a perfect day. All the fields had been cut but not yet ploughed. The gates were open and there was no need to keep to the edge. The ground wasn't too hard but it was firm and even and the stubble made a dry swish-swish as the horses cantered through it. There was just enough breeze to keep them cool and hold the flies away.

From Daylesford they dipped down to Kingham, let the horses have a drink in the river and then waded through it, the children apprehensive and excited, the grown-ups shouting at them to urge their ponies on.

David shouted across to his son, 'Hal, get her head up. She'll lie down in the water if you don't kick her on.'

The four-year-old flailed his legs valiantly and his pony reluctantly gave up hopes of a swim and waded forward. Richard could not get his pony to budge and David reached down for his bridle and led him through the stream and up the bank while the child protested that he could manage on his own.

Donald, seeing Silvano's cob similarly keen on a roll in the mud, gave him a whack on the rump so that he sprang forward, nearly unseating Silvano. There was a good deal of excitement and laughter, then everyone was on the other side and they hacked on through Bleddington and to Foscot.

The Bentley was there before them in the narrow lane at the edge of the woods. Giovanni had driven it, stuffed with the picnic, drinks, cushions, rugs and four more adults: Carlotta and Maud, Grace and Brenda, the groom, to keep an eye on the tethered horses. Giovanni had scouted out a picnic spot: a dappled clearing with a great fallen beech for the older ones to sit on, and space for two picnic rugs.

*

The fence between the lane and the woods was a sturdy wooden one and they all tied their horses to it, the novice riders carefully using the half-hitch they'd been taught. Laura watched Angelica solemnly putting her stirrups up, hooking her reins behind one of them and struggling to loosen her pony's girth. Laura went over to help her. The child looks as she does when she's cooking, she thought, all focused concentration.

Everyone was thirsty, so Maud passed out home-made lemonade for the children, while the grown-ups drank cider or Frampton's dandelion wine, now successfully on sale at local groceries as well as several London stores. After a lunch of Carlotta's cold pizza, Maud's pork pie with mustard, hard-boiled eggs, small whole tomatoes from the greenhouse, wedges of Cheddar cheese with chutney, soft buttered 'dinner rolls' made by Giovanni and Angelica's squashy greengage cake which she had made with her mother's help, they had all eaten uncomfortably much.

'Oh, that was all wonderful,' said Laura. 'Just delicious.'

Carlotta nodded. 'It's such a pleasure to finally have everything, even meat and bacon, off the ration.'

Maud agreed. 'I know, I thought it would never stop. Fourteen years of coupons and queues!' She indicated the brown paper she was carefully folding. 'But look at me! Old habits die hard.' She tucked the paper into the picnic basket. 'I suppose I'll hoard every scrap of paper or piece of string until I go to my grave.' Laura felt a sudden wave of affection for her mother. That woman is pure gold, she thought. Stalwart, loving, unselfish.

The children set off to explore the woods. Brenda kept an eye on the horses, half asleep in the sun, motionless except for the occasional stamp or swish of a tail to drive off the flies. Donald sat on the fallen tree while the rest of the adults dozed on the rugs.

Laura was at the back of the group on the ride home. As they breasted Chastleton Hill, some of the horses, sensing home and used to a good run up here on the flat, became restive, eager for some speed.

Laura was riding next to Sophie and David. Hal turned round in his saddle and shouted to David, 'Dad, can we race? Go for a gallop?'

David turned to Laura. 'What do you think? Is Angelica ready for galloping?'

Laura shook her head. 'No, I don't think so. Not on this pony anyway. And surely your two are a bit young, aren't they?'

'They'll be fine. They live in the saddle. And those ponies are good as gold. But I agree, it's not a good idea.' He raised his voice to shout to the boys.

'Sorry, lads, but no. We have too many new riders. We'll just have a controlled canter. OK?'

But Donald called from the front, 'Laura, I'm going to let Angelica off the lead. Otherwise she'll be cantering sideways the length of the hill!'

'No, Daddy. Don't. Don't.'

'Mummy, please. I'll be fine.'

Everyone was just managing to keep to a walk, except Angelica's little grey, who was cantering on the spot, to the child's delight. Donald leant forward and flipped the leading rein over the pony's head, knotting it on her neck. Immediately the pony dropped to a walk, still prancing a bit, but walking. 'There you are, Laura. She'll be fine if we just all stop fussing and give the horse its head.'

Laura didn't like it, but it was true the pony was behaving better now. She called to Jane, 'Jane, could you swap with Angelica, do you think? You are a much better rider and Angelica will be fine on Snowdrop.' But Angelica said, 'No, Mum, I'm fine. I don't want to change.'

Donald said, 'All right, everyone, let's trot and then we'll have a canter. No galloping, mind, you boys. Just a steady canter.'

They were in a fairly tight group, all cantering steadily. But before they'd gone two hundred yards Hal and Richard were leaning over their horses' necks, racing. And Angelica's little grey was behind them.

Laura's heart leapt in panic but then she noticed that Angelica was fine: standing in her stirrups, leaning forward, her reins short, and, she was glad to see, holding onto the neck strap. She looked every inch the competent rider. Laura saw her father spur his hunter on to catch up with the three galloping ponies. The rest of the party slowed to a trot and watched Donald, now in the distance, draw level with the little grey. The boys were slowing to a canter at the end of the bridal path and Laura began to breathe again. Then, as Donald reached down for Angelica's lead rein, the pony shied violently to the right, swerved past Richard and disappeared through the open gate with Angelica, half unseated, just clinging on, and Donald in pursuit.

They found her on the verge outside Chastleton House. When Laura and Sophie clattered down, they could not at first see her because Donald was obscuring their view. All they could see were Angelica's skinny legs, stretched out and absolutely still.

Laura was off her horse five yards from the motionless girl, running to fall on her knees next to her. Seeing Donald putting an arm under Angelica's bottom, Sophie barked in a voice of command, 'Leave her alone. Don't move her.'

Angelica was unconscious. 'Call an ambulance,' Sophie said to Donald. He stood looking at her, his face stricken. 'Donald, go into Chastleton House and get them to call an ambulance. Now!'

Sophie put her fingers to Angelica's neck, lifted her eyelid, put an ear to her chest.

'Her heart is fine. But she's knocked out. We'll wait for the ambulance.' She looked at Laura. 'I should think she'll be fine, Laura. But just in case she's cracked her skull . . .'

Sophie turned to David, now standing holding his horse with the rest of the party, all silent. 'Can you dash home and get Giovanni and a car? Laura will want to follow the ambulance to Moreton and Giovanni should be with her. And bring Brenda, too. She can take our horses home and help the children untack.'

Laura sat on the gravel next to her daughter, praying. Please no. Don't let her die. Don't let her back be broken. Don't let her be paralysed, please. Please.

The owner of the riding school arrived with her farmer husband in their motorcycle and sidecar. Angelica's pony had cantered into their yard and they'd come looking for his rider. But no one really wanted to talk to them, so they left again, protesting that the pony had never been known to bolt before.

David came back in the Bentley with Giovanni, ashen-faced, and Brenda. Giovanni at once sat in the dust next to Laura, his arm around her shoulders. They exchanged one anguished look and Laura said, 'Oh darling,' but nothing more. She returned her eyes to her daughter, willing her to wake up. Giovanni put his head close to Angelica's and whispered urgently in Italian to her

418

motionless face. Laura barely heard him. Neither took their eyes off their daughter until the ambulance arrived.

Angelica was taken straight through to the X-ray department and Laura and Giovanni were left in the waiting room. Laura was rigid with fear. She sat almost immobile, trying not to think. But she couldn't help it. If Angelica died, she'd never be able to bear it. And Giovanni would blame her like he blamed her for the loss of their son. And he would be right. Why hadn't she insisted on Angelica being on the leading rein? She'd known that pony was too eager. Why had she been so feeble?

Giovanni didn't ask her how the accident had happened. He sat next to her for a while, holding one of her hands in both of his. But then he couldn't bear it any longer and jumped up to ask at the desk what was happening.

'It won't be long now. The radiologist will be with you as soon as they've examined her X-rays.' Giovanni nodded. But he did not come back at once to sit with Laura. He paced up and down the floor.

Laura became aware that she was shivering. Shaking, in fact, and very cold. She called out, 'Giovanni!' Her voice sounded odd to her but Giovanni turned at once and came back to her. He leant over to put his arms round her. 'Don't worry, sweetheart, it's the shock.' He hurried back to the reception and soon someone brought her a cup of sweet tea and a blanket. Gradually the shaking stopped. But the fear increased. It had been forty minutes since they'd got here.

Eventually a young man, presumably a doctor, appeared and asked them to follow him. He took them into a small room and offered them a seat. They both shook their heads.

'Just tell us,' said Laura.

'Yes. Well, your daughter's spinal column and neck are undamaged but she has sustained considerable trauma to her head. There is a hairline fracture to her skull and a lot of bruising, though no apparent bleeding, to the soft tissue.'

'You mean to the brain?' asked Giovanni.

'Yes, the brain and neck, and the scalp, of course.'

'Is she still unconscious?' Laura asked.

'Yes, she is, and that's the difficulty. I cannot tell you when she will come round. She could wake up at any time, or it could be hours, or even days.'

'But she will come round? She won't be like this for ever . . .'

'I am sure she'll regain consciousness, Mrs . . .' – he consulted his clipboard – 'Mrs Angelotti. But of course no one can say with certainty. Cases vary.'

Eventually David came to collect Giovanni. They had decided to take it in turns to stay with Angelica so that at least one of her parents would be with her when she came to. The ward sister gave Laura a chair which she positioned close to the head of the bed so she could talk to her daughter. Laura kissed Angelica's head.

'Sleep well, my darling. And wake up whenever you like. I will be here.'

When Giovanni entered the curtained cubicle, he looked grey with fatigue. He'd obviously not slept much more than Laura had.

Laura stood and met his anxious eyes. She shook her head. No change. Nothing to report. Giovanni sat in Laura's chair and took his daughter's hand. *Angelica svegliati, piccola mia.*

In the lift, Laura looked at herself in the mirror without much interest. Her chalk-grey cheeks and unbrushed hair made her look suddenly middle-aged. Who cares? she thought.

Carlotta and the boys went back to London, but Giovanni stayed on at Chorlton. Over the next few days, David taxied his sister and her husband to the hospital, where they did alternate five-hour bedside shifts throughout the day, and one of them stayed all night. Sometimes they shared a vigil so they could talk to each other. When not at the hospital, Laura cooked and hoped and prayed, and Giovanni walked round the fields, alone. Donald sat in his study, smoking. Sophie did a giant jigsaw with the twins.

Sophie also visited the hospital every day and talked quietly to the doctors and nurses. Laura was grateful, not just because she could translate the medical opinions, but also because she was confident and cheerful. I don't believe it has crossed her mind, thought Laura, that Angelica may never wake up.

Everyone was gentle with everyone else. Grace came over to Chorlton, bringing a cake, a pot of soup or some of Frampton's wine. It's funny, thought Laura, how you give people food and drink when you're sorry for them and there is nothing you can do to help.

Donald had tried to talk to Laura, to offer sympathy and apologies or explanations about letting Angelica off the leading rein, but Laura had brushed him aside. She hadn't the energy to blame or forgive, or even discuss the matter. All she could do was be with Angelica and will her to wake up.

Three days after the accident, Donald came into the kitchen to find Maud sitting at the table, alone. He saw at once that she'd been weeping. He pulled a chair up close to hers, sat down and put his hand on her knee. 'Darling, can I help?'

Maud shook her head, sniffed, and smiled. 'I'm fine, just tired. And worried sick. We all are.'

She got up to get him some tea. He didn't really want any, but he could see she needed to busy herself with ordinary things. He sat silently, looking at her back as she moved about. Suddenly she swung round to look at him.

'Actually, Donald, there is something you could do to help.'

'What?'

'Well, I don't suppose you'll do it, or indeed could do it. But I think you should have a proper talk to Giovanni. He was just beginning to forgive us for that business over the first baby. Now I think he believes you're responsible for Angelica's accident.'

'Maud, I really wasn't. The pony was responding—'

'I believe you. I know that riding is dangerous, that there are no guarantees of safety. Anyone might have advised what you advised. But Donald, Giovanni knows nothing about riding. He just knows his daughter is in a coma. He'll be looking for someone to blame.'

Donald felt a rush of warm gratitude. For her understanding, and her loyalty.

'Does Laura blame me, too? Do you know?' he asked.

'I doubt if she has energy for finding someone to blame. All that concerns her is that Angelica comes round. But if she doesn't, or if she dies, then Laura may blame you. You'll know better than me anyway. I wasn't there when you were arguing about what to do.'

Donald's mind went back to the shouted exchange on the hill,

Laura yelling for him to keep Angelica on the leading rein, him refusing. But the pony *was* behaving better off the lead.

He shook his head. 'I doubt if Giovanni will let me talk to him, let alone listen.'

'You can but try.'

Angelica had been unconscious for almost three days. The doctors all said, and Sophie said, too, that she could wake up at any time. She did not say, 'Or she might not.' But Laura and Giovanni both knew it.

Late in the afternoon of the third day Donald came to the hospital. Angelica had been moved into a private room with a little more space for both parents and sometimes for one of the others: Maud, Sophie or Grace.

Neither Laura nor Giovanni did more than nod briefly to Donald when he entered the room. He glanced at Giovanni and Laura, then looked at the motionless Angelica.

He turned back to his daughter. 'Laura, my dear girl, I cannot tell you how sorry I am about the accident. I hope you don't think it was my fault. I'm a pretty good judge of horsemanship and I honestly thought—'

'Daddy, stop,' interrupted Laura, her voice flat and lifeless. 'You've said it all before, and what's the use?'

Her father started to protest, but Laura interrupted him, this time with more energy and a steely coldness. 'Daddy, all I know is this: if Angelica dies, or never speaks or walks again, I will never, ever, forgive you. If she recovers, well, I don't know . . .' She smiled a twisted, bitter half-smile. 'Maybe I'll say "Accidents happen", "Horses are unreliable". Who knows? I don't.'

Giovanni got up and went to stand close to Donald. 'Well,

Laura may not know, but I know. I know that you took away my first child and now you are taking away my daughter. When this is over, when Angelica is better, or when she is dead, we will go. And you will never see your daughter or your granddaughter again. Never. Never . . .'

Laura watched him push her father in the chest, a scornful, insulting shove.

Donald did not retaliate. He just stood there, staggering slightly. 'I don't blame you, Giovanni,' he said. 'You are right about the first one. I was a stubborn, stupid idiot. Pig-headed.'

'For sure,' shouted Giovanni, 'and you still are.'

'I agree,' said Donald. 'I agree. I am arrogant. And back then I didn't give you a chance. Or Laura. I assumed you were a cad and a bounder. I was so wrong. You have been the most wonderful husband to her. You have made her happy in spite of everything. And now . . . Oh . . .' He put his head in his hands. When he looked up tears were running down his face. He cried out, loudly, begging to be believed, 'But this was an accident. I—'

'It was because you didn't listen. Laura said to keep Angelica on the lead. But no, you have to—'

'No, no. I know about horses.' Both men were yelling and Laura tried to get between them.

'Stop it, Daddy. Giovanni, please, darling . . .'

Donald shouted, 'I really thought it was better . . .' Then suddenly he dropped his hands and shook his head, lowered his voice. 'Oh, God. Laura, my darling girl, what's the use?'

Laura registered, not emotionally but quite clearly as if in another part of her brain, that she had never seen her father cry and that he was suddenly old. Really old and quite frail. He looked like someone else. Someone beaten.

They stood looking at each other, a kind of hopelessness engulfing them all.

Then, in the silence they heard Angelica's voice, thin but clear.

'What's the matter, Mummy? Why are Daddy and Grandpa shouting?'

ACKNOWLEDGEMENTS

I thought I knew a good bit about food and the post-war years and imagined that anything I didn't know, Google would.

But it turned out I needed a lot of expert help. So now I must thank Mick Kernan, Ian Hollingsbee and Robin Dale for information about Cotswold POW camps and airfields; Dr John Martin, Gemma Fitzpatrick and Tom Evans for knowledge and memories of farming in the forties; Charlie Caisey and CJ Jackson for their expertise on the fish trade; Dr Mark Charnock, Sarah Dixon-Smith and Penny Hutchins for help on anaesthesia and obstetrics in 1950; Cat Gazzoli and Massimo Zorzi for checking my Italian; and Lyn Pearse for much googling.

And then, as ever, I owe huge thanks to my agent Jane Turnbull, editor Jane Wood and PA Francisca Sankson for beady-eyed editing and advice. My usual reaction to all criticisms and most suggestions is indignation followed by objection. But almost always they are right and I am wrong. So I *am* grateful. Truly. And hope they will do the same hard job for Book Two and Book Three.